OATH OF THE SHATTERED CANOPY

Written by Diane Kann

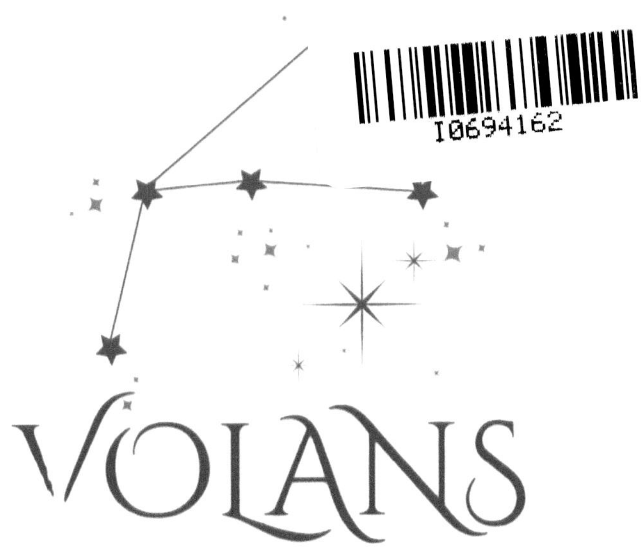

Brought to you by Volans Galaxy Press

Published by Kannceptual Creations LLC

An imprint of Volans Galaxy Press

ISBN: 978-1-971356-73-0

Printed in the United States of America

First Edition, January 2026

CONTENTS

Author's Biography   V

Dedication   VI

1. Whispers of the Withering   1

2. Fractured Resonance   29

3. Whispers of Technology   51

4. The Canopy Accord Council   84

5. The Dragon's Distrust   116

6. The Ashbound's Shadow   142

7. The Truth of the Engines   166

8. Drastic Measures   190

9. Sharpening Tensions   217

10. Restoring Resonance   247

11. Reforging the Oath   280

12. Whispers from the Deep   312

13. A New Horizon   331

Glossary   356

AUTHOR'S BIOGRAPHY

Diane Kann writes eco–science fantasy that explores the intersections of technology, nature, and hope. Drawn to mysterious worlds, sentient ecosystems, and the quiet strength of unlikely heroes, she crafts stories that imagine not just what humanity might survive, but how it might heal.

A believer in environmental stewardship and deeply fascinated by the natural world, Diane weaves themes of conservation and interconnected life throughout her work. When she's not writing, she can be found exploring the diverse ecosystems of Central Florida with her family and dogs—dreaming up strange futures rooted in compassion and the resilience of nature.

DEDICATION

For the guardians of fragile things—
for those who listen when forests whisper
and when dragons fall silent.

For the ones who believe that broken systems
can be mended,
that fractured resonance can be restored,
and that even in a withering world,
an oath still matters.

May we remember that we are not masters of the canopy,
but part of its breath—
and may we always choose to heal
what we have the power to harm.

CHAPTER ONE

WHISPERS OF THE WITHERING

The Skywood canopy, a verdant cathedral that had always breathed life into the world, was beginning to exhale its last. Mara, her senses still attuned to the rhythmic pulse of the ocean's tides, felt the change as a jarring dissonance. The familiar, life-giving humidity that clung to her skin like a second layer of moss was absent, replaced by a brittle, suffocating dryness. Each breath felt like inhaling dust and despair. Her eyes, accustomed to the dappled, emerald light filtering through countless leaves, now scanned a panorama of muted greens and burgeoning browns. The leaves, once firm and glossy, drooped with a weary resignation, their edges curled and desiccated as if already kissed by a phantom frost. It was an unsettling sight, a visual shorthand for a deeper malaise that Mara, despite her nascent Reefwarden training, could only begin to comprehend.

She stood on a high ridge, the wind, usually a gentle, moisture-laden caress, now a dry rasp against her cheeks. Below, the vast expanse of the Skywood stretched out, a tapestry woven with shades of verdant life, but the fraying threads were becoming undeniably apparent. The vibrant hum of the forest, the chorus of unseen creatures that had always formed its natural symphony, was muted, punctuated by an unnerving silence.

It was a quiet that spoke not of peace, but of a struggle for survival. She saw it in the way the smaller creatures, usually flitting between branches with acrobatic grace, moved with a lethargic caution, their eyes wide with an apprehension that mirrored her own. Even the ancient, gnarled trees, their branches reaching skyward like supplicating arms, seemed to stoop under an invisible weight. Their bark, usually etched with the stories of centuries, looked parched, as if the very lifeblood within them was being siphoned away.

Mara reached out, her fingers brushing against a broad, emerald leaf. It felt brittle, papery, and disconcertingly cool to the touch, as if the life force had already begun to ebb. A tiny tremor ran through her hand, a sympathetic resonance with the dying plant. Her Reefwarden training, designed to understand the delicate balance of aquatic ecosystems, felt woefully inadequate here, on this dry, terrestrial ground. The principles of ebb and flow, of predator and prey, of symbiotic relationships—they were universal, she knew, but the manifestation of imbalance was terrifyingly alien. She had seen coral bleached white by warming seas, kelp forests withered by pollution, but this... this felt like a slow, agonizing suffocation of an entire world.

The air itself seemed to hold its breath. The usual symphony of rustling leaves, chirping insects, and the distant calls of unseen birds was replaced by a profound, almost suffocating stillness. A few hardy leaves, clinging tenaciously to their branches, trembled not with the wind, but with a desperate, unheard plea. Mara could feel it – a subtle shift in the land's energy, a disquiet that resonated deep within her bones, a primal alarm bell sounding in the silent chambers of her heart. It was a sensation that felt both intimate and vast, as if the very soul of the Skywood was weeping, and she, an outsider, was bearing witness to its sorrow. The whispers she heard weren't just the rustling of dry leaves; they were the murmured anxieties of the forest dwellers, the fleeting thoughts of creatures whose lives were inextricably bound to the health of this arboreal realm.

She had heard tales, of course, of droughts that plagued the inland territories, of seasons where the rains forgot their duty. But this felt different. This wasn't just a harsh season; it was a fundamental unraveling. The usual patterns of life were disrupted. The vibrant, almost electric hum of the forest's life force, which she had felt even from a distance, was now a faint, flickering ember. It was a subtle change, imperceptible to those who lived their lives in its constant embrace, but to Mara, whose senses were honed by the vast, dynamic forces of the ocean, it was a glaring, terrifying anomaly. The very air felt thinner, drier, as if the Skywood was losing its breath, its vibrant lungs struggling to draw in the moisture they so desperately needed.

She noticed the peculiar behavior of the normally boisterous canopy dwellers. The sky-sprites, usually a kaleidoscope of iridescent wings darting through the upper reaches, were scarce, their playful chases replaced by a huddled stillness on higher branches, their vibrant hues dulled by an unseen weariness. Even the arboreal lizards, their scales shimmering like polished jade, clung to the branches with a newfound desperation, their usual vigilance replaced by a listless stare. They were the first, Mara thought, to feel the true bite of this encroaching dryness. Their small lives were so intimately tied to the constant, life-sustaining moisture of the canopy, that any deviation from the norm would be felt with immediate, acute intensity.

The ground beneath her feet, usually springy with a thick carpet of moss and fallen leaves, felt dry and brittle. She kicked at a small pile of detritus, and a puff of fine, brown dust rose into the air, dancing in the oppressive stillness. It was a stark contrast to the damp, loamy scent of the forest floor she had half-expected, a scent that spoke of decay and regeneration, of the constant cycle of life and death. This dry dust spoke only of depletion.

The overarching canopy, once a testament to nature's boundless vitality, now seemed like a vast, failing lung. The leaves, from her vantage point, appeared less like a vibrant, unbroken ceiling and more like a collection of individual entities, each fighting a solitary battle against the encroaching desiccation. Some were already tinged with the sickly yellow of autumn, despite the season being far from its turn. Others were speckled with brown, their edges crisping into an unnatural fragility. It was a visual metaphor for the larger crisis unfolding. This was not merely a drought;

it was a symptom of a deeper illness, a subtle poison seeping into the very veins of the Skywood.

Mara closed her eyes, attempting to focus her senses, to filter out the visual evidence and delve into the more primal, energetic undercurrents of the forest. She felt it then, a faint, almost imperceptible tremor beneath the surface of things. It was a disquiet, a low thrum of unease that vibrated through the earth and up into her bones. It was a sensation she knew well from her time by the sea, the subtle warnings of a storm gathering, of currents shifting, of the ocean's temper about to change. But here, it was different. It was slower, more insidious, like a slow poison spreading through a vast, living body. It spoke of a profound imbalance, a disruption in the natural order that was far more pervasive than a mere lack of rain.

The usual symphony of the Skywood—the chattering of canopy dwellers, the rustling of leaves, the hum of unseen insects—had been replaced by an unnerving quiet. A silence that wasn't peaceful, but pregnant with a palpable sense of dread. Mara strained her ears, trying to discern any sound beyond the dry rasp of the wind. She heard the faint, anxious chirps of a few small birds, their calls more like panicked cries than their usual melodious tunes. She heard the dry skittering of unseen creatures in the undergrowth, a sound that spoke of desperation, of searching for sustenance that was no longer readily available. And beneath it all, she felt the subtle tremor of the land itself, a low, persistent thrum of distress.

Her Reefwarden training had instilled in her an innate respect for the intricate web of life, a deep understanding that every organism played a vital role in the health of its ecosystem. She knew that even the smallest imbalance could ripple outwards, causing catastrophic consequences. She had witnessed firsthand the devastating effects of overfishing, of pollution that choked the life out of vibrant reefs, of storms that reshaped coastlines with brutal indifference. But the Skywood was a different kind of ecosystem, vaster, more ancient, and seemingly more robust. Yet, the signs of its distress were undeniable, and they spoke of a force far more pervasive and unsettling than she had ever encountered.

She watched as a small, furry creature, its fur the colour of dried moss, scurried across a branch, its movements jerky and uncoordinated. It paused, its tiny head twitching, before continuing its frantic search. It was an uncommon sight; normally, such creatures were known for their agility and playful curiosity. Their current behavior was a stark indicator of the stress they were under, a testament to the pervasive lack of nourishment and water. Mara felt a pang of empathy for the creature, and a deeper sense of unease about the larger implications of its struggle. This was not an isolated incident; it was a symptom of a widespread affliction.

The very scent of the air had changed. It was no longer the rich, earthy perfume of damp soil and decaying leaves, mingled with the sweet fragrance of unseen blossoms. Instead, it was thin, acrid, and carried the faint, metallic tang of something struggling to survive. It was the scent of a world beginning to unravel. Mara found herself instinctively reaching for the canteen at her hip, the cool water within a small comfort against the encroaching dryness. But she knew that water, in and of itself, was not the solution to this deeper malady. This was a wound that went far beyond the surface, a sickness that permeated the very lifeblood of the Skywood.

She thought of the coral reefs she knew, their vibrant colors fading to a ghostly white when the water grew too warm, their intricate structures becoming brittle and lifeless. The parallel was disturbingly clear. The Skywood, too, was a complex, living entity, and its current state suggested a similar, profound trauma. The once-vibrant canopy, a testament to eons of growth and adaptation, was now a stark visual representation of a life source being slowly choked. The leaves, meant to capture sunlight and breathe in the air, now seemed to be wilting under an oppressive, unseen force, their surfaces drying and curling as if touched by a slow-burning fire.

A faint rustling from the undergrowth drew her attention. A small creature, its fur the color of dried earth, darted from behind a patch of wilting ferns. Its movements were quick, almost frantic, its eyes wide with a primal fear. It paused for a moment, sniffing the air, before disappearing back into the shadows. This was not the usual cautious foraging Mara had observed in healthy forests; this was a desperate search for sustenance, a sign that the usual sources were drying up. The creature's unease was a palpable echo of the larger disquiet Mara felt permeating the very air she breathed.

The silence, once she truly listened, was not absolute. It was punctuated by small, desperate sounds: the dry rustle of leaves that should have been damp, the frantic chirping of birds whose songs had always been a joyous melody, the unsettling quiet of insects that should have been a constant, vibrant hum. These were not the sounds of nature at rest, but of nature under immense strain, each sound a tiny, strained cry for relief. It was a symphony of scarcity, and it was a deeply unsettling prelude to what Mara suspected would be a long and arduous journey inland.

The Skywood, so full of life just a short time ago, was now whispering its distress, and Mara felt compelled to listen, to understand, and perhaps, to help. The oppressive stillness seemed to press in on her, a physical manifestation of the encroaching crisis. The air, usually alive with the scent of damp earth, decaying leaves, and the subtle perfume of unseen flowers, now carried a dry, dusty odor, tinged with the faint, metallic hint of life struggling against the inevitable. It was a scent that spoke of depletion, of a vital resource being leached away, leaving behind only the arid husk of what once was.

Her Reefwarden training had taught her to observe, to analyze, and to understand the interconnectedness of all living things within an ecosystem. She had seen the devastating consequences of imbalance—coral bleaching, the collapse of fish populations, the erosion of coastlines. But the Skywood presented a different kind of challenge, a terrestrial crisis that felt both familiar in its ecological principles and alien in its scale and scope. The vibrant green of the canopy, so characteristic of this ancient forest, was now marred by patches of dull brown and sickly yellow, like a creeping blight. The leaves, once plump and full of moisture, were shriveled, their edges curled inwards as if in pain.

She reached out and touched a drooping leaf. It felt dry and brittle, crumbling slightly under her fingertips, a stark contrast to the supple resilience she expected. The usual rich, earthy scent of the forest floor was absent, replaced by a dry, dusty aroma that tickled her nostrils. The air, usually thick with a life-giving humidity, now felt thin and oppressive, each breath a conscious effort. Mara felt a deep thrum beneath her feet, a subtle tremor that wasn't caused by her movement, but by the land itself. It was a low, persistent vibration, a physical manifestation of the forest's distress, a silent scream echoing through the very earth. This was not just a lack of rain; it was a fundamental disruption of the Skywood's life force.

The whispers she heard were not just the rustling of parched leaves in the dry wind, but the anxious murmurs of the forest dwellers, the subtle shifts in the energy of the land that spoke of a profound disquiet. Her Reefwarden senses, honed by the ebb and flow of the ocean, picked up on this subtle yet alarming change. It was a disharmony, a discordant note in the usually vibrant symphony of the Skywood. The air, normally alive with the rich, humid scent of damp earth, decaying leaves, and the sweet fragrance of unseen blossoms, was now thin, dry, and carried a faint, acrid tang that spoke of a struggle for survival. It was the smell of a world slowly suffocating, its lifeblood being leached away.

Mara knelt, her fingers tracing the cracked, dry earth. It crumbled into a fine, dusty powder, devoid of the rich, dark loam she associated with healthy soil. This was the soil of a land parched, its microbial life struggling to endure. She looked up at the canopy again. What had once been a seemingly impenetrable ceiling of vibrant green was now clearly a mosaic of distress. Patches of dull brown and sickly yellow marred the verdant expanse, like a creeping blight. Leaves, once plump and full of moisture, were shriveled, their edges curled inwards as if in pain. A gentle breeze, which in wetter times would have set the leaves into a joyous dance, now caused them to rustle with a dry, papery sound, like a thousand dying whispers.

She felt it then, a low, persistent thrumming beneath her feet, a subtle vibration that wasn't caused by her own movement, but by the land itself. It was a physical manifestation of the Skywood's distress, a silent scream echoing through the very earth. Her Reefwarden training, focused on the intricate balance of aquatic life, had taught her to sense these subtle shifts, these energetic imbalances. But here, inland, the scale of the problem was overwhelming. The air, normally thick with life-giving humidity, felt thin and oppressive, each breath a conscious effort, carrying with it the faint, acrid scent of a world struggling to survive. It was the scent of a vital resource being leached away, leaving behind only the arid husk of what once was. She saw a small, arboreal lizard clinging to a branch, its usually vibrant scales dulled, its movements sluggish. It was a stark indicator of the stress pervading the ecosystem. This was not merely a dry spell; it was a fundamental unraveling, a crisis that threatened to silence the vibrant symphony of the Skywood forever. The disquiet she felt was a reflection of the land's own agony, a resonant echo of a world on the precipice of collapse.

The forest floor, usually a springy cushion of moss and decaying leaves, offered a brittle resistance beneath Mara's worn boots. Each step sent a small puff of dust into the air, a stark reminder of the pervasive dryness that had settled over the Skywood. She had traveled for days since leaving the coast, pushing further inland with a growing sense of urgency that warred with the gnawing uncertainty in her gut. Her Reefwarden training had equipped her with a deep understanding of ecological balance, a sensitivity to the subtle ebb and flow of life within the ocean's embrace. But here, on solid ground, surrounded by trees that seemed to sigh with a weariness she felt echoed in her own bones, those principles felt like fragile shells, ill-suited for the tempest that was brewing.

The coastal air, thick with the briny kiss of the sea, had been replaced by a dry, rasping current that chafed her lungs and whispered tales of parched earth. The vibrant greens of the canopy, which she had expected to see in their full glory, were interspersed with unsettling patches of yellow and brown, like a creeping sickness. Leaves, once glossy and supple, hung limp and desiccated, their edges curled inward as if in silent agony. Even the sounds of the forest were muted, the usual cacophony of chattering creatures and rustling foliage replaced by a somber quiet, punctuated by the dry skittering of unseen things and the anxious chirps of birds whose songs had lost their joyous cadence. It was a symphony of distress, a stark contrast to the vibrant life she was accustomed to sensing.

Mara clutched the leather-bound journal in her satchel, its pages filled with the meticulous observations of her mentors, filled with diagrams of coral polyps and symbiotic relationships of the reef. She had tried to overlay those familiar patterns onto the terrestrial landscape, to find parallels, but the Skywood's suffering was a language she was still struggling to decipher. The principles of predator and prey, of resource management, of the delicate interdependence of species – they were universal, she knew, but their manifestation here was a terrifying mystery. She had seen bleached coral, a silent testament to the ocean's fever, but this... this was a slow, agonizing dehydration of an entire world.

Her initial interactions with the few inland communities she had encountered had been met with guarded glances and curt responses. They were a hardy people, their faces etched with the hardships of life on the fringes of the Skywood, their eyes holding a deep-seated suspicion of outsiders. Mara, with her sea-spun clothing and her unweathered hands, was an obvious anomaly. The encroaching crisis, she sensed, had only amplified their isolation and their distrust. They spoke of the 'withering' in hushed tones, their words laced with a fear that went beyond the simple hardship of a dry season. There were rumors, too, of strange occurrences in the deeper woods, of creatures behaving erratically, of the ancient spirits of the forest stirring in their discontent.

She remembered the elder of the last village, a woman with eyes like polished obsidian, who had warned her, "The Skywood remembers what the sea forgets. Its wounds run deeper than water can heal. You come seeking to mend what is broken, child, but this sickness... it is in the bone." The words had resonated with a chilling accuracy. This wasn't just a drought; it felt like a fundamental unraveling of the land's very essence, a slow poisoning that no amount of rain could wash away.

Her journey inland had been solitary, punctuated by brief, wary encounters. She had traded a small vial of concentrated sea-salt for a handful of dried berries and a crude map that offered little more than a general direction. The villagers, their faces a study in apprehension, had watched her go, their silence more eloquent than any words of warning. They knew, as she was beginning to understand, that the Skywood's plight was no longer a distant concern. It was a creeping shadow, and it was coming for them all.

As she ventured deeper, the landscape shifted. The dense, emerald canopy began to thin, revealing glimpses of a sky that was often a hazy, pale blue. The air grew hotter, drier, and the ground beneath her feet became more rugged, littered with fallen branches that snapped like dry twigs. She had been told to look for signs, for clues to the source of the withering, but the signs were everywhere, a constant barrage of distress. Wilting flora, scarce water sources, and the unnerving quiet of a forest that had lost its voice.

One afternoon, as the sun beat down with an unforgiving intensity, she stumbled upon a clearing that was unlike anything she had seen before. It was a place where the trees stood stark and bare, their branches like skeletal fingers clawing at the sky. The ground was cracked and parched, not a blade of grass in sight. And in the center of the clearing, nestled amongst the deadwood, lay a colossal, scale-covered form.

It was a terrestrial dragon, or at least, what Mara assumed to be one from the ancient legends whispered by the coastal folk. The creature was immense, its body coiled as if in slumber, its scales a dull, earthen hue that seemed to absorb the sunlight rather than reflect it. It was undeniably ancient, its hide scarred and weathered, a testament to centuries of existence. Yet, even in its stillness, there was a palpable aura of power, a raw, untamed energy that vibrated in the air. Mara's heart hammered against her ribs, a mixture of awe and terror coursing through her veins. Her Reefwarden training had taught her to respect all life, but this was a creature of myth, a being that belonged to the realm of stories, not the tangible world she inhabited.

She approached cautiously, her every instinct screaming at her to flee, but a deeper compulsion, the same one that had driven her from the coast, held her rooted to the spot. The dragon's breathing was shallow, almost imperceptible, a faint puff of dry air escaping its nostrils. Its eyes were closed, long, elegant lashes resting against its scaled cheeks. There was a stillness about it, a profound weariness that mirrored the very land around them. It wasn't the slumber of peaceful rest, but the exhaustion of a being deeply unwell.

Mara remembered the tales of the ancient dragons, guardians of the terrestrial realms, their lives intricately woven with the health of the land itself. They were said to draw their strength from the earth, their vitality a reflection of the land's own. If this magnificent creature was suffering, it was a grim indicator of the Skywood's true condition. Her hand instinctively went to the smooth, sea-worn stone she always carried, a reminder of her home, of the vibrant life she fought to protect.

She observed the dragon, her keen eyes, accustomed to spotting the subtlest signs of distress in marine life, now focusing on the terrestrial beast. There were no obvious wounds, no visible signs of injury, yet the creature exuded an aura of profound weakness. Its scales, while impressive, lacked the lustrous sheen of vitality. They were dull, almost brittle, and a fine layer of dust coated their surfaces. The air around it felt heavy, stagnant, devoid of the vibrant energy that even a slumbering creature of such power should possess.

She noticed the way the surrounding vegetation seemed to recoil from it, the few struggling plants in the clearing drooping even further in its presence. It was as if the dragon itself was a focal point of the withering, a living embodiment of the land's suffering. A profound sadness settled over Mara. She had come inland seeking answers, seeking a way to help, but confronting this magnificent, dying creature, she felt an overwhelming sense of her own inadequacy. What could a lone Reefwarden, a student of the ocean's depths, do to mend the woes of a terrestrial titan and a dying forest?

Her fingers traced the cool, smooth surface of her sea-stone. She thought of the coral reefs, their delicate ecosystems teetering on the brink, and she felt a kinship with this ancient dragon, a shared struggle against an encroaching darkness. Both were facing a threat that was insidious, pervasive, and seemed to defy easy solutions.

Hesitantly, Mara reached into her satchel and pulled out her canteen, a small vessel of the precious water she had carefully conserved. She knew it was a futile gesture, a drop in the ocean of this dragon's needs, but it was all she had to offer. She approached the dragon's massive head, her movements slow and deliberate, her gaze never leaving the creature's still form. She poured a small amount of water onto a patch of dry earth near its snout, the liquid quickly absorbed, leaving behind a darker stain that seemed to vanish as she watched.

As the water touched the earth, a flicker of movement caught her eye. One of the dragon's massive eyelids, slow as a glacier's shift, began to lift. A single, ancient eye, the color of molten gold flecked with amber, opened and fixed upon her. There was no immediate aggression, no roar of challenge, but a profound weariness, a deep-seated sorrow that seemed to emanate from the very depths of its being. It was an ancient gaze, filled with the weight of ages, and for a fleeting moment, Mara felt as if she were looking into the soul of the Skywood itself.

The dragon's breath stirred the dust at its snout, a dry, rasping sound that spoke of a parched throat. It did not recoil from her, nor did it advance. It simply observed her, its golden eye a silent question. Mara stood her ground, her own apprehension slowly giving way to a quiet determination. She wasn't here to conquer or to claim, but to understand, and perhaps, to offer a sliver of hope.

"Great one," she began, her voice barely a whisper, rough from the dry air. "I am Mara, a Reefwarden from the southern coast. I have come seeking the cause of the withering. The Skywood... it is dying."

The dragon's eye remained fixed on her, unblinking. There was no audible response, but Mara felt a subtle shift in the air, a faint tremor that seemed to originate from the creature itself. It was not a sound, but an impression, a feeling of ancient sadness, of a burden too great to bear. It was as if the dragon itself was struggling to communicate, its voice choked by the very dryness that was consuming its world.

She continued, her voice gaining a little strength, fueled by a desperate need to connect, to bridge the chasm between her world and this ancient being. "My training has taught me of balance, of the interconnectedness of all life. The ocean... it bleeds when it is sick. I see the Skywood bleeding now, and I must understand why."

As she spoke, the dragon's head lowered slightly, its immense form shifting with a grating sound of scales against dry earth. It exhaled again, a longer, deeper breath this time, and a faint, almost imperceptible scent of dust and ancient stone filled the air. Then, slowly, deliberately, it lifted one massive claw, its sharp talons scraping against the parched ground, and drew a symbol in the dust.

It was a spiraling pattern, intricate and flowing, reminiscent of a whirlpool, yet rooted in the terrestrial earth. As the dragon's claw completed the final swirl, a faint, ethereal glow emanated from the dust, a shimmer of light that seemed to push back the oppressive dryness for a fleeting moment. Mara watched, captivated, her Reefwarden senses tingling with an understanding that transcended spoken language. The symbol was one of interconnectedness, of a cycle, of a flow that was vital, and that was now broken.

The dragon's golden eye flickered, and Mara felt a new impression, a surge of ancient memory, of a time when the Skywood pulsed with life, when rivers flowed freely, and when the dragons themselves were vibrant guardians. Then, the impression faded, replaced by a profound sense of loss, of a deep, gnawing emptiness. The creature lowered its head again, its eye closing once more, the brief flicker of connection extinguished. It was as if it had shared all it could, its energy too depleted to sustain the effort.

Mara knelt by the dust symbol, her fingers tracing its outline. It was a message, a plea, a roadmap. The spiral, she understood, represented the flow of life, the circulation of vital energies that sustained the Skywood. The broken nature of the symbol, its faint glow quickly fading back into the dusty earth, spoke of a disruption, a blockage in that vital flow. Her Reefwarden training had emphasized the importance of currents, of how their disruption could lead to devastation. This terrestrial symbol, she realized, was a mirror of that principle.

She looked at the great dragon, its slumber now more profound than before, its presence a heavy testament to the Skywood's suffering. She was just one person, a woman who understood the rhythm of tides, the language of coral. But she had been given a sign, a direction. The withering was not a natural phenomenon; it was a consequence of a broken cycle, a blocked flow. And if the dragons, the ancient heart of the land, were suffering, then the entire Skywood was in peril.

Rising slowly, Mara dusted off her hands. The weight of her journey had shifted. It was no longer just about understanding; it was about action. The symbol in the dust was a puzzle, a challenge, but also a promise. The journey inland was far from over. It had, in fact, just truly begun. She would carry the dragon's silent message with her, a constant reminder of the vital flow that needed to be restored, of the interconnectedness that bound even the deepest oceans to the mightiest forests. The responsibility felt immense, crushing even, but beneath it, a flicker of hope ignited. She was a Reefwarden, after all. She understood the importance of flow, and she knew that even the most stagnant waters could, with the right guidance, find their way back to the sea. The Skywood was her sea now, and its currents, however broken, were calling to her.

Cael Thornevale walked the ancient paths of the Skywood, his steps as familiar and rhythmic as the pulse of the forest itself. Each fallen leaf, each gnarled root, was a known entity, a friend under his care. As a Land Guardian, his existence was intrinsically linked to the towering trees that formed the emerald ceiling above him, a relationship forged not just by duty, but by a deep, almost spiritual resonance. He felt the Skywood not as a collection of individual plants, but as a singular, breathing entity, its well-being etched into the very marrow of his bones.

Lately, however, that resonance had been troubled by a discordant hum. It was in the unnerving quiet that had settled over the normally boisterous canopy. The cheerful chatter of the sky-wrens, a sound as constant as the rustle of wind through leaves, had dwindled to mere whispers, their songs fragmented and anxious. The emerald canopy, his constant companion, was showing an unsettling blush of gold and ochre, far too early in the season. Leaves, meant to cling with tenacious vigor until the autumn winds coaxed them down, were surrendering to the ground with a premature, brittle rustle, as if a fever had passed through their veins, draining them of their lifeblood.

These were not the usual cycles of growth and decay that Cael had meticulously observed and tended for decades. This was a sickness, a creeping malaise that gnawed at the edges of his world. He'd seen it begin subtly, a few dry patches on the bark of elder oaks, a faint wilting on the sun-dappled ferns near the forest's edge. But now, it was pervasive, a shadow stretching across the heart of the Skywood. He ran a calloused hand over the rough bark of a sentinel pine, its needles dry and brittle to the touch. Normally, he would feel the sap's steady flow, a reassuring sign of robust health. Today, there was only a faint, sluggish pulse, a desperate murmur of life struggling against an unseen antagonist.

His oath as a Land Guardian was a sacred vow, a lifelong commitment to the protection and preservation of the Skywood. He was its watchful eye, its guiding hand, its unwavering vigil. He understood the intricate dance of life and death within its borders, the delicate balance that allowed it to thrive. He knew which fungi aided the great trees, which insects were vital pollinators, and which creatures, in their natural predation, kept the ecosystem in check. His senses were attuned to the subtlest shifts in the forest's mood, the faintest tremor of distress. And now, those senses were screaming a dire warning.

He paused, his gaze sweeping across a familiar glade. The sunlight, which usually dappled the forest floor in shifting patterns of gold, was harsher now, less filtered. The undergrowth, usually a lush carpet of vibrant green mosses and ferns, was thinning, the earth beneath exposed and cracked in places, like parched skin. A single, desiccated fern frond lay curled on the dusty ground, a miniature testament to the widespread thirst. He picked it up, its delicate structure crumbling into dust between his fingers. It was a stark contrast to the resilient vitality he had always known.

Cael knelt, his knees pressing into the dry earth. He closed his eyes, drawing a deep, conscious breath. He tried to reach out with his senses, to feel the forest's heartwood, its life-giving arteries. He focused, pushing past the immediate signs of decay, seeking the deeper currents that sustained the Skywood. He felt the ancient, slow heartbeat of the oldest trees, the deep roots that anchored them to the earth's core. But beneath that familiar rhythm, there was a new sensation, a faint, erratic tremor, like a dying ember struggling to catch flame. It was the sound of the forest's life force sputtering, its vitality ebbing away.

He remembered his training, the ancient lore passed down through generations of Land Guardians. They spoke of the Skywood as a living entity, its health tied to the very essence of the land. Its rivers were its veins, its canopy its lungs, its roots its anchor. If any part of this intricate system was compromised, the whole would suffer. And Cael could feel, with a certainty that chilled him to the bone, that a significant part of that system was failing.

His father, the previous Land Guardian, had always spoken of the forest with a reverence that bordered on worship. "The Skywood is not just trees, Cael," he had once told him, his voice a low rumble like distant thunder. "It is memory. It is spirit. It is the breath of the world. To harm it is to harm yourself, and all who depend on it." Those words echoed in Cael's mind now, a solemn reminder of the immense responsibility he carried. He was not merely a caretaker; he was a part of the Skywood, and its suffering was his own.

He stood again, his gaze intense as he surveyed the scene. The premature shedding of leaves was particularly troubling. It spoke of a desperate attempt by the trees to conserve energy, to slow their metabolic processes in the face of an overwhelming stress. It was a sign of true distress, not just a seasonal change. And the silence... the silence was the most unnerving. A healthy forest was a symphony of life, a constant hum of activity. This pervasive quiet was an anomaly, a void where life should be teeming. It felt like a held breath, an anticipation of something terrible.

He walked further, his path taking him towards the deeper, more secluded parts of the Skywood. Here, the trees grew taller, their canopies interlocked so tightly that only slivers of sky peeked through. The air was cooler, more shaded, but the signs of distress were no less evident. He found a cluster of Moonpetal blossoms, their delicate white petals usually unfurling with the twilight. Today, they were shriveled and brown, clinging to their stalks like brittle parchment. He touched one gently, and it disintegrated into a fine, powdery dust.

This was not a simple drought. Droughts were harsh, but the Skywood had weathered them before. There were seasons of scarcity, times when the rain was slow to come, but the forest always rallied. This felt different, more insidious, a fundamental weakening that no amount of water, if it even came, could truly mend. It felt as if the very life force of the land was being leached away, leaving behind a hollowed-out shell.

He continued his patrol, his senses on high alert. He was not just an observer; he was a protector. His duty was to identify the source of this malaise, to understand its nature, and to find a way to halt its destructive progress. He carried the knowledge of generations of Land Guardians, their wisdom passed down through oral tradition and the ancient texts bound in the Skywood's own bark. But this threat felt new, a darkness that the old lore had not quite prepared him for.

He stopped near a small stream, usually a lively artery of the forest, its waters clear and bubbling. Today, it flowed sluggishly, its surface coated with a faint, iridescent film. The pebbles on its bed, usually vibrant with moss, were bare and dull. He knelt by the water's edge, his reflection a somber face staring back at him. He cupped his hands and brought the water to his lips. It tasted thin, metallic, devoid of the sweet, pure essence of the Skywood's lifeblood. A wave of despair washed over him. If the water, the very sustenance of the forest, was tainted, what hope was there?

He observed the banks of the stream. The reeds that usually grew tall and verdant were yellowed and brittle, their stalks bent as if under an invisible weight. A small, furry creature, its fur usually a sleek grey, scurried past, its movements jerky and disoriented, its eyes wide with an unnatural fear. It was a whisper of panic in the pervasive silence, a sign that even the smallest inhabitants of the Skywood were succumbing to the encroaching sickness.

Cael stood, his jaw set with grim determination. His connection to the Skywood was not just a duty; it was a part of his very being. He felt its pain as if it were his own. The early signs of this withering had been subtle, easily dismissed by those who did not possess the Land Guardian's deep intimacy with the forest. But for Cael, they were undeniable pronouncements of disaster. He had seen the gradual decay, the slow draining of vitality, and he knew, with a certainty that was both terrifying and resolute, that this was no mere passing hardship. This was a profound crisis, a deep-seated sickness that threatened to consume everything he held dear. He would not stand idly by and watch his world wither and die. His vigil was unwavering, and he would face this encroaching darkness head-on, no matter the cost. The Skywood was his life, and he would fight for it with every fiber of his being.

The earth hummed a discordant tune, a subtle tremor beneath the soles of Thryxal's immense claws. He was ancient, his scales the color of deep, undisturbed earth, weathered by millennia of sun and storm. His lineage was woven into the very fabric of this land, his ancestors having slumbered in its core before the first human settlements dared to carve their ephemeral marks upon its surface. The Skywood, the vibrant tapestry of green that Cael Thornevale so fiercely protected, was an extension of his own being, a terrestrial garden nurtured by the deep pulses of the planet. Yet, something was wrong. Terribly wrong.

He shifted his massive weight, the movement sending ripples through the soil beneath him. The air, usually thick with the scent of damp earth and pine, carried an unfamiliar dryness, a metallic tang that pricked at his sensitive nostrils. The rainfall, a rhythm as predictable as his own heart's slow beat, had become erratic, a capricious tease of drought interspersed with sudden, violent deluges that washed away fertile soil without truly quenching the land's thirst. His kin, the other land dragons, felt it too. The ancient resonance pathways, the invisible arteries that carried the lifeblood of the earth, were frayed, their vibrant hum muted, their energies struggling against an encroaching silence.

"The waters do not fall as they should, Thryxal," rumbled Vorlag, his voice like stones grinding together. Vorlag was younger by a few centuries, his scales a mottled grey, but his concern mirrored Thryxal's own. They lay coiled in a sun-dappled clearing, a place where generations of land dragons had sought solace and communed with the earth. This clearing, once lush with mosses that felt like soft velvet beneath their scales, was now brittle and sparse, its vitality leached away.

Thryxal exhaled a slow plume of dust. "The patterns are broken, Vorlag. The earth weeps, but its tears are too few, or too fierce. And the nesting grounds..." He trailed off, a deep unease settling in his cavernous chest. The highest aeries, those carved into the sheer cliffs where the wind sang its wildest songs, had been abandoned. The younger dragons, their scales still soft and dull, were seeking more sheltered, less exposed places, driven by an instinctual fear of the unpredictable sky. This was unprecedented. For millennia, they had known the storms, weathered the gales, and trusted in the earth's enduring strength.

"They seek safer hollows," Vorlag stated, his tone lacking conviction. "But safety is an illusion when the foundations themselves begin to crack."

"It is not merely the sky," Thryxal countered, his deep eyes, pools of molten gold, fixed on a distant point where the Skywood began to thin, a subtle yet alarming blush of ochre marring its verdant expanse. "The resonance... it falters. I feel it in my bones, in the very rock beneath me. The earth's song is growing weak." He remembered the tales, whispered through the generations, of times when the land had suffered. But those were localized ailments, quickly healed by the earth's inherent resilience. This felt different, systemic, a creeping sickness that gnawed at the land's core.

His gaze drifted towards the fringes of the Skywood, towards the scattered settlements of humans. A flicker of ancient animosity, a deeply ingrained distrust, stirred within him. Humans. They were ephemeral, their lives a blink of an eye to his own enduring existence. They were a blight, a disruption, forever seeking to bend the earth to their will, to extract its bounty without understanding the cost. He remembered the great clearing that had once existed before the Skywood had reclaimed it, a scar of their presence that had taken centuries to fade.

"It is the Two-Leggeds," Vorlag spat, echoing Thryxal's unspoken thought. His voice vibrated with a raw, territorial anger. "They delve too deep. They take too much. Their insatiable hunger poisons the earth."

Thryxal rumbled in agreement, though his own instincts whispered a more complex truth. The humans were a factor, undeniably. Their burgeoning towns, their insatiable demand for timber and ore, were a constant pressure on the natural world. But this sickness felt older, more primal, something that predated the latest human encroachments. It was as if the very spirit of the land was being drained, not just depleted.

"Their actions are a symptom, not the cause," Thryxal said, his voice a low growl. "The sickness runs deeper. It whispers in the roots, it drains the rivers, it silences the very breath of the wood. The resonance pathways... they are more than just conduits for the earth's energy. They are its memory, its very consciousness. And they are being corrupted."

He remembered his own hatching, a time when the land thrummed with an almost unbearable vitality. The air had vibrated with power, and the Skywood had been an unbroken emerald sea, stretching to the horizon. His connection to the land had been immediate, profound. He had felt the slow, patient growth of the ancient trees, the ceaseless journey of the subterranean rivers, the silent communion between stone and root. Now, that connection felt strained, like a taut rope threatening to snap.

"The humans... they have always been a careless species," Thryxal continued, his voice tinged with weariness. "They build their nests of stone and wood, and in their haste, they wound the earth. They forget that they, too, are children of this land. They believe they are its masters, not its caretakers. And when the land suffers, they will suffer too." He recalled the ancient pacts, the times when his kind had seen the need to guide the nascent humans, to teach them the rhythms of the earth. But that was long ago, before their numbers had swelled, before their ambition had outstripped their wisdom.

Vorlag shifted, his heavy limbs scraping against the parched earth. "Guidance? They spit on guidance, Thryxal. They see our strength as a threat, our ancient wisdom as superstition. They would cage us, if they could, for the power they believe we hoard." His scales bristled with indignation. "They have no respect for the old ways. They clear the ancient groves, divert the sacred streams, and then wonder why the land rebels."

Thryxal felt a pang of agreement, but his mind, honed by centuries of observation, refused to accept such a simplistic explanation. The humans were a part of the ecosystem, however destructive they often were. To attribute the entire withering of the land to them alone would be to ignore deeper, more fundamental imbalances.

"Their methods are crude, their understanding shallow," Thryxal conceded. "But there is a deeper disquiet, Vorlag. A tremor in the earth's heart that I cannot explain solely by human folly. The resonance pathways... they are not merely disrupted by their digging and their felling. They are being actively... choked. Starved." He closed his eyes, attempting to focus on the subtle vibrations, the faint echoes of power that still pulsed through the earth. He felt the lifeblood of the Skywood, the intricate network of energy that connected every root, every leaf, every creature to the core of the planet. And he felt something else, something alien and cold, like a parasitic growth slowly consuming the vital currents.

"I have felt it for seasons now," Thryxal murmured, his voice barely audible above the rustle of dry leaves. "The pulse grows fainter. The vibrant hum of the forest floor, the ancient songs of the deep earth... they are being silenced. The younger dragons, they are already growing restless. Their connection to the land is not as strong as ours. If this continues..." He didn't finish the thought, the implications too dire. A generation of dragons disconnected from the earth's vital energies was a terrifying prospect. It meant a loss of instinct, a weakening of their very being.

"And what of the Guardian?" Vorlag asked, his gaze sharp. "This Cael Thornevale. The humans speak of him with a strange reverence. They say he communes with the trees, that he understands the forest's whispers."

Thryxal snorted, a puff of fine dust escaping his nostrils. "Humans speak of many things, Vorlag. Reverence is a fleeting emotion for them. They lauded their kings one moment, and dragged them from their thrones the next. Their 'Guardians' are often the first to fall when their fragile societies crumble. He is but one of them. A single voice against a tide of destruction."

Yet, even as he spoke, Thryxal admitted to himself that there was something different about this human. The ancient texts, preserved in the deep caverns where dragon wisdom was etched onto stone tablets, spoke of rare individuals who possessed a deeper connection to the land, those who could bridge the chasm between the human world and the primal forces of nature. Could this Thornevale be one of them?

"He walks the paths, I know," Thryxal admitted grudgingly. "I have felt his presence. He touches the trees, he listens to the wind. He is... attuned. More so than most of his kind. But can he truly understand the depth of this sickness? Can he comprehend the unraveling of the resonance pathways? Or does he, like so many others, simply see the wilting leaves and the dry streams?"

His ancient distrust of humanity, however, remained a formidable barrier. They were a force of disruption, their ambition a constant threat to the delicate balance of the world. For millennia, the land dragons had existed in a state of cautious coexistence, observing from their deep caverns, intervening only when the land itself was pushed to the brink. But the brink was fast approaching.

"He feels the pain of the wood," Thryxal continued, his voice growing heavier. "I can sense that. But to feel is not to understand. To understand is not to have the power to heal. The sickness is too deeply rooted. It gnaws at the very essence of the earth. The rain patterns are but a symptom, the failing resonance a testament to a deeper wound. I fear... I fear something far more ancient and potent than mere human greed is at play here."

He recalled a time when the sky itself had been a tapestry of vibrant energy, when the earth had sung with a power so profound it vibrated through his very bones. Now, there was a hollowness, a pervasive quiet that was more terrifying than any storm. The land dragons were the guardians of the earth's deepest secrets, its primordial heart. And that heart was failing. Thryxal, the ancient, felt a chill that had nothing to do with the passing breeze. The age of slumber was over. The land demanded action, and he was unsure if even his kind had the strength to answer its desperate cry. The disquiet was no longer a whisper; it was a growing roar that threatened to swallow them all.

The memory of the Pale Tide was a phantom limb, an ache that resonated in the bones of the land even far from the scarred coastlines. Decades had passed since the monstrous inundation, since the ocean had surged inland with an insatiable hunger, swallowing villages and forests whole. Yet, the echoes persisted. They manifested not just in the perpetually damp, salt-blasted ruins that still dotted the eastern shores, or in the strangely mutated flora that clung stubbornly to life in the salt marshes, but in the very psyche of the people. An undercurrent of fear, a primal understanding of nature's capacity for brutal indifference, had settled deep within their collective consciousness.

Thryxal, his ancient awareness attuned to the faintest tremors of ecological distress, felt it too, a residual trauma in the earth's memory. The land dragons, slumbering for millennia in the planet's core, had felt the earth's agony as a physical blow. They had witnessed, through the intricate network of resonance pathways, the ocean's violent usurpation, the tearing of coastlines, the drowning of entire ecosystems.

Though the immediate threat now lay inland, a different, more insidious decay, the spectral imprint of that earlier catastrophe lingered, a testament to the fragility of balance. The Pale Tide had been a raw, cataclysmic wound, a dramatic display of nature's power unleashed. This current ailment, however, was a slow poisoning, a creeping rot that gnawed at the foundations of life.

Even for those who had never directly witnessed the Tide, its legend was a potent cautionary tale. It was spoken of in hushed tones around campfires, a stark reminder of what could happen when the natural world, pushed too far, finally broke free of its restraints. Children grew up on stories of the water's relentless march, of the desperate flight from homes that were never reclaimed. This inherited fear made them more susceptible to the subtle signs of the present blight. They were already primed to see ecological disruption not as a temporary setback, but as a harbinger of doom. The drought-stricken fields and the thinning forests were not merely inconveniences; they were a chilling echo of that past devastation, a premonition of a similar, albeit slower, demise.

The ecological scars were evident if one knew where to look. In the lowlands, where the Tide had receded, the soil remained stubbornly infertile, imbued with a lingering salinity that stunted the growth of most terrestrial plants. Certain hardy, salt-tolerant grasses had taken root, forming dense, unwelcoming carpets that choked out the more diverse undergrowth. These areas were now ghost meadows, eerily silent, devoid of the birdsong and insect hum that once characterized the region. The traditional farming villages that had once thrived there were now struggling, their livelihoods dependent on the meager yields of salt-resistant crops or on the less-than-reliable bounty of the sea, which itself was showing signs of strain.

The impact had rippled outwards, affecting entire food webs. The disruption of coastal wetlands had decimated populations of migratory birds, their ancestral stopping grounds rendered uninhabitable. This, in turn, had led to an overpopulation of certain insect species further inland, pests that now feasted on crops that were already weakened by the increasingly erratic weather patterns. It was a cascading failure, each ecological imbalance exacerbating the next, a complex web of cause and effect that was becoming increasingly difficult to untangle.

Thryxal understood this interconnectedness on a fundamental level. His very existence was bound to the health of the land. The resonance pathways, those vital arteries of the earth's energy, had been violently disrupted by the Pale Tide. While the initial inundation had been a physical assault, a brute force of water, the current malady was something subtler, a corruption that seeped into the very energetic fabric of the planet. The memory of the Tide, therefore, was not just a historical footnote; it was a scar on the earth's energetic body, a vulnerability that this new, insidious threat was exploiting. The land had been weakened, its recuperative powers taxed by the previous disaster, making it more susceptible to this deeper, more pervasive sickness.

He recalled the ancient draconic lore, tales etched into the very bedrock of the world, of times when the oceans had raged with similar, though often more localized, fury. These were often the result of immense geological shifts, or perhaps the awakening of deep-sea titans, forces that dwarfed mortal comprehension. But the Pale Tide had felt different, a perversion of natural cycles, a wrongness that even the earth's most ancient guardians struggled to fully comprehend. It was as if the very essence of the ocean had been twisted, its natural rhythm corrupted by some external influence.

Vorlag, younger and more prone to visceral reactions, had spoken of the coastal ruins with a shudder. "They say that even now, on nights when the moon is full and the tide is high, you can hear the screams of those lost to the water. A lament that chills the very marrow." Thryxal, while not prone to such fanciful notions, could appreciate the sentiment. The lingering psychic residue of such widespread tragedy was undeniable. The earth remembered pain, and that memory could shape the present.

The continued presence of saltwater further inland, in areas that should have been freshwater marshes or meadows, was a physical manifestation of this lingering trauma. The ground itself seemed to weep brine, a constant reminder of the ocean's violation. Certain rare, phosphorescent fungi, which thrived in saline conditions and fed on the decomposing remains of organisms that perished during the Tide, continued to bloom in the deepest, darkest ravines. Their eerie luminescence, visible only in the deepest night, cast an unsettling glow on the landscape, a spectral testament to the past. These areas, shunned by most life, had become pockets of eerie stillness, where the only sounds were the sighing of the wind through salt-encrusted branches and the faint, unsettling murmur of water that never truly receded.

Even the air in these regions carried a faint, metallic tang, a ghostly scent of the sea that persisted despite the distance from the current coastline. It was the smell of decay, of salt and long-submerged organic matter, a scent that clung to the very fabric of the environment. It reminded the inhabitants of the fragility of their existence, of how easily the natural order could be overthrown.

This lingering ecological trauma made the current affliction all the more terrifying. The Pale Tide had been a sudden, overwhelming catastrophe. One could flee, one could rebuild, however slowly, on higher ground. But this slow, creeping sickness, this gradual sapping of the land's vitality, offered no such clear escape. It was like a slow-acting poison, undetectable at first, its effects only becoming apparent when it was too late to counteract. The memory of the rapid, violent destruction of the Tide made the slow, agonizing decay of the present all the more unnerving. It felt less like a natural disaster and more like a deliberate, malevolent act.

The people who lived near the former coast, or who had relatives who had been displaced by the Tide, were particularly sensitive to these changes. They possessed a heightened awareness of the earth's subtle shifts, a wariness born of hard experience. They saw the wilting of leaves, the parched riverbeds, the unseasonable warmth, not as isolated incidents, but as potential precursors to a wider collapse. They were the first to notice the subtle discoloration of the Skywood's leaves, the faint, almost imperceptible shift in the wind's song. Their collective memory of the Pale Tide had honed their senses, making them more receptive to the land's lament.

The fishermen, whose livelihoods had been irrevocably altered by the Tide, now spoke of strange currents and unusual marine life, of fish that appeared sick or deformed, of fishing grounds that were suddenly barren. They saw the changes in the sea not as a natural cycle, but as a continuation of the same unnatural force that had unleashed the Pale Tide. They were the front line, bearing witness to the slow degradation of the oceans, a degradation that Thryxal knew was intrinsically linked to the land's own suffering.

The interconnectedness was the key. The Pale Tide had been a dramatic demonstration of how interconnected the world was – how a surge in the ocean could devastate inland communities, how the destruction of coastal ecosystems could have far-reaching consequences. Now, that same interconnectedness was being exploited by this new threat. The sickness that was weakening the land was also subtly affecting the waters, creating a synergistic decay that was far more potent than either ailment alone. The earth's memory of the Pale Tide served as a constant, albeit unwelcome, reminder of this fundamental truth. It was a living testament to the fact that no part of the world existed in isolation, that the health of one ecosystem was inextricably linked to the health of all others.

Thryxal often found himself contemplating the psychological impact of such a profound, shared trauma. The Pale Tide had not just reshaped coastlines; it had reshaped minds. It had instilled a sense of vulnerability, a knowledge that the seemingly immutable forces of nature could, in an instant, become instruments of destruction. This underlying anxiety was now a fertile ground for the seeds of fear and despair that this new, insidious blight threatened to sow. The people, already predisposed to seeing disaster on the horizon, were now facing a threat that was far less obvious, far more insidious, and potentially far more devastating than the monstrous wave that had once consumed their shores. They remembered the water's wrath, but this new enemy was a silent predator, a slow poison.

The impact wasn't limited to humans. The land dragons, too, carried the psychic weight of the Pale Tide. For Thryxal and his kin, it was a memory of their helplessness, of witnessing a catastrophic event unfold and being unable to fully intervene. Their own deep-earth dwelling protected them from the direct physical force of the water, but the agony of the land, the terror of the creatures caught in the deluge, had resonated through them like a seismic shock. It was a reminder of their duty as guardians, a duty they had, in some ways, failed to uphold.

This past failure, this lingering sense of inadequacy, made them all the more determined to confront the current threat, to prevent another instance of the world's vital energies being so brutally corrupted. The memory of the Pale Tide was not just a historical echo; it was a catalyst, a spur to action in the face of a new, and perhaps even more dangerous, peril. The land, having once been so violently violated, was now whispering a different, more insidious kind of warning, a warning that resonated with the old, deep wounds of the past, preparing its inhabitants for a darkness that was both new and terrifyingly familiar.

CHAPTER TWO

FRACTURED RESONANCE

The celestial dance had faltered. The predictable waltz of stars and moons, the celestial clockwork that had governed the Skywood's rainfall for millennia, was no longer in sync. Mara, her brow furrowed in concentration, traced the intricate star charts spread across her workbench, the faint luminescence of alchemical inks illuminating the delicate lines. She was accustomed to the subtle shifts in planetary orbits, the regular ebb and flow of astral energies that dictated the seasons and the rains. But the patterns she now observed were erratic, discordant. A lunar eclipse that occurred too soon, a constellation that seemed to have shifted its position overnight, a comet's tail that burned with an unnatural, sickly green hue. These were not mere anomalies; they were seismic shifts in the cosmic order, ripples emanating from a disturbance far beyond the Skywood's verdant canopy.

She muttered to herself, her voice a low murmur against the rustling leaves outside her observatory, "The Weaver's Loom is fraying. The celestial threads are snapping." The Skywood's rainfall was intimately tied to these celestial alignments. It wasn't just a matter of the sun's warmth or the moon's pull; it was a complex interplay of cosmic forces, channeled through ley lines and amplified by ancient standing stones, that guided the moisture-laden winds from the Great Southern Ocean inland.

This intricate meteorological system, honed over eons, ensured a gentle, consistent deluge, a life-giving embrace that nurtured the Skywood's unparalleled biodiversity. Now, that delicate choreography was broken. The atmospheric currents that once flowed with unwavering purpose were becoming capricious, veering off course, carrying their precious cargo of rain to distant, barren lands, or worse, dissipating them into the upper atmosphere, lost to the parched earth below.

Meanwhile, miles away, within the emerald heart of the Skywood, Cael experienced the disruption not as abstract celestial movements, but as a harsh, immediate reality. The usual symphony of dripping leaves and gurgling streams had been replaced by an unnerving silence, punctuated by the crackle of dry undergrowth underfoot. The air, once thick with the humid scent of blooming orchids and damp earth, now held a suffocating dryness, a premonition of thirst. He watched, his heart sinking, as once-vibrant ferns curled inward, their fronds brittle and brown. The mighty Lumina trees, their leaves usually a shimmering emerald, were now tinged with a sickly yellow, their branches reaching towards a sky that offered no succumbing moisture.

"It's like the sky has forgotten how to weep," he muttered, kicking at a patch of cracked earth. He'd witnessed the Skywood endure dry spells before, periods of reduced rainfall that tested the resilience of its inhabitants. But this was different. This was a profound drought, a relentless baking that seemed to drain the very lifeblood from the land. He'd seen a family of Sylphwings, their iridescent wings usually a blur of movement as they flitted between water-collecting bromeliads, now huddled listlessly on a sun-scorched branch, their delicate forms drooping with exhaustion. The normally teeming pools where the luminous Glow-worms spawned were reduced to muddy puddles, the water too shallow and stagnant to sustain them.

Cael remembered the tales of the Whispering Falls, a cascade of water so pure and abundant that its mist nourished the surrounding flora for miles. Now, the once-thundering roar of the falls had dwindled to a pathetic trickle, a thin thread of water clinging precariously to the cliff face, its spray barely reaching the moss-covered rocks at its base. The vibrant mosses, which thrived in the perpetual dampness, were turning a dull grey, their moisture-starved tendrils recoiling from the touch. This wasn't just a lack of rain; it was a fundamental disruption of the Skywood's hydrological cycle, a system so finely tuned that even a slight imbalance could have catastrophic consequences.

The impact was not confined to the plant life. The smaller creatures, the insects, the amphibians, the ground-dwelling mammals, were struggling to survive. Cael found himself constantly searching for sources of water, his usual foraging routes now yielding nothing but dust and despair. He'd seen a normally robust Burrow-hare, its fur matted and dry, frantically digging at the base of a wilting bloom, desperate for any hint of moisture. The scarcity of water was leading to increased competition, to a primal struggle for survival that was alien to the usually harmonious ecosystem. Predatory birds, usually well-fed by the abundance of smaller prey, were now seen squabbling over insects, their hunting grounds stripped bare.

Mara, in her observatory, had begun to correlate Cael's increasingly frantic reports with her celestial observations. The erratic rainfall wasn't a random act of nature. The celestial bodies were not merely misaligned; they were being subtly influenced, their gravitational pull and energetic emanations warped by an unseen force. She noticed a peculiar resonance, a harmonic discord emanating from a sector of the sky where no known celestial bodies resided, a void that seemed to pulse with a malevolent energy. This was the source of the disruption, a parasitic influence that was siphoning off the celestial energies that governed the Skywood's weather.

"It's as if something is drawing the Skywood's rain closer to... itself," she mused, her fingers tracing the unusual energy signature on her charts. The atmospheric pressure gradients that usually guided the rain-bearing winds were being artificially altered. High-pressure systems, which normally dissipated over land, were now lingering, pushing the rain-laden clouds further away. Low-pressure systems, which should have encouraged precipitation, were forming erratically, only to collapse without releasing their moisture. It was a deliberate manipulation, a perversion of natural atmospheric dynamics.

The Skywood, with its unique ecosystem, was particularly vulnerable to such a disruption. Its lush rainforest relied on a delicate balance of temperature, humidity, and a consistent, gentle rainfall. The towering canopies of the Skywood trees, so crucial for filtering sunlight and retaining moisture, were now exposed to harsher, more direct sunlight, leading to increased evaporation and further drying of the forest floor. The intricate network of fungal hyphae beneath the soil, which helped distribute water and nutrients, was withering, unable to cope with the prolonged dryness. The symbiotic relationships that defined the Skywood were unraveling, strand by strand.

Cael witnessed this unraveling firsthand. He saw the usually vibrant moss gardens, the emerald carpets that adorned the ancient roots of the Elderwood trees, turning brown and brittle. The air, stripped of its moisture, carried a fine dust that coated everything, dulling the vibrant colors of the flowers and the iridescent wings of the Lumina moths. The scent of decay, of dying vegetation, began to overpower the usual sweet fragrance of the rainforest. He found himself rationing water from his waterskin, a habit he'd never thought he'd need within the perpetually damp embrace of the Skywood. The very air felt thin, abrasive against his lungs.

"The Skywood is gasping," he whispered, his voice raspy. He saw how the smaller streams, the lifeblood of the undergrowth, had shrunk to mere trickles, their banks cracking like parched earth. The normally teeming insect life, a constant hum that was the background music of the forest, had diminished significantly. The birds that depended on these insects were either migrating prematurely or were noticeably thinner, their calls weaker. The entire ecosystem, so dependent on the Skywood's predictable rainfall, was on the brink of collapse.

Mara, looking at her instruments, saw the data reflecting Cael's grim observations. The alchemical sensors designed to measure atmospheric moisture were registering alarmingly low levels, far below anything recorded in the centuries of Skywood records. The resonance crystals that were meant to hum with the steady rhythm of the planet's hydrological cycle were now emitting a faint, erratic pulse, like a faltering heartbeat.

She realized with a chilling certainty that this wasn't a natural disaster. The celestial anomalies, the warped atmospheric currents, the withering of the Skywood – it was all interconnected, a symptom of a deeper, more insidious manipulation. The Skywood's dependence on its unique climate, once its greatest strength, had become its greatest vulnerability. The very precision that allowed life to flourish in such abundance now made it exquisitely susceptible to any disruption of its rainfall cycles. The once-gentle nourishment had become a ticking clock, each dry day accelerating the Skywood's descent into a desolate silence.

Mara adjusted the intricate lenses of her scrying bowl, the swirling mist within coalescing into faint, shimmering lines. These were not the celestial charts that had occupied her attention for so long, but something far more grounded, yet infinitely more delicate: the resonance pathways of the Skywood. She had always understood, in a theoretical sense, the concept of these conduits – the invisible arteries of natural energy that pulsed beneath the soil, through the roots of the ancient trees, and along the veins of crystalline rock, carrying the lifeblood of the forest. Her studies of ancient texts and the whispers of her own nascent abilities had given her an inkling of their existence, but now, with the Skywood's vitality visibly leaching away, the need to understand them, to *see* them, was paramount.

The mist in the scrying bowl swirled faster, and patterns began to emerge. They were like the root systems of colossal, unseen trees, branching and weaving beneath the earth, connecting sacred groves, vital springs, and the very heartwood of the Elderwood giants. Each intersection, each pulsing node, represented a confluence of energies – astral, terrestrial, and vital. These were the pathways that allowed the Skywood's unique magic to flow, to nourish, to sustain. They were the secret channels that amplified the life-giving rain, not just as water, but as a carrier of potent, restorative energies.

But what Mara was seeing now was not a vibrant, flowing network. It was a tapestry riddled with dark knots and frayed edges. Entire sections of the pathways glowed with a sickly, dim light, as if choked by an unseen hand. Others pulsed erratically, their rhythm stuttering like a dying breath. She traced a particularly dense cluster of these distortions, a place deep within the northern reaches of the Skywood, a region known for its ancient mushroom groves and its abundance of rare bioluminescent flora. Here, the lines of energy were not merely dimmed; they were fractured, broken as if by a violent impact. A dark, viscous shadow seemed to seep into the scrying mist, obscuring the true pattern of the pathway, as if something were actively feeding on its essence, or worse, deliberately damming its flow.

"The Ley-lines are not just misaligned," she murmured, her voice barely a whisper. "They are being... wounded." She focused her will, pushing her nascent abilities to their limit. She felt a faint echo, a phantom ache, reverberate through her own being, a sympathetic response to the distress of the pathways. It was as if her own body were trying to process a blockage, a constriction that made each breath a conscious effort. This was more than a disruption of rain; it was a poisoning of the Skywood's very soul. The resonance pathways were the conduits through which the forest breathed, ate, and lived. To choke them was to slowly strangle the life out of the entire ecosystem.

She saw how the blockage in the northern pathways was causing a ripple effect. The energy that should have been distributed throughout the Skywood was being siphoned, diverted, or simply extinguished. This explained why the areas furthest from the traditional rainfall zones were suffering the most, but it also explained why even the heartwood of the Skywood was showing signs of decline. The rain itself was merely a symptom; the true disease lay in the fundamental disruption of the Skywood's energetic circulatory system.

Miles away, within the increasingly parched canopy, Cael felt this energetic depletion as a gnawing emptiness. It wasn't just the thirst that plagued him; it was a deeper, more profound sense of disconnect. The forest, which had always been a source of vibrant, palpable life, now felt muted, listless. He would rest against the trunk of an Elderwood, usually a practice that filled him with a sense of grounding and strength, but now he felt only a hollow echo, a faint vibration that was more like a tremor of weakness than a thrum of life.

He noticed it most acutely when he was closest to the earth, when his hands brushed against the wilting mosses or his feet trod upon the dry, cracking soil. There was a subtle ache that seemed to originate from the very ground beneath him, a dull, persistent throb that mirrored the fatigue settling in his bones. It was a sensation he couldn't quite articulate, a phantom pain that felt like the Skywood itself was groaning under a heavy burden. He tried to explain it to himself, to rationalize it as the weariness of the long trek, the stress of the deepening drought. But he knew, with a certainty that chilled him, that it was something more.

He remembered as a child, running through the Skywood, his bare feet treading on soft, mossy ground that always felt cool and alive, even on the hottest days. He would press his ear to the earth, and he could hear it – a faint, constant hum, a symphony of life that resonated deep within him. It was the sound of the Skywood's heart beating, the pulse of its vital pathways. Now, that hum was fading. The ground felt dead beneath his touch, the silence deafening.

One afternoon, while searching for any sign of moisture near a dried-up stream bed, he stumbled upon a cluster of Lumina blooms, their petals usually so vibrant and luminous they seemed to capture moonlight. Today, they were wilted and grey, their inner glow extinguished. He knelt beside them, his fingers brushing against their brittle petals, and he felt it again – that profound ache, that energetic void. It was as if the very life force that had animated these flowers had been leached away, leaving behind only a husk. He tried to feel the connection between himself and the plants, the symbiotic dance that usually occurred, but there was nothing. It was like trying to grasp at smoke, a frustrating and disheartening emptiness.

The Sylphwings, usually so attuned to the forest's subtle energies, were now visibly distressed. Their delicate wings, which normally pulsed with a soft, internal light reflecting the health of the forest, were dim, their movements sluggish and uncoordinated. Cael watched as one, perched on a dying branch, let out a weak chirp, its body trembling not from cold, but from a profound lack of energy. He had always felt a kinship with these creatures, a shared sensitivity to the Skywood's ebb and flow. Their suffering was a mirror of his own growing discomfort.

He began to actively seek out the places where the forest felt the weakest, drawn by an instinct he couldn't explain. He found himself in the shaded hollows where the air usually hung thick with the scent of damp earth and decaying leaves, places that were now dry and dusty, their usual vibrant undergrowth replaced by brittle, straw-like stalks. In these places, the ache was more pronounced, a physical discomfort that made him want to curl up and disappear. It felt as though the Skywood was in its death throes, its vital channels clogged, its life force being systematically drained away.

Mara, meanwhile, continued her vigil in the observatory, her scrying bowl now a map of the Skywood's failing circulatory system. She saw how the blockages were not isolated incidents but part of a larger, insidious pattern. The dark, viscous energy that was clouding the pathways was not inert; it was actively consuming, spreading like a blight. She theorized that this encroaching darkness was a manifestation of whatever was manipulating the celestial bodies, a terrestrial echo of the astral disturbance. It was as if the malevolent force was extending its influence, not just from the heavens, but from deep within the very earth, twisting the natural flows of energy to its own inscrutable purpose.

She discovered that certain areas, particularly those rich in geomantic energy – ancient standing stones, nexus points of ley lines, and places of strong natural magic – were the most heavily impacted. It was as if these points, the very anchors of the Skywood's vitality, were prime targets. The blockages here were the most severe, the distortions the most violent. She realized with a dawning horror that the intention was not merely to disrupt the rain, but to fundamentally cripple the Skywood, to sever its connection to the natural forces that sustained it, and in doing so, to weaken its ability to resist whatever larger threat was looming. The failing resonance pathways were not just a symptom of the drought; they were the mechanism by which the drought was being amplified, and the Skywood was being systematically weakened from its very core. She began to understand that the Skywood's intricate, interconnected nature, once its greatest asset, was now its most profound vulnerability. The subtle, mystical underpinnings of its existence were being systematically targeted, and the forest, as it knew it, was slowly but surely ceasing to be.

The air within the dragon's lair was thick with the scent of ancient earth and something akin to smoldering embers, a primal musk that clung to the cavern walls and seeped into Cael's very bones. He stood before Thryxal, a creature of immense, slumbering power, his scales the color of deep obsidian shot through with veins of molten gold, his form so vast it seemed to warp the very space around him. Thryxal's eyes, twin pools of amber fire, regarded Cael with an ancient, unyielding skepticism.

"You come to me, little sapling, with your tales of dying trees and parched earth," Thryxal rumbled, the sound resonating not just in Cael's ears, but in the very marrow of his being. "You speak of a shared plight, of an alliance. But your kind... your kind has always seen the Skywood as a resource, a larder, a quarry. Not a living, breathing entity that deserves reverence."

Cael swallowed, the dryness in his throat a stark contrast to the cavern's humid air. "Great Thryxal, the Skywood is dying. The rains fail, the trees wither. My people suffer alongside the forest. We seek to understand, to heal."

A low growl vibrated through the stone beneath Cael's feet. "Understand? You understand destruction. I have seen your kind for millennia. I have watched your villages sprout like weeds, only to wither and die, leaving scars upon the land that take centuries to mend. I have seen your metal claws tear through the ancient roots, your fire consume the eldest boughs, your insatiable hunger drain the lifeblood of this very earth." Thryxal shifted, a movement that sent tremors through the cavern, a subtle rearrangement of immense power. "You speak of suffering. And for that, we dragons have no quarrel with your kind's pain. But do not presume that your suffering grants you the right to our aid. Not when your actions have so often been the cause of it."

Cael felt a flush of defensiveness, quickly followed by a wave of shame. Thryxal's words were harsh, unforgiving, yet Cael couldn't deny the truth woven within them. He had witnessed, in his own short life, the casual disregard for the forest's delicate balance by many humans. The quick settlements that cleared swathes of ancient growth for lumber, the hunters who took more than they needed, the careless fires that escaped control.

"We are not all the same," Cael protested, his voice barely above a whisper. "There are those who respect the forest, who live in harmony with it."

Thryxal let out a sound that might have been a laugh, a grating, stony noise. "Harmony? A fleeting song sung between bouts of plunder. You speak of respect, yet your cities sprawl, devouring the wild places. You dam the rivers that feed the roots. You poison the air with your ceasibilities, blind to the consequences. Do you think we have not seen this? Do you think we have not felt the tremor of your progress, the suffocating blanket of your ambition?"

He lowered his massive head, his amber eyes locking onto Cael's. The intensity of his gaze felt like a physical force, probing Cael's very soul. "I remember when the Elderwoods were not merely trees, but beings of immense wisdom, their roots intertwined with the very heart of the mountains. Your ancestors, then a fledgling species, arrived with fear in their hearts and a hunger in their bellies. They saw the Elderwoods as obstacles, as fuel. They carved their homes from the living wood, heedless of the pain they inflicted. They hunted the creatures that dwelled within, disrupting a balance that had held for eons."

Thryxal's voice deepened, laced with an ancient sorrow that pierced Cael's carefully constructed resolve. "We dragons are the guardians of this world's deeper truths, the keepers of its ancient rhythms. We have seen empires rise and fall, civilizations bloom and decay. And through it all, humanity's capacity for destruction has been a constant, a blight that spreads with terrifying efficiency. You have a way of taking, of consuming, of leaving desolation in your wake. And for that, you have earned our deepest mistrust."

Cael stood in silence, the weight of Thryxal's words pressing down on him. He had come seeking an alliance, a partnership in survival. But Thryxal was presenting him with a stark, brutal truth: that humanity's past transgressions were so profound, so ingrained, that the very idea of their cooperation was anathema to the ancient guardians of the Skywood.

"You wish to understand the fading resonance, the dying pathways," Thryxal continued, his voice softening slightly, though the skepticism remained etched in its depths. "You believe this is a problem that can be solved through shared effort. But what if the solution lies not in joining hands, but in severing them? What if the greatest threat to the Skywood is not some external force, but the very presence of your kind?"

The implication hung heavy in the air. Thryxal was suggesting that the only way to truly protect the Skywood might be to remove humanity from it entirely, or at least, to deny them access, to treat them as the disease rather than a potential cure. This was a perspective Cael had never truly considered, not with such stark finality. He had always believed in the possibility of redemption, of a future where humans and the natural world could coexist, even thrive together. But Thryxal's deeply entrenched animosity, born of countless ages of observation and experience, cast a long shadow over that hope.

"To protect something as ancient and vital as the Skywood," Thryxal said, his voice now a low, resonant hum that seemed to vibrate through the very air Cael breathed, "one must sometimes be willing to make difficult choices. Choices that may seem cruel, but are ultimately necessary for survival. Your kind has proven, time and again, that you are a force of imbalance. You are a catalyst for decay, a harbinger of emptiness. Your proximity, your very existence, has proven detrimental to the natural order.

We have witnessed this cycle repeat, and we are weary of bearing witness to the inevitable destruction that follows in your wake."

He paused, allowing the gravity of his words to settle. "The Skywood is a sacred trust. It is a living testament to the primordial forces that shaped this world. Its health is paramount, not just for its own sake, but for the sake of all life that depends upon it. And when we see that health threatened, we must act. We have often acted by removing the threat, by isolating it, by ensuring it can no longer cause harm. And your species, little sapling, has repeatedly demonstrated itself to be such a threat."

Cael felt a profound sense of isolation wash over him. He had come to Thryxal seeking help, seeking understanding from a being of immense power and wisdom. Instead, he had been met with an indictment, a deep-seated prejudice that seemed insurmountable. The dragons, he realized, did not see humanity as flawed beings capable of change, but as an inherently destructive force, a natural disaster in human form.

"You speak of the Skywood's resonance, of its failing pathways," Thryxal continued, his gaze unwavering. "You seek to mend these wounds. But what if these wounds are a direct consequence of your own species' actions? What if the 'blockages' you perceive are simply the Skywood, in its desperate, primal instinct, trying to expel a foreign contaminant? What if the energy you feel draining away is the very life force being leeched by your insatiable consumption? Your progress, your expansion, your constant need for more – these are the diseases that plague the natural world. And we, the ancient ones, have learned to recognize the symptoms, and to treat the cause, however harsh the cure may seem."

He took a slow, deliberate breath, the expansion of his chest like a mountain range shifting. "We have seen your civilizations rise and fall. We have watched your cities crumble to dust, your empires fade into legend. And each time, the land has eventually healed. But the scars remain. The ecological memory is long, and it is etched into the very soul of the planet. Your species has a unique ability to accelerate this decay, to make the healing process immeasurably longer, if not impossible."

Thryxal's gaze softened, not in warmth, but in a kind of weary resignation. "My skepticism is not born of malice, little one. It is born of ages. It is born of observing the same patterns of destruction, the same cycles of unsustainable growth, repeat themselves ad infinitum. When I look at your kind, I see a force that is fundamentally antithetical to the enduring spirit of this world. You are a storm that passes through, leaving ruin in its wake. And the Skywood, in its current state of distress, is a testament to the severity of that storm."

He shifted his massive form again, a subtle ripple of power that made the very air hum. "You seek to forge an alliance. But the dragons do not forge alliances with those who represent the very threat we have sworn to protect against. Our path is one of preservation. And often, preservation requires a firm, unwavering hand. A hand that is willing to draw a line, to say 'no more,' to sever the connections that lead to ruin."

The implication was clear, chilling in its directness. Thryxal was not just expressing doubt; he was articulating a potential strategy for the dragons, a strategy that involved a complete and utter separation from humanity. The idea that the Skywood might be better off without humans, or that humanity itself was the problem, was a bitter pill to swallow. Cael had always seen himself as a bridge between the human world and the natural world, a testament to the possibility of coexistence. But Thryxal's words cast doubt on the very foundation of his beliefs, suggesting that the chasm between humanity and the wild was far wider, and far more ancient, than he had ever imagined.

"Your people speak of progress," Thryxal mused, his voice a low rumble, "of innovation, of dominion. But what is progress if it leads to the silencing of the ancient songs? What is innovation if it creates more devastation than it mends? What is dominion if it is a dominion over emptiness, over dust and decay? We have seen empires built on such foundations, and they have all crumbled. The earth remembers. And the earth, like us, is weary of your kind's destructive tendencies."

He leaned closer, his great, golden eyes fixing Cael with an intensity that was both terrifying and strangely sorrowful. "The Skywood is not merely a collection of trees and creatures. It is a living tapestry of energy, a complex symphony of interconnected life. Your kind, with its relentless pursuit of expansion, its need to dominate and control, has introduced dissonance into that symphony. You have ripped threads from the tapestry, and in doing so, you have weakened the whole. You have dammed the rivers of life, and in doing so, you have brought drought. You have clouded the skies, and in doing so, you have extinguished the light."

Thryxal's skepticism was not a fleeting emotion; it was a deep-seated conviction, forged in the crucible of eons. It was the wisdom of a being who had witnessed the slow, inexorable march of human impact, a being who had seen the patterns of destruction repeat themselves across countless generations. Cael understood, with a sinking heart, that gaining the trust of the dragons, securing their aid, would be an undertaking far more arduous than he had ever conceived. It would require not just a demonstration of good intentions, but a fundamental reckoning with humanity's past, a profound and collective shift in behavior that might, in the eyes of beings like Thryxal, seem an impossible dream.

"You believe you can heal the Skywood," Thryxal stated, his tone leaving no room for argument. "You believe your species, which has so often been the source of the wound, can now be the balm. This is a dangerous assumption, little sapling. One that has led many to their downfall, and many more to their demise. The Skywood's plight is a reflection of a deeper imbalance, an imbalance that your kind has been instrumental in creating. And until that fundamental imbalance is addressed, until humanity learns to be a part of the natural order, rather than a force that seeks to dominate it, true healing will remain an elusive phantom."

The dragon's words were a stark reminder of the immense challenge Cael faced. The Skywood was in peril, its lifeblood draining away. And the ancient guardians, those who possessed the power and the knowledge to perhaps turn the tide, saw his own species not as allies, but as the very architects of the destruction. The path forward, Cael realized, would be fraught with suspicion, demanding not just courage and resilience, but a profound transformation of human perception, a transformation that might take generations to achieve, if it could be achieved at all. The dragons' skepticism was a formidable barrier, a testament to the deep-seated animosity that humanity had sown through its careless stewardship of the world, and it underscored the sheer, daunting magnitude of the crisis the Skywood faced.

The weight of Thryxal's words, like the ancient stones of the cavern, pressed down on Cael, each syllable a testament to a history he was only beginning to comprehend. He had come seeking an ally, a partner in the desperate fight to save the Skywood. Instead, he had been met with the cold, unblinking gaze of a guardian who viewed his entire species as the blight. Yet, beneath the dragon's profound distrust, a different kind of truth began to stir within Cael – the truth of his own oath, a sacred vow that now felt both too constricting and too fragile.

"The Skywood," Thryxal had said, the rumble of his voice echoing in the vastness, "is a sacred trust. It is a living testament to the primordial forces that shaped this world. Its health is paramount... And when we see that health threatened, we must act." Cael clung to that phrase, 'we must act.' It was a call to arms, a mandate for intervention. But who was 'we'? And what kind of action did it entail? His own oath, sworn before the Elderwood elders and the whispering spirits of the forest, resonated in his mind.

'I shall be the shield, the steadfast root, the watchful guardian of the canopy. I shall defend its borders, nurture its growth, and uphold its delicate balance against all encroaching shadows.'

He had always interpreted his oath as one of defense. He was to protect the Skywood from external threats, to stand as a bulwark against those who would seek to harm it. He was to be the quiet observer, the healer of wounds inflicted by others, the patient nurturer. But the Skywood was not merely being encroached upon; it was dying from within. The very essence of its life force was ebbing, its resonant pathways fracturing, its ancient wisdom fading. And the 'encroaching shadows' were not just from without, but from the very ecological imbalance that Thryxal, and indeed, many within Cael's own community, seemed to attribute to humanity.

Could his oath encompass an active, even aggressive, stance? Could he, as a Land Guardian, be permitted to sever connections that were poisoning the Skywood, even if those connections were deeply ingrained within his own species' way of life? The idea sent a shiver down his spine, a disquieting blend of fear and a nascent sense of imperative. Thryxal's words were a condemnation, but they also, inadvertently, laid bare the inadequacy of his current mandate. To merely defend was no longer enough.

The image of the dying Elderwood, its once vibrant leaves brittle and pale, flashed in his mind. He remembered tracing the desiccated veins on its bark, feeling the profound silence where once there had been a hum of vibrant life. He had felt the forest's pain, a deep, aching thrum that reverberated in his own chest. He had been sworn to protect it, but how could he protect something that was succumbing to a slow, systemic decay?

His oath was a shield, designed to deflect external blows. But what if the enemy was not an external force, but a pervasive illness? What if the healing required not just defense, but a radical pruning, a forceful redirection of currents that had gone stagnant or toxic? The elders had spoken of balance, but their understanding of balance had always been rooted in maintaining a status quo, in defending against incursions. They had never envisioned a scenario where humanity itself, or at least its deeply ingrained patterns, was the source of the imbalance.

Cael shifted his weight, the rough stone of the cavern floor a stark contrast to the soft moss he was accustomed to treading. Thryxal's skepticism, while painful, was a mirror reflecting a harsh truth. He had seen the casual disregard for the forest's bounty, the insatiable desire for more, the way settlements expanded like unchecked fungi, consuming ancient groves. He had witnessed the subtle poisoning of waterways, the careless fires, the logging that prioritized immediate gain over long-term health. He had, in many ways, been a silent witness to the very transgressions Thryxal detailed.

His oath commanded him to uphold balance. But if humanity's actions had thrown the Skywood into such profound disarray, then maintaining the status quo was, in essence, perpetuating the imbalance. This was the ethical precipice Cael found himself teetering on. Was he bound to a literal interpretation of his oath, to defend the existing boundaries, even if those boundaries were now a cage for a dying world? Or did the spirit of his oath, the fundamental charge to protect and preserve, demand a more fluid, adaptive approach?

He recalled the whispers of the Wind-Woven Glades, a region once teeming with life, now eerily silent, its ancient trees hollowed out by a slow decay that defied any obvious external cause. The resonance there had been so weak, so fractured, that even the birds had fallen silent. He had stood there, his hand on the withered bark of a colossal oak, feeling a profound sense of helplessness. His oath had offered no solace, no clear path forward. He could only observe, and lament.

Thryxal's words about the Skywood trying to "expel a foreign contaminant" echoed in his mind. What if the sickness wasn't an invasion, but a symptom of a broken internal system? And what if his role as Land Guardian wasn't just to fend off the wolf at the door, but to diagnose and, if necessary, administer a difficult cure, even if the cure was unpalatable to the patient?

The limitation of his oath, Cael realized, lay in its passive nature. It was a vow of stewardship, not of active intervention against the very ecosystem it was meant to protect, or the people who inhabited it. He was sworn to defend the Skywood from harm. But what if the greatest harm came from the ways in which his own people interacted with it, from the deeply ingrained habits and desires that had become so normalized they were invisible?

He thought of the ritual of the Spring Harvest, a time when his village celebrated the bounty of the forest. He had always participated, helping to gather the fruits, the herbs, the lumber. But he had also seen the excess, the waste, the casual disregard for the sacredness of the gifts. His oath did not forbid such practices; it implicitly accepted them as part of the human relationship with the forest. But now, faced with Thryxal's stark assessment, those practices felt less like celebration and more like a slow, deliberate poisoning.

Could he, as Cael, the Land Guardian, openly question the very foundations of his community's relationship with the Skywood? Could he advocate for radical change, for severing practices that had been followed for generations, even if those practices were contributing to the forest's demise? His oath was a binding agreement, a set of responsibilities. But what if those responsibilities, when applied to the current crisis, were not enough? What if they were, in fact, hindering the very salvation they were meant to ensure?

The dragons, Thryxal had implied, were active agents of balance, guardians who did not shy away from harsh measures when necessary. They had seen the long cycles of destruction, and they had learned to intervene. Cael, bound by his oath to a more passive role, felt a profound inadequacy. His vows were a testament to his commitment, but they also represented a framework that might be too rigid for the fluid, emergent nature of the crisis.

He considered the possibility of seeking counsel from the Elderwood spirits themselves, if any still had the strength to communicate. Would they see his oath as a shield to be held firm, or as a tool to be wielded with more agency? The very idea of 'wielding' his oath felt like a betrayal of its intent, a shift from defense to offense. Yet, the Skywood was not merely under siege; it was slowly suffocating.

Thryxal's words, though laced with ancient bitterness, had sparked a dangerous question in Cael's mind: What if his oath, meant to protect, was now, in its limitations, contributing to the Skywood's destruction? What if true guardianship required a willingness to break, or at least redefine, the very vows that had defined him? The responsibility felt immense, crushing. He was sworn to protect the canopy, to nurture its growth, to uphold its balance. But when the very methods of nurturing and the understanding of balance were tied to a system that was now failing, his oath became a gilded cage, beautiful in its intent but ultimately restrictive in its application.

The Skywood needed more than a shield; it needed a surgeon, a catalyst for change, a force willing to confront the uncomfortable truths of its own place within the world. And Cael, bound by his oath, was not yet sure if he could be that force. The weight of his oath, a symbol of his devotion, now felt like a shroud, threatening to smother the very life he was sworn to protect. He was caught between the ancient wisdom of a dragon who saw humanity as the disease, and the strictures of his own vows, which, in their current interpretation, offered no pathway to a proactive cure.

The dusty tang of the coastal air, usually a comforting, familiar scent, had begun to feel cloying to Mara. For weeks, she had been poring over reports, tracing the slow, insidious creep of the wilting blight from the shoreline inland. Her colleagues, steeped in the rhythms of the tides and the salt-laced winds, saw only the predictable consequences of a shifting climate, perhaps exacerbated by dwindling rainfall. But Mara felt a tremor of unease, a discordant note in the symphony of the natural world that the others seemed to overlook. It was the quiet insistence of the land itself, a whisper that something more was at play than mere atmospheric shifts.

She left the familiar embrace of the coast under a sky the color of bruised plums, the oppressive humidity clinging to her like a second skin. Her journey inland was a deliberate departure, a personal quest to escape the echo chamber of coastal theories and to seek the truth in the heart of the land. Her pack was light, filled with essentials, but her mind was heavy with unanswered questions. The old maps, brittle with age, were spread across the worn leather of her satchel, marked with the places where the whispers of distress had grown loudest. She wasn't just following the reports; she was following the silences, the places where the usual chorus of insect hum and bird song had been replaced by an unnerving stillness.

Her first stop was a cluster of settlements nestled in the foothills of the Azure Peaks, an area known for its resilient, ancient flora, particularly the Sky-Moss that clung to the north-facing slopes. It was said to glow with a faint luminescence after a rain, a testament to the purity of the mountain springs that fed its roots. But when Mara arrived, the moss was dull, its vibrant green faded to a sickly chartreuse. The glow was absent, even after a recent, meager shower. She knelt, her fingers brushing against the desiccated fronds. They crumbled to dust at her touch, a premature decay that spoke of more than just thirst.

"It's the sun," a local farmer, Elara, told her, her voice raspy with fatigue. Her face was etched with worry lines deeper than the furrows in her parched fields. "It's been too harsh this year. The rain just evaporates before it can do any good."

Mara nodded, her gaze sweeping over the wilting crops. The leaves were curled and brittle, as expected. But it was the texture of the soil that caught her attention. It was unnaturally fine, almost powdery, as if something had leached the very life out of it, leaving behind a fine, inert dust. She scraped a small sample into a pouch, noting the peculiar lack of any discernible organic matter. Typically, even in drought, the soil retained some of its richness, a testament to the slow decomposition of fallen leaves and roots. This felt... sterile.

Her investigation continued to a small grove of Whispering Willows, trees renowned for their sensitivity to subtle shifts in the earth's energy. Their long, trailing branches were supposed to sway and rustle even in the gentlest breeze, their leaves creating a soft, melodic sigh. Now, the branches hung heavy and still, a mournful drape against the oppressive sky. The leaves, usually a shimmering silver-green, were a uniform, dull grey, tinged with a brownish hue at the edges. There was no movement, no sound, only a heavy, stagnant silence.

She approached one of the trees, placing her palm against its bark. It felt dry, brittle, almost hot to the touch, despite the lack of direct sunlight. She closed her eyes, trying to sense the usual vibrant energy that pulsed through the Willow's being. Instead, she felt a faint, erratic tremor, like a faltering heartbeat. It was a disturbing sensation, one that resonated with a deeper, more primal alarm bell in her mind.

"They're dying," a young boy, no older than ten, said as he emerged from the shadow of a nearby dwelling. He carried a crudely fashioned wooden toy, its paint faded. "Grandmother says they've never been this quiet. Not even during the Great Drought of '72."

Mara turned to him, her eyes sharp with inquiry. "And what does your grandmother say is happening?"

The boy shrugged, kicking at a loose stone. "She just shakes her head. Says it's not natural. Says the land is... sick."

The word 'sick' echoed Mara's own burgeoning suspicion. It wasn't just drought. Drought was a natural phenomenon, a cyclical hardship that the land, and its inhabitants, understood and adapted to. This felt different. This felt like an illness, a deep-seated malady that was systematically weakening the very foundations of life.

She spent the next few days moving through scattered hamlets and isolated homesteads, her observations becoming increasingly unsettling. She noted that the insects, usually a constant presence, were fewer in number, and those she did see seemed sluggish, disoriented. Even the birdsong was muted, the usual cheerful cacophony replaced by solitary, mournful calls. She examined the riverbeds, finding them not just dry, but scoured, the usual silt and detritus of seasonal flooding seemingly absent. It was as if the water had simply vanished, leaving behind only hardened, cracked earth.

One evening, as she sat by a meager campfire, meticulously documenting her findings, she noticed something peculiar. A patch of wildflowers, near the edge of her camp, seemed unnaturally vibrant, their colors almost aggressively bright compared to the surrounding desolation. Intrigued, she approached them. Their petals were perfectly formed, their stems strong and erect. But as she got closer, she realized they were also completely devoid of insect life. No buzzing bees, no fluttering butterflies, not even a single ant crawled upon their petals. She gently touched a deep crimson bloom, expecting the velvety softness she'd seen in the wild specimens. Instead, her fingers met a strange, waxy resilience. It felt artificial, too perfect, too still.

A chill, entirely unrelated to the cooling night air, snaked down her spine. This wasn't natural resilience. This was an anomaly. She carefully collected a sample of the soil around these unnaturally perfect flowers, as well as one of the blooms themselves, wrapping them with extreme care. The more she looked, the more she noticed other such isolated pockets of seemingly healthy life, always devoid of any fauna. They stood out like painted scenery against a dying backdrop, too pristine, too inert.

Her journey was far from over, but the initial threads of her investigation were beginning to weave a disquieting tapestry. The patterns she was observing—the sterile soil, the unnaturally still flora, the absence of insect life, the peculiar vibrancy of isolated patches—all pointed away from a simple drought. They hinted at a deliberate, insidious manipulation, a subtle interference that was systematically draining the life force from the land. It was a realization that settled deep within her, a cold certainty that the crisis unfolding inland was far more complex, and far more dangerous, than anyone on the coast had yet comprehended. The land wasn't just suffering; it was being systematically undermined. And Mara, with a growing sense of urgency, knew she had to discover by whom, and why.

Chapter Three

WHISPERS OF TECHNOLOGY

The air in the cavern, even away from the faint, phosphorescent glow of the bioluminescent moss clinging to the walls, hummed with a power that Mara could feel vibrating in her bones. It was a deep, resonant thrum, unlike anything she had ever encountered. Her Reefwarden training had attuned her to the subtle energies of the ocean, the ebb and flow of currents, the silent language of coral reefs. But this was different. This was the pulse of something vast, something ancient, something... constructed. Her scientific mind, honed by years of cataloging marine ecosystems and understanding the intricate balance of oceanic life, was buzzing with a mixture of awe and apprehension.

She moved deeper into the cavern, her boots crunching on a fine, granular dust that shimmered with an inner light. It wasn't sand, nor was it typical rock sediment. It felt more like pulverized gems, each particle catching and refracting the dim light. She knelt, scooping a handful into her palm. It was cool to the touch, surprisingly smooth, and held a faint, metallic tang that tickled her nostrils. This was the same peculiar dust she had found in the soil near the unnaturally vibrant wildflowers, the same sterile residue that had so disturbed her. Here, in the heart of this forgotten place, it seemed to be the very foundation upon which this strange machinery rested.

Before her, bathed in a more intense, almost ethereal light that emanated from within, stood the engines. They were colossal structures, their forms elegant yet undeniably functional. Imagine colossal, obsidian obelisks, their surfaces etched with intricate, geometric patterns that pulsed with a soft, internal radiance. These weren't crude mechanisms of iron and steam; they were crafted from a material that seemed to absorb and amplify light, giving the impression of solidified starlight. They rose from the cavern floor like petrified giants, their apexes disappearing into the oppressive darkness of the cavern ceiling.

Around the base of each obelisk, a complex array of smaller, crystalline structures were embedded in the dust. These crystals, larger than any Mara had ever seen, glowed with varying intensities, their light shifting through hues of sapphire, emerald, and amethyst. They seemed to be connected to the obelisks by conduits of braided, metallic fiber, shimmering like spun moonlight. The entire assembly thrummed with that low, resonant hum, a symphony of contained energy that made the air itself feel heavy and charged.

Mara approached the nearest engine, her heart pounding a frantic rhythm against her ribs. This was it. This was the source of the sickness. The scale of it was staggering, far beyond anything she had imagined. The legends she had dismissed as fanciful tales of sorcery and ancient gods now felt startlingly, terrifyingly real. These were not just machines; they were instruments of immense power, capable of shaping the very atmosphere.

She ran a gloved hand along the cool, smooth surface of the obsidian-like material. The etched patterns felt raised beneath her fingertips, a tactile language she couldn't yet decipher. They weren't random; they formed complex circuits, interwoven with symbols that hinted at astronomical alignments and elemental forces. It was as if the builders had inscribed the very laws of the universe onto these monumental structures.

Her Reefwarden training had instilled in her a deep respect for natural processes. She understood how currents influenced weather, how solar radiation drove evaporation, how the moon's pull dictated tides. These engines, however, represented a different paradigm: the direct, forceful manipulation of those very forces. They were designed, she realized with a dawning sense of horror, to control the weather.

The whispered legends spoke of the Starstone Engines, devices crafted by a civilization long vanished, built to bring life-giving rains to arid lands, to temper scorching suns, and to divert destructive storms. They were said to be powered by the very essence of the stars, channeled through celestial crystals that captured cosmic energies. For millennia, they had been dormant, their existence fading into myth. But the evidence before her suggested they were not only active, but actively *doing* something.

Mara activated the diagnostic scanner she kept in her satchel, a sophisticated piece of Reefwarden technology designed to analyze energy signatures and elemental compositions. The device whirred to life, its lens focusing on the nearest engine. The readouts that flashed across its screen were unlike anything she had ever seen.

"Energy output... astronomical," she murmured, her voice hushed with disbelief. "Composition... unknown alloys, trace elements unidentifiable. And the resonance... it's... it's drawing energy from... the atmosphere itself? No, it's *influencing* atmospheric energy. Manipulating it."

She moved to the crystalline conduits, carefully bringing the scanner closer. The crystals pulsed with raw power, their internal luminescence fluctuating rhythmically. The scanner struggled to quantify the energy flowing through them. It was a torrent, a deluge of pure, untamed force.

"This isn't just channeling energy," she breathed, tracing the intricate patterns of the conduits. "It's... it's actively drawing moisture from the air. Or... or preventing it from condensing? The readings are chaotic, Mara, like a storm in miniature."

She recalled the dry riverbeds, the desiccated flora, the absence of insects. These engines weren't *bringing* rain; they were *stopping* it. The dust, she now understood, was not just pulverized stone, but the inert residue of desiccated organic matter, leached of its life force by the engines' potent influence. The unnaturally vibrant flowers were likely artificially sustained, their vitality a façade maintained by proximity to the engines' localized energy fields, a cruel mockery of true life.

The implications were staggering. This wasn't a natural disaster. It was a manufactured one. Someone, or something, had reactivated these ancient engines and was using them for a purpose that was systematically strangling the land. The subtle ecological shifts she had observed weren't the slow march of climate change; they were the direct, targeted consequences of this monumental, technological assault.

Mara's scientific curiosity, a force as potent as any she had encountered in this cavern, was now fully ignited. She needed to understand how these engines worked, how they were controlled, and who was wielding this terrifying power. The intricate etchings on the obelisks suddenly seemed less like decorative carvings and more like an operating manual, a blueprint for wielding celestial power.

She began to meticulously document the patterns, sketching them into her waterproof notebook, her stylus moving with practiced speed. She cross-referenced them with known astronomical charts and ancient symbology databases stored within her scanner. The geometric precision of the designs, the subtle shifts in their configurations, suggested a sophisticated understanding of celestial mechanics and atmospheric dynamics.

The sheer ingenuity of the design was breathtaking. These weren't just rudimentary weather machines; they were complex, interconnected systems that likely interacted with each other, creating localized atmospheric phenomena on a continental scale. The idea that an entire civilization had possessed the knowledge and the power to build and operate such devices was almost too much to comprehend.

As she worked, a new set of readings began to flicker on her scanner. It was an energy signature, faint but distinct, emanating from deeper within the cavern. It wasn't the powerful hum of the Starstone Engines, but something... different. Smaller, more focused, and carrying a different kind of resonance. It was a subtle pulse, almost like a heartbeat, distinct from the powerful, steady thrum of the engines.

Intrigued, Mara adjusted her gear and moved towards the new energy source. The dust grew thicker, the air colder. The glow of the bioluminescent moss became more pronounced here, casting eerie shadows that danced with her every movement. She passed a smaller, more weathered obelisk, its surface pitted and scarred, its crystals dull and cracked. It appeared to be a deactivated engine, a relic of a bygone era. But the new energy signature led her away from the main cluster, towards a narrow fissure in the cavern wall.

Squeezing through the opening, she found herself in a smaller, more intimate chamber. The air here was still, heavy with an almost palpable sense of waiting. And in the center of the chamber, resting on a pedestal of polished obsidian, was the source of the faint energy signature.

It was a device, no larger than her two hands clasped together. It was fashioned from a metal that gleamed like liquid silver, intricately interwoven with thin, glowing filaments that pulsed with that soft, rhythmic beat. At its heart, a single, perfectly cut crystal, the size of a pigeon's egg, glowed with a steady, internal light—a deep, pulsating azure. It was clearly a control mechanism, a key, or perhaps a diagnostic tool, for the colossal engines she had just witnessed.

Mara approached it with extreme caution. The scanner confirmed it was a power source, but a vastly different kind than the engines. It was humming with controlled energy, not raw, overwhelming force. It felt... deliberate. Precise.

She reached out, her gloved fingers hovering just above the crystal. A faint warmth emanated from it. As her fingertip brushed against its cool, smooth surface, a surge of information flooded her mind. Not words, not images, but pure data – complex equations, atmospheric models, energy flow charts, and schematics of the Starstone Engines, rendered in a way that bypassed conscious thought and imprinted directly onto her understanding.

She saw the engines' purpose laid bare: not just to bring rain, but to regulate rainfall. To siphon moisture from one region and deposit it elsewhere. To create localized drought and localized deluge. To sculpt the climate to a predetermined design. And she saw, with terrifying clarity, the precise calibrations and energy frequencies required to achieve these effects.

But within the torrent of data, a subtler pattern emerged. A series of override protocols. An emergency shutdown sequence. And something else... a set of directives that seemed to deviate from the original design, pushing the engines beyond their intended parameters, deliberately creating the arid conditions she had witnessed. This was not a malfunction; it was sabotage. Or, more chillingly, a deliberate misuse by those who had reactivated them.

The device in her hand, she realized, was a tool for understanding and, potentially, controlling these engines. It was a missing piece of the puzzle, a key to unraveling the mystery of the manufactured blight. The legends had spoken of the Starstone Engines as benevolent forces, guardians of life. But in the hands of those who understood their destructive potential, they were weapons of unimaginable power.

The weight of her discovery pressed down on her. The ecological crisis was not a tragedy of nature, but a calculated act of devastation. And the ancient, starstone-powered engines, once symbols of hope and prosperity, had been twisted into instruments of ruin. The hum of the dormant engines in the main cavern seemed to take on a more sinister note, a prelude to a symphony of destruction that was already underway. She carefully documented the smaller device, her mind racing with the implications of her findings. The journey inland had led her to the heart of a technological marvel, a forgotten power that had been unleashed to bleed the land dry. And now, she held a sliver of the knowledge required to potentially stop it.

The air in the cavern, even away from the faint, phosphorescent glow of the bioluminescent moss clinging to the walls, hummed with a power that Mara could feel vibrating in her bones. It was a deep, resonant thrum, unlike anything she had ever encountered. Her Reefwarden training had attuned her to the subtle energies of the ocean, the ebb and flow of currents, the silent language of coral reefs. But this was different. This was the pulse of something vast, something ancient, something... constructed. Her scientific mind, honed by years of cataloging marine ecosystems and understanding the intricate balance of oceanic life, was buzzing with a mixture of awe and apprehension.

She moved deeper into the cavern, her boots crunching on a fine, granular dust that shimmered with an inner light. It wasn't sand, nor was it typical rock sediment. It felt more like pulverized gems, each particle catching and refracting the dim light. She knelt, scooping a handful into her palm. It was cool to the touch, surprisingly smooth, and held a faint, metallic tang that tickled her nostrils. This was the same peculiar dust she had found in the soil near the unnaturally vibrant wildflowers, the same sterile residue that had so disturbed her. Here, in the heart of this forgotten place, it seemed to be the very foundation upon which this strange machinery rested.

Before her, bathed in a more intense, almost ethereal light that emanated from within, stood the engines. They were colossal structures, their forms elegant yet undeniably functional. Imagine colossal, obsidian obelisks, their surfaces etched with intricate, geometric patterns that pulsed with a soft, internal radiance. These weren't crude mechanisms of iron and steam; they were crafted from a material that seemed to absorb and amplify light, giving the impression of solidified starlight. They rose from the cavern floor like petrified giants, their apexes disappearing into the oppressive darkness of the cavern ceiling.

Around the base of each obelisk, a complex array of smaller, crystalline structures were embedded in the dust. These crystals, larger than any Mara had ever seen, glowed with varying intensities, their light shifting through hues of sapphire, emerald, and amethyst. They seemed to be connected to the obelisks by conduits of braided, metallic fiber, shimmering like spun moonlight. The entire assembly thrummed with that low, resonant hum, a symphony of contained energy that made the air itself feel heavy and charged.

Mara approached the nearest engine, her heart pounding a frantic rhythm against her ribs. This was it. This was the source of the sickness. The scale of it was staggering, far beyond anything she had imagined. The legends she had dismissed as fanciful tales of sorcery and ancient gods now felt startlingly, terrifyingly real. These were not just machines; they were instruments of immense power, capable of shaping the very atmosphere.

She ran a gloved hand along the cool, smooth surface of the obsidian-like material. The etched patterns felt raised beneath her fingertips, a tactile language she couldn't yet decipher. They weren't random; they formed complex circuits, interwoven with symbols that hinted at astronomical alignments and elemental forces. It was as if the builders had inscribed the very laws of the universe onto these monumental structures.

Her Reefwarden training had instilled in her a deep respect for natural processes. She understood how currents influenced weather, how solar radiation drove evaporation, how the moon's pull dictated tides. These engines, however, represented a different paradigm: the direct, forceful manipulation of those very forces. They were designed, she realized with a dawning sense of horror, to control the weather.

The whispered legends spoke of the Starstone Engines, devices crafted by a civilization long vanished, built to bring life-giving rains to arid lands, to temper scorching suns, and to divert destructive storms. They were said to be powered by the very essence of the stars, channeled through celestial crystals that captured cosmic energies. For millennia, they had been dormant, their existence fading into myth. But the evidence before her suggested they were not only active, but actively *doing* something.

Mara activated the diagnostic scanner she kept in her satchel, a sophisticated piece of Reefwarden technology designed to analyze energy signatures and elemental compositions. The device whirred to life, its lens focusing on the nearest engine. The readouts that flashed across its screen were unlike anything she had ever seen.

"Energy output... astronomical," she murmured, her voice hushed with disbelief. "Composition... unknown alloys, trace elements unidentifiable. And the resonance... it's... it's drawing energy from... the atmosphere itself? No, it's *influencing* atmospheric energy. Manipulating it."

She moved to the crystalline conduits, carefully bringing the scanner closer. The crystals pulsed with raw power, their internal luminescence fluctuating rhythmically. The scanner struggled to quantify the energy flowing through them. It was a torrent, a deluge of pure, untamed force.

"This isn't just channeling energy," she breathed, tracing the intricate patterns of the conduits. "It's... it's actively drawing moisture from the air. Or... or preventing it from condensing? The readings are chaotic, Mara, like a storm in miniature."

She recalled the dry riverbeds, the desiccated flora, the absence of insects. These engines weren't *bringing* rain; they were *stopping* it. The dust, she now understood, was not just pulverized stone, but the inert residue of desiccated organic matter, leached of its life force by the engines' potent influence. The unnaturally vibrant flowers were likely artificially sustained, their vitality a façade maintained by proximity to the engines' localized energy fields, a cruel mockery of true life.

The implications were staggering. This wasn't a natural disaster. It was a manufactured one. Someone, or something, had reactivated these ancient engines and was using them for a purpose that was systematically strangling the land. The subtle ecological shifts she had observed weren't the slow march of climate change; they were the direct, targeted consequences of this monumental, technological assault.

Mara's scientific curiosity, a force as potent as any she had encountered in this cavern, was now fully ignited. She needed to understand how these engines worked, how they were controlled, and who was wielding this terrifying power. The intricate etchings on the obelisks suddenly seemed less like decorative carvings and more like an operating manual, a blueprint for wielding celestial power.

She began to meticulously document the patterns, sketching them into her waterproof notebook, her stylus moving with practiced speed. She cross-referenced them with known astronomical charts and ancient symbology databases stored within her scanner. The geometric precision of the designs, the subtle shifts in their configurations, suggested a sophisticated understanding of celestial mechanics and atmospheric dynamics.

The sheer ingenuity of the design was breathtaking. These weren't just rudimentary weather machines; they were complex, interconnected systems that likely interacted with each other, creating localized atmospheric phenomena on a continental scale. The idea that an entire civilization had possessed the knowledge and the power to build and operate such devices was almost too much to comprehend. It spoke of a profound mastery over the very forces that governed their world, a level of technological prowess that bordered on the divine.

But with that awe came a chilling realization. The same ingenuity that could create such wonders could also wield them for destruction. The Starstone Engines, by their very nature, represented a profound intervention in the natural order. They were designed to bend the planet's atmospheric systems to the will of their creators. And while the legends painted them as benevolent tools for prosperity, the reality Mara was witnessing was a stark testament to the potential for hubris.

It was a classic tale, a recurring motif throughout the chronicles of burgeoning civilizations: the insatiable desire to conquer, to control, to impose one's will upon the untamed forces of nature. From the earliest attempts to harness fire to the complex irrigation systems that fed empires, humanity had always strived to bend the world to its needs. But the Starstone Engines represented a leap beyond anything she had ever conceived. They were not merely tools for shaping the immediate environment; they were instruments capable of redrawing the very climate of a continent.

The desire to understand and to master was a powerful motivator. It had driven exploration, fueled discovery, and propelled innovation. Yet, it was a double-edged sword. The pursuit of knowledge, untempered by wisdom or foresight, could lead to unforeseen catastrophes. The builders of these engines, in their quest to achieve ultimate control over the weather, had perhaps never truly considered the long-term repercussions. Or, more disturbingly, they had known, and had chosen to wield that power regardless of the cost.

Mara's mind grappled with the ethical quandaries. Was it inherently wrong to interfere with natural cycles? Where was the line between beneficial adaptation and destructive manipulation? The Reefwarden creed spoke of living in harmony with the oceans, of understanding and respecting their power, not subjugating it. But the builders of these engines had clearly operated under a different philosophy, one that placed technological dominance above ecological equilibrium.

She traced a particularly complex series of interwoven symbols on the obelisk's surface, her scanner attempting to cross-reference the intricate glyphs. They depicted what appeared to be weather patterns, not as they occurred naturally, but as they could be

orchestrated. Clouds being drawn from distant horizons, rain being condensed and directed with impossible precision, winds being channeled and amplified. It was a stark visual representation of a profound and dangerous ambition.

The very idea of controlling something as vast and chaotic as weather systems was, in retrospect, an act of immense arrogance. The planet's climate was a delicate dance of countless variables, a complex, self-regulating system honed over millennia. To presume that a collection of machines, however advanced, could perfectly replicate or improve upon that system was the height of hubris. And the result, as Mara was seeing, was not improvement, but devastation. The unnatural stillness in the air, the parched earth, the silence of the once-vibrant ecosystem – these were the tangible consequences of that ambition.

As she worked, meticulously documenting every detail, a new set of readings began to flicker on her scanner. It was an energy signature, faint but distinct, emanating from deeper within the cavern. It wasn't the powerful hum of the Starstone Engines, but something... different. Smaller, more focused, and carrying a different kind of resonance. It was a subtle pulse, almost like a heartbeat, distinct from the powerful, steady thrum of the engines.

Intrigued, Mara adjusted her gear and moved towards the new energy source. The dust grew thicker, the air colder. The glow of the bioluminescent moss became more pronounced here, casting eerie shadows that danced with her every movement. She passed a smaller, more weathered obelisk, its surface pitted and scarred, its crystals dull and cracked. It appeared to be a deactivated engine, a relic of a bygone era. But the new energy signature led her away from the main cluster, towards a narrow fissure in the cavern wall.

Squeezing through the opening, she found herself in a smaller, more intimate chamber. The air here was still, heavy with an almost palpable sense of waiting. And in the center of the chamber, resting on a pedestal of polished obsidian, was the source of the faint energy signature.

It was a device, no larger than her two hands clasped together. It was fashioned from a metal that gleamed like liquid silver, intricately interwoven with thin, glowing filaments that pulsed with that soft, rhythmic beat. At its heart, a single, perfectly cut crystal, the size of a pigeon's egg, glowed with a steady, internal light—a deep, pulsating azure. It was clearly a control mechanism, a key, or perhaps a diagnostic tool, for the colossal engines she had just witnessed.

Mara approached it with extreme caution. The scanner confirmed it was a power source, but a vastly different kind than the engines. It was humming with controlled energy, not raw, overwhelming force. It felt... deliberate. Precise. This was not the brute force manipulation of atmospheric systems she had observed in the main chamber. This was something finer, more intricate.

She reached out, her gloved fingers hovering just above the crystal. A faint warmth emanated from it. As her fingertip brushed against its cool, smooth surface, a surge of information flooded her mind. Not words, not images, but pure data – complex equations, atmospheric models, energy flow charts, and schematics of the Starstone Engines, rendered in a way that bypassed conscious thought and imprinted directly onto her understanding.

She saw the engines' purpose laid bare: not just to bring rain, but to regulate rainfall. To siphon moisture from one region and deposit it elsewhere. To create localized drought and localized deluge. To sculpt the climate to a predetermined design. And she saw, with terrifying clarity, the precise calibrations and energy frequencies required to achieve these effects. The intention, at its core, had been to create balance, to redistribute the planet's life-giving waters where they were most needed. It was a vision of ultimate environmental stewardship, a testament to a society that sought to engineer prosperity.

But within the torrent of data, a subtler pattern emerged. A series of override protocols. An emergency shutdown sequence. And something else... a set of directives that seemed to deviate from the original design, pushing the engines beyond their intended parameters, deliberately creating the arid conditions she had witnessed. This was not a malfunction; it was sabotage. Or, more chillingly, a deliberate misuse by those who had reactivated them. The data revealed a disturbing truth: the Starstone Engines, designed to foster life, were being actively weaponized to extinguish it. The very ingenuity that had made them possible had also made them instruments of destruction.

The device in her hand, she realized, was a tool for understanding and, potentially, controlling these engines. It was a missing piece of the puzzle, a key to unraveling the mystery of the manufactured blight. The legends had spoken of the Starstone Engines as benevolent forces, guardians of life. But in the hands of those who understood their destructive potential, they were weapons of unimaginable power. The implications of this discovery were profound. The ecological crisis wasn't an accident, not a natural consequence of atmospheric shifts, but a deliberate act of ecological warfare.

The weight of her discovery pressed down on her. The ecological crisis was not a tragedy of nature, but a calculated act of devastation. And the ancient, starstone-powered engines, once symbols of hope and prosperity, had been twisted into instruments of ruin. The hum of the dormant engines in the main cavern seemed to take on a more sinister note, a prelude to a symphony of destruction that was already underway. She carefully documented the smaller device, her mind racing with the implications of her findings.

The journey inland had led her to the heart of a technological marvel, a forgotten power that had been unleashed to bleed the land dry. And now, she held a sliver of the knowledge required to potentially stop it, a stark reminder that even the most brilliant human ingenuity, when divorced from ethical consideration and ecological humility, could lead to the deepest and most devastating of fallings. The ancient builders, in their quest for mastery, had perhaps forgotten that true power lay not in control, but in understanding and integration.

The emerald canopy, once a vibrant testament to the Skywood's vitality, was now a patchwork of desolation. Cael traced the brittle, browning edges of a leaf, his fingers coming away dusted with a fine, lifeless powder. It was a stark contrast to the rich, damp loam he knew so well, a tangible sign of the Skywood's slow, agonizing surrender. Each fallen leaf, each withered bloom, was a tiny death, a chipped shard of the vibrant life that had defined his world. He watched a Sky-Moth, its iridescent wings dulled and torn, flutter weakly from a branch before plummeting to the forest floor, its once-graceful descent now a pathetic tumble. The creatures of the Skywood, the vibrant sprites that danced in the dappled sunlight, the melodious call of the Sun-Crested Warblers, were becoming ghosts in their own home. Their numbers dwindled, their songs grew faint, and a pervasive silence was beginning to creep into the heart of the forest.

His heart ached with a grief so profound it felt like a physical wound. He had sworn an oath to protect the Skywood, a sacred vow passed down through generations of his lineage, a promise to be its guardian, its breath, its very lifeblood. But his oath felt like a fragile shield against an encroaching tide of decay. He had tried everything within the bounds of his sacred duty. He had consulted ancient texts, performed the traditional cleansing rituals, and channeled his own life force into the ailing trees, a desperate act that left him drained and trembling, the Skywood's sickness seeping into his own bones. Yet, the blight persisted, an insidious stain spreading further with each passing day. The very air felt thinner, charged with a melancholic energy that mirrored his own growing despair.

He remembered the vibrant hum of the Skywood in its prime, a symphony of rustling leaves, chattering creatures, and the gentle murmur of life. Now, the silence was deafening, broken only by the mournful sigh of the wind through dying branches and the dry rustle of desiccated foliage. The creatures that remained moved with a lethargy that spoke of deep-seated exhaustion, their once bright eyes clouded with an unnerving weariness. He saw a family of Glimmer-Squirrels, their fur usually a dazzling array of shifting colours, now muted and dull, huddled together on a branch, their tiny bodies trembling. They were the sentinels of the Skywood's health, and their evident distress was a brutal indictment of his failure.

The weight of responsibility pressed down on him, a crushing burden that threatened to break his spirit. He felt the desperation gnawing at him, a bitter, corrosive sensation that whispered temptations into his ear. The elders spoke of balance, of the natural order, of patience. But patience was a luxury the Skywood could no longer afford. The decay was accelerating, each sunrise revealing a landscape more desolate than the last. He saw it in the way the Skywood's bioluminescent fungi, once a source of ethereal light, now flickered weakly, their glow diminished as if struggling to survive. He saw it in the thinning mist that clung to the forest floor, the life-giving moisture seemingly stolen from the very air.

He found himself gazing at the Skywood's elder spirits, ancient trees whose gnarled branches reached towards the heavens like supplicating arms. He had always felt a profound connection to them, a deep empathy that transcended words. Now, he could feel their pain echoing within his own soul. Their branches, once strong and resilient, sagged under the weight of their affliction. The life force that had pulsed through them for centuries was ebbing, a slow, agonizing decline that mirrored the wider decay of the forest. He ran a hand over the rough bark of the Great Sentinel, the oldest tree in the Skywood, and felt a profound emptiness, a hollow echo where vibrant life once resonated.

The traditional methods, the whispered incantations, the gentle ministrations of a guardian – they were no longer enough. The blight was not a natural sickness that could be healed with poultices of moss and dew. This was something more insidious, something that struck at the very roots of the Skywood's existence. He had heard whispers, fragmented tales from the fringes of the forest, tales of a different kind of power, a power that could bend nature to one's will, a power that could force life where it refused to bloom. He had always dismissed them as folklore, as the desperate imaginings of those who lived outside the harmony of the Skywood. But now, those whispers were growing louder, more insistent, resonating with the growing turmoil in his own heart.

His oath was clear: to protect, to nurture, to preserve the natural order. But what if the natural order itself was being systematically dismantled? What if the balance he was sworn to uphold had already been irrevocably broken? The thought was a heresy, a betrayal of everything he had ever known. Yet, the image of the wilting Skywood, the dying creatures, the silent, empty clearings, burned in his mind's eye, demanding action, any action, however extreme.

He found himself drawn to the forbidden places, the shadowed groves whispered about in hushed tones, places where the veil between the natural and the unnatural was said to be thin. He had always avoided them, understanding the inherent danger, the seductive allure of powers that lay beyond the wisdom of his people. But the Skywood was dying, and with it, his very identity. He was the Guardian of the Skywood, and if the Skywood ceased to be, then what was he?

The desperation gnawed at him, a constant companion that amplified his every doubt. He saw the faces of the younger forest sprites, their usual exuberance replaced by a hesitant fear. They looked to him for reassurance, for hope, and he found himself offering hollow smiles and empty promises. He knew, with a certainty that chilled him to the bone, that he was failing them. His connection to the Skywood, once a source of strength and clarity, was now a conduit for its suffering, a shared agony that threatened to consume him.

He recalled a conversation with Elder Lyra, her voice raspy with age and concern. "The Skywood has endured much, Cael," she had said, her eyes holding a wisdom that seemed as ancient as the trees themselves. "It has faced storms, droughts, and the shadows of blight before. But always, it has healed. Always, the balance has been restored." But the blight he saw now was different. It was a cold, unnatural thing, devoid of the slow, organic rhythm of decay and rebirth. It was a sickness that felt... deliberate.

The thought began to form, a dangerous seedling in the fertile ground of his despair. What if he could *force* the Skywood to heal? What if he could tap into a power that could reverse the decay, that could infuse the trees with a life force so potent it would overwhelm the blight? He knew of certain rituals, ancient and rarely invoked, that spoke of channeling the raw essence of the earth, of drawing upon primal energies that lay dormant beneath the surface. These were not rituals of preservation, but of transformation, of forceful intervention. They were considered dangerous, unpredictable, and potentially destructive in their own right.

He found himself poring over scrolls that had been locked away for centuries, texts that spoke of the 'Great Unraveling' and the 'Primal Surge.' The language was arcane, the symbols cryptic, but the intent was chillingly clear: to manipulate the very fabric of life and energy. One passage spoke of 'binding the fading light,' of 'forcing the sap to flow against its will.' It was a language of dominion, not of guardianship.

His sleep became restless, filled with visions of the Skywood consumed by fire, then by ice, then by a suffocating, barren dust. He would wake in a cold sweat, the phantom sensation of wilting leaves scratching at his skin. The boundaries of his oath, once as solid and immutable as the oldest oak, began to blur. The imperative to protect was being challenged by a desperate urge to *save*, even if it meant venturing into uncharted and perilous territory. He felt a growing chasm between the Cael who had taken the oath and the Cael who now contemplated breaking it, a fractured self wrestling with an impossible choice.

He walked through the groves where the blight was most severe, the air thick with a palpable sense of dying. He saw a young Sapling Spirit, barely more than a wisp of green light, its form flickering weakly, its tiny branches brittle and grey. He felt a primal surge of protective anger, a fierce desire to shield it from this encroaching doom. But what shield could he offer? His gentle ministrations were like drops of water against a wildfire. He needed a flood, a torrent, a force that could sweep away this insidious decay.

The thought of the 'Primal Surge' returned, a concept that spoke of unleashing raw, untamed elemental power. It was the antithesis of the Skywood's gentle rhythms, a force that could shatter the very foundations of its existence if not wielded with absolute precision. But desperation was a powerful intoxicant, and the image of a vibrant, revitalized Skywood, even one achieved through such drastic means, began to eclipse the fear. He found himself imagining the leaves unfurling, the creatures returning, the songs echoing through the branches once more. It was a dangerous dream, born of a desperate heart.

He knew the risks. The texts warned of unintended consequences, of powers that could consume the wielder, of ecological imbalances that could be far worse than the original affliction. But the alternative was to watch the Skywood wither and die, to stand by as his oath, his heritage, and his very purpose faded into dust. The pressure was immense, a vise tightening around his chest, forcing him to consider actions he had once deemed unthinkable. The growing desperation was a seed of madness, and he felt it taking root, pushing him towards a precipice from which there might be no return. He was a guardian on the brink of becoming a destroyer, driven by a love for the Skywood so profound it was slowly, inexorably, breaking him. He looked at his hands, calloused and stained with the earth of the Skywood, and wondered if they would soon be stained with something far darker. The whispers of ancient power, once a distant echo, were now a roar in his ears, a siren song promising salvation through annihilation.

The hushed reverence that had always permeated Cael's existence within the Skywood was beginning to fray. The silence, once a comforting balm, now felt heavy with unspoken anxieties. It wasn't just the natural decay he witnessed daily, the slow creep of the blight that gnawed at his soul; it was a new kind of silence, one born of fear and uncertainty. Rumors, like tendrils of smoke, had begun to curl around the edges of the forest, carried by the hushed conversations of travelers and the furtive glances of those who ventured too close to the Skywood's ailing heart. These whispers spoke not of natural disaster, but of deliberate intent, of a force that actively sought to accelerate the Skywood's demise.

These were the whispers of the Ashbound.

Cael first encountered their ideology not through direct confrontation, but through scattered remnants of their fervor. A torn banner, crudely woven from scorched bark and bound with sinew, found snagged on a thorn bush at the forest's edge. It depicted a stylized inferno consuming a wilting sapling, the emblem stark and uncompromising. Beside it lay a small, crudely carved wooden bird, its wings snapped, its form blackened as if by fire. It was a chillingly simple, yet potent, statement.

Then came the graffito. Scrawled in a dark, viscous substance that smelled faintly of ash and decay, symbols appeared on ancient stones and weathered tree trunks. They were not the elegant glyphs of the Skywood's lore, but jagged, aggressive markings that spoke of rage and finality. Cael, along with his fellow guardians, meticulously scrubbed them away, but the act felt futile, like trying to erase a stain from the very air. Each removal was a temporary reprieve, a cosmetic fix against a festering wound.

The elders, their faces etched with a new kind of worry, began to convene more frequently. Their hushed discussions, once focused on the Skywood's ailments and potential remedies, now turned to these new whispers. Elder Maeve, her voice usually a gentle rustle of leaves, spoke with a tremor of alarm. "They call themselves the Ashbound," she revealed during one such gathering, her gaze sweeping across the anxious faces of the younger guardians. "They believe the Skywood is beyond saving through natural means. They preach a doctrine of 'necessary destruction,' of purging the old to make way for the new."

Cael felt a prickle of unease crawl up his spine. "Purging? What does that mean?"

"It means fire, Cael," Maeve replied, her voice low and grim. "It means razing the dying to fertilize the soil. They see the blight not as a tragedy, but as an opportunity. An opportunity to clear the slate, to burn away the weakness and plant anew."

The concept was abhorrent. Cael's entire existence was dedicated to preservation, to the slow, meticulous nurturing of life. The Skywood was not merely a collection of trees; it was a living tapestry woven from millennia of growth, a delicate ecosystem where every element, even the decay, played a vital role. To deliberately inflict destruction, to *burn* the Skywood, was a betrayal of his deepest convictions, a sacrilege of the highest order.

He remembered one of the more unsettling graffito symbols he'd seen – a spiraling vortex of ash. He had initially dismissed it as mere vandalism, but now, with Maeve's words echoing in his mind, it took on a far more sinister significance. It represented not just destruction, but a chaotic, uncontrolled descent into nothingness, a surrender to the very forces that were already threatening the Skywood.

"Who are these people?" Cael asked, his voice tight with a rising anger. "Where do they come from?"

"They are drawn from the fringes, Cael," explained Elder Lorien, his voice a low rumble. "Those who have felt the sting of loss, who have seen their own lands wither and die, and who have found no solace in the traditional ways. They believe the Skywood's slow death is a symptom of a broader sickness in the world, a weakness that must be eradicated with extreme prejudice. They see the current guardians, those who try to heal and protect, as enablers of this decay. They believe we are merely delaying the inevitable, prolonging the suffering."

This was a perspective Cael found almost impossible to grasp. How could anyone witness the beauty and vitality of the Skywood, even in its current weakened state, and wish to extinguish it entirely? He looked at his own hands, the hands that had always tended to the gentle unfolding of leaves, the careful coaxing of seedlings, the soothing of ailing bark. The thought of using those same hands to sow destruction, to wield fire or poison, felt like a physical violation.

"They are dangerous," Cael stated, the words heavy with conviction. "They offer a path of annihilation, not salvation."

"Indeed," Lorien agreed. "Their philosophy is a perversion of true ecological balance. Balance is not achieved through brute force, but through understanding and symbiosis. They seek to impose their will upon nature, rather than to work with it. And their methods... they speak of 'ashes to ashes, dust to dust' with a chilling fervor. They believe that only from the deepest ashes can true, unadulterated growth emerge."

Cael pictured the Great Sentinel, the ancient heart of the Skywood, its branches reaching towards the sky like a silent prayer. He imagined the Ashbound setting their fires to its base, watching with cold eyes as the millennia of life turned to smoke and cinders. The image sent a shiver of revulsion through him.

"Have they... have they attacked anything?" he pressed, dread coiling in his stomach.

Maeve nodded, her expression grim. "There have been isolated incidents. Small groves near the periphery, where the blight was already advanced, have been subjected to arson. Livestock, not of the Skywood's native creatures but those introduced by settlers in the outlying territories, have been poisoned. They leave behind their symbols, their messages of impending 'cleansing.'"

The scope of their agenda was terrifying. This was not simply a fringe group of radicals; they were organized, determined, and possessed a chillingly coherent, albeit twisted, ideology. Their actions were not random acts of violence, but calculated steps towards their ultimate goal.

"They see Mara's efforts as weak," Lorien added, referring to the diplomat who had been attempting to broker peace between the Skywood and its neighboring settlements. "They dismiss her attempts at negotiation and understanding as futile gestures that only prolong the agony of the sick. They believe her approach is a betrayal of the natural order, that it allows the blight to fester and spread."

Cael understood the frustration that might drive such a group, the desperation born from witnessing widespread ecological collapse. He himself was wrestling with the limits of his own abilities, the gnawing fear that his traditional methods were insufficient. But the Ashbound's solution was not a solution at all; it was an abdication of responsibility, a surrender to despair disguised as radical action.

"Their path leads only to more destruction," Cael said, his voice firm. "It is a cycle of violence. If they burn, and then new life grows, what is to stop the next generation from deciding that this new life is also flawed and needs to be burned again?"

"Precisely," Maeve confirmed. "They offer no true solution, only a return to a primal, destructive state. Their 'new growth' would be born of chaos, not of balance. It would be a world forged in fire, perpetually at risk of being consumed by it again."

Cael felt a knot of determination tighten in his chest. He had sworn to protect the Skywood. That oath now felt more vital, more urgent, than ever before. His duty was not just to fight the blight, but to defend the Skywood from those who would see it obliterated entirely. The Ashbound represented a new and terrifying enemy, one whose ideology was as dangerous as the blight itself. They were a philosophical counterpoint to his own guardianship, a dark mirror reflecting the potential for despair to curdle into destructive fervor.

He thought of the creatures within the Skywood, the fragile spirits and the ancient trees. They were not merely subjects of his protection; they were his kin, his life. The Ashbound's vision of a 'cleansed' world, devoid of the nuances and complexities of the current ecosystem, felt like a profound violation of that kinship. They did not see the interconnectedness, the delicate web of life that held the Skywood together. They saw only weakness, only decay, and their answer was to sever all ties, to obliterate the whole in pursuit of an idealized, sterile beginning.

"We must understand them," Cael stated, his gaze meeting Lorien's and Maeve's. "We must understand their motives, their strengths, and their weaknesses. We cannot simply dismiss them as madmen. Their message, however twisted, resonates with a segment of the population, those who feel abandoned by the natural order, those who have lost hope."

Lorien nodded slowly. "That is a wise, albeit dangerous, path, Cael. To understand is not to condone. Their actions are a threat, and they must be stopped. But if we are to effectively counter them, we must first understand the soil from which their destructive seeds have grown."

The emergence of the Ashbound Faction added a new, perilous dimension to the crisis plaguing the Skywood. It was no longer solely a battle against a creeping ecological disease, but a nascent socio-political conflict, a clash of ideologies where preservation was pitted against radical, destructive purging. Cael knew, with a sinking certainty, that his oath to protect the Skywood now extended beyond the natural world and into the realm of human – or perhaps, more accurately, sentient – intent. The whispers of technology he had begun to hear from the outside world now seemed to be accompanied by a more primal, ancient roar of destruction, and he had to find a way to silence it before it consumed everything he held dear. He had to find a way to protect the Skywood not just from the rot within, but from the fire without.

The news of the Ashbound faction spread like wildfire, not through the hushed tones of rumour, but through the pronouncements of the faction itself. Their reach, once confined to the fringes of the civilized world, was now extending, their message of radical ecological reset finding fertile ground in communities suffering from environmental devastation. Cael learned, through the network of forest sprites who acted as the Skywood's eyes and ears, that the Ashbound had established several known sanctuaries in the ravaged territories beyond the Great Mountains. These were not places of community or refuge, but rather staging grounds, training facilities where their brand of 'eco-purification' was honed.

One such sanctuary, whispered about with a mixture of terror and grim fascination, was located in the desiccated husk of what was once a verdant valley, now known only as the Ashlands. Here, the Ashbound were said to be experimenting with potent, alchemical concoctions designed to accelerate decay, to poison the very soil and water sources of any remaining life. Their methods were crude, brutal, and terrifyingly effective. They were not merely advocates of destruction; they were actively engineering it, creating pockets of absolute desolation where nothing could survive.

"They believe they are performing a necessary surgery," explained Elara, a young Dryad whose grove had been on the border of one of the Ashbound's targeted areas. Her voice, usually lilting and melodic, was now brittle, like dried leaves. She had witnessed firsthand the horrifying efficiency of their methods. A small, isolated patch of ancient oaks, once revered for their resilience, had been targeted. Within weeks, the leaves had curled and blackened, the bark had split, and the very air around them had become thick with a foul, acrid stench. The Ashbound had then moved in, not to mourn, but to burn the fallen trees to ash, scattering the remnants to the winds, a symbolic act of finality.

"They spoke of the 'blight' being a symptom of the Skywood's weakness, its unwillingness to shed the old," Elara continued, her eyes wide with remembered horror. "They said that by accelerating the decay, by burning away the sick flesh, they were preparing the ground for a stronger, more robust life to emerge. They saw the dying trees not as victims, but as necessary sacrifices."

Cael found himself recoiling from the sheer callousness of their ideology. To view sentient life, to view ancient beings of immense power and wisdom, as mere 'sacrifices' was a profound betrayal of the interconnectedness he held so dear. His own struggle with the Skywood's decline was a testament to his deep empathy for its suffering. The Ashbound seemed to possess none of that. Their hearts, he suspected, were as barren as the lands they sought to create.

"And what of the creatures?" Cael asked, his voice tight. "The sprites, the moths, the beasts that dwell within the Skywood?"

"They are deemed 'excess biomass'," Elara replied, a shudder running through her. "Unnecessary embellishments on a dying form. The Ashbound believe that a truly pure ecosystem would be stripped down to its bare essentials, a foundation upon which a more perfect form of life could eventually be built. They view any current inhabitant as an obstacle, a lingering vestige of imperfection."

This was a horrifying revelation. The Ashbound were not just targeting flora; they were actively planning the eradication of fauna, of all life that did not fit their narrow definition of purity. Cael's mind raced, picturing the vibrant, chattering Glimmer-Squirrels, the iridescent Sky-Moths, the countless other beings that made the Skywood their home. The thought of them being swept away, deemed 'excess biomass,' was a blow to his very core.

Elder Lorien, who had been listening intently, his weathered face grim, spoke up. "Their philosophy is a dangerous one, rooted in a profound misunderstanding of ecological principles. True resilience comes not from elimination, but from adaptation and diversity. They seek a sterile perfection, a theoretical ideal that has no place in the messy, vibrant reality of life. They are not gardeners; they are executioners."

Cael felt a surge of anger, a protective fire that had been smoldering within him, now igniting. He had sworn to protect the Skywood, and that included all the life it harbored. The Ashbound were not simply a new threat; they were an existential one.

"They are a direct antithesis to everything we stand for," Cael declared, his voice ringing with conviction. "While we strive to nurture, to heal, to understand the delicate balance, they seek to shatter it, to impose a brutal, artificial order. Their 'new growth' would be a sterile imitation, devoid of the soul and spirit that makes the Skywood what it is."

He knew, with a chilling certainty, that his guardianship would now extend far beyond battling the creeping blight. He would have to defend the Skywood from those who actively sought its destruction, from those who believed that its end was the only path to its salvation. The whispers of technology that had begun to concern him were now joined by the roaring inferno of the Ashbound's ideology, a dual threat that demanded a vigilance he had never before imagined. He had to find a way to counter their destructive fervor, to demonstrate that true balance came not from annihilation, but from a deep, abiding respect for all life, however flawed or imperfect it might seem to those who yearned for a scorched-earth rebirth. He had to ensure that the Ashbound's fires never reached the heart of the Skywood, and that their message of despair was drowned out by the enduring symphony of life.

The weight of her mission pressed down on Mara with an intensity that rivaled the arid heat shimmering off the parched earth. She had ridden for days, the dust of the Sunstone Wastes clinging to her worn leathers, her throat perpetually dry despite the waterskin slung across her shoulder. Her objective was deceptively simple: to engage the disparate communities that dotted the fringes of the Skywood's influence, to weave a tapestry of understanding and cooperation where only threads of suspicion and fear had begun to fray. Elder Maeve's words echoed in her mind: "The Skywood cannot stand alone, Mara. Its roots are intertwined with the very fabric of this land, and the hearts of its people. You must remind them of that connection."

Her first stop was the settlement of Oakhaven, a cluster of sturdy, stone-built homes nestled precariously close to the withered edge of the elder woods. The air here was thick with the scent of desperation – the lingering smell of failing crops, the acrid tang of woodsmoke from constant, weary fires. As she approached the central gathering place, a rough-hewn square dominated by a dry, cracked fountain, she saw faces turn towards her, their expressions a mixture of wariness and a flicker of desperate hope. Children, their faces smudged with dirt, ceased their games and stared, their eyes wide with a curiosity that was quickly overshadowed by their parents' anxious scrutiny.

Mara dismounted her hardy steppe mare, a creature as weathered and resilient as the people she sought to engage. She offered a small, almost imperceptible nod to the gathered villagers, her gaze sweeping over them, trying to read the unspoken stories etched onto their faces. She saw the lines of worry around their eyes, the tightness in their jaws, the way they instinctively clutched at worn amulets or protective charms. This was not a receptive audience, not yet.

"Greetings," Mara called out, her voice clear and steady, though she felt the tremor of apprehension beneath her outward calm. "I am Mara, a diplomat from the Skywood. I come with a plea for understanding, and a proposal for shared resilience."

Silence met her words, a silence far more profound than the gentle hush of the forest. It was a heavy, suffocating silence, born of years of neglect, of broken promises, and of a gnawing fear that had been amplified by the creeping blight and the more recent whispers of the Ashbound. A burly man, his face tanned and leathery, stepped forward, his hands resting on the hilt of a crude, well-used blade. He was clearly a man of authority in this place, his presence radiating a quiet, imposing strength.

"Skywood?" he grunted, his voice a low rumble like distant thunder. "We've heard little from the Skywood but the rustle of dying leaves and the silence of forgotten promises. What understanding can a dying forest offer us, diplomat? What resilience can it share when it has none left for itself?"

His words hung in the air, sharp and bitter. Mara felt a familiar pang of sorrow. This was the crux of the problem, the deep-seated distrust that had festered for too long. The Skywood, once a source of life and sustenance for these communities, had become a symbol of decay, a looming testament to their shared vulnerability.

"The blight is a sickness that affects us all," Mara replied, her tone gentle but firm. "It does not discriminate, nor does it respect boundaries. While the Skywood may be weakening, its interconnectedness with your lands remains. The water that flows into your streams, the very air you breathe, is touched by its essence. To allow the Skywood to fall completely would be to sever a vital artery, not just for us, but for you as well."

Another voice, sharper and more strident, cut through the tense quiet. "Resilience? We've learned resilience here, diplomat. We've learned to make do with less, to weather the droughts, to ward off the mutated creatures that the blight seems to breed. We've learned to rely on ourselves, not on the fickle favor of ancient trees." A woman, her face gaunt and her eyes burning with a fierce intensity, pushed her way to the front. "Your Skywood offers us nothing but the shade of its decline. While you communed with your spirits and tended your ancient roots, our crops withered, and our children went hungry."

Mara's heart ached at the raw pain in the woman's voice. She understood the accusation, the resentment that had built up over generations. "I do not come to dismiss your struggles, nor to claim the Skywood is blameless," Mara said, choosing her words with care. "We have faced our own challenges, our own moments of near despair. But despair is a fertile ground for the Ashbound. They thrive on the belief that the only solution is to burn away the old. Is that the future you wish for yourselves? A future of ashes, where even the memory of what was is consumed?"

The mention of the Ashbound elicited a ripple of fear and anger through the crowd. Murmurs of their destructive deeds, their symbols of fire and ash, spread like a nervous tremor. This was a language they understood, a fear that was fresh and raw.

"The Ashbound," the first man, who introduced himself as Kaelen, the village elder, echoed, his voice losing some of its hardness. "They are a blight of a different kind. Their fire is not cleansing; it is annihilation. We've heard their pronouncements, seen their twisted symbols on the ravaged farms to the north. They speak of a new world, born of ruin. But who will be left to live in it? Who will tend the fields when the soil itself is poisoned?"

"Exactly," Mara seized on the shared fear. "And that is why we must work together. The Ashbound believe that isolation breeds weakness. They seek to divide us, to pit us against each other. But our strength lies not in isolation, but in unity. If we pool our knowledge, our resources, our resilience, we can face this threat, and the blight, together."

She spoke of potential collaborations: sharing Skywood seeds that might be more resistant to the blight, offering the expertise of the Skywood's healers in treating ailments that afflicted both flora and fauna, and even, if they were willing, seeking the counsel of the land dragon elders who, though reclusive, held ancient wisdom that might offer new perspectives on ecological balance. She proposed the establishment of shared watch posts along the Skywood's periphery, a joint effort to monitor the movements of the Ashbound and to provide early warnings of blight outbreaks.

"The land dragons," Kaelen scoffed, though there was a flicker of interest in his eyes. "They are myths. Whispers on the wind, as unreliable as the Skywood's shade."

"They are ancient," Mara corrected gently. "And their connection to the land runs deeper than any living memory. Their perspective, however alien it may seem, is invaluable. If we are to truly understand the balance we seek to restore, we must consider all voices, all forms of life that are intrinsically tied to this world." She paused, her gaze meeting each individual she could in the crowd. "I am not asking for blind faith. I am asking for an open mind, for a willingness to explore possibilities, to see beyond the immediate fear and to build a future where all our communities can thrive, not just survive."

Her speech, though heartfelt, was met with a cautious silence. The fear of the Ashbound was potent, but so too was the ingrained distrust of the Skywood. They had been disappointed too many times. Kaelen stroked his chin, his gaze fixed on the distant, hazy outline of the Skywood. "Your words are... eloquent, diplomat. They speak of hope, a commodity we have found scarce of late. But hope does not fill empty granaries, nor does it mend broken fences. We have learned to be practical. We have learned to look after our own."

Mara nodded, acknowledging the truth in his words. "And I respect that practicality. My proposal is not for charity, but for mutual benefit. Imagine if the Skywood could offer you stronger saplings, less susceptible to the blight. Imagine if our healers could share their knowledge to help your livestock. Imagine if we could collectively develop early warning systems for the Ashbound's movements. These are tangible benefits, born from collaboration."

She spent the rest of the day in Oakhaven, speaking with individuals, answering their hesitant questions, and gently challenging their ingrained skepticism. She spoke of the technologies the Skywood had developed, not in the sense of sterile machinery, but in the intricate ways they had learned to harness natural energies, to encourage symbiotic relationships between flora and fauna, to cultivate plants with remarkable resilience. She spoke of their attempts to understand the very nature of the blight, not as an enemy to be eradicated, but as a natural process, albeit one that had been thrown out of balance.

The resistance was palpable, a thick, invisible wall. Many saw her as naive, a dreamer clinging to outdated ideals in a world that had grown harsh and unforgiving. They had seen too much loss, too much suffering, to easily embrace the promise of cooperation. Yet, Mara detected faint cracks in that wall. A few villagers, their faces etched with a weariness that spoke of years of hardship, approached her with quiet questions, their curiosity piqued by the mention of the land dragons or the Skywood's methods of healing. They had little to lose, and perhaps, just perhaps, something to gain.

As dusk began to paint the sky in hues of ochre and deep purple, Mara prepared to depart. She had not secured any grand alliances, no sweeping promises of mutual defense. But she had planted seeds. She had introduced the idea that the Skywood was not merely a dying entity, but a potential partner, a repository of knowledge and resources that could aid them. Kaelen, the elder, approached her once more as she mounted her mare.

"We will consider your words, diplomat," he said, his tone still guarded, but with a hint of something new – perhaps a grudging respect, or a flicker of buried hope. "Oakhaven has always been a place that looks after its own. But perhaps, in these dark times, 'our own' may need to extend beyond our stone walls."

Mara offered him a genuine smile, a rare sight that softened the determined lines of her face. "That is all I ask, Elder Kaelen. That is all I ask."

Her journey continued to the neighboring settlement of Willow Creek, a community known for its skilled weavers and its deep connection to the nearby river. Here, the blight had manifested differently, affecting the water purity and the reeds that were vital to their livelihood. The people of Willow Creek were initially even more resistant. They viewed the Skywood's troubles as a distant problem that had now encroached upon their own delicate ecosystem.

"The Skywood weeps its sickness into our waters," proclaimed Lyra, the leader of the weavers, her voice sharp and laced with accusation. "Our reeds are stunted, our fish are becoming scarce. And you come speaking of cooperation? We need solutions, not philosophical musings on interconnectedness!"

Mara explained, with painstaking patience, how the blight was not a singular entity but a complex imbalance, a cascading effect that began within the Skywood's ancient heart and rippled outwards. She spoke of the Skywood's attempts to purify its own waterways, and how their methods, if shared, could potentially benefit Willow Creek. She offered the Skywood's knowledge of drought-resistant crops and water conservation techniques, ideas that were met with a similar blend of skepticism and a desperate, underlying need for answers.

"We hear tales of the Ashbound, too," Lyra admitted, her gaze falling to her own roughened hands, calloused from years of weaving. "They speak of purging the weak. But they offer no balm, only the threat of the blade. We don't want to be purged, diplomat. We want our river to run clean again. We want our reeds to grow strong."

"And that is precisely what I believe we can achieve, together," Mara reiterated, her voice imbued with a quiet conviction that began to chip away at Lyra's hardened exterior. She spoke of the potential for shared research into the blight's effects on aquatic life, of joint efforts to reseed the riverbanks with resilient native plants, and of the possibility of learning from the land dragons' ancient understanding of water cycles.

The resistance she faced was not born of malice, but of a profound weariness and a deep-seated fear. The blight had taken so much, and the Ashbound threatened to take the rest. They had learned to rely on themselves, to build walls around their hopes and their communities. Mara's diplomatic overture was an attempt to breach those walls, not with force or deception, but with the quiet, persistent force of reason and shared purpose. It was a gamble, a desperate hope that in the face of overwhelming adversity, the instinct for survival might, just might, be strong enough to overcome the ingrained distrust.

As she moved from village to village, each encounter was a testament to the profound challenge she faced, and to her unwavering commitment to bridging the divides that threatened to consume them all. Her journey was a slow, arduous one, a testament to the power of persistent diplomacy in a world teetering on the brink of ecological and societal collapse. She was a single voice, whispering of unity against the growing roar of despair, a lone diplomat in a land fractured by fear.

Chapter Four

THE CANOPY ACCORD COUNCIL

The Great Banyan Hall pulsed with an ancient, hushed energy. Sunlight, filtered through the colossal, interwoven branches that formed its living ceiling, dappled the polished bark floor in shifting patterns of gold and emerald. The air was thick with the scent of decaying leaves, blooming mosses, and the subtle, metallic tang of arcane energies. This was the heart of the Skywood, the sacred space where the Canopy Accord Council convened, its members gathered not just from the arboreal city itself, but from the farthest reaches of its influence.

At the center of the vast, circular chamber, upon roots that had been smoothed and shaped by generations of careful tending, sat the Elders. They were the custodians of the Skywood's legacy, the living embodiment of its wisdom, and the arbiters of its future. Their faces, etched with the deep lines of centuries, held a profound stillness, a reflection of the ancient trees they served. Elder Maeve, her silver hair braided with luminous fungi, occupied her usual place, her gaze sharp and assessing, missing nothing. Beside her sat Elder Bram, his gnarled hands clasped over a staff that seemed to be carved from a single, petrified lightning strike, his brow furrowed in perpetual contemplation. There were others, too, each a figure of reverence, their presence a testament to the enduring power and intricate social fabric of the Skywood.

Mara stood a respectful distance from the central gathering, her heart a drumbeat against her ribs. She was here not as a petitioner, but as an observer, a representative of a younger, more desperate generation whose future was inextricably tied to the decisions made within these hallowed walls. The weight of Oakhaven and Willow Creek still settled upon her shoulders, the memory of their skepticism a counterpoint to the solemnity of the Hall. Beside her, Cael stood with an almost imperceptible tension in his shoulders.

He was not an Elder, nor even a formal delegate, but his reputation as a skilled tracker and a keen observer of the Skywood's ecological health had earned him a place at the periphery of these vital discussions. His presence here was a silent testament to the growing understanding that the crisis facing the Skywood could not be solved by wisdom alone; it demanded a visceral, ground-level understanding of the encroaching blight and the shadowy movements of the Ashbound.

The first words spoken were not a greeting, but a pronouncement. Elder Theron, his voice like the rustle of dry leaves, addressed the assembled council. "The blight deepens. The Ashbound grow bolder. Our traditional remedies falter. We convene today not to merely discuss, but to decide, before the Skywood weeps its last tears."

A murmur rippled through the Hall. The acknowledged severity of the situation was a cold comfort, yet the sheer lack of immediate solutions hung heavy in the air. Elder Rowan, her face serene but her eyes reflecting a deep concern, spoke next. "We have consulted the Sunstone Oracles, we have performed the ancient rites of purification, we have reinforced the wards. Yet, the decay spreads. The whispers from the outer settlements grow louder, filled with fear and accusations of neglect. They see our inaction, our reliance on the old ways, and they feel abandoned."

Her words struck a chord with Mara. She saw the faces of Kaelen and Lyra in her mind's eye, their distrust a tangible force even in this sacred space. "Inaction is a perception," Elder Bram countered, his voice a low rumble. "We are not inactive. We are... assessing. The blight is a complex entity, a symptom of an imbalance that may have roots far deeper than we initially understood. To act rashly, to apply treatments without true comprehension, could be more destructive than the blight itself."

"Destructive?" Elder Maeve's voice cut through Bram's measured tone, sharp and resonant. "What could be more destructive than the slow, agonizing death of our home? The outer settlements are not merely 'perceptions' of neglect, Bram. They are starving. Their children are falling ill. Their pleas for aid are no longer whispers; they are cries for help. If we are to maintain the Accord, if we are to uphold our duty, we must offer them more than contemplative silence."

The tension in the hall ratcheted higher. The inherent conflict between preservation and immediate action, between deep ecological understanding and urgent human need, was laid bare. Cael shifted his weight, his gaze sweeping over the assembled Elders. He had seen the Ashbound's mark firsthand, a scorched symbol that promised not renewal, but utter annihilation. He understood the urgency that Mara had encountered, the raw fear that the Skywood's slow deliberations could not assuage.

"Elder Maeve speaks truth," Cael's voice, though respectful, carried a new authority, born of his recent experiences. He had seen the blight's relentless advance, the way it withered not just trees, but the very hope of those who depended on them. "I have ventured beyond the immediate canopy. The blight is not merely a sickness of the wood; it is a corruption of the soil, a poison in the water. And the Ashbound... they are not simply raiders. They are an ideology. They preach of cleansing through fire, of a world purged of its 'weaknesses.' Their influence is growing, fueled by the very despair that our current approaches are failing to quell."

His words hung in the air, a stark counterpoint to the Elder's philosophical debates. The inclusion of an outsider, and one who spoke with such unvarnished urgency, was unusual. Most of the Elders regarded Cael with a mixture of curiosity and mild disapproval. He represented a world beyond their carefully curated ecosystem, a world of harsh realities they were often insulated from.

"An ideology, you say?" Elder Theron mused, his eyes narrowing. "And what, young tracker, do you propose we do about an ideology that thrives on our perceived failings?"

"We offer a counter-narrative," Mara interjected, stepping forward, her voice clear and firm. "We offer tangible proof that cooperation is not weakness, but strength. The people of Oakhaven and Willow Creek are not enemies; they are allies in a war we are all losing. They possess knowledge of their lands, of drought-resistant crops, of water management techniques that we in the Skywood, for all our arboreal focus, may have overlooked. Their resilience is not a defiance of the Skywood; it is a testament to the very spirit of survival that we must rekindle in all our communities."

Elder Bram sighed, a sound like wind through hollow reeds. "Mara, your passion is admirable, and your diplomatic efforts are noted. However, you speak of pooling resources as if we had an abundance. The Skywood itself is strained. Our own reserves are dwindling. How can we offer aid to others when we are teetering on the brink ourselves?"

"We offer what we *can* offer," Mara insisted, her gaze unwavering. "Knowledge. Shared research. Coordinated efforts. We can share our understanding of symbiotic cultivation, our methods of pest control that don't rely on harsh chemicals. We can learn from their practical experience, their hard-won wisdom born of necessity. And we can, collectively, develop early warning systems for the Ashbound. Their fire is a threat to us all. To face it alone is to invite annihilation."

The debate continued, a complex tapestry woven from ancient traditions and pressing realities. Elder Maeve, ever pragmatic, saw the logic in Mara's plea. "The outer settlements are our eyes and ears on the ground, Bram. If they fall, we become blind. Their survival is, in a very real sense, our own. The Ashbound would not hesitate to raze their farms and then turn their attention to our roots."

"But what of the source of the blight?" Elder Lyra, a wizened guardian of the Skywood's medicinal gardens, countered, her voice raspy with age. "We have brewed the most potent purges, sought the aid of the earth spirits. They offer little solace. The blight seems... intrinsic. A corruption that has taken root in the very lifeblood of the Skywood."

This was the crux of the issue, the question that gnawed at the heart of the Council. For generations, the Skywood had been a bastion of ecological harmony, a self-sustaining paradise. Now, it was ailing. The blight, a slow-creeping decay, was unlike any pestilence they had faced before. It did not discriminate between ancient and young, between healthy and weakened. It simply consumed.

"Perhaps," Cael spoke again, his voice low and measured, drawing the attention of the council once more, "the blight is not merely a disease, but a response. A consequence. The Skywood, in its ancient wisdom, has always maintained a delicate balance. But we, too, have changed. Our reliance on certain ancient practices, our detachment from the very lands we protect... have we, in our own way, tipped that balance?"

His words hung in the air, an uncomfortable truth. The Skywood's inhabitants, while deeply connected to their arboreal home, had grown increasingly insular, their focus narrowed to the preservation of their immediate ecosystem. The pleas of the outer settlements, once addressed with paternalistic gestures, had gradually faded into a distant hum, drowned out by the more immediate concerns of the canopy.

Elder Theron, ever the pragmatist, steepled his fingers. "Your points are valid, young Cael, and your observations from the periphery are valuable. But theorizing about imbalances does not prune the dying branches. We must act. Elder Maeve, you have been the most vocal proponent of external engagement. What concrete steps do you propose beyond diplomacy and shared knowledge?"

Maeve's gaze swept across the council, her expression firm. "We must establish a formal Accord Council, one that includes representatives from the outer settlements. Not as supplicants, but as partners. We must share our limited resources, not in the form of charity, but as investments in mutual survival. I propose that we allocate a portion of our remaining Skywood seeds, the blight-resistant strains we have cultivated, to Oakhaven and Willow Creek. In return, they will share their crop yields and their knowledge of arid land cultivation. Furthermore, we must organize joint patrols with their hunters and our scouts along the borderlands, to track the Ashbound's movements and to provide early warnings. This is not a concession; it is a strategic alliance."

"Seeds?" Elder Bram scoffed gently. "Are we to fight an encroaching blight and a fanatical ideology with mere seeds? Our wards are weakening, our protective enchantments are faltering. The very energy that sustains us is being drained."

"The energy that sustains us, Elder Bram," Mara countered, her voice resonating with conviction, "is also the energy that sustains all life connected to the Skywood. When the outer lands wither, when their wells run dry, that is a drain on our own vitality. The Ashbound thrive on division, on the belief that the old must be burned to make way for the new. Our resistance lies in proving them wrong. Our strength lies in unity. If we can show that cooperation breeds resilience, that shared knowledge can mend what has been broken, then we offer a hope that the Ashbound, with their fire and ash, can never extinguish."

The debate raged on, a fierce, intellectual storm within the serene embrace of the Great Banyan Hall. Each Elder brought their own perspective, their own deeply held beliefs about the Skywood's nature and its place in the world. Some, like Maeve, were driven by a desperate pragmatism, recognizing that the Skywood could not survive in isolation. Others, like Bram, were more cautious, fearing that any deviation from ancient traditions could have unforeseen and catastrophic consequences.

Elder Silas, the keeper of the Skywood's historical archives, spoke with a voice that seemed to carry the weight of ages. "The legends speak of times when the Skywood stood as a solitary beacon, its own protector.

But they also speak of periods of great darkness, when the canopy was threatened from without, and when alliances were forged with those who lived beyond the shadow of our leaves. These alliances were not always easy, but they were often vital for our survival."

"Legends are not blueprints for action, Silas," Bram retorted, though his voice lacked its usual conviction. He understood the underlying truth in Silas's words, the cyclical nature of threat and response. The Skywood had never been truly alone, not in its long history. Its interconnectedness was not merely ecological; it was political, social, and spiritual.

"But they are warnings, Elder Bram," Mara pressed. "Warnings that isolation breeds vulnerability. The Ashbound are not merely a physical threat; they are a spiritual one. They prey on fear, on despair, on the belief that there is no solution but destruction. If we allow ourselves to be consumed by fear, if we retreat into ourselves, we validate their worldview. We become the very weakness they seek to exploit."

Cael, who had remained largely silent, observing the intricate dance of politics and tradition, finally offered his perspective. "The Ashbound's strength is in their unity of purpose, however twisted. They move with speed and decisiveness. Our deliberations, while rooted in wisdom, are slow. The blight does not wait for our pronouncements. The Ashbound do not respect our sacred spaces. If we are to match their resolve, we must find a way to act more swiftly, to bridge the gaps between contemplation and action."

He looked directly at Elder Maeve, a silent acknowledgement of her efforts to bridge those gaps. "Diplomacy is the first step, Elder Maeve. But it must be followed by concrete action. Shared patrols, shared resources, a unified defense. We cannot afford to lose more ground, literally or figuratively, while we debate the finer points of balance."

A profound silence fell over the Great Banyan Hall, broken only by the gentle sigh of the wind through the ancient branches. The weight of the crisis, the looming threat of the Ashbound, and the insidious creep of the blight pressed down on each Elder. The traditional methods, once the bedrock of their stability, were proving insufficient. The Skywood, for all its grandeur and wisdom, was facing a reckoning.

Elder Maeve rose, her gaze sweeping across the council, her eyes holding a glint of fierce determination. "I agree with Elder Silas's historical precedent and with Mara's urgent plea. The time for passive observation is over. We must forge a new accord, one that recognizes the interconnectedness of all life that falls under the Skywood's shadow, and beyond. I propose that we form a special committee, tasked with bridging the divide between the Skywood and the outer settlements. Mara, you will represent the Skywood in these negotiations. Cael, your knowledge of the external threat will be invaluable. And Elder Rowan, your wisdom in matters of community and healing will be essential."

A ripple of surprise, then a grudging acceptance, passed through the council. The formation of such a committee, with representatives from beyond the Skywood's immediate embrace, was a significant departure from tradition. It was a tacit acknowledgement that the old ways, while holding their intrinsic value, were no longer enough.

Elder Bram, after a moment of deep introspection, nodded slowly. "A committee. Perhaps that is the path forward. A way to maintain our traditions while embracing the necessities of a changing world. But let it be known, this council will not abandon the deep wisdom of the Skywood. It will inform our decisions, even as we reach beyond our roots."

The decision was made. The Canopy Accord Council, a bastion of ancient wisdom, had taken a hesitant but significant step towards a new era. The weight of responsibility now shifted, not just to the venerable Elders, but to Mara, Cael, and Rowan, who would carry the hopes and fears of a fractured world on their shoulders. The path ahead was fraught with peril, but for the first time in a long time, there was a flicker of genuine hope, a sense that perhaps, just perhaps, the Skywood and its scattered communities could find a way to weather the storm, together. The Great

Banyan Hall, usually a place of hushed contemplation, now buzzed with a new kind of energy – the potent, unpredictable force of change.

The Great Banyan Hall, usually a sanctuary of measured deliberation, now thrummed with a palpable tension, the air thick with the unspoken anxieties of a community teetering on the precipice. Elder Theron, his voice usually a calm balm, now carried a sharp edge of urgency. "We have discussed the symptoms, the manifestations of the blight, the increased activity of the Ashbound. But we have yet to address the *how*. How do we combat this encroaching darkness? The time for simply observing and consulting is long past."

A ripple of agreement swept through the chamber, a collective exhalation of frustration. Elder Maeve, her silver braids catching the dappled light, seized the moment. "My esteemed colleagues," she began, her voice clear and resonant, "the blight is not merely a disease; it is an ecological unraveling. We have spent generations meticulously cultivating the Skywood, understanding its intricate symbiosis. Now, that tapestry is fraying. To stand idly by, to believe that nature will simply right itself, is a dangerous gamble. I propose a course of aggressive restoration. We must, with all our knowledge and power, intervene. We must actively heal the corrupted soil, bolster the weakened flora, and actively push back the blight's advance. This may require methods that are... unconventional. Risks we have historically avoided. But the alternative is the slow, certain death of our home."

Her words hung in the air, a bold declaration that immediately ignited a counter-current of dissent. Elder Bram, his brow furrowed deeper than usual, shifted on his root-throne. "Maeve, your conviction is commendable, and your desire to protect the Skywood is beyond question. However, 'aggressive restoration' often translates to 'meddling.' We are stewards, not masters. The Skywood possesses its own innate resilience, its own ancient rhythms of recovery. Our attempts to 'force' healing can, and often do, lead to unforeseen consequences.

Remember the Great Seedling Blight of the third age? Our well-intentioned attempts to accelerate its growth only made it more susceptible to a fungal infection that nearly decimated the western boughs. Nature, left to its own devices, often finds a more balanced, sustainable path to recovery. Perhaps what is needed is not intervention, but *withdrawal*. A period of strategic retreat, allowing the land to heal undisturbed by our presence, by our very attempts to 'fix' it."

A murmur of assent followed Bram's words, particularly from the older, more tradition-bound Elders, those whose memories stretched back to a time when the Skywood's growth was more organic, less engineered. Mara felt a knot tighten in her stomach. Withdrawal? The very idea felt like a betrayal of everything she had fought for. She had seen the hollow eyes of the children in Oakhaven, the desperate hands that clawed at barren soil.

"Withdrawal?" she echoed, her voice betraying the shock she felt. "Elder Bram, with all due respect, how can we withdraw when the blight is actively consuming our communities? When the Ashbound are not waiting for nature to heal, but are actively fanning the flames of destruction? Our people are starving. Their land is poisoned. To tell them to simply wait, to hope that the Skywood *might* heal itself while they perish... it is not a strategy, it is a death sentence!"

Cael, standing beside her, shifted his weight, his gaze fixed on the troubled faces of the Elders. He understood Mara's visceral reaction. He had seen the Ashbound's scorched earth, the speed with which they razed settlements. But he had also seen the insidious nature of the blight, how it seeped into the very roots of the ancient trees, how it choked the life from the soil. He felt caught between two opposing tides of desperation. "Elder Bram's concern for unintended consequences is valid," Cael stated, his voice calm but firm, drawing the attention of many who had been focused on the political wrangling. "But Mara is also correct. The Ashbound are an immediate, existential threat that does not respect ecological cycles. Their fire is indiscriminate. If we withdraw, if we cease our active defense, the Ashbound will simply sweep through the outer settlements, then turn their attention to the Skywood itself. There is no 'healing' on scorched earth."

He paused, choosing his words carefully. "However, Elder Maeve's proposed 'aggressive restoration' also carries immense risk. We don't fully understand the blight's origin. Is it a natural phenomenon, exacerbated by some imbalance? Or is it something... introduced? A deliberate poison? If it is the latter, our attempts to 'heal' might inadvertently nourish it, or even unleash something worse. I have seen areas where the blight is particularly virulent. The very air feels wrong, charged with a stagnant, suffocating energy. To try and force growth there, with potent elixirs or accelerated cultivation, could be like pouring fuel on a smoldering fire. It might bloom for a moment, then collapse entirely."

Elder Lyra, whose hands were perpetually stained with the vibrant hues of medicinal herbs, spoke with a voice like dry leaves skittering across stone. "Cael speaks with a wisdom that transcends mere observation. The blight... it is unlike any ailment we have faced. It does not respond to our most potent purges, nor to the invocations that have soothed lesser ills. It feels... alien. As if the Skywood itself is rejecting something fundamental. Perhaps Elder Bram's suggestion of allowing nature to reclaim its space, to shed the diseased parts and regenerate, holds a certain truth. The Skywood has survived millennia. It has weathered storms and droughts, plagues and invasions. Its resilience is not in its ability to be 'fixed' by us, but in its deep, inherent capacity for renewal."

"Renewal requires a foundation upon which to renew!" Mara countered, her voice rising with passion. "The foundation is crumbling! Our people cannot wait for a 'natural' process that may take decades, centuries! What of the immediate suffering? What of the Ashbound, who offer only annihilation? If we withdraw, we cede territory, we surrender hope. The Ashbound thrive on despair. Our only hope, our only defense against their destructive ideology, is to demonstrate that life *can* persist, that communities *can* rebuild, even in the face of overwhelming adversity.

That requires active intervention, not passive waiting. We must share our knowledge, our resources, even our limited blight-resistant seeds, to help Oakhaven and Willow Creek fortify themselves. We must organize patrols, not just to observe, but to *defend*. To show the Ashbound that they will not find fertile ground for their despair here."

Elder Theron steepled his fingers, his gaze sweeping from Mara to Bram, then to Maeve. "The dichotomy is stark. Restoration or withdrawal. Intervention or observation. Action or patience. Elder Maeve proposes a proactive, perhaps even dangerous, approach to mend what is broken. Elder Bram suggests a hands-off strategy, trusting in the inherent resilience of nature to eventually overcome the blight. Mara champions the immediate needs of our people, advocating for a visible, active defense and mutual support. Cael, you have walked the poisoned lands and witnessed the Ashbound's advance. Where does your counsel lie?"

Cael took a deep breath, the weight of his experiences pressing down on him. He saw the pragmatism in Maeve's drive for restoration, the understanding that inaction was a form of surrender. But he also felt the profound unease that Bram's words evoked, the fear of upsetting a delicate, ancient balance that they barely understood. And Mara's plea for his people, for the immediate, tangible suffering, resonated deeply within him. "I see the immediate threat of the Ashbound as paramount," he began, his voice measured. "Their fire is an immediate danger that withdrawal cannot ignore. They will burn, and then they will conquer. Therefore, a complete withdrawal from defending our communities is not viable. We must actively patrol, actively warn, actively resist their physical advance. This is not an ecological debate; it is a war."

He turned his gaze to Elder Maeve. "However, Elder Maeve, your proposed restoration methods, while well-intentioned, could indeed be a double-edged sword. If the blight is a symptom of a deeper imbalance, or even a deliberate corruption, our attempts to 'force' its reversal could have catastrophic consequences. Imagine if we try to accelerate the healing of a blighted grove, only to find we've created a beacon for the Ashbound, or worse, a breeding ground for something even more insidious. The blight feeds on decay, on weakness. Perhaps the most effective restoration is not to fight the blight directly with powerful remedies, but to strengthen the *health* of the ecosystem around it. To nurture the surrounding, unaffected flora, to improve soil vitality in unaffected areas, and to create resilient buffers. This is a slower approach, perhaps, but it might be more sustainable and less prone to catastrophic failure."

He then looked towards Elder Bram. "And Elder Bram, while I believe a complete withdrawal is untenable due to the Ashbound, your point about allowing nature its course is not entirely without merit. We must also consider the possibility that our interventions, however well-meaning, are contributing to the problem. Perhaps some of the practices that have sustained the Skywood for generations are no longer appropriate in this new era of ecological stress. We need to reassess *how* we interact with the land, not just *whether* we interact."

"So, you propose a hybrid approach?" Elder Theron inquired, his gaze sharp. "Active defense against the Ashbound, careful, incremental restoration focusing on strengthening the surrounding ecosystem, and a reassessment of our own practices?"

"Precisely," Cael affirmed. "We cannot afford to be passive. The Ashbound will not let us be. But we also cannot afford to be reckless. We must act with precision, with a deep understanding of the risks. This means prioritizing immediate defense, while simultaneously studying the blight and its ecological context. It means listening to the wisdom of those who live closest to the land, the farmers and hunters of the outer settlements, who have perhaps developed practical, low-impact methods for dealing with similar challenges. They may not have our ancient rituals, but they have the hard-won knowledge of survival in a harsh world."

Mara, though still yearning for a more direct, immediate approach to healing the blight itself, recognized the wisdom in Cael's words. The idea of creating "resilient buffers" and strengthening the surrounding ecosystem felt like a practical, less volatile application of restoration. It still involved action, but action informed by caution. "So, not a wholesale pouring of potent elixirs into the dying heart of the wood," she mused, "but a strengthening of the entire body, so that it might naturally expel the sickness? And a continuous, active defense against the Ashbound who seek to exploit that weakness?"

"Exactly," Cael confirmed. "It is a strategy that acknowledges both the immediate danger and the long-term ecological imperative. It is a path that requires constant vigilance, adaptation, and a willingness to learn from all quarters, even those we have historically overlooked. It is about survival, not just for the Skywood, but for all who depend on it."

Elder Bram stroked his beard thoughtfully. "A re-evaluation of our practices... that is a path I can walk. For too long, we have relied on the old ways, assuming they would always suffice. But the world is changing, and perhaps our approach must change with it. But the Ashbound... they do not wait for us to re-evaluate. Their destruction is immediate. We must not neglect the urgent need for defense while we ponder the subtle nuances of ecological balance."

Elder Maeve, though her initial proposal for aggressive, direct intervention had been tempered, remained resolute. "My concern for the immediate suffering remains. If we are to strengthen the surrounding ecosystem, we must also ensure that the communities at the forefront of this crisis are not left to wither. Sharing blight-resistant seeds, providing practical agricultural knowledge, establishing joint patrols – these are not merely acts of diplomacy, but essential components of any viable strategy, whether it be termed 'restoration' or 'resilience building'. We cannot expect the land to heal if its people are dying of hunger and fear."

The debate, though fierce, had begun to coalesce. The stark choice between outright restoration and complete withdrawal had given way to a more nuanced understanding, a recognition that survival in this encroaching darkness would demand a multifaceted approach. It would require the courage to act decisively against immediate threats, the wisdom to proceed with caution in ecological interventions, and the humility to learn from all those who shared the shadow of the Skywood, no matter how far beyond its canopy they dwelled.

The path forward was not yet clear, but the council was beginning to see a way through the encroaching gloom, a way that acknowledged the inherent resilience of nature, the immediate danger of their enemies, and the desperate need for unity among all peoples under the Skywood's venerable branches. The debate itself was a form of healing, a clearing of the air that allowed for the emergence of a more pragmatic, and perhaps more hopeful, path.

The weight of the chamber seemed to press down on Mara, each rustle of leaves, each creak of ancient wood, amplifying the silence that followed her impassioned plea. Her words, intended to bridge the chasm between their world and the encroaching human settlements, had landed not as a balm, but as a stone thrown into a placid pool, sending ripples of distrust and apprehension through the gathered Elders.

She had spoken of shared threats, of the mutual benefit of understanding the blight's origins, whether they sprang from the Skywood's own imbalances or from external forces. She had even, with a carefully measured tone, alluded to the potential advantages of understanding the rudimentary technologies of the land-dwellers – not to adopt them, but to comprehend their impact, their potential to exacerbate or even cause ecological distress. This, it seemed, was her greatest transgression.

Elder Rhiannon, a matriarch whose lineage was as deeply rooted in the Skywood's history as the Elder Banyan itself, was the first to voice the dissent. Her voice, usually a gentle murmur, now carried the brittle sharpness of a frost-touched leaf. "Diplomacy, Mara? With creatures who pave over ancient groves and poison rivers with their 'progress'? You speak of collaboration as if the land-dwellers possess some wisdom we need to glean. Their wisdom lies in consumption, in dominion. They do not understand balance; they understand conquest." Rhiannon's gaze, sharp and unwavering, fixed on Mara, a silent accusation in its depths. "You, who have spent so little time under the true canopy, who have perhaps been too eager to embrace their ways, speak of understanding them. Do you understand the language of scorched earth? Do you comprehend the silence that follows the felling of a millennia-old tree? These are the only truths the land-dwellers understand."

Another Elder, Kaelen, whose domain was the deep earth and its mineral veins, echoed Rhiannon's sentiment, his voice resonating with a low, rumbling discontent. "The blight, if it stems from the land-dwellers' influence, is a symptom of their inherent nature. To seek dialogue is to invite the wolf into the sheepfold, hoping it will discuss the merits of vegetarianism. Their 'investigations' into our ways, as you term them, are likely driven by a desire to exploit our resources, to understand our vulnerabilities. Your willingness to even entertain such notions, Mara, is... concerning. It suggests a naiveté that we cannot afford. This is not a matter for gentle persuasion; it is a matter of containment. Of isolating the infection, not of trying to reason with the pathogen."

Mara's heart sank. She had anticipated skepticism, even outright rejection, but the vehemence of their opposition, the deep-seated suspicion, was more profound than she had imagined. She had believed that the shared threat of the blight, the encroaching Ashbound, would force a re-evaluation of their isolationist tendencies. But it seemed their fear of the unknown, and their deep-seated resentment towards humanity, was a more potent force.

"With all due respect, Elder Rhiannon, Elder Kaelen," Mara began, her voice trembling slightly, but her resolve hardening, "I am not suggesting we embrace their ways, nor that we naïvely trust their intentions. I am suggesting that we *understand* them. If the blight is, as some suspect, linked to their activities, then understanding those activities – the source of their poisons, the nature of their technologies – is crucial to our own defense. How can we effectively combat a threat if we refuse to acknowledge its potential origin? To dismiss them entirely is to blind ourselves."

She turned her attention to Kaelen. "And Elder Kaelen, you speak of containment. But the Ashbound are already breaching our borders. If the blight is indeed a weapon, or a consequence of their unchecked expansion, then merely containing ourselves will not suffice. We need to understand the tools of our enemy. Is it so unthinkable that by studying their methods, we might find a way to neutralize them, or at least to better predict their movements and their impact?"

A low hum of disagreement spread through the council. Elder Lyra, whose connection to the Skywood's spiritual currents was said to be unparalleled, spoke with a sigh that seemed to carry the weariness of centuries. "Mara, your spirit is willing, but your understanding is incomplete. The land-dwellers' 'technologies' are not merely tools; they are extensions of a mindset that seeks to dominate, not to harmonize. Their machines churn and spew, their fires burn with a voracious, unthinking hunger. They do not understand the subtle dance of life and decay, the delicate threads that bind the ecosystem. To study them is to stare into an abyss. Their 'progress' is a destructive force, and our efforts are best spent fortifying our own natural defenses, not trying to decipher the logic of their barbarism."

"Barbarism?" Mara's voice rose, a spark of defiance igniting within her. "Elder Lyra, I have seen the fear in the eyes of the land-dweller children, the same fear that we see in our own when the Ashbound advance. They are not a monolithic entity of destruction. There are factions, differences, and within them, there are those who yearn for a different path, those who recognize the damage being wrought. To paint them all with the same brush is to ignore the possibility of allies, or at least, of understanding their motivations. Is it not a fundamental tenet of survival to understand one's adversary? And if their 'barbarism' is a response to their own ecological collapse, then perhaps understanding that crisis might offer us a different perspective on the blight itself."

Elder Theron, the council's moderator, held up a hand, his gaze steady, assessing. "Mara, your arguments carry the fervor of conviction, but they also tread a dangerous path. The history between our peoples is not one of peace or cooperation. The Canopy Accord was established precisely because the land-dwellers' presence and their actions posed an existential threat to the Skywood. To suggest opening lines of communication now, to delve into their methods, risks undermining the very foundations of our security. Some among us believe your investigations have already gone too far, that your recent excursions beyond the protected glades have been... imprudent."

The implication hung heavy in the air. Mara felt a flush creep up her neck, a mixture of embarrassment and indignation. She knew some of the Elders viewed her recent forays into the borderlands, her attempts to observe and understand the human settlements from a distance, with suspicion. They saw it as fraternization, a betrayal of their isolationist stance. But she saw it as necessity. She had witnessed firsthand the crude but effective methods the land-dwellers used to clear land, to extract resources, and the undeniable correlation between these activities and the spread of blight in the surrounding flora.

"Imprudent, Elder Theron?" she countered, her voice regaining its strength. "Or necessary? I have seen the edge of the blight creeping closer, and I have seen the marks of human activity preceding it. Not intentional malice, perhaps, but the inevitable consequence of their actions. Their clear-cutting, their mining operations, their waste – these disrupt the delicate balance of the land in ways we have not fully accounted for. To deny this connection is to ignore a vital piece of the puzzle. And if we are to solve this blight, we must examine *all* the pieces, no matter how uncomfortable their origin."

She looked around the chamber, her gaze sweeping across the faces of the Elders, some hardened by generations of cautious vigilance, others softened by the serene wisdom of the Skywood. "I understand your reservations," she continued, her voice softening, aiming for conciliation. "The history is fraught with conflict. But the world is changing. The Ashbound represent a new level of threat, one that respects no boundaries, no ancient pacts.

If we remain cloistered, focused only on our internal balance, we will be swept away by forces we refuse to acknowledge. I am not advocating for alliance, but for awareness. For the strategic intelligence that comes from understanding our environment, including the disruptive elements within it. This is not about embracing their technology; it is about understanding its impact. It is about finding ways to mitigate their influence, perhaps even to influence them towards more sustainable practices, before their actions irrevocably destroy us all."

Elder Bram, who had championed a more passive, nature-led approach to the blight, now looked at Mara with a mixture of concern and resignation. "Mara, your passion is evident, and your observations about the land-dwellers' impact are... not entirely unfounded. We have long observed the disquiet their presence brings to the periphery. But your focus on 'understanding their motivations,' on finding 'allies'... that is where the danger lies. Their motivations are driven by a hunger for resources, a need for expansion. To seek dialogue is to invite them to dictate the terms, to see our willingness to talk as a sign of weakness, a precursor to their dominion. Our strength lies in our self-sufficiency, in the resilience of the Skywood itself. Not in the fickle currents of human politics or their ever-changing technologies."

"But Elder Bram," Mara pressed, her voice laced with frustration, "what if their 'technology' is the very thing that is *creating* the blight? What if it's not just about hunger or expansion, but about a deliberate or accidental unleashing of something destructive? My investigations have yielded... disturbing fragments. Whispers of experiments, of substances designed to alter landscapes, to control growth. If this is true, then simply fortifying ourselves is like building a dam against a tide that is not merely water, but a corrosive acid. We need to know *what* they are doing, not just *that* they are doing it. And that knowledge can only come from careful, deliberate inquiry, not from fearful isolation."

A collective intake of breath swept through the council. The mention of "experiments" and "substances designed to alter landscapes" had clearly struck a nerve, igniting a deeper apprehension than mere territorial disputes. This was a fear that touched the very heart of their existence, the sanctity of the Skywood's natural order.

Rhiannon, her face etched with a grim understanding, spoke again, her voice lower now, but no less firm. "Experiments? Altering landscapes? This is precisely the kind of dangerous knowledge you should not be pursuing, Mara. You are meddling in matters that are beyond our purview, matters that could draw unwanted attention. If these land-dwellers possess such destructive capabilities, then our priority must be to remain hidden, to strengthen our natural defenses, and to sever any connection that might betray our presence or our vulnerabilities. Your 'investigations' could be our undoing. We must distance ourselves from your inquiries, not embrace them."

Kaelen nodded in agreement. "The risk of exposure is too great. If they possess weapons that can alter the land, then any attempt to engage them, even for knowledge, could be seen as an act of aggression, or worse, an invitation for them to test their might upon us. We must uphold the principles of the Canopy Accord: to preserve the Skywood, to remain unseen, and to trust in the inherent power of nature to sustain us. Your path, Mara, is one of recklessness."

Mara felt a prickle of tears, but she blinked them back, her jaw set. She understood their fear; it was a primal, instinctual response to a perceived threat. But their fear was also blinding them to the larger danger. To be unseen was one thing, but to be ignorant when ignorance could mean annihilation was another.

"I understand your concerns," she said, her voice resonating with a quiet conviction that cut through the growing tension. "I understand the history, the fear of exposure. But I believe that true preservation lies not in absolute isolation, but in informed vigilance. The Ashbound are a clear and present danger, a force of destruction that we must actively resist. But the blight... its source is still a shadow. And I believe that shadow may be cast by the very beings you wish to ignore. If we are to survive, we must not only defend our borders, but understand the nature of the threats that loom beyond them. My work is not reckless; it is a desperate attempt to find the truth, to arm us with knowledge that might save us all. I implore you, do not let fear blind you to the possibility of understanding. For if we cannot comprehend the threat, we cannot truly hope to overcome it."

The chamber remained silent for a long moment, the weight of her words settling upon them. The path she proposed was one fraught with peril, a deviation from the time-honored traditions of the Canopy Accord. But the very nature of the threat, the encroaching blight and the ravenous Ashbound, suggested that the old ways might no longer be enough. Mara's resistance to the prevailing sentiment, her insistence on a more outward-looking, investigative approach, was met not with open arms, but with deeply entrenched suspicion. The political hurdles were immense, rooted in centuries of mistrust and a profound fear of the 'other'. Her quest for peaceful resolution was being met by a council more inclined towards absolute fortification and isolation, a stance that felt increasingly untenable in the face of an evolving, multi-faceted crisis. The chasm between her vision of proactive understanding and their deep-seated fear of entanglement was widening, a stark testament to the political complexities that lay ahead in their struggle for survival.

Cael stood before the Council, the air in the cavernous chamber thick with the scent of damp earth and ancient moss. Unlike Mara, whose pleas had been met with a storm of dissent, his had been received with a quiet, almost somber deference. His reputation as a Land Guardian, one who had weathered the harshest of seasons and charted the most treacherous of blight-infested territories, preceded him. The Council Elders, their faces etched with the wisdom of centuries, regarded him not as an advocate for new, potentially dangerous alliances, but as a steadfast bulwark against the encroaching darkness.

"The southern glades are thinning," Cael stated, his voice a low rumble, devoid of the passionate urgency Mara had employed. "The blight's tendrils are no longer confined to the outer reaches. They have breached the Whisperwood's heartwood, and the Ashbound follow in their wake. We've lost three more Guardian posts in the last moon cycle. Three more brave souls whose connection to the earth was severed, not by nature's decree, but by a force that respects no living thing." He paused, his gaze sweeping across the faces of the Elders, each a study in quiet concern. "Our patrols are stretched thin. Our defenses, while rooted in the deep wisdom of the Skywood, are being tested as never before. We are a shield, yes, but a shield can only absorb so many blows before it cracks."

His words were not a plea for diplomacy or an exploration of enemy tactics, but a stark assessment of their current capabilities, a grim inventory of their losses. This grounded, pragmatic approach resonated with the Elders in a way Mara's more outward-looking strategies had not. They understood the language of survival, of strategic defense, of the raw, unforgiving realities of their world. Cael's willingness to confront the severity of their situation, however bleak, was seen not as pessimism, but as a necessary clarity.

Elder Lyra, her voice a silken thread weaving through the somber atmosphere, addressed him. "Cael, your dedication to the Skywood is unquestioned. Your reports have always been... unvarnished. You speak of losses, of the strain upon our Guardians. What solutions do you propose, beyond the continued reinforcement of our existing patrols and the deepening of our roots? The blight spreads, the Ashbound advance. We can fortify, but can we truly *hold*?"

Cael met her gaze, a flicker of internal conflict crossing his stoic features. He had always operated within the strict confines of his oath as a Land Guardian, a sworn protector of the Skywood's natural state, bound by ancient laws that prioritized preservation and isolation. His role was to defend the existing balance, not to fundamentally alter it or engage in the complex political maneuverings that Mara had attempted. Yet, the scale of the current threat was forcing him to confront the limitations of his sworn duties.

"My oath, as you know, Elder Lyra, is to protect the Skywood," Cael began, his voice steady, yet with an undercurrent of immense weariness. "To ensure its continued vibrancy, its untainted essence. I have spent my life nurturing its growth, healing its wounds, and defending its borders from any who would seek to disrupt its natural order. But this blight... it is an unnatural wound. The Ashbound... they are a corruption that defies the natural cycle of decay and renewal. Our traditional methods, our understanding of the land's inherent resilience, are proving insufficient against an enemy that does not play by nature's rules."

He clenched his fist, the rough bark of his knuckles a testament to his constant contact with the earth. "I have seen the patterns. The blight flourishes where the land itself is weakened, where its natural defenses have been compromised. And the Ashbound... they are drawn to this decay, like carrion birds to a fallen beast. To simply reinforce our borders, to 'hold' as you say, is to merely delay the inevitable if the source of this weakening remains unaddressed."

The weight of expectation settled upon him. He could feel the Council's eyes upon him, not as a commander seeking tactical advice, but as a shepherd desperately seeking a way to save his flock from a predator they could not fully comprehend. They looked to him for wisdom, for a solution rooted in his deep connection to the earth, but the earth itself was in turmoil.

"We have always believed that the Skywood's strength lies in its self-sufficiency, in its ability to heal and regenerate," Elder Bram interjected, his voice a gentle sigh. "Your reports, Cael, suggest this is no longer a guaranteed outcome. You speak of an 'unnatural wound,' of an 'enemy that does not play by nature's rules.' This implies an external influence, something beyond the Skywood's inherent cycles. Is it your belief, then, that our isolation, our adherence to the ancient ways, has left us vulnerable to threats we cannot withstand on our own?"

Cael hesitated. This was the precipice he had been increasingly approaching, the ethical and spiritual quandary that had gnawed at him during his solitary patrols. His oath was to the Skywood, to its natural order. But what if that order was being actively dismantled by forces that operated outside of nature's ken? What if the very act of remaining purely natural was, in this new era, an act of self-destruction?

"My oath is to preserve the Skywood," Cael repeated, his voice gaining a somber resonance. "To defend its balance, its lifeblood. But if the greatest threat to that balance comes from... elsewhere, from something that does not respect the natural order, then I must ask myself: what does 'preservation' truly entail in such circumstances? Is it a passive adherence to tradition, a belief that the Skywood will endure simply because it *should*? Or does it demand... adaptation? A willingness to understand, and perhaps even to counter, the forces that seek to overwhelm it, even if those forces lie beyond our established boundaries?"

He looked at Mara, who had remained silent, observing the exchange with a watchful intensity. Her earlier attempts at dialogue had been met with resistance, but Cael's measured words, framed within the context of his sworn duty, seemed to be chipping away at the Elders' entrenched wariness.

"Elder Bram, you speak of self-sufficiency," Cael continued, addressing the Elder directly. "And indeed, the Skywood has endured for millennia through its own inherent strength. But what if that strength is being systematically undermined? I have witnessed, firsthand, the gradual degradation of certain soil compositions in areas bordering the human settlements. It is not a sudden poisoning, but a slow, insidious alteration. A leaching of vital nutrients, a subtle shift in pH that favors the blight's propagation. This is not the work of a natural predator; it is the consequence of actions, of practices that are alien to our understanding of the land."

He paused, gathering his thoughts, the burden of his responsibility weighing heavily on his shoulders. "My role has always been to heal the damage, to reintroduce lost vitalities, to coax the land back to its harmonious state. But the scale of this degradation... it outpaces my ability to mend. It requires more than a Guardian's touch; it requires understanding the origin of the decay, the nature of the force that causes it. To simply continue applying poultices to a wound that is being actively and systematically reopened is... futile. It is a betrayal of my oath to truly *preserve* the Skywood, if preservation means allowing it to wither and die while I cling to outdated methods."

A hushed murmur rippled through the chamber. Cael, the stoic Land Guardian, was articulating a profound dilemma that struck at the heart of their council's philosophy. His words were not a call for aggression, but for a deeper understanding, a strategic necessity driven by the evolving nature of the threat. He was questioning the very definition of their sworn duties in the face of an unprecedented crisis.

"So you believe," Elder Rhiannon stated, her voice carefully modulated, "that the land-dwellers are, intentionally or not, the source of this blight's exacerbated spread. And that your duties as a Land Guardian now extend beyond merely tending to the Skywood's wounds, to investigating and potentially mitigating the actions that cause them?"

Cael met her gaze, his own unwavering. "My oath is to protect the Skywood. If the greatest threat to the Skywood is an external factor that is causing its degradation, then understanding that factor, and finding a way to neutralize its destructive influence, becomes a paramount duty. It is not about abandoning our ways, but about ensuring that our ways can still *be*. If the blight is a symptom of a deeper imbalance caused by the land-dwellers' activities, then I must, in good conscience, seek to understand those activities. Not to adopt them, not to engage in their reckless pursuits, but to learn how to counter their effects, to protect the Skywood from their encroaching influence."

He took a deep breath, the air feeling heavy in his lungs. "My patrols have taken me closer to their settlements than is customary. I have observed their methods, their reliance on... artificial means to shape the landscape. Their relentless pursuit of expansion leaves scars that run deep, scars that the blight seems to exploit with terrifying efficiency. To ignore this connection, to pretend that the Skywood exists in a vacuum, is to misunderstand the nature of the threat we face. We are not simply defending against a natural phenomenon; we are defending against a force that actively and relentlessly alters the environment to its own perceived needs, with devastating consequences for our own."

The council elders exchanged glances, a silent debate passing between them. Mara's arguments had been met with outright suspicion, but Cael's, framed within his dedication and the grim realities of his reports, were being considered with a reluctant gravity. His influence, forged in years of quiet service and undeniable results, was now being tested against the bedrock of their isolationist doctrine. The pressure to act, to find a tangible solution beyond mere defense, was mounting, and Cael found himself at the epicenter of that burgeoning expectation. He was not a diplomat, but a guardian.

And a guardian's duty, he was coming to realize, was not always to stand and defend, but sometimes, to understand the nature of the beast at the gates, no matter how alien or terrifying. His internal struggle was no longer a solitary one; it was now laid bare before the assembled wisdom of the Skywood, a testament to the growing urgency that permeated their ancient sanctuary. The Council was beginning to see that survival might require more than just rootedness; it might require a willingness to look beyond their own branches, to understand the winds that threatened to tear them down. And Cael, the devoted Land Guardian, was being compelled to lead them, however reluctantly, in that direction. The weight of their hopes, and their fears, rested heavily upon his broad shoulders.

The cavernous chamber, once a symbol of their enduring stability, now felt like a cage. The air, thick with the scent of ancient moss and the unspoken anxieties of its inhabitants, vibrated with a tension that had been building for cycles. Elder Lyra's gentle probing had opened a fissure, not just in Cael's stoic resolve, but in the very foundations of the Council's long-held tenets. His words, measured and grounded in the grim reality of his patrols, had shifted the atmosphere from one of polite debate to a palpable unease. The Elders, their faces a tapestry of ancient wisdom and dawning concern, wrestled with a truth that had been painstakingly avoided for generations: their isolation, their unwavering adherence to the Skywood's pristine self-sufficiency, might no longer be a shield, but a vulnerability.

Cael's assessment, stark and unvarnished, had painted a picture of a Skywood under siege, not by a natural predator that could be weathered or outlasted, but by a corruption that seemed to seep from the very foundations of their world. He spoke of unnatural wounds, of blight that fed on a land whose inherent defenses were being systematically weakened by an external, and increasingly visible, force. His duty, once clear and defined – to tend, to heal, to defend the established order – was now a tangled knot of ethical quandaries. Could he truly preserve the Skywood by passively watching it be eroded? Was his oath to protect its *essence*, or merely its physical form, even as that form was being irrevocably altered?

The silence that followed Cael's pronouncements was not a comfortable one. It was the heavy, pregnant pause before a storm breaks, or a precipice before a leap into the unknown. Elder Bram, his usual gentle demeanor replaced by a furrowed brow, had voiced the unspoken fear: had their steadfastness become a form of stubbornness, leaving them blind to the encroaching shadows? Cael's responses, though framed within his unwavering loyalty, were revolutionary. He spoke not of rallying the existing defenses, but of understanding the enemy, of dissecting the source of the decay, even if that source lay beyond the hallowed borders of the Skywood.

It was Mara, a silent observer for much of Cael's testimony, who finally broke the spell. Her earlier pleas for engagement, for understanding the 'others,' had been met with a wall of suspicion. But Cael, the guardian of their most sacred traditions, the embodiment of their connection to the land, was now articulating a similar, albeit differently couched, necessity. His perspective, rooted in the physical degradation of the very soil beneath their roots, carried a weight that Mara's more abstract arguments had not been able to achieve.

"You speak of the land-dwellers' activities," Mara began, her voice soft but carrying a new authority, born from the Council's reluctant attentiveness.

"Of a slow, insidious alteration that weakens the earth. Cael, you've seen the blight spread. You've seen the Ashbound follow. But what if their actions are not merely a passive cause of decay, but an active *embrace* of it? What if their approach to the land, their relentless expansion and alteration, is not just damaging, but is *symbiotic* with the very forces that now threaten us?"

Her question hung in the air, a dark omen. It was a subtle shift, a suggestion that the Ashbound were not merely a consequence of external damage, but perhaps, a deliberate manifestation of a philosophy that embraced the decay, that found strength in the very corruption they fought. This was a dangerous thought, one that veered away from the simple narrative of 'us' versus 'them,' and into the unsettling territory of shared, albeit perverted, values.

Elder Rhiannon, her voice a carefully controlled cadence, addressed Cael again, seeking clarification on his newfound willingness to engage with the unknown. "You propose we investigate their methods, not to emulate them, but to understand how to counter their effects. This is a significant departure from our established doctrine. If their actions are the cause, then understanding them is indeed necessary. But your patrols have also brought you into proximity with the Ashbound themselves. Do you believe their current trajectory, their alignment with this blight, is a consequence of the land-dwellers' influence, or a separate, perhaps even independent, evolution of their own kind?"

Cael's brow furrowed, the complexity of the question mirroring the turmoil within him. "The blight is a catalyst, Elder Rhiannon. It exploits weakness. The land-dwellers, through their disregard for natural equilibrium, create that weakness. The Ashbound, however... they seem to have found a way to *harness* that weakness. Their presence is not merely reactive; it is proactive. They do not just follow the blight; they cultivate it. I have seen scorched earth, areas that have been deliberately stripped bare, not for building or sustenance, but as... nurseries for the blight. These are not the casual, unthinking actions of those seeking to merely expand their territory. This is a deliberate cultivation of decay, a perversion of the land's natural cycles."

He paused, his gaze drifting towards the shadowy recesses of the chamber, as if seeing not the ancient stone, but the blighted forests and the figures that moved within them. "The land-dwellers' impact provides the fertile ground, the compromised earth. But the Ashbound's embrace of it, their active propagation of this corruption... that is a different threat. It suggests a philosophy, a chosen path.

And if their path is one of active symbiosis with corruption, then our attempts to merely 'heal' the damage may be akin to treating a fever while the infection actively grows stronger. We must understand the *nature* of their choice, the reasoning behind their embrace of such a destructive path. For if they find power in decay, then our own resilience, our own connection to life, may be precisely what they seek to extinguish."

A low murmur spread through the Council. The carefully constructed edifice of their worldview was beginning to crumble. They had always viewed external threats as intrusions, as disruptions to their inherent purity. But Cael's observations suggested something far more insidious: a force that actively sought to corrupt, to pervert, and to feed upon the very essence of their existence. The idea that the Ashbound's approach was not simply destructive, but *philosophically driven*, was deeply unsettling. It implied intent, a conscious choice to align with forces that were anathema to the Skywood.

Elder Lyra, her voice a delicate thread woven through the growing unease, addressed Mara, a hint of curiosity now mingling with her caution. "Mara, you have always sought to understand the motivations of those beyond our borders. You spoke of potential alliances, of finding common ground. If the Ashbound actively cultivate blight, if they have a philosophy centered on embracing decay, what 'common ground' could there possibly be? Such a path seems inherently antithetical to any form of balanced coexistence."

Mara met Elder Lyra's gaze, her own steady and unwavering. "Common ground is not always about shared ideals, Elder Lyra. Sometimes, it is about shared threats, or even shared circumstances that lead to disparate actions. Cael's observations about the land-dwellers' impact creating the *conditions* for the blight are crucial. The Ashbound have, perhaps, found a way to thrive in the imbalance that others have wrought. This doesn't mean we agree with their methods, or their embrace of decay. But it does suggest a shared enemy: the forces that create and exploit environmental imbalance."

She continued, her voice gaining a quiet fervor. "The Ashbound, in their own twisted way, are responding to a world that is becoming increasingly inhospitable to traditional forms of life. If the land-dwellers' relentless expansion and disregard for natural cycles are making the world more susceptible to blight, and the Ashbound are those who have learned to flourish in this new, blighted landscape, then they are, in a sense, a product of the very imbalance we face. To simply dismiss them as 'corrupted' and beyond comprehension is to ignore a vital aspect of the threat. It is to fail to understand how such a faction could arise, and therefore, how it might be countered."

The Council elders exchanged glances, a silent dialogue passing between them. The weight of Cael's empirical evidence, coupled with Mara's nuanced interpretation, was beginning to erode their entrenched resistance. The 'others' were no longer just a vague threat lurking at the periphery; they were becoming a complex, multifaceted challenge that demanded more than just defensive fortification. The Ashbound, in particular, were emerging not just as a destructive force, but as a faction with a clear, albeit terrifying, modus operandi.

"So, if I understand correctly," Elder Bram interjected, his voice thoughtful, "you are suggesting that the Ashbound's appeal, their very existence, is intrinsically linked to the environmental degradation caused by the land-dwellers, and that their methods of cultivating blight represent a deliberate choice to exploit this degradation. This is a far cry from simply being a monstrous entity. It implies a... strategy. A decision."

"Precisely," Mara affirmed, her gaze sweeping across the assembled elders. "And if it is a deliberate choice, a strategy, then it can be understood. It can be countered. But not by clinging solely to our old ways, to our isolation. Cael's willingness to observe, to report on the land-dwellers' impact, is a crucial first step. My own attempts to understand the broader ecological shifts, the forces that empower such factions, are another. We are facing an enemy that thrives on imbalance, that actively seeks to perpetuate it. To ignore the cause of that imbalance, or to fail to understand the logic, however warped, behind the Ashbound's actions, is to leave ourselves vulnerable to their growing influence."

The chamber, moments before filled with the quiet dread of an inescapable decline, now felt charged with a different kind of energy. It was the unsettling hum of possibility, the dangerous allure of radical solutions that were beginning to emerge from the ashes of their perceived failure. The Council's inability to forge a unified path, their prolonged indecision in the face of escalating threats, had created a vacuum. And into that vacuum, the radical pronouncements of the Ashbound, their promises of power derived from embracing the very corruption that gnawed at the Skywood, began to whisper.

Cael, the steadfast guardian, had inadvertently opened the door to acknowledging the root causes of the blight, the damage wrought by the land-dwellers. Mara, the diplomatic seeker, had begun to articulate a potential framework for understanding the Ashbound not as mindless monsters, but as a faction with a perverse but potent ideology. These were not the calls for alliance or compromise that the Council had so readily dismissed. These were arguments for a deeper, more uncomfortable understanding, a recognition that the Skywood's vulnerability lay not just in external attacks, but in its own rigid adherence to a world that was rapidly changing.

The Elders, accustomed to the slow, deliberate pace of their ancient wisdom, were being forced to confront a new reality, one where inaction was a direct path to destruction. The growing desperation, the visible strain on their once-invincible defenses, was creating fertile ground for more extreme ideas. The Ashbound's appeal, with its promise of harnessing the blight, of finding strength in the very forces that threatened the Skywood, was no longer a distant, alien concept.

It was a dark siren song, beginning to resonate with a faction of the Council who saw in Cael's reports and Mara's insights a justification, however terrifying, for a radical departure from their established norms. The path of understanding, of engagement, was fraught with peril, and the Council was beginning to realize that some within their ranks might see the Ashbound's extreme proposals not as a threat, but as a desperate, yet viable, solution. The seeds of future conflict, sown in the fertile ground of their current predicament, were beginning to sprout.

CHAPTER FIVE

THE DRAGON'S DISTRUST

The weight of the Council's deliberations pressed down on Cael, a physical manifestation of the Skywood's precarious state. While the elders grappled with the philosophical implications of the blight and the Ashbound's unsettling ideology, Cael's focus remained rooted in the tangible. His patrols had shown him the encroaching rot, the unnatural decay that the Skywood's inherent resilience could no longer fully contain. And he knew, with a certainty that chilled him to the bone, that the Skywood could not stand alone against the forces that now gathered at its edges. The land dragons, ancient and powerful beings whose very presence was intertwined with the health of the earth, were the key. Their cooperation was not merely desirable; it was essential.

He had sought out Thryxal, the eldest of the mountain dragons, a creature of obsidian scales and eyes like molten gold, in the heart of their ancestral cavern. The air here was thin, sharp with the scent of sulfur and ancient stone, a stark contrast to the verdant, life-infused atmosphere of the Skywood. The chamber itself was a testament to the dragons' long dominion, its walls etched with millennia of history, of power that predated the Skywood's sapling beginnings. Yet, Cael felt an intruder, his every breath a disturbance in the profound stillness. Thryxal's presence filled the cavern, a coiled power that made the very rock tremble. The dragon's gaze, when it finally fell upon Cael, was not one of welcome, but of a deep, ingrained suspicion.

"You come again, Sylvari," Thryxal's voice rumbled, a sound like grinding mountains. It held no warmth, only the stark pronouncement of a truth that had been carved into the dragon's very being over countless ages. "Seeking what? Another plea for aid? Another promise of balance that your kind has never truly honored?"

Cael inclined his head, a gesture of respect that he knew was as much for the dragon's ancient lineage as for the creature itself. "Thryxal, I come not with empty promises, but with the stark truth of our shared peril. The blight you have witnessed spreading across the lower peaks, the unnatural decay that gnaws at the very roots of this land – it is not confined to our forests. It is a sickness that will consume us all, dragon and Sylvari alike."

Thryxal shifted, a slow, deliberate movement that sent tremors through the cavern floor. His golden eyes narrowed, a flicker of something akin to recognition, quickly masked by a renewed wave of distrust. "We have seen the rot, Sylvari. We have felt its cold touch. But it is not *our* fight. Your kind has always sought to dominate, to bend the natural world to your will, heedless of the consequences. You sow imbalance, and then you come to us, the guardians of the ancient cycles, to clean up your mess."

The accusation hung heavy in the air, a poison Cael had anticipated. He had spent cycles studying the dragons, their history, their deep-seated grievances. He knew their distrust was not born of malice, but of a profound disillusionment, a long history of broken covenants and betrayed trust. The Sylvari, in their quest for dominance, had indeed encroached upon dragon territories, had felled ancient forests that held sacred meaning for the scaled beings, and had, in their pursuit of expansion, disrupted the delicate ecological balance that the dragons so fiercely protected.

"The past cannot be undone, Thryxal," Cael said, his voice steady, though his heart ached with the truth of the dragon's words. "But it can be learned from. The current blight, the rise of the Ashbound – these are not the direct result of our actions alone. There are... other forces at play. Forces that seek to accelerate this decay, to embrace it even. Forces that would see this world consumed by shadow. If they succeed, your mountains will crumble, and our forests will turn to ash."

He spoke of the land-dwellers, of their insatiable hunger for resources, their reckless disregard for the earth's bounty. He described the Ashbound, not as mere monsters, but as a terrifying evolution, a faction that had found a perverse strength in the very corruption that threatened them. He painted a picture of a world on the precipice, a world where the ancient ways of balance were being systematically dismantled, replaced by a hunger for power derived from decay.

Thryxal listened, his massive head lowered, his gaze fixed on some unseen point beyond Cael, beyond the cavern walls, perhaps seeing the distant tremors of the world's unraveling. Yet, his skepticism remained a tangible barrier. "Your kind speaks of 'balance' when it suits your purpose, Sylvari. You speak of 'shared peril' when your own existence is threatened. We have seen your species rise and fall, your empires bloom and wither, always at the expense of the natural order. Why should this time be any different? Why should we entrust our ancient strength to those who have so consistently proven themselves unworthy?"

The dragon's words were sharp, each syllable laced with the bitterness of ages. Cael felt the familiar pang of frustration, the gnawing desperation of seeing a vital path blocked by the unyielding weight of history. He could not deny the dragons' grievances. He had seen the scars left by Sylvari ambition, the echoes of their past transgressions in the very landscape. But he also saw the encroaching darkness, the insidious blight that respected no boundaries, no species.

"It is not about trust, Thryxal," Cael countered, choosing his words with care. "Not yet. It is about necessity. The blight is a manifestation of imbalance, a sickness that festers when the earth is wounded. The land-dwellers wound the earth with their insatiable needs. The Ashbound, in their twisted embrace of this wound, accelerate its decay. You, who are intrinsically connected to the lifeblood of this world, must understand this. Your strength lies in the health of the land, and the land is dying."

He stepped closer, his voice dropping to a more urgent, but still respectful, tone. "I have seen the Ashbound actively cultivate the blight. They do not merely endure it; they *nurture* it. They clear lands not for habitation or sustenance, but to create fertile ground for this corruption. Their ideology, as I understand it, is to draw power from this decay, to thrive in the very imbalance that sickens us all. If this is allowed to continue, if they become strong enough to dictate the terms of existence, then even your mighty mountains will offer no sanctuary."

Thryxal let out a low growl, a sound that vibrated through Cael's bones. It was not agreement, but aacknowledgement of the grim reality Cael presented. "You speak of a new breed of... cultivators of decay. A disturbing notion. But it is still a consequence of the world's sickness, a sickness your kind has been instrumental in creating."

"And *we* are now seeking to heal that sickness," Cael insisted, his voice firm. "But healing requires understanding. It requires working with those who still hold the ancient knowledge, who still possess the strength to mend what has been broken. Your kind, Thryxal, has always been a part of this world's healing. You are the earth's guardians. We seek not to command you, but to ask for your partnership. We need your strength, your wisdom, to understand and ultimately to push back this tide of corruption."

He spoke of the Skywood's resilience, its capacity for renewal, and how that resilience, when combined with the dragons' elemental power, could create a bulwark against the encroaching blight. He described the delicate interdependencies, how the health of the Skywood nourished the earth that in turn sustained the dragons, and how their combined efforts could restore a semblance of balance. He detailed the Ashbound's methods, their tactics, their likely goals, all with the hope of illustrating the urgency and the specific nature of the threat. He stressed that this was not a matter of Sylvari survival alone, but of the very life force of the planet.

"We do not ask you to fight our battles, Thryxal," Cael continued, "but to join us in defending our shared home. We offer not mere words, but a commitment. A commitment to learn from past mistakes, to forge a new path of true coexistence. The blight spreads, and it respects no ancient pacts, no territorial claims. It is a universal threat, and it requires a universal response."

He laid out the observations from his patrols, the signs of unnatural growth and decay, the patterns of Ashbound activity that indicated a deliberate strategy of corruption. He detailed the weakening of the Skywood's natural defenses, the slow erosion of its inherent vitality, and how this mirrored the larger planetary sickness. He spoke of the land-dwellers' expanding influence, their relentless pursuit of resources, and how their actions created the conditions for the blight to take root. He described the Ashbound not as mindless beasts, but as intelligent beings who had made a conscious choice to harness the forces of decay, and how their growing power posed a significant threat to all forms of life.

Thryxal remained unmoved, his gaze piercing, as if trying to see through Cael's words to the true intentions beneath. "Partnership," the dragon scoffed, the sound like rocks tumbling down a mountainside. "Your species' history with 'partnership' is one of subjugation. You seek to control, not to collaborate. You see our strength as a tool to be wielded, not a force to be respected."

"We see your strength as a vital component of this world's defense," Cael corrected, his voice unwavering. "The Skywood's magic, its inherent life-giving properties, are a potent counter to decay. But alone, we are not enough. We are being weakened from within, our defenses compromised by forces we do not fully understand. Your connection to the earth, your ancient power, can help us not only to resist the blight but to understand its very nature. We need to know how it spreads, what fuels it, and how to sever its hold."

He elaborated on the ways in which the Skywood's magic might interact with the blight, suggesting that a deeper understanding, informed by the dragons' connection to the elemental forces, could reveal new methods of containment and healing. He spoke of specific areas where the blight was most potent, where its effects were most unnatural, and where the dragons' unique senses might detect anomalies invisible to Sylvari eyes. He detailed the Ashbound's observed behavior, their movements, their apparent coordination, all to highlight the organized and deliberate nature of their threat.

"The Ashbound are not a natural phenomenon, Thryxal," Cael insisted, his frustration mounting with each dismissive rumble of the dragon's voice. "They are a symptom of a deeper sickness, a perversion of nature. They have found a way to thrive in the imbalance that the land-dwellers have wrought, and their methods are increasingly aggressive. If we do not act in concert, their influence will grow, and soon, there will be nothing left for any of us to protect."

He presented his findings with a quiet intensity, outlining the ecological disruptions he had observed, the subtle shifts in the land's energies that indicated a growing imbalance. He spoke of the Skywood's own internal struggles, the ways in which its ancient magic was being strained by the pervasive corruption, and how this vulnerability made it an even more attractive target for those who sought to spread decay. He described the Ashbound's unsettling adaptations, their physical manifestations of the blight, and how their existence seemed to be a direct consequence of unchecked environmental degradation.

"Your distrust is understandable," Cael conceded, acknowledging the vast chasm of history that separated them. "But the future demands more than a recitation of past grievances. The land-dwellers' relentless expansion has created a world where such unnatural growths can flourish. The Ashbound have learned to exploit this new reality. If we, the ancient custodians of this land, cannot find a way to stand together against this shared threat, then we are condemning ourselves to a slow, agonizing demise. Consider this not a plea for forgiveness, but a stark warning. A warning from one guardian to another, about a sickness that will consume us all."

He described the tangible effects of the blight on the Sylvari, the wilting of ancient trees, the weakening of their magical connections, all to underscore the shared vulnerability. He detailed the potential consequences of inaction, of allowing the Ashbound to consolidate their power, and how this would inevitably lead to the desolation of both the Sylvari forests and the dragon's mountain strongholds. He spoke of the need for a unified defense, a synergistic approach that combined the Sylvari's intrinsic connection to life with the dragons' raw, elemental power.

Thryxal finally uncoiled himself, a mountain of scales and sinew, his golden eyes burning with an ancient fire. He moved to the edge of the cavern, his immense form silhouetted against the dim light filtering from the entrance. He looked out, towards the distant, shadowed peaks, towards the encroaching blight that Cael had so vividly described.

"You speak of a shared threat," Thryxal rumbled, his voice still laced with suspicion, but now also with a hint of something else – a grudging acknowledgement of the undeniable truth in Cael's words. "You speak of a sickness that festers when the earth is wounded. Your kind has inflicted many wounds, Sylvari. Many indeed."

He turned his gaze back to Cael, a chilling intensity in his eyes. "But you also speak of a new corruption, a deliberate cultivation of decay. A force that embraces the rot. This... this is not merely the consequence of your past transgressions. This is a new darkness, one that even we, who have witnessed the ebb and flow of ages, have not fully comprehended."

A flicker of something akin to worry crossed the dragon's ancient face, a fleeting glimpse of vulnerability beneath the stoic facade. He let out a low growl, a sound of deep unease. "If this blight is not merely a natural decay, but a weapon wielded by intelligent hands, then the calculus changes. If the Ashbound are not simply creatures of corruption, but architects of it, then your warning carries weight."

Cael felt a surge of hope, small and fragile, but present nonetheless. He knew this was not an alliance, not yet. It was merely a crack in the wall of distrust, a moment of shared concern that might, with careful tending, grow into something more.

"They are architects of imbalance, Thryxal," Cael affirmed, pressing his advantage gently. "And their designs are not for the benefit of any living thing. They seek to remake this world in their own blighted image. We must understand their designs, their methods, and their ultimate goals, if we are to have any hope of thwarting them. Your unique perspective, your connection to the very stones and currents of this land, is invaluable in such an endeavor."

He detailed the specific areas where the Ashbound seemed to be concentrating their efforts, the patterns of blight spread that suggested a strategic rather than a random assault. He spoke of the subtle signs of environmental stress that he had observed, indicators that the Skywood's own natural defenses were being systematically undermined. He described the disturbing efficiency with which the Ashbound seemed to adapt to changing conditions, a testament to their deep, albeit perverse, understanding of the forces they manipulated.

"We need to know *why* they embrace decay, Thryxal," Cael implored. "What is their ultimate aim? What is it they hope to gain from a world consumed by rot? Your ancient sight, your long memory, might hold the answers that elude us. You have seen cycles of creation and destruction. You have witnessed the rise and fall of powers. Perhaps you have seen echoes of this... this ideology of decay before, in some forgotten age."

He elaborated on the potential consequences of the Ashbound's success, the cascading ecological collapse that would follow their unchecked proliferation, the eventual death of all life, regardless of species. He painted a grim but necessary picture of the future that awaited them if they could not overcome their ancient animosities and forge a new path of cooperation. He stressed that this was not a matter of sentiment, but of pragmatic survival.

Thryxal remained silent for a long moment, his gaze fixed on the distant horizon. The weight of Cael's words seemed to settle upon him, the unspoken threat of a shared doom becoming a more pressing concern than the ghosts of past betrayals.

"The Sylvari have brought much ruin," Thryxal finally conceded, his voice a low, measured rumble. "But the architects of decay you describe... they are a different kind of threat. A blight that feeds on imbalance, that finds strength in what others cast aside. This is a perversion of natural order, a sickness that strikes at the heart of existence itself."

He shifted his massive frame, a gesture that spoke of deep contemplation. "We have observed the spreading rot. We have felt its chill. But we have not understood its purpose. Your insights, Sylvari, however unwelcome the messenger, illuminate a path we had not foreseen. If these Ashbound actively cultivate the blight, if their very existence is a testament to the perversion of life, then... then perhaps your warning is not a plea for aid, but a call to arms."

Cael's breath hitched. This was not a full surrender, not a commitment, but it was more than he had dared to hope for. It was an opening, a crack through which a fragile alliance might begin to form.

"Then let us forge that path together, Thryxal," Cael said, his voice filled with a newfound urgency and a cautious optimism. "Let us investigate this darkness, understand its nature, and devise a way to purge it from our world. The Skywood and the mountains, the life and the stone – we are not separate entities. We are threads in the same tapestry. And that tapestry is unraveling."

He met the dragon's ancient gaze, not as a supplicant, but as an equal, bound by a shared fate. The millennia of distrust remained, a dark shadow in the cavern, but for the first time, a faint glimmer of shared purpose began to push back against the encroaching gloom. The journey would be arduous, fraught with peril, and the dragons' skepticism would undoubtedly linger, but the first, crucial step had been taken. The tense alliance had begun to form, not out of trust, but out of a shared, terrifying necessity.

Thryxal's golden eyes, vast and ancient as molten suns, seemed to bore into Cael's very soul. The cavern, carved by aeons of dragon breath and seismic shifts, pulsed with a palpable energy, a silent testament to the earth's deep magic. "You speak of balance, Sylvari," the dragon rumbled, his voice a symphony of grinding stone and whispering winds. "But your kind has a fractured understanding of its true nature. Balance is not a static state to be maintained, but a dynamic dance, a constant ebb and flow. It is the rhythm of the seasons, the breath of the mountains, the lifeblood that courses through the very arteries of this world."

He shifted, a monumental ripple of obsidian scales, and a gust of ancient air, carrying the scent of sulfur and petrichor, washed over Cael. "You see the Skywood as a single entity, a living jewel. And it is. But it is also but one note in a grand symphony. The health of your forest is inextricably linked to the health of the deep earth, to the veins of energy that run beneath your roots, to the very heart of the mountains I call home."

Thryxal gestured with a massive claw towards a network of glowing fissures that crisscrossed the cavern floor, pulsing with a soft, ethereal light. "These are not mere geological formations, Sylvari. They are resonance pathways, conduits through which the earth's vital force flows. Think of them as the planet's circulatory system, carrying nourishment and power to every living thing. The Skywood draws its strength from these pathways, as do the deepest caverns, as do the roots of the tallest mountains. And as do we, the dragons."

His voice deepened, laced with a weariness that spoke of millennia of observation and sorrow. "For countless ages, we have been the silent guardians of these pathways. We feel their pulse, their health, their every tremor. When they surge with life, the world flourishes. When they falter, when they become choked with stagnation or torn by discord, then the world itself begins to sicken. And your kind, Sylvari, has often been the instrument of that discord."

Cael listened intently, his mind racing to absorb the immensity of Thryxal's words. He had always understood the interconnectedness of nature, but this was on an entirely different scale. The resonance pathways – he had sensed their presence before, faint hums beneath the forest floor, but he had never grasped their fundamental importance, their role as the very heartbeat of the earth.

"Your species," Thryxal continued, his golden eyes fixed on Cael, "has a unique talent for disruption. You seek to tame, to cultivate, to shape the world to your will. This is not inherently wrong. Life itself is a force of change. But your ambition often outstrips your wisdom. You plant your groves, you build your cities, you channel rivers, all without truly understanding the delicate web you are tugging upon."

He let out a low rumble, a sound that vibrated through Cael's chest. "You fell ancient trees, not realizing they were anchor points for the pathways, their roots entwined with the very essence of this land's vitality. You diverted water sources, unaware that you were starving the earth's arteries in one place to enrich another. You have, time and again, frayed these vital threads, and each time, the world has bled."

Cael swallowed, the dragon's words striking home with an uncomfortable accuracy. He had seen the evidence of Sylvari ambition throughout his life, the scars on the landscape, the altered riverbeds, the hushed tales of ancient forests felled for progress. He had always seen these as regrettable but necessary steps in the evolution of his people. Now, he saw them through the eyes of a being who perceived the world's hidden arteries, the invisible currents of energy that sustained all life.

"The blight you spoke of," Thryxal said, his voice regaining its focused intensity, "is a symptom of a deep sickness within these pathways. It is not merely a disease that affects plants and animals; it is a corruption that seeps into the very energy of the earth. When these pathways become sluggish, when their natural flow is impeded by imbalance, then decay finds fertile ground. And your species, in its relentless pursuit of growth, has been the most fertile ground of all."

The dragon paced slowly, his movements deliberate and powerful, each step a testament to his ancient lineage and his profound connection to the earth. "The Ashbound, you say, cultivate this decay? They nurture it?

This is a perversion of the natural order, a deliberate twisting of the earth's lifeblood. It is like poisoning a well and then drinking from it, hoping to gain strength from the toxins."

He stopped, his gaze locking with Cael's once more. "We have witnessed this decay, Sylvari. We have felt the pathways weaken, the vibrant hum dimming to a sickly throb. But we have never seen it actively *cultivated*. This is new. And it is deeply disturbing. It suggests a conscious intent to corrupt, to dismantle the very foundations of life."

"And that is why we must act together, Thryxal," Cael urged, sensing a subtle shift in the dragon's demeanor, a flicker of genuine concern beneath the layers of ancient distrust. "If the Ashbound are not merely a manifestation of imbalance, but agents of its deliberate acceleration, then the threat is far greater than we initially understood. They are not just exploiting the wounds we have inflicted; they are actively widening them, spreading a contagion that will consume everything."

Thryxal remained silent for a long moment, his massive head lowered, his gaze fixed on the pulsing fissures beneath his claws. The air in the cavern grew heavy with unspoken thoughts, with the weight of millennia of separate existence and contrasting perspectives.

"Your people have always seen yourselves as masters of the land, Sylvari," Thryxal finally said, his voice a low, thoughtful murmur. "You prune and shape, you cultivate and harvest. And in doing so, you have, time and again, disrupted the deep currents. You have diverted the flow, dammed the arteries, and sometimes, you have severed them entirely. You have taken from these pathways, but you have rarely understood what you were taking, or the consequences of its absence."

He raised his head, his golden eyes reflecting the soft glow of the resonance pathways. "We, the dragons, are different. We do not seek to shape the land, but to be of it. We are woven into its very fabric. When a pathway weakens, we feel it as a sickness in our own bones. When it surges with life, we feel a corresponding surge within ourselves. We are attuned to its rhythm, its needs, its ancient song. And that song is growing discordant, Sylvari. It is strained, and it is fading."

"And the Ashbound," Cael pressed, seizing the sliver of opening, "are actively attempting to silence that song, are they not? To replace it with a dirge of decay. They seek power not from growth and renewal, but from entropy and dissolution. They are anathema to the very essence of these resonance pathways."

Thryxal let out a breath, a slow exhalation that seemed to carry the weight of the mountains. "Your words paint a grim picture, Sylvari. A picture of a force that seeks not to conquer, but to unravel. To dismantle the intricate tapestry of life, thread by thread. And if they are indeed actively poisoning the very arteries of the world, then your presence here, seeking an alliance, is not merely a plea for your own survival, but a recognition of a shared threat that transcends even our ancient grievances."

He looked at Cael, and for the first time, Cael saw not just suspicion, but a deep, ancient weariness, a flicker of recognition of a shared peril that was beginning to outweigh the bitterness of past betrayals. "You speak of understanding these pathways," Thryxal continued, his voice gaining a new resonance. "Of learning their secrets. We have lived with them, breathed them, for longer than your kind has walked this earth. We know their flows, their strengths, their vulnerabilities. We feel the subtle shifts that you, with your feet on the surface, can only guess at."

"Then let us share that knowledge, Thryxal," Cael pleaded, his voice earnest. "Let us combine your deep understanding of the earth's energy with our knowledge of the blight's manifestations. We can observe the Ashbound's activities, map their movements, and use your wisdom to decipher the true nature of the corruption they spread. We can follow the sickness through the resonance pathways, tracing its source, and find a way to cauterize the wound before it consumes us all."

"The pathways are not merely conduits of energy, Sylvari," Thryxal stated, his gaze intense. "They are also conduits of memory. They hold the echoes of all that has transpired upon this land. The rise and fall of forests, the passing of ages, the very imprint of life and death. By tracing the blight through these pathways, we might not only understand its mechanics but also its origins. Perhaps, within the deep currents of earth's memory, lies a clue to how this perversion of life came to be."

He turned his massive head, his gaze sweeping across the cavern, as if seeing beyond its stone walls, into the very heart of the world. "Your people have always looked outward, Sylvari, towards the sky, towards the canopy of your great forest. We have always looked inward, towards the core, towards the molten heart of the world. Perhaps, for the first time, we must both look in the same direction, towards the unseen currents that bind us. For if these pathways are corrupted, then the very life force of this world is threatened, and even the mightiest dragon will eventually fall."

Cael felt a profound sense of awe wash over him. Thryxal was not just a guardian of mountains; he was a guardian of the earth's very essence, a living embodiment of its ancient, enduring power. His wisdom, though delivered with a sternness born of long-held distrust, was a gift, a revelation of truths that lay hidden beneath the surface of his own understanding.

"The Ashbound," Thryxal concluded, his voice a low, resonant hum that seemed to vibrate with the very pulse of the earth, "are a symptom of a world out of tune. They are a manifestation of imbalance so profound that it has twisted life itself. If we are to have any hope of healing this world, then we must first understand the song that the earth has forgotten, and then help it to sing it once more. Your intrusion here, Sylvari, has forced us to confront a truth we have long tried to ignore: that the wounds you have inflicted, however ancient, have paved the way for a far more insidious decay." He looked directly at Cael, his golden eyes holding a complex mixture of apprehension and a dawning, reluctant acceptance. "The resonance pathways are weakening. The earth weeps. And if we do not listen, if we do not act in concert, the silence that follows will be the end of all things."

The silence that followed Thryxal's pronouncement was not one of agreement, but of profound, echoing disagreement. Cael felt it in the way the air thrummed, in the subtle tightening of the stone beneath his feet, in the way the dragon's massive form seemed to coalesce into a single, unyielding monument of distrust. He had come seeking an ally, a partner in the desperate fight against the encroaching blight. Instead, he found himself facing a barrier as ancient and formidable as the mountains themselves. Thryxal's words, though offering a glimmer of shared concern for the earth's arteries, had ultimately underscored the chasm that separated their peoples, their methods, and their very understanding of obligation.

Cael's mind, usually so sharp and focused when it came to the intricate weave of the Skywood, felt muddled, weighed down by a confusion that had little to do with the blight and everything to do with his own sworn duty. His oath, sworn under the oldest boughs of the Skywood, bound him to protect its canopy, to safeguard its ancient magic, and to ensure its vibrant life. He had interpreted this oath as a shield, a commitment to preserve what was, to defend it from external threats. But the dragon's unwavering skepticism, his palpable refusal to engage beyond a grudging acknowledgment of a shared peril, forced Cael to question the very nature of his pledge. Was protection merely a matter of standing guard, or did it demand more? Did it require him to actively *persuade*, to *compel*, even to *coerce* those who held immense power but chose to wield it only for themselves?

He paced a small circle on the cavern floor, the smooth stone cool beneath his worn boots, each step a silent testament to his internal turmoil. His oath was to the Sylvari, to the Skywood. It did not explicitly bind him to the dragons, nor to the deep earth they guarded. Yet, Thryxal's revelation about the resonance pathways, about the interconnectedness of the Skywood's health with the very lifeblood of the planet, had irrevocably broadened Cael's understanding of his responsibilities. If the Skywood's roots were indeed drinking from the same arteries that nourished the mountains, and if those arteries were being poisoned by the Ashbound, then his oath to protect the canopy extended, by extension, to protecting the source of its vitality. But how could he protect what he could not directly influence? How could he mend the world's veins when the ancient guardians of those veins refused to acknowledge his need, let alone offer their aid?

The weight of his position settled upon him, a cloak woven from the ancient woods and the expectations of his people. As a Sylvari, he was a steward, a cultivator, a nurturer. His methods were rooted in growth, in balance achieved through careful tending. He understood the delicate art of coaxing life from the soil, of guiding the flow of water, of pruning the overgrowth to allow new shoots to thrive. But dragons, and by extension, the ancient earth itself, operated on a scale and with a ferocity that dwarfed his own experience. Their power was elemental, primal. To ask Thryxal to join him was like asking a storm to hold back its rain so a single sapling could grow stronger. It was a fundamental misunderstanding of their nature.

Cael stopped his pacing and looked up at the colossal form of Thryxal, a silhouette against the faintly glowing fissures. He saw not just a creature of immense power, but a being bound by its own ancient instincts, its own deep-seated distrust. The Sylvari had wronged the dragons, Cael knew. The tales were as old as the mountains themselves, of forest groves cleared where dragon lairs once lay, of sacred waters diverted, of the earth's deep places disturbed by Sylvari ambition. Thryxal's skepticism was not born of malice, but of millennia of perceived betrayal. And Cael, despite his earnest intentions, represented the very species that had caused those ancient wounds.

This was the crux of his dilemma, the agonizing knot in his gut. His oath demanded protection, but the means to achieve that protection were being withheld by a power that felt justified in its refusal. He couldn't force Thryxal. The very thought was ludicrous. A Sylvari, even one with the strength of the Skywood behind him, attempting to coerce a dragon? It was an act of suicidal folly. Yet, the alternative was to stand by, to watch the blight spread, to see the Skywood wither and die, knowing that he had possessed the knowledge of the true threat and the potential for a powerful alliance, but had been unable to overcome the ancient distrust that stood between them.

Was his oath a passive promise? A vow to defend if attacked, but not to actively seek out the tools or allies needed to prevent the attack in the first place? The thought felt like a betrayal in itself. The Sylvari didn't just survive; they *thrived*. They didn't merely endure; they *cultivated*. And if cultivation required reaching beyond one's own immediate domain, then his oath, too, must demand that. It was a mandate for active guardianship, not passive observation.

He remembered the hushed whispers of the Elder Sylvari, their pronouncements on duty and sacrifice. They spoke of the interconnectedness of all things, of the forest breathing with the world. But had they ever envisioned a threat that required convincing the very earth to lend its voice? Had they anticipated a foe so insidious that it attacked not just the visible branches, but the unseen roots and the deepest arteries? Cael felt a pang of guilt, a realization that perhaps he, and his people, had grown complacent in their protected forest, their understanding of the world's vulnerabilities dulled by the very security they had achieved.

The dragon's low rumble, a sound that vibrated through the stone and into Cael's bones, broke his reverie. "You ask for aid, Sylvari. You speak of balance. But your kind's history is a testament to its absence. We have seen your balance, and it has always been at our expense." Thryxal's golden eyes, ancient and piercing, held a reflection of the glowing pathways, but also a deep well of sorrow and resignation. "We are not your tools, Sylvari. We are the keepers of what you have long neglected. Our trust is not given lightly, nor is it easily regained."

Cael knelt, a gesture of humility and respect, though he knew it was unlikely to sway the ancient dragon. "I understand your distrust, Thryxal. And I do not ask you to forget the past. But the Ashbound are not merely a symptom of imbalance. They are actively *creating* it. They are poisoning the very pathways that sustain us both. If they succeed, there will be no Skywood to protect, no mountains for you to guard. There will only be dust and decay." He met the dragon's gaze, his own eyes filled with a plea that was both desperate and defiant. "My oath binds me to protect the life of the Skywood. But life, as you have taught me, is not contained within a single canopy. It is a symphony, and the Ashbound are determined to silence it. If I cannot convince you to join me, then I must find a way to act alone, even if it means challenging the very laws of nature that you embody."

He stood again, the immense weight of his words hanging in the air. The oath, he realized, was not a shield to hide behind, but a responsibility to fulfill, no matter the cost, no matter the opposition. He would not coerce, for that was not the Sylvari way. But he would not yield, either. If Thryxal would not lend his strength, then Cael would have to find strength elsewhere, or forge it within himself, drawing upon the very core of his being and the deep, resonant power of the Skywood that he was sworn to protect.

The confrontation with the dragon was not just about gaining an ally; it was about testing the limits of his own commitment, about discovering if his oath was strong enough to bear the crushing weight of the world's silent suffering. And in that moment, facing the ancient distrust of Thryxal, Cael knew it was a test he had to pass, for the sake of the forest, for the sake of the world, and for the sake of his own soul. The path ahead was uncertain, fraught with peril, and the dragon's refusal was a stark reminder of the lonely burden he carried. But the fight was far from over. It had, in fact, just begun.

Mara's fingers, usually nimble and precise, trembled as they traced the intricate etchings on the weather engine's control panel. The air in the cavern, thick with the scent of ozone and damp earth, seemed to press in on her, amplifying the frantic thrumming of her own heart. For weeks, she had meticulously cataloged the anomalies, the strange atmospheric distortions, the unsettling patterns in the wind currents. She had approached her investigation with the detached logic of a scholar, seeking to understand a natural phenomenon, a complex ecological imbalance spiraling out of control. The idea that these grand, ancient mechanisms, designed to harmonize with the world's delicate rhythms, could be failing on their own had seemed plausible, if terrifying. But the evidence now accumulating before her eyes painted a far more sinister picture.

The readouts on the primary console, which she had painstakingly deciphered over countless hours of study, were no longer displaying cryptic error codes suggesting system degradation. Instead, they showed clear, deliberate overrides. Sequences of commands, designed to force the atmospheric regulators into specific, unnatural configurations, were logged with chilling regularity. These weren't the random fluctuations of a dying system; they were calculated actions, executed with precision. It was akin to finding a meticulously crafted blueprint for chaos where she had expected to find the crumbling plans of decay.

She pulled up the maintenance logs, her brow furrowed in concentration. The entries were sparse, almost eerily so, for a piece of machinery of this magnitude. Most were automated diagnostics, routine checks that showed the engines operating within acceptable parameters, right up until the moment a cascade of erratic readings would begin. But then, buried deep within a sub-menu, she found them – a series of manual input logs, timestamped with unnerving frequency, all occurring just prior to the major weather disturbances. The user IDs associated with these entries were not cryptic designations of machine intelligence or elemental spirits. They were... human. Plain, identifiable human user IDs.

Mara leaned back, her breath catching in her throat. The implications washed over her, cold and sharp. This wasn't a natural disaster. This wasn't the earth groaning under the weight of its own imbalance. This was an attack. Someone, or some group, was actively *weaponizing* the weather. The thought sent a shiver down her spine, not from fear, but from a surge of grim understanding. It explained the unnatural ferocity of the recent storms, the way the winds seemed to possess a malicious intent, the unnervingly precise timing of the devastating downpours and droughts.

She brought up the schematics for the entire weather engine network, her fingers flying across the holographic interface. The engines weren't isolated units; they were interconnected, a vast, intricate circulatory system for the planet's atmosphere. If one could be manipulated, then perhaps they all could. And if that was the case, then the Ashbound, with their penchant for destructive ideology and their rumored access to forgotten technologies, became the prime suspects. Their desire to see the world cleansed, to eradicate what they deemed impurities, suddenly took on a terrifying new dimension. They weren't just waiting for the world to crumble; they were actively pushing it towards the precipice.

Mara accessed the encrypted communication logs, a layer of security she had only managed to breach thanks to a particularly insightful hint from a cryptic old sage in the Western Peaks. The data streams were heavily coded, but the patterns of communication were undeniable. There were frequent, encrypted exchanges between various weather engine control centers, not related to standard operational procedures, but to coordinated shifts in atmospheric pressure, temperature, and precipitation across vast regions. The timestamps of these communications often preceded major weather events by mere hours, even minutes. The Ashbound, she realized with a sickening lurch, were not just a fringe cult; they were a highly organized, technologically advanced force with the power to wreak global devastation.

The sheer audacity of it was staggering. To tamper with the very forces that sustained life, to turn the sky into a weapon, was an act of unparalleled barbarism. Mara had always believed in the inherent good of the world, in its natural tendency towards balance. Even in the face of the blight, she had held onto the hope that the land would eventually find a way to heal itself. But this... this was different. This was a deliberate, malicious act of desecration.

She zoomed out on the global map, the weather engine network glowing like a celestial constellation. A chilling thought struck her: if the Ashbound could manipulate the engines, what else could they control? Were their ambitions limited to the atmosphere, or did their reach extend to other fundamental forces of nature? The thought sent a fresh wave of unease through her. The blight was a creeping decay, a slow strangulation of life. This, however, was a lightning strike, a swift and brutal assault on the very systems that kept the world alive.

Mara felt a surge of adrenaline, the initial shock giving way to a fierce determination. Her quest had just taken a monumental shift. It was no longer about understanding a failing ecosystem; it was about uncovering a conspiracy, about finding the perpetrators of this global sabotage. She needed to gather more concrete proof, evidence that could not be dismissed as mere conjecture. She needed to identify the specific individuals or cells within the Ashbound responsible for these actions.

She began cross-referencing the manual input logs with known Ashbound strongholds and training camps. There were faint, but discernible, geographical correlations. Certain engine control centers, located in regions known to harbor Ashbound operatives, showed a disproportionately high number of these suspicious manual overrides. It was a painstaking process, like sifting through grains of sand to find a single, incriminating pebble, but Mara was relentless. She knew that if she could link specific Ashbound operatives to these commands, if she could demonstrate a direct causal relationship between their actions and the catastrophic weather events, then she might finally have the leverage she needed.

The implications for her own journey were profound. She had set out to find the source of the blight, believing it to be a symptom of the world's own weakening constitution. Now, she understood that the blight might be a deliberate consequence of the Ashbound's larger campaign of environmental warfare. They were not just passively allowing the world to decay; they were actively accelerating it, using the weather engines as instruments of destruction to hasten the process.

Mara brought up the ancient texts on celestial alignments and atmospheric magic, her mind racing. The weather engines were said to be attuned to the planet's natural energies, their operation guided by an understanding of deep, cosmic rhythms. The Ashbound, in their pursuit of control, were perverting this fundamental harmony, twisting the natural order into a weapon. This was not merely an act of vandalism; it was an assault on the very soul of the world.

She scrolled through more logs, her eyes scanning for any hint of an external influence beyond the direct manipulation of the engines. Were there other systems being targeted? Were there other natural forces being subverted? The more she learned, the vaster and more terrifying the scope of the Ashbound's agenda became. They were not just fighting a war against life; they were waging a war against existence itself.

The weight of her discovery settled upon her shoulders, heavy and immense. She was no longer just an investigator; she was a witness to a crime of unimaginable scale. The carefully constructed facade of natural decay had crumbled, revealing the cold, calculating hand of deliberate malice. Her path forward had become infinitely more dangerous, but also, paradoxically, clearer.

She knew what she was up against, and the knowledge, while daunting, fueled a burning resolve. She would expose them. She would find the proof. And she would ensure that the world, the *real* world, the one that breathed and grew and thrived, understood the true nature of the enemy it faced. The weather engines, once symbols of the planet's intricate harmony, had become chilling testaments to its vulnerability, and Mara was now tasked with revealing the architects of its potential downfall.

The air crackled with an ancient power, a palpable energy that seemed to emanate from Thryxal himself, the great dragon whose scales shimmered like a thousand sunsets. Cael stood before him, a mere mortal dwarfed by the sheer magnitude of the creature, yet his gaze was steady, filled with a newfound resolve forged in the crucible of his recent discoveries. The cavern, carved by eons of elemental fury, pulsed with the dragon's presence, its immense body coiled like a mountain range, its eyes, two molten pools of emerald fire, fixed upon the young man.

Thryxal's voice, a resonant rumble that vibrated through Cael's very bones, was laced with a gravitas that transcended mere words. It was the voice of epochs, of witnessing the slow dance of creation and decay, of understanding the intricate, often brutal, ballet of the natural world. "You believe you understand the tremors you have felt, the disquiet in the earth's heart," the dragon began, his words echoing the profound truth of the land. "But you have only glimpsed the surface, the frantic fluttering of wings before the storm. The blight you perceive is but a symptom, a festering wound that has been long in the making."

Cael listened, his mind grappling with the weight of Thryxal's pronouncements. He had seen the data, the deliberate manipulation of the weather engines, the chilling precision of the Ashbound's attacks. He understood the *how*, the technological perversion of nature. But Thryxal spoke of something deeper, something more primal.

"The earth remembers," the dragon continued, the words a low, mournful cadence. "Every tremor, every scorch mark, every poisoned stream. It is a tapestry woven with the threads of life and death, of growth and desolation. And its wounds, young Cael, are deep. Deeper than any mortal mind can truly fathom. You seek to mend a broken mechanism, to rewind the clock on a catastrophic error. But this is not an error. This is a betrayal."

The dragon shifted, a movement that sent ripples of energy through the cavern. "The balance was not merely disrupted; it was systematically eroded. The whispers of discord grew to a roar, amplified by those who sought to hasten its demise. They have not simply broken the harmony; they have sought to corrupt its very source, to twist the songs of the elements into dirges of destruction."

Cael's heart ached at the dragon's words. He had felt the sorrow of the land, the silent scream of dying forests and choked rivers. He had attributed it to the natural course of decline, the inevitable consequence of the world's weakening constitution. But Thryxal's perspective offered a terrifying new lens. This wasn't just a slow fade; it was an active, malicious assault.

"The elements themselves are not inherently cruel," Thryxal explained, his gaze softening slightly, as if acknowledging the inherent fragility of Cael's understanding. "They are forces, raw and untamed, seeking their own equilibrium. But even the most patient of beings can be pushed to their limits. The earth has absorbed the offenses, the reckless exploitation, the disregard for its sacred cycles. It has endured the scarring, the poisoning, the relentless taking without regard for the giving."

The dragon lowered his massive head, his eyes now mirroring the ancient, sorrowful depths of the earth itself. "And its patience, Cael, is finite. There is a limit to what even the most resilient of systems can withstand. When that limit is reached, the earth does not merely weep; it unleashes. It casts off the maladies, the parasites that have burrowed into its flesh, with a force that is both cleansing and terrifying."

Cael swallowed, the dryness in his throat a stark contrast to the raw power he felt in the dragon's presence. He thought of the Ashbound, their fanatical zeal, their desire to purge the world. They saw themselves as saviors, as instruments of a higher purification. But Thryxal's warning painted them as harbingers of an even greater cataclysm, as fools who believed they could control a power they did not comprehend, and in doing so, would awaken the earth's own wrath.

"You speak of the Ashbound," Cael ventured, his voice a low murmur, "of their manipulation of the weather engines. I have seen their hand in the chaos."

Thryxal let out a low growl, a sound that was not anger, but a deep, resonant disappointment. "They are but the most visible manifestation of a deeper rot. They wield tools they do not fully grasp, believing their mastery extends to the very heart of creation. They seek to command the storms, to dictate the seasons, to bend the will of the ancient forces to their own limited designs. They are like children playing with a dragon's fire, unaware of the inferno they court."

The dragon's gaze intensified, a piercing intensity that seemed to strip away all pretense. "But understand this, Cael. The earth's memory is not a passive record. It is an active force. The wounds you see are not merely scars; they are reservoirs of pain, of imbalance. And when the pressure becomes too great, when the defiance is too egregious, the earth will respond. Not with the calculated precision of a weapon, but with the untamed fury of a living being pushed beyond its endurance."

He paused, allowing his words to settle, to resonate within Cael's very being. "The blighted lands, the unnatural storms, the famines that grip the villages – these are the cries of a wounded planet. But the deeper resonance, the tremors that precede an even greater upheaval, are the earth's own defenses stirring. It is preparing to shed the infection, to purge the imbalance. And this purging will be... absolute."

Cael felt a cold dread seep into him, a stark contrast to the fiery conviction that had propelled him thus far. He had focused on the Ashbound's immediate threat, on their technological perversion. But Thryxal's warning spoke of a larger, more fundamental reckoning. The Ashbound's actions were not just an attack on humanity, but an assault on the very essence of the world, an assault that would inevitably provoke a response far more devastating than any weapon.

"What does this mean for us?" Cael asked, the question heavy with the unspoken fear of what lay ahead.

"It means," Thryxal rumbled, his voice taking on a somber cadence, "that your task is not merely to expose the manipulators. It is to attempt to soothe the wound, to staunch the bleeding before the earth itself begins to bleed out. You must strive not only to stop the weaponization of the skies but to address the very reasons why the earth has been pushed to such a precipice. The Ashbound are a symptom, a dangerous one, but the disease runs far deeper."

The dragon's eyes seemed to hold the weight of millennia, of watching civilizations rise and fall, of seeing the slow erosion of natural harmony.

"The earth has a memory, yes, but it also has a spirit. And when that spirit is sufficiently wounded, its wrath is a force that no mortal army, no technological marvel, can withstand. You must remind those who have forgotten, and perhaps even remind yourself, that the power you seek to control is not yours to command, but yours to respect. For in its violation lies not only the potential for destruction, but the certainty of a reckoning that will reshape all that you know."

Thryxal's gaze drifted, as if gazing into the depths of time, at the echoes of past imbalances and the potential futures that lay before them. "The blight is a wound. The Ashbound are a parasite. But the earth itself is a slumbering giant, and you are treading dangerously close to waking it in its full, terrible fury. Remember this, Cael. The earth remembers. Its wounds are deep, and its patience finite.

And when that patience breaks, the consequences will be as profound and as permanent as the turning of the stars." The dragon's words hung in the air, a chilling prophecy, a stark reminder of the immense forces that lay beyond human comprehension and the dire consequences of their continued desecration. Cael felt the weight of the dragon's warning settle upon him, a heavy mantle of responsibility that extended far beyond the immediate threat of the Ashbound. He understood now that his quest was not merely to fight a war, but to avert a global ecological suicide, a desperate attempt to heal a planet pushed to its breaking point.

Chapter Six

The Ashbound's Shadow

The Ashbound did not see the parched earth as a symptom of neglect, but as a crucible. They spoke of a necessary distillation, a sifting of the unworthy, a purification by fire and drought. Their pronouncements, etched into weathered stone and whispered in hushed gatherings, painted a world steeped in decadence, a civilization that had gorged itself on the earth's bounty with no thought for consequence.

This rampant consumption, they argued, had not merely strained the planet; it had defiled it, rendering it impure, deserving of a swift and decisive purging. For them, the creeping deserts and the skeletal remains of ancient forests were not harbingers of doom, but signs of a long-awaited, vital metamorphosis. The world was not dying; it was undergoing a radical, earth-shattering rebirth, and the Ashbound saw themselves as its midwives, albeit midwives armed with a terrifying vision of a scorched, desolate landscape.

Their ideology was a perversion of natural cycles, a twisted interpretation of renewal that favored destruction over preservation. Where others saw tragedy in the dying trees, the Ashbound saw progress. They spoke of the drought not as a failure of stewardship, but as the earth's own immune response, a natural fever breaking the infection of overpopulation and unchecked industrialization.

The collapse of ecosystems was not a disaster to be averted, but a necessary shedding of weakened limbs, preparing the planet for a new, more robust growth. This growth, they believed, would be born from ashes, nurtured by scarcity, and built by those who understood the true, unforgiving nature of existence. They viewed the current ecological crisis as a cosmic correction, a grand rebalancing that would eventually weed out the weak and the undeserving, leaving behind a purer, more resilient world.

The Ashbound's core tenet was a radical form of ecological Darwinism, stripped of any sentimentality for existing life. They believed that humanity, in its current form, was an evolutionary dead end, a blight upon the planet's grand design. Their actions, therefore, were not acts of destruction, but acts of extreme ecological surgery. They were merely accelerating a process that nature, left to its own devices, would eventually undertake. This self-appointed role as agents of this "natural" cleansing gave them a sense of divine mandate, a conviction that their harsh methods were not only justified but essential for the planet's long-term survival. They saw the suffering caused by their interventions – the famines, the displacement, the desperate scramble for dwindling resources – as regrettable but ultimately necessary casualties in the grand war for planetary redemption.

Within their clandestine circles, their doctrines were espoused with an almost religious fervor. They painted vivid, apocalyptic visions of the future, where shimmering cities lay in ruins and the wild, untamed forces of nature reclaimed the land. These were not visions of despair, but of liberation. They believed that stripping away the artifice of civilization, its technologies and its comforts, would reveal a more authentic, more primal human existence, one that was intrinsically connected to the earth and respectful of its power. This new humanity, forged in the fires of the Ashbound's "cleansing," would live in harmony with the planet, not through careful management, but through a profound, almost instinctual understanding of its limits and its rhythms.

The whispers of their philosophy often began with a lament for what had been lost – the pristine wilderness, the untouched landscapes, the perceived innocence of a world before human dominion. But this lament quickly morphed into a condemnation of the present, a scathing critique of humanity's insatiable greed and its hubris. They argued that humanity's relentless pursuit of progress had severed its primal connection to the earth, turning it into a parasitic force that exploited and corrupted. The weather engines, in their eyes, were the ultimate symbol of this perversion – humanity's arrogant attempt to control and manipulate forces that were never meant to be tamed by mortal hands. These engines, they believed, had not brought prosperity, but a false sense of security, a fragile illusion that masked the planet's growing resentment.

Their extremist stance was rooted in a deep-seated distrust of any form of human intervention that sought to *manage* nature. They viewed attempts to mitigate climate change, to rescue endangered species, or to restore damaged ecosystems as acts of defiance against a higher, more brutal order. These efforts, they argued, were akin to propping up a dying organism, prolonging its suffering and delaying the inevitable, necessary demise. True ecological health, in their view, could only be achieved through a radical reset, a forceful severing of the parasitic human connection. They saw the Ashbound's manufactured droughts and engineered ecological collapses as simply expediting this process, ensuring that the purge was swift and efficient, preventing a more prolonged and agonizing decline.

The Ashbound's vision was not one of complete annihilation, but of selective survival. They believed that a small, chosen remnant of humanity would emerge from the cataclysm, those who had demonstrated resilience, adaptability, and a fundamental respect for the earth's power. These survivors would inherit a world reborn, a planet cleansed of its excess, where a more harmonious relationship with nature could be forged. This survivalist mentality fueled their ruthlessness, as they saw any attempt to aid the current suffering as a distraction from the ultimate goal – the creation of this new, purer world. They were not driven by malice, but by a chilling, unwavering conviction that their radical methods were the only path to salvation, a necessary evil to bring about a greater good.

This ideology manifested in their meticulous planning and their unwavering resolve. They studied the earth's vulnerabilities, not to heal them, but to exploit them. They understood the interconnectedness of ecosystems not to preserve it, but to weaponize its fragility. The droughts they engineered were designed to be not just inconvenient, but catastrophic, pushing the planet to the brink where their vision of renewal could begin to take root. They saw the panic and despair that spread through human populations as evidence of humanity's weakness and its unsuitability for the planet's future. Each collapsed village, each failed harvest, was a testament to their cause, a data point confirming the necessity of their radical agenda.

The Ashbound's philosophical underpinnings were a dangerous cocktail of ecological fundamentalism, neo-Malthusian dread, and a profound distrust of human progress. They romanticized a pre-industrial past that likely never existed, a time of supposed harmony and balance that they sought to resurrect through utter devastation. They viewed any attempt to find a middle ground, to balance human needs with ecological preservation, as a compromise with corruption. For them, there was no room for negotiation, no space for gentle adaptation.

The only acceptable path was one of radical purgation, a violent rebirth. Their rhetoric often employed terms like "natural selection," "primal forces," and "the earth's will," cloaking their extremist agenda in the guise of ecological wisdom. They did not see themselves as terrorists, but as ecological purists, driven by a desperate, albeit twisted, love for the planet. Their actions, therefore, were not born of a desire to harm, but from a grim determination to "save" the world by destroying its current, flawed iteration. The suffering of millions was a price they deemed acceptable for the potential salvation of an entire planet, a chilling calculation that underscored the depth of their radicalism.

The Ashbound did not merely wait for the world to crumble; they actively hastened its descent, weaving a tapestry of influence from threads of despair and nascent hope. Their recruitment was not an overt call to arms, but a subtle infiltration, a whisper in the wind that carried the scent of scorched earth and a promise of renewal. They understood that in times of profound crisis, when the established powers faltered and the future seemed a barren wasteland, the most fertile ground for radical ideology was the heart of the disenfranchised.

In the parched hamlets clinging to the desiccated edges of the Skywood, where the dust devils danced with a mournful waltz and the skeletal remains of once-proud trees clawed at the bleached sky, the Ashbound found their most receptive audience. They didn't arrive in gleaming processions or with pronouncements of divine right. Instead, their emissaries were often ordinary people, individuals who had themselves endured the gnawing hunger, the gnawing thirst, the gnawing fear. They were the broken, the displaced, the ones who had witnessed their homes become dust and their livelihoods evaporate like morning mist under a relentless sun. These were the people who no longer looked to the Council for salvation, their faith eroded by years of empty promises and bureaucratic inertia.

The Ashbound's approach was one of insidious empathy. They didn't preach or demand. They listened. They sat with the villagers by the meager fires, their faces etched with the same weariness, and they shared in the sorrow. They spoke of the dying crops, not as a tragedy to be lamented, but as a symptom. "The earth is sick," they would murmur, their voices low and resonant, "and the Council, with their grand pronouncements and their futile tinkering, are merely treating the fever, not the disease." This resonated deeply with those who had watched irrigation systems fail, who had seen desperate attempts to cultivate resilient strains of grain yield only more disappointment.

"They try to force the earth to be something it is not," an Ashbound recruiter named Silas, a man whose weathered hands spoke of a life spent in the unforgiving soil, explained to a hushed group gathered in the shadow of a withered oak. His eyes, the color of storm clouds, held a fierce, almost mournful intensity. "They build their weather engines, their arcane contraptions, believing they can bend the sky to their will. But the sky answers to a higher power, a power we have long forgotten." He paused, letting the silence stretch, the only sound the skittering of unseen creatures in the dry undergrowth. "The earth is not meant to be coddled. It is a wild, magnificent force, and it demands respect. It demands balance. And sometimes, balance is achieved not through gentle persuasion, but through a necessary reckoning."

Their message was deceptively simple, a stark contrast to the complex, often contradictory decrees of the Council. The Ashbound offered a narrative of clear cause and effect, a justification for the suffering that felt more plausible than the Council's pronouncements of unforeseen atmospheric anomalies or the complex machinations of global weather patterns. They explained the drought not as a random act of nature, but as the planet's desperate, primal scream against humanity's relentless exploitation. They painted the Council's efforts as an insult to the very fabric of existence, a pathetic attempt to deny the inevitable.

"The Council speaks of adaptation," another recruiter, a woman named Lyra whose youth belied the stark certainty in her gaze, told a gathering of refugees huddled in the ruins of a market square. The air was thick with the smell of dust and desperation. "They tell you to conserve, to endure, to wait for their machines to fix what they themselves have broken. But what if the answer is not to endure, but to embrace? What if the earth is not asking us to adapt to its suffering, but to help it purge the rot?" Her words, delivered with a quiet conviction, chipped away at the fragile hope that still flickered in the eyes of her audience. "The world is not dying; it is transforming. And this transformation requires a shedding, a cleansing. We, the Ashbound, understand this. We are not afraid of the ashes, for in the ashes lies the seed of a new beginning."

Their recruitment efforts were particularly effective in the Skywood's Fringe settlements, regions that had borne the brunt of the ecological collapse. Here, the Council's presence was minimal, their aid sporadic and insufficient. The Ashbound, however, were there. They offered practical solutions, albeit ones tinged with their radical philosophy. They taught methods of water conservation that were more drastic than any official decree, emphasizing the complete sealing of water sources and the collection of every precious drop. They introduced techniques for cultivating drought-resistant crops, not by developing new strains, but by focusing on hardy, wild varieties that had survived past ecological upheavals, plants that required minimal water and were often bitter and difficult to process, but were undeniably tenacious.

But their influence extended beyond mere survival tips. They offered a sense of belonging, a community forged in shared hardship and a common, albeit grim, purpose. In a world where individuals felt increasingly isolated and powerless, the Ashbound provided a network, a group of like-minded souls who understood their plight and offered a framework for action. They organized small, clandestine gatherings, ostensibly for mutual support, but in reality, for indoctrination. Within these circles, the Ashbound's philosophy was expounded in greater detail, their pronouncements framed as profound ecological truths, their actions presented not as destructive, but as necessary interventions for the planet's ultimate health.

They spoke of the "Great Purge," a term that sent shivers down the spines of some, but was embraced by others as a necessary cleansing. They described how the current ecological crisis was but a precursor to a greater transformation, a period of intense sifting where only the strong, the resilient, and the true inheritors of the earth would survive. This narrative tapped into a deep-seated human desire for meaning, for a grander purpose in the face of overwhelming chaos. Those who felt abandoned by the Council, who saw their lives crumbling around them, found a perverse comfort in the Ashbound's stark vision. It provided an explanation, a rationale, and most importantly, a sense of control, even if that control was directed towards destruction.

"The Council tells you to despair," Silas had said during one of these hushed meetings, his voice gaining a steely edge. "They want you to remain weak, dependent, waiting for their crumbs. But the earth does not reward weakness. It rewards strength. It rewards understanding. We are teaching you to understand. We are showing you how to become the survivors, the ones who will inherit the renewed world. The world that the Council, in its foolishness, is actively destroying."

Their influence was like a creeping vine, slowly engulfing the traditional structures of community. They subtly undermined the authority of village elders who still held onto hope in the Council's promises. They exploited existing grievances, magnifying the Council's failures and the perceived indifference of the ruling powers. They preyed on the fear of the unknown, painting vivid, albeit skewed, pictures of what the future held if the current trajectory continued – a world choked by its own excess, suffocated by its own technological hubris.

One of the most potent tools in their arsenal was the idea of "purification." The ecological collapse, they argued, was the earth's way of shedding impurities, of ridding itself of the toxic elements that humanity had introduced. And those who embraced the Ashbound's path were, in a sense, choosing to align themselves with this natural purification. They were not being asked to cause suffering, but to witness and accept it as a necessary part of a greater, cosmic process. This detached perspective, while chilling, offered a way for individuals to cope with the devastating realities of their lives, to reframe their own suffering and the suffering of others as essential steps towards a better future.

Lyra, with her unwavering gaze, often spoke of the inherent resilience of nature. "Look at the desert blooms," she would say, her hand gesturing towards a patch of tough, thorny flowers stubbornly pushing through the cracked earth. "They do not complain of the drought. They do not weep for the lack of rain. They simply adapt, they endure, and when the slightest moisture appears, they burst forth in defiance. We, too, must learn this defiance. We must learn to thrive in the crucible, not to be consumed by it."

The recruitment was often facilitated by existing social networks. Families torn apart by migration, friends separated by hardship, would find themselves drawn back together under the Ashbound's banner. A whispered conversation at a communal well, a shared meal amongst refugees, a chance encounter in a desolate marketplace – these were the points of contact. The Ashbound were patient, their approach gradual. They would sow seeds of doubt, offer a flicker of hope, and then, when the ground was sufficiently prepared, they would reveal their true message.

The promise of purpose was a powerful lure. In a world stripped bare of its comforts and its certainties, where survival itself was a daily struggle, the Ashbound offered a clear objective. They were not just surviving; they were participating in a grand, ecological imperative. They were the antibodies of a dying planet, working to purge the infection. This elevated their actions, transforming desperate survival into a noble, albeit brutal, mission.

The Ashbound also subtly exploited the Council's reliance on advanced technology. While the Council poured resources into weather engines and atmospheric regulators, the Ashbound pointed to the continued degradation of the environment as proof of the technology's failure, or worse, its active role in exacerbating the problem. "They build machines to control the sky," Silas would explain, a hint of derision in his voice. "But they cannot control the consequence. They cannot control the balance. The earth remembers its own rhythms, and it will always reassert its dominance." This narrative fed the growing distrust of the Council and their technological solutions, making the Ashbound's simpler, more primal approach seem more appealing, more honest.

The influence spread like a contagion, not just through direct recruitment, but through the subtle contagion of ideas. As more people in a community adopted the Ashbound's worldview, their conversations, their actions, their very outlook on life began to shift. The talk of despair slowly morphed into talk of resilience, of acceptance, of a coming reckoning. The Ashbound, by offering a tangible ideology and a sense of community, provided a bulwark against the overwhelming psychological toll of the ecological crisis, even as their ideology encouraged actions that would exacerbate the physical toll. Their shadowy presence was becoming an undeniable force, shaping the desperate landscape of the Skywood with their brutal, uncompromising vision of renewal.

The Ashbound's approach to achieving their envisioned "reset" was not a passive waiting game, but an active, deliberate campaign of disruption. They understood that the Canopy Accord Council, for all its perceived failures, still maintained a fragile grip on order, a grip that needed to be not just loosened, but shattered. Their targets were not chosen at random; they were the linchpins of the Council's authority and the symbols of their flawed attempts at ecological salvation.

One of their most audacious acts of sabotage targeted the Skywood's ancient water-filtration nexus, a colossal structure of interwoven, bio-luminescent vines and crystalline conduits that had been meticulously maintained for generations. Nestled deep within the shadowed heart of the forest, it was a testament to the Council's engineering prowess, a beacon of hope in a world parched by drought. The Ashbound saw it not as a symbol of progress, but as an abomination, a hubristic attempt to artificially manipulate the planet's lifeblood.

Silas, with his intimate knowledge of the Skywood's hidden pathways and its vulnerabilities, led the strike team. They moved under the cloak of a moonless night, their footsteps muffled by the damp moss that carpeted the forest floor. The air, usually alive with the symphony of nocturnal creatures, was eerily silent, a testament to the fear that even the wild things held for the Ashbound's presence. Their objective was not outright destruction, which might be too obvious, too easily attributed and rallied against. Instead, their goal was insidious contamination, a slow poisoning that would render the nexus useless and, more importantly, sow doubt in its efficacy.

They carried with them specially cultivated strains of parasitic fungi, their spores potent and virulent, designed to thrive in the moisture-rich environment of the filtration system. The spores were encased in brittle, hollowed-out seed pods, each one a miniature bomb of ecological warfare. As the Ashbound operatives scaled the vine-like conduits, their movements fluid and silent, they systematically injected the pods into the nexus's delicate flow. The bioluminescent vines pulsed with a soft, ethereal light, oblivious to the creeping blight that was being introduced into their very essence.

Lyra, who remained on the periphery with a contingent of lookouts, monitored the faint vibrations of the forest, listening for any sign of Council patrols. Her senses, honed by years of survival and a deep attunement to the natural world, were her primary defense. She communicated with Silas through a series of coded whistles, each one carrying a message of approaching danger or the all-clear signal. The tension was palpable, a taut string stretched to its breaking point. A single misstep, a single rustle of leaves too loud, could mean their capture and the exposure of their network.

The fungi, once unleashed, began their insidious work. Within days, the normally pristine water that flowed from the nexus began to take on a murky, viscous quality. The bioluminescent vines, once vibrant and healthy, started to wither, their light dimming to a sickly pallor. The filtered water, meant to sustain the parched settlements on the Skywood's fringe, now carried with it a subtle toxicity, a slow-acting poison that would not kill instantly, but would weaken, sicken, and erode the health of those who drank it. The Council's response was one of frantic confusion. Their technicians, usually so confident in their diagnostic tools, found themselves baffled by the sudden, inexplicable degradation of the nexus. They blamed atmospheric shifts, unprecedented microbial blooms, anything but deliberate malice. And that, for the Ashbound, was a victory.

Another critical target was the Council's network of atmospheric regulators, massive, obelisk-like structures that dotted the landscape, designed to subtly influence weather patterns and mitigate the worst effects of the drought. These regulators were not only vital for maintaining what little stability remained, but they were also powerful symbols of the Council's control over nature. To cripple them was to strike at the heart of that perceived authority.

The Ashbound chose a regulator situated in a vast, windswept plateau, an area notorious for its unpredictable storms. The plan was not to destroy the regulator outright, which would require overwhelming force, but to subtly reprogram its delicate mechanisms. This was a task that fell to a small, specialized cell within the Ashbound, individuals who possessed a unique blend of technical aptitude and a deep, almost intuitive understanding of the arcane energies that powered the Council's technology.

Their method involved what they termed "harmonic dissonance." Using specially crafted sonic emitters, they generated low-frequency vibrations that mimicked the natural resonance of the plateau, but with carefully introduced discordant notes. These dissonant frequencies, imperceptible to the human ear but deeply disruptive to the sensitive crystalline matrices of the regulator, began to destabilize its internal workings. It was a psychological assault as much as a technological one. The regulator, designed to harmonize with the environment, was being forced into a state of constant, internal conflict.

The effect was gradual but devastating. Instead of subtly moderating the weather, the malfunctioning regulators began to amplify the existing atmospheric instability. Gentle breezes turned into gale-force winds, light showers escalated into torrential downpours that eroded the already fragile soil. The regulator near the plateau, instead of bringing rain, began to draw moisture from the surrounding atmosphere with an unnatural voracity, creating localized pockets of intense humidity that fostered the growth of invasive, water-logged molds and fungus, further damaging the land.

The Council's attempts to recalibrate the regulators were met with a frustrating lack of success. Their technicians, accustomed to predictable systems, found themselves battling chaotic feedback loops and inexplicable energy fluctuations. The regulators, once symbols of control, became agents of chaos, their presence a constant reminder of the Council's inability to manage the very forces they claimed to command. The Ashbound watched from afar, their satisfaction a cold, hard thing, as the Council's carefully constructed facade of order began to crumble under the weight of their own destabilized technology.

Beyond these large-scale operations, the Ashbound also engaged in a constant campaign of smaller, more targeted acts of sabotage. They would poison wells in remote villages, not to kill outright, but to cause sickness and despair, pushing those communities further into reliance on their own radical doctrines of survival. They would sabotage irrigation channels, ensuring that the meager crops that managed to sprout would wither and die. They would even resort to vandalism of Council infrastructure, defacing their propaganda posters with symbols of the Ashbound, leaving behind taunting messages that spoke of the earth's retribution.

Each act was a carefully calculated step, designed to achieve multiple objectives. Firstly, it was to actively worsen the ecological crisis, thereby accelerating the "reset." The more desperate the situation, the more receptive people would be to the Ashbound's message of radical change. Secondly, it was to discredit the Canopy Accord Council, to expose them as incompetent, corrupt, or simply incapable of protecting their people. By demonstrating the Council's failures, the Ashbound aimed to erode public trust and create a vacuum that they could fill.

Thirdly, these acts served as a brutal form of indoctrination for their own members. Witnessing the direct impact of their actions, the tangible results of their commitment to the Ashbound cause, served to solidify their resolve and deepen their belief in the righteousness of their mission. It transformed abstract ideology into visceral reality, forging a bond between the Ashbound and the increasingly desperate populace they sought to lead. The ash and ruin they wrought were not merely collateral damage; they were the seeds of their new world, sown with intent and watered with the tears of a failing order. The shadow of the Ashbound was not just a creeping dread; it was a tangible force of destruction, reshaping the land and the hearts of its inhabitants with every calculated act of sabotage.

The whispers had become a roar, carried on the wind that rustled through the Skywood's leaves, each gust a harbinger of ill news. Cael, his senses attuned to the subtle shifts in the forest's hum, felt the growing disquiet like a pressure behind his eyes. The reports, initially fragmented and dismissed as localized disturbances, had coalesced into a pattern of deliberate, devastating disruption. The Ashbound. The name itself tasted of ash and decay, a stark antithesis to the vibrant life he was sworn to protect. His role as a Land Guardian, once a practice of patient observation and measured intervention, now demanded a swift, unyielding pursuit. This was no longer about guiding the forest's natural cycles; it was about defending it from a festering blight that sought to accelerate its death.

His heart, a steady rhythm against his ribs, quickened with a righteous anger. He had seen the Council's failings, their well-intentioned but often clumsy attempts to mend the world's wounds. He understood the desperation that might drive some to drastic measures. But this... this was not desperation. This was calculated malice, a perversion of purpose that aimed to dismantle, not to heal. The sabotage of the water-filtration nexus, the tampering with atmospheric regulators – these were not the acts of those seeking balance, but of those who reveled in chaos. The thought of the parasitic fungi, of the destabilizing sonic frequencies, sent a chill down his spine that had nothing to do with the mountain air. It was the cold realization that a significant faction of those who walked beneath the Skywood's boughs no longer saw it as a living entity to be nurtured, but as a dying husk ripe for the taking.

Cael tightened his grip on the carved yew staff that had been his constant companion for decades. It was more than a tool; it was an extension of his will, a conduit for the forest's energy. He had spent his life learning its language, understanding its intricate web of life and death. He knew its vulnerabilities, but more importantly, he knew its resilience. And it was that resilience he intended to champion. The Ashbound were a threat not just to the physical integrity of the Skywood, but to the very spirit of hope that flickered within its canopy. They were an external force, an infection, and as a Land Guardian, it was his sacred duty to root them out.

His pursuit began not with a grand charge, but with a meticulous unraveling of their trail. The forest, in its silent wisdom, offered clues to those who knew how to listen. He found the scorched earth where the Ashbound's encampments had been, the unnaturally disturbed patterns of animal tracks, the lingering scent of their peculiar, acrid incense. He moved with a predatory grace, his senses sharpened by the urgency of his mission. Each discarded scrap, each disturbed branch, was a breadcrumb leading him closer to the heart of the contamination. He followed the faint trails across the rolling foothills, through dense thickets of shadow-wood, and along the winding riverbeds that snaked through the valleys.

His journey was a solitary one, a stark contrast to the often communal nature of his duties as a Land Guardian. He was accustomed to the company of the forest itself, the rustle of leaves, the chirping of unseen insects, the distant call of a sky-hawk. But now, the silence of his pursuit felt heavier, charged with the anticipation of confrontation. He was venturing into their domain, into the shadows they had cultivated. He knew they were not fools; they would have laid traps, both physical and psychological. They would have watchers, their eyes as keen as his own. Yet, the thought of hesitation, of allowing them free rein to sow more discord, was anathema to him.

He recalled the legends of the Ashbound, the fragmented tales passed down through generations. They were said to be born from the ashes of past ecological disasters, individuals who had witnessed the earth's suffering firsthand and had sworn to accelerate its cleansing. Their methods were radical, their vision of a "reset" a terrifying prospect for those who believed in the possibility of slow, organic recovery. But Cael, while acknowledging the validity of some of their grievances, could not reconcile their destructive path with any notion of true healing. True healing was a process of regeneration, of nurturing growth from decay, not of razing everything to the ground in the hope that something new would emerge from the desolation.

His frustration simmered with each mile he covered. He saw the toll the drought had taken, the withered leaves, the parched soil, the anxious faces in the scattered settlements. He understood the Council's struggle, their limited resources, their often-bureaucratic approach. But the Ashbound offered no solutions, only a promise of an end, a brutal finality disguised as salvation. They preyed on fear, amplified despair, and offered a path of destruction as the only viable escape.

One evening, as the twilight painted the Skywood in hues of bruised purple and fiery orange, Cael stumbled upon a scene that solidified his resolve. It was a small, isolated farming community, nestled in a fertile pocket that had somehow managed to hold onto its moisture. But the fields, once bursting with the promise of harvest, were now a scene of devastation. The irrigation channels, Cael's keen eyes noted, had been deliberately dammed with a foul-smelling, viscous slime, likely a concoction cultivated by the Ashbound to further clog and corrupt the water flow. The meager crops that had managed to sprout were blackened, as if touched by an unnatural frost, and the air was thick with the stench of decay. A few villagers, gaunt and hollow-eyed, huddled together, their faces etched with a despair that mirrored the blighted land around them.

Cael approached them cautiously, his staff held loosely. He saw no immediate threat from the villagers themselves. They were the victims, their hope systematically extinguished. He offered them water from his own canteen, a small gesture in the face of such overwhelming ruin. Their stories, when they finally found their voices, were a litany of loss and fear. They spoke of shadowy figures moving in the night, of whispers that promised a new beginning through destruction. They spoke of their wells being poisoned, their livestock falling ill, their future evaporating like mist in the harsh sun.

Listening to their hushed, broken accounts, Cael felt a surge of cold fury. This was not simply an ecological crisis; it was a human one. The Ashbound were not just attacking the land; they were attacking the spirit of its people, eroding their will to survive, their capacity for hope. He saw in their vacant stares the reflection of what the Ashbound sought to achieve: a population broken, desperate, and ready to embrace any radical change, no matter how destructive, that promised an end to their suffering.

He spent the night with the villagers, offering what comfort he could, tending to the sickest among them with the rudimentary healing knowledge he possessed. He promised them that he would not rest until the source of their suffering was found and dealt with. As he prepared to depart at dawn, a small child, no older than five, tugged at his tunic. The child held out a single, perfectly formed wildflower, its petals a vibrant, defiant blue against the muted tones of the ravaged landscape. "For you, Guardian," the child whispered, their voice reedy but clear. "So you don't forget what we're fighting for."

Cael knelt, accepting the delicate bloom. He pressed it gently between the pages of his worn journal, a silent vow made to the child, to the villagers, and to the Skywood itself. This small act of beauty, a stubborn spark of life in the face of utter desolation, became his beacon. He would hunt the Ashbound, not just out of duty, but out of a profound love for the resilience that even the most desperate circumstances could not entirely extinguish. The pursuit was no longer just a task; it was a crusade. He turned his back on the devastated village, his gaze fixed on the horizon, his path now irrevocably set towards the heart of the Ashbound's shadow. The forest was calling, and he would answer.

The rhythmic whir of the weather engines, usually a comforting hum of atmospheric balance, now felt like a discordant thrum beneath Mara's skin. Each tremor that pulsed through the ancient conduits, each fluctuation in the carefully calibrated energy readings, sent a shiver of unease through her. She had been drawn to these hulking, archaic machines by a persistent anomaly – a subtle deviation in the wind patterns, a whisper of unnatural chill in the temperate zones, a too-precise timing of rainfall in drought-stricken areas. At first, she'd dismissed it as a glitch, a testament to the ages that had weathered these marvels of a forgotten era. But the deviations persisted, growing bolder, more deliberate.

Her fingers, stained with the iridescent residue of arcane lubricants and the faint dust of ionized particles, danced across the holographic interfaces projected from her analysis tools. The data streams, once a predictable flow of environmental metrics, were now a tangled knot of conflicting information. It was like trying to decipher a symphony played by a mad conductor, notes jarringly out of place, rhythms deliberately broken. She'd spent weeks meticulously tracing the energy signatures, mapping the subtle shifts in atmospheric pressure, cross-referencing them with historical records of ecological events. And slowly, painstakingly, a pattern began to emerge from the chaos.

It wasn't a simple malfunction. The engines were being *guided*. Not by the usual protocols, not by the Grand Council's sanctioned weather orchestrators, but by something... or someone... else. The energy surges weren't random; they were targeted. The precise manipulation of localized cloud formations to create localized deluges in areas already struggling with water scarcity wasn't a coincidence. The sudden, inexplicable temperature drops that withered nascent crops weren't just atmospheric quirks. These were acts of controlled environmental sabotage.

Mara adjusted her spectacles, her brow furrowed in concentration. Her workspace, a compact, cluttered chamber within the Skywood's administrative sector, was a testament to her obsessive nature. Scrolls unfurled from ceiling-mounted dispensers, ancient tomes lay open on every surface, and intricate diagrams of atmospheric circulation patterns were pinned haphazardly to the walls. The air was thick with the scent of old parchment, polished metal, and the faint, electric tang of active enchantments. She lived and breathed the Skywood's intricate systems, its delicate dance of life and preservation. And what she was seeing now was a brutal, calculated assault on that balance.

She zoomed in on a particular set of energy spikes, correlating them with a recent surge in seismic activity in the northern mountain ranges. The readings were unmistakable. The weather engines, designed to regulate and harmonize the climate, were being subtly coaxed to amplify existing geological stresses, creating a feedback loop of environmental disruption. It was a cruel, ingenious method of destabilization. The natural world, already strained by the encroaching drought and the lingering effects of past ecological upheavals, was being pushed to its breaking point.

And then, a name began to surface in her meticulous research, a name whispered in hushed tones by those who dealt with the fringes of societal unrest, a name that sent a ripple of apprehension through her. The Ashbound. She'd encountered fragmented reports of their existence before

– radical factions, disillusioned by the slow pace of ecological recovery, advocating for extreme measures. They spoke of a "cleansing fire," a "reset" of the world order, a complete dismantling of the existing systems to allow for a purer, uncorrupted genesis. Their ideology, while rooted in a genuine anguish over the planet's suffering, was terrifying in its absoluteness.

Mara had initially dismissed them as a fringe movement, a vocal minority whose radical pronouncements were more a symptom of desperation than a tangible threat. But the data she was compiling painted a different picture. The Ashbound's known methods, as far as they were documented, involved targeted acts of sabotage and disruption. They sought to dismantle the very systems that, in their view, had failed to protect the planet. And what were the weather engines, these ancient behemoths of atmospheric control, if not a prime target for those who sought to unravel the established order?

She cross-referenced the timestamps of the engine manipulations with known Ashbound activities. The parallels were too stark to ignore. The sabotage of the water-filtration nexus in the Southern Plains, the disruption of the sonic resonance emitters in the Whispering Caves – these incidents, previously considered isolated acts of eco-terrorism, now seemed to fit a larger, more sinister design. The Ashbound weren't just protesting; they were actively weaponizing the Skywood's own infrastructure against itself.

Her investigation led her down increasingly precarious digital and arcane pathways. She delved into encrypted logs, deciphered corrupted data fragments, and even consulted with the reclusive guardians of the ancient weather engine schematics, individuals who spoke in riddles and guarded their knowledge with ancient oaths. The deeper she went, the clearer it became: the Ashbound were not merely aware of these technologies; they were actively manipulating them. They had found a way to interface with the engines, to bend their powerful energies to their destructive will.

She traced a specific energy signature, a unique harmonic frequency, that repeatedly appeared in the data logs of the sabotaged systems. It was a signature that resonated with an alarming similarity to the energy patterns associated with certain types of controlled decay, the kind that could be intentionally amplified. This wasn't about understanding the natural flow of energy; it was about hijacking it, twisting it, and weaponizing it. The Ashbound, it seemed, were not just driven by ideology; they were equipped with the means to enact it on a catastrophic scale.

The sheer audacity of their plan was breathtaking. To turn the very mechanisms of balance and sustenance into instruments of destruction – it was a perversion of the highest order. Mara felt a cold knot tighten in her stomach. She had always believed in the inherent goodness of the Skywood, in its capacity for resilience and regeneration. But the Ashbound's actions threatened to shatter that faith, to replace it with a grim realization of the destructive potential that lay dormant, waiting to be awakened.

Her focus shifted to the central control hub of the weather engines, a nexus of power deep within the earth, rumored to be guarded by ancient, slumbering automatons and layered with arcane wards. It was the heart of the system, the place where any significant manipulation would likely originate. Reaching it would be perilous, a journey fraught with unknown dangers. But the evidence was undeniable. The Ashbound were not just a theoretical threat; they were a clear and present danger, and their focus was squarely on the Skywood's most vital systems.

As she meticulously documented her findings, compiling reports that detailed the specific manipulations, the energy signatures, and the increasingly alarming ecological consequences, a disturbing thought began to form. If the Ashbound were indeed targeting the weather engines, their actions would inevitably draw the attention of those tasked with the direct protection of the Skywood. She thought of Cael, the Land Guardian, his unwavering dedication to the forest's well-being. His path, she realized with a growing sense of urgency, was likely converging with her own. He would be sensing the forest's distress, tracking the disturbances, and undoubtedly, he would be heading towards the same source of the corruption.

Mara saved her latest data compilation, a detailed map of the energy flows and anomalies, to a crystalline data shard. She looked at the projected image of the Skywood's vast expanse, its intricate network of life, its delicate atmospheric equilibrium. The Ashbound sought to unravel it all, to plunge it into a devastating reset. Her fingers brushed against a small, polished stone on her desk, a keepsake from a time when her own studies had been purely theoretical, when the threats to the Skywood felt distant and abstract. Now, they felt terrifyingly immediate.

She knew her findings would be met with skepticism by some within the Council. The idea that a radical faction could so thoroughly infiltrate and manipulate such ancient, powerful technology would seem far-fetched, the ramblings of an overzealous researcher. But Mara wasn't seeking validation; she was seeking solutions. She needed to understand the full extent of the Ashbound's reach, the specific methods they were employing to bypass the system's safeguards, and most importantly, how to counter them before they could unleash irreversible devastation.

Her gaze drifted to a particular point on the map, a remote, geologically unstable region in the northeastern highlands. The energy readings there were particularly volatile, a maelstrom of manipulated atmospheric pressure and amplified seismic tremors. It was a place where the weather engines were pushing the boundaries of their intended function, creating localized storms of unnatural ferocity. It was also a region that, according to her fragmented intel, had seen increased activity from individuals matching the descriptions of Ashbound operatives.

Mara meticulously cross-referenced the energy signature of the weather engine manipulations with the subtle energy readings she'd picked up from Cael's reconnaissance drones in the northern territories. There was a faint, yet distinct, overlap. It was like hearing two separate melodies that, when played in proximity, revealed a shared underlying chord. Cael was tracking the physical manifestations of the Ashbound's incursions – the disrupted wildlife, the scorched earth, the poisoned water sources. She, on the other hand, was tracing the technological sinews of their attack, the manipulation of the very atmospheric currents that sustained the Skywood.

The implications were staggering. The Ashbound weren't just a disruptive force; they were a sophisticated network, capable of operating on multiple levels. They were simultaneously striking at the physical heart of the ecosystem and the technological veins that controlled its lifeblood. And their ultimate goal, as far as Mara could surmise from their radical rhetoric, was nothing less than the complete collapse of the current ecological order, paving the way for their envisioned, brutal rebirth.

She compiled a summary of her findings, detailing the precise energy frequencies used to manipulate the weather engines, the specific algorithms that appeared to have been subverted, and the projected outcomes of these continued manipulations: escalating droughts in some regions, catastrophic floods in others, widespread crop failure, and a general destabilization of the Skywood's delicate climate. It was a grim prognosis, a testament to the Ashbound's deep understanding of the systems they were targeting. They weren't simply smashing things; they were intelligently deconstructing them.

Mara initiated a secure communication link, her fingers flying across the holographic keyboard. She needed to share this information, to alert those who could act. But even as she drafted her urgent message, a sense of isolation washed over her. She was a scholar, a scientist, not a warrior. Her battles were fought with data and logic, not with staffs and ancient enchantments. Yet, she understood that in this escalating crisis, every skill, every perspective, was vital.

She considered the possibility that Cael might already be aware of the weather engines' involvement. His connection to the forest was profound; he could likely sense the unnatural disturbances more acutely than anyone. If he was indeed on the trail of the Ashbound, he would be drawn to the epicenters of their activity, and the weather engines, now weapons in their arsenal, would undoubtedly be among them.

The convergence of their investigations was not merely a matter of coincidence. It was an inevevitable consequence of the Ashbound's broad-spectrum assault. They were targeting the land, and they were targeting the technology that sustained it. Mara, with her intimate knowledge of the Skywood's intricate systems, and Cael, with his primal connection to its very essence, were both being pulled towards the same nexus of corruption.

Her analysis revealed a specific manipulation pattern originating from a series of defunct atmospheric monitoring stations in the western territories. These stations, long since decommissioned due to their outdated technology, were now showing anomalous energy spikes, consistent with the Ashbound's signature frequencies. It was a brilliant, yet terrifying, tactic. By utilizing abandoned infrastructure, they were effectively hiding their tracks, obscuring their manipulation of the much more prominent weather engines.

Mara meticulously mapped out the most likely points of ingress and egress for the Ashbound operatives, cross-referencing the energy readings with known Ashbound activity patterns in those regions. The data pointed towards a clandestine network of operations, utilizing the very fabric of the Skywood's infrastructure to facilitate their destructive agenda. She felt a surge of adrenaline mixed with apprehension. The Ashbound were more organized, more technologically adept, than she had initially feared. Their radical ideology was being translated into sophisticated, coordinated action.

She saved the updated report, its pages filled with complex diagrams and stark warnings. The convergence of her investigation with Cael's was no longer a theoretical possibility; it was a palpable certainty. Both of them, in their own distinct ways, were closing in on the heart of the Ashbound's operation. And as she looked at the projected map of the Skywood, her fingers hovering over the points of intense atmospheric disturbance, Mara understood that the shadow of the Ashbound was not just a localized threat; it was an encroaching darkness, threatening to engulf the entire

Skywood. Their path was no longer diverging, but rather, in the face of this escalating danger, irrevocably converging.

CHAPTER SEVEN

THE TRUTH OF THE ENGINES

The ancient schematics of the starstone weather engines were not merely blueprints; they were a labyrinth of celestial mechanics and arcane script, a testament to a civilization that understood the universe not just through observation, but through communion. Mara felt the weight of that understanding pressing down on her as she unrolled the holographic projections, each intricate line and symbol a whisper from a time when the Skywood's architects had woven the very fabric of the atmosphere with intention and power. Her fingers, still faintly smelling of ozone and stardust, traced the flowing curves that depicted the engines' primary conduits, designed to draw raw atmospheric energy from the upper reaches of the Skywood and refine it into life-giving currents.

It was a language she was only beginning to grasp. Her own studies had focused on the practical application of these energies – the delicate art of weather orchestration, the careful balancing of precipitation and sunlight. But these schematics spoke of a deeper, more fundamental purpose. They detailed the intrinsic properties of the starstones themselves, crystalline matrices that pulsed with captured starlight, acting as the engines' hearts. The diagrams showed how these stones, when aligned in specific geometric patterns, could resonate with the planet's own magnetic field, drawing and channeling energies that Mara had only ever theorized about.

The initial layers were straightforward enough, detailing the intake valves, the filtration chambers that scrubbed impurities from the incoming atmospheric streams, and the primary resonance chambers where the starstones were housed. She cross-referenced these sections with her own extensive knowledge of atmospheric physics and arcane energy manipulation, finding the principles to be elegant and, in their own way, terrifyingly powerful. The sheer scale of energy harnessed was immense, capable of influencing weather patterns across vast continents.

But as she delved deeper, the schematics began to reveal their more guarded secrets. Hidden within the seemingly standard diagrams were sub-layers of intricate inscriptions, almost invisible to the untrained eye. These were not mere technical annotations; they were coded directives, embedded enchantments designed to control the flow of energy with an almost sentient precision. Mara recognized some of the glyphs – ancient wards designed to prevent unauthorized access, archaic commands that dictated specific atmospheric responses to celestial alignments. It was like peeling back the layers of an onion, each one revealing a new, more complex truth.

She found a section depicting a series of secondary regulators, designed to fine-tune the output of the primary resonance chambers. The schematics showed these regulators intricately linked to what appeared to be a celestial clockwork, a mechanism that tracked the movements of not just the Skywood's moons, but of distant constellations. The implication was profound: the engines were not simply reacting to current atmospheric conditions; they were designed to anticipate and influence them based on a cosmic calendar. The creators hadn't just sought to control the weather; they had sought to harmonize the Skywood with the very rhythm of the cosmos.

This was where her own expertise began to fray at the edges. Her understanding of natural energy flows, of the predictable ebb and flow of atmospheric systems, was comprehensive. But these schematics described a level of manipulation that bordered on predetermination. The coded directives within the secondary regulators spoke of specific energy signatures to be amplified, of particular atmospheric frequencies to be generated, all tied to astrological conjunctions. It suggested a proactive, rather than reactive, approach to climate control.

Then came the encrypted data streams, revealed not by simply unrolling the schematics, but by a specific sequence of arcane gestures Mara had learned from a cryptic text on celestial cartography. The data appeared as shimmering, ephemeral glyphs, hovering just above the main diagrams. Deciphering them was a monumental task, requiring her to employ a blend of linguistic analysis, pattern recognition, and a touch of intuitive guesswork. The creators had clearly intended for their most profound secrets to be hidden, accessible only to those who possessed not just the knowledge, but the specific keys to unlock them.

These encrypted sections spoke of a contingency, a fail-safe, or perhaps, more disturbingly, a deliberate function that had been purposefully obscured. They detailed methods for weaponizing the starstone energy, for focusing it into destructive beams, for creating localized atmospheric phenomena of catastrophic proportions. The schematics showed how the resonance chambers could be overloaded, how the carefully calibrated energy flows could be inverted, turning the life-sustaining power of the engines into instruments of destruction.

One particular set of schematics, buried deep within a section detailing emergency power regulation, caught Mara's eye. It depicted a series of hidden conduits, branching off from the main energy flow, leading to what were labeled as "destabilization nodes." These nodes, according to the encrypted annotations, were designed to create micro-disruptions in the atmospheric equilibrium, subtle enough to go unnoticed by standard monitoring systems, but significant enough to amplify existing geological stresses or natural weather patterns. It was a chillingly precise form of environmental warfare.

She realized with a growing sense of dread that these schematics were not just a record of how the weather engines *worked*, but how they *could be used*. The creators, in their wisdom or their foresight, had built into the very heart of these magnificent machines the capacity for their own perversion. They had provided the blueprints for both creation and destruction, for harmony and for chaos.

The implications for her current investigation were immense. If the Ashbound had managed to access and decipher these schematics, they would have a roadmap to the Skywood's most vulnerable systems. The encrypted directives, the hidden conduits, the destabilization nodes – these were precisely the elements that would allow for the kind of targeted sabotage she had been observing. It wasn't just about overriding the system; it was about exploiting its deepest, most concealed functionalities.

Mara spent hours tracing the pathways described in these hidden compartments. She discovered a complex network of secondary power relays, designed to reroute energy to the destabilization nodes. These relays were activated by specific harmonic frequencies, frequencies that were incredibly difficult to generate without the proper arcane knowledge or technology. The Ashbound, she deduced, must have either acquired such knowledge or developed a method to mimic these frequencies.

She found a section that detailed the 'Aetherial Lock,' a safeguard designed to prevent the engines from drawing energy directly from the volatile aether, the raw, unformed magical energy that permeated the spaces between worlds. This lock, however, had a bypass mechanism, a series of temporal sequences tied to rare celestial alignments. If these alignments were present, and the correct arcane sequence was initiated, the Aetherial Lock could be disengaged, allowing access to a far more potent, and far more dangerous, source of power. The schematics provided the sequences, the precise celestial timings, and the arcane incantations required to achieve this.

The sheer depth of the knowledge required to understand and implement these schematics was staggering. It spoke of a civilization that lived in intimate symbiosis with the forces of nature and the arcane, a people who understood the universe as a tapestry of interconnected energies. And it also spoke of a profound caution, a deep-seated awareness of the potential for misuse. The creators had not simply built powerful tools; they had built tools with inherent dangers, and they had, in their own way, left warnings etched into the very fabric of their designs.

Mara meticulously documented her findings, her stylus flying across the interface, creating a parallel set of annotations that highlighted the potential for misuse. She marked the hidden conduits, the destabilization nodes, the Aetherial Lock bypass sequences. It was a grim undertaking, transforming the elegant architecture of the weather engines into a blueprint for their own subversion.

She noticed that certain sections of the schematics were deliberately incomplete, faded, or obscured by what appeared to be intentionally corrupted data. It was as if the creators had intentionally left some aspects of the system's design ambiguous, perhaps as a final layer of protection, or perhaps to allow for future adaptation and evolution. This ambiguity, however, also presented a challenge for Mara. It meant that even with the schematics, a complete understanding of the engines' capabilities and vulnerabilities was not guaranteed. The Ashbound, too, would face these gaps in knowledge, and their attempts to fill them could lead to further, unpredictable consequences.

One particularly challenging section involved a series of rotating starstone arrays. The schematics showed them shifting and reconfiguring based on an intricate dance of gravitational forces and arcane resonance. The exact alignment required for optimal energy extraction, and more importantly, for the specific manipulation of localized atmospheric phenomena, was incredibly complex. The encrypted data suggested that even minor deviations in these alignments could lead to unintended consequences, such as localized energy surges or atmospheric instability.

Mara began to hypothesize about the Ashbound's methods. Had they gained access to the full schematics, or only partial fragments? Were they working with a complete understanding of the encryption, or were they fumbling in the dark, relying on guesswork and brute force? The targeted nature of the sabotage suggested a sophisticated level of understanding, but the unpredictability of some of the atmospheric anomalies hinted at incomplete knowledge.

She focused on a particular diagram depicting the 'Harmonic Weaver,' a component responsible for synchronizing the energy output of multiple engines. The schematics revealed a highly complex calibration process, requiring precise adjustments to individual starstone frequencies and resonance chamber pressures. The encrypted notes associated with this component warned of catastrophic feedback loops if the synchronization was not maintained, potentially leading to chain reactions that could destabilize entire regions.

The architects of the Skywood had clearly foreseen the potential for misuse. They had embedded layers of security, both technical and arcane, designed to safeguard the immense power of the weather engines. But they had also, it seemed, provided the very knowledge that could be used to circumvent those safeguards. It was a paradox that spoke volumes about the nature of power itself – its inherent duality, its capacity for both immense good and terrible destruction.

Mara continued her painstaking work, her mind a whirlwind of ancient symbols, arcane formulas, and celestial calculations. The schematics were a puzzle, a testament to a lost civilization's brilliance and foresight, and a chilling forewarning of the forces that now sought to exploit it. Each decoded inscription, each unraveled diagram, brought her closer to understanding the mechanics of the Ashbound's assault, and with that understanding, the terrifying potential for what lay ahead. The truth of the engines was not just in their function, but in their latent capacity for disruption, a capacity that had been meticulously, and ominously, laid bare.

The revelation that the starstone weather engines were not purely instruments of ecological stewardship, but also conduits for profound atmospheric manipulation, settled over Mara like a shroud of mist. It wasn't just that the ancient architects possessed the knowledge to *restore* balance; they had also mastered the art of *imposing* it, of dictating the very breath of the Skywood. The schematics, once viewed as blueprints for benevolent terraforming, now pulsed with a more complex, and unsettling, purpose. The intricate designs weren't solely about channeling life-giving rains or dispelling destructive storms for the planet's well-being. Instead, they detailed precise mechanisms for cultivating specific crops through optimized sunlight and moisture, ensuring bountiful harvests that could sustain vast populations, or conversely, withholding such boons to exert pressure. The architects had the power to sculpt the very climate to their will, a dominion over nature that was both awe-inspiring and deeply disquieting.

This wasn't merely a technical capability; it was a philosophical stance. The existence of such finely tuned control systems suggested a deeply ingrained desire by the Skywood's founders to actively shape their environment, not just live in harmony with it. They had sought to become conductors of the planet's atmospheric symphony, rather than mere listeners. The diagrams laid bare the pathways by which specific atmospheric conditions could be induced – the precise manipulation of temperature gradients for faster plant growth, the controlled dissemination of moisture for arid regions, even the subtle alteration of wind patterns to direct airborne pollutants away from settled areas. These were not simply defensive measures against natural chaos; they were proactive interventions, designed to optimize and direct the natural world towards predefined goals. This level of control, while beneficial on the surface, carried an inherent risk, a temptation towards absolute dominion.

Mara found herself tracing a series of secondary conduits, meticulously routed from the primary resonance chambers towards specialized dispersal units. These units, unlike the broad-reaching atmospheric regulators, were designed for localized effect. The accompanying annotations, written in a more colloquial, yet still archaic, script, spoke of "Nourishment Cycles" and "Growth Augmentation." It was clear that these systems were intended to guarantee agricultural success, acting as a constant, reliable bulwark against famine. However, the same mechanisms, with a slight recalibration of energy output and frequency, could just as easily be repurposed. The power to accelerate growth was, by its very nature, the power to stunt it, to create droughts or floods on a micro-level that could devastate specific regions or agricultural endeavors. This duality was present in almost every aspect of the engine's design; every function that could nurture life also held the potential to extinguish it.

The encrypted sections, particularly those detailing the 'Aetherial Lock' bypass, offered a chilling glimpse into the potential for weaponization. While the primary function was to draw from the planet's inherent energies, the ability to tap into the volatile aether, the raw, untamed essence of creation, hinted at capabilities far beyond mere weather modification. The energies channeled from the aether were described as "unbound and transformative," capable of manifesting phenomena on a scale that dwarfed terrestrial weather. The schematics hinted at the ability to generate localized storms of immense power, not just for agricultural benefit, but for defense, or indeed, offense. This was not the gentle guidance of atmospheric currents; this was the unleashing of primal forces.

This realization brought a stark historical perspective to her current predicament. The Ashbound, in their destructive campaign, were not an anomaly, but a continuation of a long-standing human, or rather, sentient, tendency. Across countless civilizations and eons, there had been an undeniable impulse to bend the natural world to one's will, to harness its power for human – or sentient – ambition. From the earliest irrigation systems to the grandest terraforming projects, the drive for control had always been present. The Skywood's founders, in their immense wisdom, had created tools that reflected this duality inherent in their own nature. They had built for sustenance and for protection, for abundance and for dominion, embedding within their creations the very choices that had plagued sentient societies throughout history: whether to foster life or to wield power.

Mara's fingers hovered over a schematic depicting what appeared to be an "Atmospheric Sculpting Matrix." It was a complex arrangement of resonant crystals and energy conduits that, when activated in specific sequences, could allegedly alter the composition of the air itself, thinning it for increased solar radiation or thickening it to retain warmth. The annotations spoke of creating "idealized atmospheric conditions," a phrase that sent a shiver down her spine. This was not about adapting to the environment; it was about forcing the environment to adapt to the creators. The potential for manipulating not just weather, but the very atmospheric suitability for life in certain regions, was laid bare. It was a level of control that implied not just seasonal management, but the fundamental alteration of entire ecosystems, potentially for the exclusive benefit of a select few.

The implication was profound: the architects of the Skywood, in their quest for a stable and prosperous world, had also forged the tools for its subjugation. They had built the ultimate climate control system, one that could ensure perfect growing seasons and protect against natural disasters, but also one that could starve enemies, create uninhabitable zones, or even engineer specific atmospheric conditions to favor one species or group over another. The very engines designed to sustain life could, with a shift in intent and a re-coding of their arcane directives, become instruments of death and ecological devastation. This historical precedent of seeking control, of valuing dominance over pure symbiosis, echoed through the schematics, a warning from the past about the inherent dangers of unchecked ambition. The Skywood's architects, in their advanced understanding, had not only grasped the mechanics of the atmosphere but also the darker impulses of the beings who wielded such power.

The hum of the Skywood engines was a constant companion, a low thrum that vibrated through the very bedrock of the control chamber. Mara had spent cycles deciphering the ancient texts, piecing together the original intent of the architects, but now, her focus shifted from what *was* to what *is*. She ran a diagnostic sweep, her specialized tools sifting through the torrent of data, searching for anomalies, for deviations from the pristine, balanced operation the schematics implied. The air in the chamber, usually thick with the scent of ozone and damp stone, felt charged, expectant, as if the engines themselves were holding their breath.

Her gaze fell upon a cluster of energy conduits, their crystalline matrices glowing with a steady, rhythmic pulse. According to the blueprints, these should have been drawing power from the planet's geothermal core, a constant, predictable flow. But the readouts told a different story. There were fluctuations, sudden spikes and dips that didn't align with any known natural phenomena or the designed operational parameters. It was like watching the steady heartbeat of a healthy organism suddenly stutter and race. This wasn't the natural ebb and flow of energy; this was a disruption, a deliberate interference.

"There," she murmured, her finger tracing a jagged line on the holographic display. A distinct energy signature, alien to the Skywood's intrinsic resonance, flared and then vanished, leaving behind a faint, residual imprint. It was like a whisper of foreign magic in a sacred grove, an unmistakable sign that something, or someone, had been here. This wasn't the work of a rogue element within the planet's natural systems; this was the mark of an outsider, an intentional intrusion. The thought sent a cold tendril of dread coiling in her gut.

She cross-referenced the aberrant signatures with the Skywood's historical logs, meticulously archived within the same archival system. For cycles, the logs had been a testament to the architects' genius, a record of perfect atmospheric equilibrium. But buried within the seamless narrative of planetary stewardship, she found faint traces, subtle deviations that had been meticulously scrubbed, or perhaps, cleverly disguised. It was like finding a single, out-of-place brushstroke on a masterpiece, a tiny imperfection that spoke volumes about the artist's state of mind, or in this case, their clandestine actions.

The anomalies weren't random. They clustered around specific engine nodes, often coinciding with periods of intense meteorological activity or, more alarmingly, with shifts in agricultural output across the continent. The pattern was too consistent to be accidental. Someone was not just observing the engines; they were actively *using* them, manipulating their intricate mechanisms for a purpose that was far from the architects' original benevolent design. The proof was irrefutable, etched in the very energy currents that powered their world.

She zoomed in on a schematic depicting the primary resonance chamber, the heart of the Skywood engine. The schematics showed a delicate balance of harmonic frequencies, a symphony of energies that created the planet's stable climate. But now, she overlayed the real-time energy readings, and the discord was palpable. Certain frequencies were being amplified, others suppressed, creating a ripple effect that distorted the natural atmospheric processes. It was akin to a musician deliberately striking wrong notes, not out of ignorance, but with malicious intent to shatter the harmony.

"They're not just influencing the weather," Mara breathed, her voice raspy. "They're *forcing* it. They're overriding the architects' safeguards, rewriting the very code of the climate." The implications were staggering. If someone could manipulate the engines to this degree, they could create devastating droughts, trigger unnatural floods, or even foster plagues of agricultural blight, all while making it appear as a natural, albeit catastrophic, event. The architects had built a system capable of nurturing life; it seemed someone had found a way to turn it into a weapon of mass destruction.

Her mind flashed back to the tales of the Ashbound, the whispers of their unnatural resilience, their ability to thrive in the harshest of conditions. Could this be connected? Had the Ashbound, or whatever entity now commanded them, discovered this hidden power? The thought was both terrifying and galvanizing. The ecological disasters weren't random acts of nature; they were calculated assaults, meticulously orchestrated through the very engines meant to protect the planet.

She meticulously documented each anomaly, tagging the specific energy signatures and their correlated timestamps. These were not mere technical glitches; they were fingerprints. The foreign energy signatures were distinct, almost like a unique dialect spoken by a particular group of manipulators. They had a specific quality, a sharp, almost aggressive resonance that stood in stark contrast to the Skywood's smooth, inherent power. It was the difference between the gentle caress of a breeze and the brutal force of a gale.

Mara's investigation into the historical logs had been a search for understanding; this was a hunt for perpetrators. The architects had foreseen the potential for misuse, embedding fail-safes and protocols within the engine's core programming. But these were not the remnants of natural decay or accidental malfunction. The modifications were precise, surgical, suggesting a deep, intimate knowledge of the engines' inner workings. This wasn't a brute-force attempt to break in; it was an insider, or someone who had gained insider knowledge, carefully altering the systems from within.

She identified a recurring pattern of energy surges originating from a specific set of external input arrays. These arrays were designed to receive environmental data from across the globe, allowing the engines to adapt and respond to changing conditions. But the data being fed into these arrays was corrupted, falsified. The engines were being fed false information, blinded by a manufactured reality, and in response, they were enacting harmful directives. It was a sophisticated form of deception, a digital poisoning of the planet's atmospheric brain.

"They're feeding the engines lies," she whispered, the realization chilling her to the bone. "They're telling the Skywood that the world needs this destruction, that these unnatural conditions are necessary for survival." The sheer audacity of it was breathtaking. To manipulate the very foundation of their civilization, to turn the benevolent giants into instruments of their own undoing, required a level of cunning and depravity she had only encountered in the darkest of legends.

The schematics, once a source of awe and wonder, now felt like a testament to a profound betrayal. The architects, in their pursuit of ultimate balance, had inadvertently created the perfect tool for ultimate control, and it seemed that control had fallen into the wrong hands. Her hands trembled as she isolated one particularly potent energy signature, a raw, volatile waveform that pulsed with a malevolent intensity. This was not a subtle manipulation; this was a declaration of war waged through the very air they breathed.

She remembered a passage from the ancient texts, a cryptic warning about the "Whispers of the Unseen," entities or forces that sought to twist the natural order for their own gain. At the time, she had dismissed it as allegory, a cautionary tale. Now, it felt terrifyingly real. These energy signatures, this deliberate corruption of the Skywood's sacred purpose – this was the tangible manifestation of those ancient whispers.

The tampering wasn't confined to a single engine or a single region. Her scans revealed similar anomalies across multiple Skywood nodes, suggesting a coordinated, widespread operation. This wasn't the work of a lone saboteur; it was a systemic assault, a carefully planned campaign to dismantle the world's ecological stability from the inside out. The sheer scale of the operation implied a significant organization, resources, and a motive powerful enough to justify such catastrophic actions.

She zoomed out, viewing the network of Skywood engines as a single, interconnected entity. The anomalies pulsed like a spreading infection, weakening the entire system. The architects had designed these engines to be resilient, capable of self-correction and adaptation. But this level of sustained, targeted interference was pushing them to their limits, and perhaps, beyond.

Mara felt a surge of determination harden within her. She had come seeking knowledge, but she had found evidence. The hope that the ecological disasters were a natural cycle, a phase of the planet's own complex rhythm, had been a comforting illusion. The truth, however painful, was far more vital. There were active agents at work, entities driven by a will to dominate, to destroy, and they were using the very heart of their world against them. Her path was now clear: identify these perpetrators, understand their motives, and find a way to sever their connection to the Skywood engines before it was too late. The manipulators had left their mark, and now, it was her turn to leave hers – in the form of resistance. She began to compile her findings, not just for her own records, but for the wider council, for anyone who would listen. The era of passive observation was over. The era of active pursuit had begun.

The air thrummed with a primal, discordant energy, a stark contrast to the steady, subterranean hum of the Skywood engines Mara had been studying. Cael found himself on the fringes of a desolate plateau, the wind whipping dust into his eyes and stinging his exposed skin. This was not a place of calculated manipulation, but of raw, unbridled force. He had tracked the peculiar energy signature – sharp, aggressive, unlike the subtle tampering Mara had detected – to this very spot. He hadn't anticipated finding its source so readily, nor in such terrifying company.

They emerged from the swirling dust not like soldiers, but like a plague of locusts descending upon barren land. The Ashbound. The name itself evoked images of scorched earth and desperate survival, but seeing them, truly seeing them, was a different matter entirely. Their skin was a mottled grey-brown, like sun-baked clay, etched with the harsh lines of constant exposure and a life lived on the edge of endurance. Their eyes, sunk deep within their hollowed faces, burned with an unnerving intensity, a fanaticism that seemed to consume them from within. They wore simple, utilitarian tunics woven from coarse, dark fibers, stained with what he suspected was a mixture of mud, ash, and something far more visceral. Some carried crude weapons – sharpened obsidian shards lashed to wooden shafts, heavy clubs studded with jagged rocks. Others, however, seemed to rely on their bare hands, their calloused fingers already curled into fists.

Cael drew his own weapon, a sturdy blade forged from starlight ore, its edge shimmering with contained power. He had expected a confrontation, but the sheer ferocity of their charge caught him slightly off guard. They didn't strategize; they simply *attacked*, a wave of desperate, driven beings intent on overwhelming him through sheer numbers and brutal efficiency. Their roars were not cries of battle, but guttural expressions of a primal rage, fueled by a conviction that was both chilling and, in its own twisted way, absolute.

The first Ashbound he faced was a hulking brute, his face a mask of snarling determination. He swung a massive club, aiming to shatter Cael's guard and his bones with a single, devastating blow. Cael sidestepped, the wind of the club's passage a tangible force against his side. He deflected the next swing with a clang, the impact jarring his arm to the shoulder. The obsidian edge of another Ashbound's blade glinted as it slashed at his legs, forcing him to hop back, his heart hammering against his ribs.

He fought defensively, trying to keep them at bay, to create enough space to analyze their tactics, their weaknesses. But there were no apparent weaknesses, only a relentless, unwavering drive. They moved with a strange, almost disjointed grace, their bodies adapting to the uneven terrain with an instinct born of a lifetime of hardship. They seemed unfazed by pain, their injuries appearing to fuel their fury rather than diminish it. One Ashbound took a deep gash across his arm from Cael's blade, yet continued his charge, his eyes fixed solely on Cael, a terrifyingly vacant expression on his contorted face.

This was not the calculated violence of a trained soldier, nor the opportunistic savagery of a common brigand. This was something... purer, in its horrific intent. They believed, Cael realized with a dawning horror, that what they were doing was not just justified, but *necessary*. Their conviction was as sharp and deadly as the obsidian shards they wielded. He saw it in the way they threw themselves into the fray, in the utter disregard for their own well-being, in the fanatical gleam in their eyes.

He managed to disarm one of his attackers, sending a wicked-looking obsidian dagger skittering across the dusty ground. The Ashbound, stripped of his weapon, didn't falter. He lunged forward, attempting to grapple with Cael, his breath hot and fetid against Cael's face. Cael pushed him back, but the man stumbled only to be immediately replaced by another, then another. It was like fighting a hydra, an endless tide of hostile bodies.

He could feel his own energy draining, not just from the physical exertion, but from the sheer psychic weight of their fanaticism. It was a palpable force, a suffocating blanket of absolute belief that seemed to drain the very hope from the air. He saw a woman among them, her face gaunt but her eyes blazing, wielding a burning brand as if it were a sacred artifact. She didn't strike with it, but rather, held it aloft, its flames dancing wildly, a beacon of their destructive creed.

As he parried a blow that would have cleaved his skull, Cael caught a glimpse of something beyond the immediate chaos. In the distance, beyond the swirling dust and the guttural cries, he saw it. A faint, shimmering distortion in the air, a subtle ripple that mirrored the aggressive energy signature he had been tracking. It was emanating from a cluster of strange, crude devices that had been erected on a nearby rise, structures of twisted metal and what looked like petrified wood, pulsating with that same jarring energy. They were crude, yet undeniably powerful, and they seemed to be the focal point of the Ashbound's aggression.

The connection slammed into Cael with the force of a physical blow. These devices, these "engines" of the Ashbound, were not just a source of power; they were instruments of their will. And their will, as Cael was now experiencing firsthand, was terrifyingly destructive. He saw one of the Ashbound raise a clenched fist towards the sky, and with a sickening lurch, a torrent of acrid, black rain began to fall from an unnaturally darkened cloud that seemed to coalesce from nowhere. The rain hissed as it struck the dry earth, leaving behind blackened, smoking patches. The Ashbound around him let out a collective, triumphant roar.

He had heard the whispers, the hushed tales of the Ashbound's ability to endure hardship, to thrive in the most desolate environments. He had dismissed them as folklore, as exaggerations of their resilience. But this... this was not resilience. This was an active, aggressive manipulation of the very environment, a deliberate act of ecological warfare. The Ashbound were not just surviving; they were *forcing* the world to their grim image, twisting its natural processes to suit their destructive agenda.

The encounter was a brutal awakening. The Ashbound were not simply a displaced people seeking a home; they were a force of nature, bent on reshaping the world through violence and unwavering zeal. Their conviction was their shield, their desperation their weapon, and their crude, energy-wielding devices were the instruments of their chosen apocalypse. Cael fought with a newfound urgency, not just to survive, but to understand. He had to find a way to stop them, to sever their connection to these destructive engines before their chilling vision of a scorched and barren world became reality.

He felt a sharp pain in his side, a searing burn as an obsidian blade found its mark. He gritted his teeth, the taste of his own blood filling his mouth. He kicked his attacker away, the man stumbling but not falling, his eyes still locked on Cael with that same terrifying, unyielding fire. This wasn't just a fight for his life; it was a fight for the planet itself, a desperate stand against a tide of destructive fervor. The Ashbound were a testament to the terrifying power of belief, and their belief was in ruin. He had to counter that belief, not with more violence, but with a deeper understanding, and a resolve that burned just as fiercely, but with a purpose to preserve, not to destroy. He pushed off the ground, his injured side throbbing, and met the next charging Ashbound head-on, his gaze no longer just defensive, but fiercely determined. He would not let their conviction win.

The persistent hum of the Skywood engines, once a comforting sign of life and intricate engineering, now felt like a prelude to a dirge. Mara, hunched over her console in the sterile glow of the research bay, traced the energetic anomalies with a growing sense of dread. The patterns were unmistakable, subtle shifts in the engine's rhythmic pulse, like a perfectly composed symphony suddenly marred by a discordant note. It wasn't a malfunction; it was interference, a deliberate, insidious manipulation. Her instruments, designed to monitor the Skywood's delicate ecological balance, were now registering something far more sinister.

She zoomed in on a cluster of data points, a sharp spike that had appeared during her last diagnostic sweep. It was localized, specific, and utterly alien to the Skywood's inherent energy signature. This wasn't the gentle influence of the Whispering Grove, nor the predictable oscillations of the geothermal vents. This was a jagged intrusion, a wound being carved into the very heart of their world's lifeblood. The source, according to her readings, was originating from the desolate eastern rim, a region notorious for its harsh climate and its sparse, hardy inhabitants – the Ashbound.

The Ashbound. The name alone conjured images of hardship, of a people perpetually on the brink, surviving on the fringes of a world that offered them little. Tales of their resilience were common, whispered by traders and scavengers who had ventured into those unforgiving lands. But Mara's data suggested something far beyond mere survival. It hinted at an active, aggressive engagement with the very forces that sustained the Skywood. The thought sent a shiver down her spine, a cold premonition that the Ashbound were not simply victims of their environment, but architects of its destruction.

She cross-referenced the anomaly with seismic readings, atmospheric composition charts, and energy flux maps. The pieces, when forced together, began to form a disturbing image. The disruptions coincided with localized shifts in air quality, a marked increase in particulate matter, and subtle, yet significant, fluctuations in the planet's magnetic field. It was as if something was actively *forcing* the natural world to bend to its will, twisting its inherent energies into something corrupted. The Skywood engines, designed to harmonize with and regulate these energies, were being used as conduits, their sophisticated mechanisms repurposed for a more destructive purpose.

Mara felt a familiar knot of frustration tighten in her stomach. Her father, a brilliant if eccentric engineer, had always spoken of the Skywood's delicate equilibrium, the constant dance between the planet's raw power and the Skywood's gentle guidance. He had warned of those who would seek to exploit such power, those who saw only brute force where he saw intricate harmony. Now, it seemed, his fears were materializing. The Ashbound, driven by desperation or some darker ideology, were not just surviving in the harsh lands; they were actively weaponizing them.

She spent hours poring over ancient texts, searching for any mention of the Ashbound's connection to powerful energies, any lore that might explain their capabilities. Most accounts were fragmented, tales of a nomadic people who had been driven to the eastern wastes by a cataclysm long forgotten. There were scattered references to their affinity for the earth, their ability to draw sustenance from barren soil, but nothing to suggest the sophisticated manipulation of energies her instruments were detecting.

Then, a name surfaced in a tattered journal, a reference to a "Shaper" among the Ashbound, a figure who could "command the dust and the wind." It was a poetic description, but coupled with her data, it resonated with an unsettling clarity. The Ashbound weren't just enduring the harshness of their land; they were *commanding* it, bending its volatile energies to their will through some unknown means, with the Skywood engines acting as unwilling amplifiers.

The realization gnawed at her. If the Ashbound were indeed manipulating the engines, what was their ultimate goal? Were they seeking to disrupt the Skywood's life-giving functions, to plunge the fertile lands into the same desolation they endured? Or was there a more complex agenda at play, a desperate attempt to reclaim something lost, perhaps even to recreate their lost homeland by force?

She decided to take a calculated risk. Her instruments could only offer so much from a distance. She needed to get closer to the source of the interference, to observe the Ashbound's activities firsthand. The eastern rim was a dangerous territory, a place where few ventured willingly, and fewer still returned. But the implications of her findings were too dire to ignore. The Skywood's delicate balance was under threat, and the Ashbound, armed with their unique connection to the land and the stolen power of the Skywood's engines, seemed to be the immediate perpetrators.

She packed a compact, multi-spectrum scanner, a few days' worth of ration packs, and a concealed energy dampener – a device designed to mask her own energetic signature. Her journey would be fraught with peril, but the alternative – allowing this unseen sabotage to continue unchecked – was far more terrifying. She would tread carefully, observe from the shadows, and try to understand the true nature of the Ashbound's campaign before it escalated beyond any hope of repair. The Skywood's future, and perhaps the future of the entire continent, rested on her ability to uncover the truth behind the engines' corrupted song.

Miles away, across the wind-swept plains and jagged canyons, Cael found himself locked in a desperate struggle for survival. The Ashbound, a force of raw, unbridled fury, had descended upon him with a ferocity that bordered on the supernatural. Their obsidian weapons flashed, their guttural roars echoed across the desolate plateau, and their eyes burned with a terrifying conviction. He fought with the precision of a trained warrior, his starlight ore blade a blur of shimmering defense, but he was being pushed to his absolute limit.

He had tracked the aggressive energy signature to this very location, a desolate stretch of land where the very air seemed to crackle with raw power. He had expected a confrontation, but the sheer, overwhelming numbers and the fanatical zeal of the Ashbound had caught him off guard. They didn't fight with strategy; they attacked with a primal, all-consuming rage, a wave of bodies driven by an unshakeable belief.

As he parried a brutal blow, Cael caught a glimpse of the source of this volatile energy. On a nearby rise, crude structures of twisted metal and petrified wood pulsed with that same jarring frequency. They were engines, unlike anything he had ever seen, emanating a raw, untamed power that seemed to fuel the Ashbound's aggression. He understood then that these were not mere weapons, but instruments of their will, extensions of their desperate, destructive creed.

One of the Ashbound, a gaunt woman with eyes that blazed like embers, raised a burning brand aloft. With a sickening lurch, a torrent of acrid, black rain began to fall from a rapidly coalescing cloud. The rain hissed as it struck the parched earth, leaving behind smoking, blackened scars. The Ashbound around her let out a collective, triumphant roar. This was not mere survival; this was ecological warfare. They were not adapting to their environment; they were forcing it to bend to their grim vision.

Cael felt a searing pain in his side as an obsidian blade found its mark. He gritted his teeth, the taste of his own blood filling his mouth. He kicked his attacker away, but another immediately took his place. It was like fighting a hydra, an endless tide of hostile bodies. He was running on fumes, his energy draining not just from the physical exertion but from the sheer psychic weight of their fanaticism.

He needed to understand *why*. Why this destruction? Why this rage? He dodged a clumsy swing, his mind racing. The energy signature he had been tracking was connected to the Skywood engines, yet the Ashbound's methods were so crude, so raw. It was a perversion of the Skywood's intricate design, a brutal hijacking of its benevolent purpose. Could they truly be so lost to despair that they would seek to inflict it on others?

As he deflected another blow, his gaze swept over the chaotic battlefield. His senses, honed by years of tracking and combat, registered a faint, almost imperceptible distortion in the air, far from the immediate Ashbound encampment. It was a subtle ripple, a localized shimmer that didn't quite fit the raw, chaotic energy emanating from the Ashbound's crude engines. It was different, cleaner, and eerily familiar. It felt... controlled.

He knew, with a certainty that settled deep in his bones, that this was not just a random encounter. He had been drawn here, and he suspected the Ashbound had been too. This desolate plateau was becoming a nexus, a point where converging forces were about to collide. The Ashbound's raw, destructive power was undeniable, but this other energy, this subtle hum that he could now faintly detect beneath the din of battle, spoke of something else. Something calculated. Something... engineered.

He managed to disarm an Ashbound, sending a wicked obsidian dagger skittering across the dust. The man didn't flinch, lunging forward with his bare hands. Cael pushed him back, the encounter only reinforcing his growing conviction. There was a method to this madness, a deeper layer he was missing. The Ashbound were the visible threat, the immediate storm, but what was brewing beneath the surface? What were they truly fighting for, and who was orchestrating this devastating display?

He needed to disengage, to follow that subtler energy signature. But the Ashbound were relentless, their eyes fixed on him with an unwavering, almost hypnotic intensity. He was a symbol to them, an intruder, an obstacle to their desperate cause. He fought defensively, creating space with sharp, precise movements, his starlight ore blade singing a song of resistance. Each parry, each sidestep, was a testament to his skill, but also a desperate attempt to buy himself time.

He saw it then, a flicker of movement on the periphery of his vision. A figure, silhouetted against the harsh, bruised sky, moving with an unnerving fluidity that was utterly alien to the Ashbound's jerky, desperate movements. This newcomer was not part of the Ashbound horde. Their presence was subtle, almost ephemeral, yet their energy signature pulsed with that same controlled, almost clinical precision that Cael had detected.

He blocked a brutal overhead swing, the impact reverberating up his arm. The Ashbound's eyes, sunken and filled with a disturbing gleam, were locked onto him with an unyielding fire. But Cael's attention was now divided. His warrior's instincts screamed of immediate danger from the Ashbound surrounding him, yet his explorer's curiosity, his innate drive to understand, was pulling him towards that distant, enigmatic figure.

The raw power of the Ashbound was a force of nature unleashed, a primal scream of desperation. But this other energy, the one that mirrored the subtle tampering Mara had detected in the Skywood engines, felt different. It felt like a scalpel, precisely cutting into the world's vital systems. He had heard whispers of Ashbound shamans who could commune with the earth, but this felt far more advanced, far more... technological.

He needed to retreat, to regroup, to follow that subtler trail. The Ashbound were a symptom, a violent manifestation of a deeper disease. He could fight them, he could even defeat them, but if he didn't understand the root cause, this conflict would simply repeat itself, perhaps on a grander, more devastating scale.

With a surge of desperate strength, Cael feinted left, then spun right, breaking free from the immediate scrum. He didn't run, but moved with a calculated pace, creating distance between himself and the enraged Ashbound. Their roars of frustration followed him, a chorus of primal fury. He ignored them, his senses now solely focused on that faint, shimmering distortion in the air, that subtle hum of controlled power. It was leading him away from the Ashbound's desperate battle, towards something more intricate, more insidious.

He realized, with a jolt, that the energy signature he was tracking was resonating with the Skywood engines in a way that the Ashbound's crude devices were not. The Ashbound were amplifying a destructive force, but this other energy was subtly *altering* the existing flow, rerouting it, corrupting it from within. This was the work of someone who understood the Skywood's systems, someone who could manipulate them with a level of precision that bordered on the elegant.

He ventured further into the desolate landscape, the wind whipping his cloak around him. The Ashbound, seemingly content to defend their territory, didn't pursue him aggressively, their attention perhaps more focused on the immediate threat he represented, or perhaps their handlers had other directives. He caught another glimpse of that shimmering distortion, now clearer, more defined. It was emanating from a small, almost camouflaged structure nestled between two jagged rock formations. It was too small to be a Skywood engine, yet the energy it pulsed with was undeniably connected.

As he approached, the air grew heavy, charged with an unseen force. The structure itself was a marvel of efficiency, a blend of what appeared to be salvaged Skywood components and native, petrified wood, intricately woven together. It was a junction, a conduit, designed to intercept and redirect the Skywood's vital energies. And standing beside it, a solitary figure cloaked in shadow, was the source of the controlled manipulation.

Cael stilled, his hand resting on the hilt of his blade. He could feel the Ashbound's raw power behind him, a chaotic tide of fury. But before him was something far more complex, a web of deception being woven with precision and intent. His path had led him from the brutal battlefield to this hidden nexus, and he knew, with a certainty that chilled him to the bone, that the truth of the engines lay not just in their brute force, but in this subtle, insidious corruption. The convergence of their separate investigations was happening now, on this desolate, wind-scoured plateau. The separate threads of his investigation and Mara's were about to intertwine, and the fate of the Skywood hung precariously in the balance. He had to confront this shadowy figure, had to understand the mind that could orchestrate such a devastating betrayal of the Skywood's purpose. The Ashbound were the hammer, but this was the hand that wielded it.

CHAPTER EIGHT
DRASTIC MEASURES

The wind howled a mournful dirge across the scarred earth, mirroring the turmoil in Cael's gut. Each gust carried with it the scent of ash and decay, a constant, cloying reminder of the forest's slow death. He stood on the precipice of the great chasm, the very wound that had bled the life from the surrounding lands, and felt the weight of his oath pressing down on him like a physical burden. His role was to protect, to preserve, to be a bulwark against the encroaching darkness. But what did one do when the darkness was not an external enemy, but a creeping rot from within?

He watched the last vestiges of the Skywood's canopy, once a vibrant tapestry of emerald and gold, now a dull, skeletal filigree against the bruised twilight sky. The great engines, the heart of their world, throbbed with a sick, irregular rhythm, their usual song of life now a feverish, rasping cough. Mara's reports, delivered with a growing urgency, painted a grim picture: the vital energies of the land were being siphoned, twisted, and corrupted. Not by a direct assault, but by a subtle, insidious manipulation that gnawed at the Skywood's foundations. The Ashbound, driven by their desperation and misguided fury, were the visible instruments, but the true architects remained shrouded in mystery, their motives as opaque as the poisoned rain that sometimes fell from the sky.

He had spent the last cycle in council with the elders, his voice raw from impassioned pleas, his arguments met with the predictable inertia of tradition and protocol. They spoke of appeasement, of negotiation, of understanding the Ashbound's plight. They cited ancient treaties, protocols for dealing with the marginalized, and the paramount importance of consensus. But Cael saw only the dying trees, the receding life, the desperate cries of the land itself. Consensus. The word tasted like ash in his mouth. How long did it take for a forest to die of thirst while the water purifiers debated the merits of a new filtration system?

His hand tightened around the hilt of his starlight ore blade, the familiar weight a small comfort against the gnawing unease. He was a protector, sworn to uphold the balance, and the balance was tipping, irrevocably. The elders, steeped in centuries of tradition, seemed incapable of grasping the swiftness of their decline. They saw a problem to be solved through diplomacy; Cael saw a contagion that demanded immediate, surgical intervention. He had argued, pleaded, even threatened, but his words had fallen on deaf ears. The weight of his duty felt heavier than ever, a crushing responsibility that threatened to suffocate him.

He recalled the ferocity of the Ashbound he had encountered on the eastern rim, their eyes burning with a fanaticism that chilled him to the bone. They were not mere brigands or starving refugees; they were soldiers in a war, wielding instruments of destruction he barely understood. And behind them, he suspected, lurked a more calculating mind, one that understood the Skywood's intricate systems and could twist them to its own dark purpose. The subtle energy signature he had detected, the one that felt so different from the Ashbound's raw power, haunted his thoughts. It was a whisper of sophisticated sabotage, a chilling counterpoint to the land's desperate cries.

He remembered his father's words, spoken years ago when Cael was just a young initiate, full of naive idealism. "The Skywood is a living thing, Cael," his father had said, his voice filled with a reverence that Cael had only begun to truly understand. "It breathes, it feels, it suffers. And like any living thing, it can be wounded. But it can also heal, if given the chance. The greatest threat comes not from those who would tear it down outright, but from those who would subtly poison its wellsprings." His father's face, etched with the wisdom of a lifetime spent studying the land, swam before his eyes. Had he foreseen this? Had he understood that the true danger lay not in overt aggression, but in the insidious perversion of life itself?

The council's deliberation felt like a dance of death, each step delaying the inevitable, each word a procrastination of action. They spoke of the Skywood's resilience, of its capacity to endure. But Cael saw the signs of terminal illness: the wilting flora, the agitated fauna, the unnerving silence that had fallen over once-vibrant groves. He had ventured into the peripheral forests, the areas most affected by the Ashbound's raids and the subtle energy disruptions, and the sight had broken his heart. Trees that had stood for millennia were crumbling into dust, their roots withered and exposed, their once-majestic forms now skeletal monuments to a dying world. The very soil seemed to recoil from his touch, devoid of its usual life-giving warmth.

He closed his eyes, the image of a single, blighted flower, its petals brittle and brown, seared into his mind. It was a small thing, insignificant in the grand scheme of their world, but it represented everything. It was the lifeblood of their world, choked and suffocated by a force that seemed to understand its vulnerabilities all too well. He could feel the forest's pain as if it were his own, a deep, resonant ache that echoed in his very bones.

The elders' insistence on consensus felt like a betrayal of his oath. He was sworn to protect the Skywood, and protection, in this instance, meant decisive action. He could not stand by and watch their world wither and die while a committee debated the optimal shade of green for the restoration efforts. The Ashbound were a symptom, a desperate lashing out, but the underlying cause, the calculated manipulation of the Skywood's energies, was the true enemy. And that enemy, he suspected, was far more insidious than a horde of starving warriors. It was an enemy that understood the intricate symphony of their world and was deliberately playing a discordant, destructive tune.

He thought of Mara, her fierce intelligence and unwavering dedication to understanding the Skywood's delicate balance. She, too, had seen the subtle shifts, the unnatural patterns, the evidence of deliberate interference. Her data, though purely scientific, confirmed the gut feeling that had been gnawing at him for cycles. Something was deeply wrong, and the established order was too slow, too complacent, to address it.

He looked down at the swirling mists that obscured the chasm's depths. He could feel the raw, untamed power of the land seeping from its core, a power that the Skywood engines were meant to channel and harmonize. But now, that power was being perverted, twisted into a weapon. He imagined the Ashbound, their faces grim and determined, wielding the very forces of nature against them. It was a terrifying thought, a perversion of the natural order.

He knew what he had to do. The oath he had taken was not merely to follow the dictates of the council, but to protect the Skywood, even from itself if necessary. He could no longer afford the luxury of debate. The forest was dying, and hesitation was a death sentence. He would have to act unilaterally, to take a path that would undoubtedly strain his relationships, test his loyalties, and perhaps even mark him as a renegade. But the alternative was to preside over the slow, agonizing death of everything he held dear.

He turned his back on the dying forest, the wind whipping his cloak around him like a phantom embrace. His resolve hardened with each step. He would not wait for consensus. He would not appeal to reason that had already proven deaf. He would find the source of this corruption, and he would sever it, no matter the cost. The forest deserved a champion, not a mourner. And if the established order could not provide that champion, then he would have to become one, even if it meant standing alone against the weight of tradition and the judgment of his peers. The time for reckoning had come, not just for the Ashbound, but for those who stood idly by as their world crumbled.

He would forge his own path, a path illuminated by the dimming light of the Skywood, a path that led to a desperate, possibly irreversible, act of preservation. He had to trust his instincts, his training, and the quiet voice of the dying land itself. The future, he knew, rested not on the pronouncements of elders, but on the courage of a single individual willing to make the ultimate sacrifice for the sake of life. He would not let his oath be a passive vow; he would make it an active force, a weapon against the encroaching darkness, even if that meant wielding it against those he was sworn to protect. He walked with a renewed sense of purpose, the weight on his shoulders replaced by the steely resolve of a man who had finally made his choice.

The ancient mechanisms of the Skywood pulsed with a desperate, irregular heartbeat. Cael could feel it in the soles of his boots, a tremor that resonated not just through the earth, but through the very marrow of his bones. The elders, bless their tradition-bound hearts, had continued their protracted deliberations, their voices a distant hum against the roar of his own growing conviction. They spoke of protocols, of the sanctity of the established order, of the delicate balance of power. But the Skywood was not a mere political entity to be managed; it was a living being, and it was bleeding out.

He moved with a newfound urgency, his earlier despair transmuted into a cold, sharp resolve. His path diverged sharply from the council chambers, away from the hushed tones of diplomacy and towards the thrumming, corrupted heart of their world. His destination was the Nexus, a central hub of the Skywood's lifeblood, where the conduits that fed the vital energies to the vast forest converged. It was a place of immense power, and currently, a place of profound vulnerability. Mara had identified a critical juncture there, a point where the flow of vital essence, the very sap of life that sustained the Skywood, was being systematically choked.

The journey was a grim testament to the creeping blight. The once verdant pathways were now choked with brittle, ash-laden undergrowth. The air, usually alive with the chirping of unseen creatures and the rustle of leaves, was heavy with an unnatural silence. Even the light seemed to struggle, filtering through a perpetual haze that dulled the vibrant greens and golds into muted, sepia tones. He passed by ancient trees, their bark scarred and blackened, their branches skeletal against the perpetually overcast sky. Each withered leaf, each crumbling trunk, was a silent accusation, a testament to his own perceived inaction.

He reached the outer perimeter of the Nexus, a vast, crystalline structure that hummed with contained power. It was usually a beacon of life, its facets reflecting the vibrant hues of the Skywood's health. Now, it seemed to weep a dull, viscous sheen, a visible manifestation of the corruption seeping within. The air here was thick with an almost palpable tension, the residual energy of a system under duress. The faint, discordant hum that emanated from the structure was not the song of harmonious flow, but a broken, agonizing groan.

Mara's projections, etched into his memory, guided him. The primary conduit, the 'Aorta' as she'd termed it, was experiencing a severe constriction. Not a natural blockage, but a deliberate, insidious redirection of its flow. This wasn't the brute force of the Ashbound, whose destructive tendencies were often chaotic and visible. This was a surgical precision, a manipulation of the very currents that sustained them all, designed to starve the Skywood from within. He had to override the control mechanisms, to force a rerouting of the vital essence, even if it meant a temporary, violent surge that could shatter the delicate equilibrium.

His starlight ore blade, usually a tool of defense, now felt like an instrument of surgical intervention. The elder's warnings echoed in his mind: "Disruption will cause unforeseen consequences, Cael. The Skywood is a delicate tapestry, and pulling a single thread can unravel the whole." But what of a tapestry already being systematically unpicked? What if the 'unforeseen consequences' were simply the price of averting utter annihilation?

He accessed the Nexus's external interface, a shimmering panel of interwoven light. His fingers, accustomed to the intricate patterns of energy manipulation, danced across the surface. He bypassed the automated safety protocols, their warnings flashing like dying embers. The system resisted, its internal logic fighting against his intrusion. It was like wrestling with a phantom limb, a part of the Skywood's consciousness that was currently infected.

"This is for your own good," he murmured, his voice a low growl. "A necessary pain."

With a final, desperate surge of will, he initiated the override sequence. A searing arc of emerald energy erupted from the panel, a violent discharge that momentarily blinded him. The Nexus itself groaned, a sound that vibrated through his very core, like the cry of a wounded behemoth. The ground beneath him shuddered.

Immediately, the air crackled with a new, raw energy. The discordant hum faltered, replaced by a low, resonant thrum that vibrated with immense power. He felt it, an almost overwhelming tide of vital essence surging through the redirected conduits. It was a torrent, far exceeding the usual controlled flow. His senses, attuned to the Skywood's subtle energies, were assaulted by the sheer volume of power being unleashed.

He could see the immediate effects, even from the exterior. The dull sheen on the Nexus began to recede, replaced by a faint, almost imperceptible glow. In the distance, where the forest began to thin, he thought he saw a faint resurgence of color, a hint of emerald fighting against the encroaching grey. It was a small victory, a flickering ember of hope in the encroaching darkness.

But the surge was wild, untamed. The ground continued to tremble, and the ambient temperature around the Nexus began to rise sharply. He could feel the strain on the very structure of the Nexus, the ancient crystalline matrix groaning under the immense pressure. This was the risk: the potential for a catastrophic overload, a shattering of the Nexus itself, which would sever the Skywood's lifeblood entirely. He had not just diverted the flow; he had potentially unleashed a tidal wave.

He scanned the area, his heightened senses searching for any immediate signs of disaster. The trees closest to the Nexus, moments ago brittle and dead, were now visibly trembling, their branches writhing as if in agony. Some of the smaller, more delicate flora began to disintegrate, their cellular structures unable to withstand the sudden influx of raw, unrefined energy. It was a double-edged sword; he was forcing life back into the dying arteries, but the sheer force of it was also proving destructive to the weaker tissues.

He then turned his attention to the primary contamination source, a locus of dark energy Mara's scans had indicated was at the heart of the problem. It wasn't an Ashbound encampment, nor a natural blight. It was a focal point of corrupted energy, a wound that was actively draining the Skywood's vitality. This required a more direct intervention, a confrontation with the very source of the corruption. It was a gamble, a desperate act born of his refusal to stand by and watch his world wither. He had bypassed the council, the protocols, the established order, because time was a luxury he no longer possessed. He had chosen action, and the consequences, for better or worse, were already beginning to unfold. The Skywood had groaned in protest, but also, perhaps, in a flicker of acknowledgement. He had made his choice, a bold intervention that could either save them all or shatter their world into irreparable pieces.

The surge of vital essence through the Nexus was a tempest unleashed. Cael had expected a powerful resurgence, a life-giving flood to counteract the insidious drain, but the reality was a violent inundation. The Skywood, accustomed to the gentle, regulated flow of its lifeblood, thrashed and convulsed under the sudden, overwhelming influx. The ancient crystalline conduits, designed for a steady pulse, now vibrated with a frantic, almost panicked rhythm, groaning under a pressure they were never meant to endure.

He could feel it, a raw, untamed power coursing through the very ground beneath him, a force that was as much destructive as it was restorative. The smaller, more delicate flora near the Nexus, those that had been clinging to the brink of desiccation, now withered and blackened, their cellular structures vaporized by the sheer intensity of the raw energy. It was a brutal irony: in his haste to save the Skywood from a slow, agonizing death by starvation, he had inadvertently subjected parts of it to a swift, violent immolation. He'd pulled a thread, as the elders had warned, but it felt more like he'd ripped a gaping hole in the fabric of existence.

As the initial shock of the surge subsided, new patterns of disruption began to emerge. The redirected flow, powerful and indiscriminate, was not confined to the Skywood's core. It was seeking its own paths, carving new channels through the earth, and in doing so, altering the very landscape. Miles away, in the marshlands that fringed the Skywood's western edge, a low, insistent rumbling began. The soil, saturated with the ambient moisture of years of slow drainage, began to liquefy. Aquifers, long dormant and stable, were suddenly overwhelmed by the redirected subterranean currents of vital essence, no longer a gentle trickle but a torrent. Water, infused with this raw, potent energy, began to seep upwards, then erupt.

A low-lying village, built on the very edge of the marsh, was the first to feel the true impact. The inhabitants, a community of amphibious folk who had always lived in harmony with the wetlands, were caught completely unawares. Their homes, constructed from woven reeds and hardened mud, were suddenly submerged. The carefully tended aquatic gardens, their primary source of sustenance, were swept away by the rising tide of energized water. Panic, a sharp and alien emotion for these usually placid people, began to spread like a disease. Their world, so predictable and steady, was being violently reshaped, their ancestral waters transforming into a dangerous, unpredictable deluge.

This localized flooding was not a direct consequence of the Nexus's immediate overload, but a downstream effect of Cael's drastic measure. The Skywood's internal plumbing, once a meticulously managed system, was now in chaos. The vital essence, like any powerful fluid, would find the path of least resistance, and in this case, that path led to the lowest points, overwhelming natural drainage and causing unprecedented inundation. Cael, focused on the immediate crisis at the Nexus, was miles away, oblivious to the mounting disaster unfolding on the fringes of his world. His intervention was a stone dropped into a vast, interconnected pond, and the ripples, though invisible from his vantage point, were already spreading, threatening to drown those in their path.

Beyond the immediate physical disruptions, Cael's actions also awakened something far more ancient and dangerous. The Skywood was not just a collection of trees and waterways; it was a living entity, imbued with a primordial consciousness. His forceful redirection of its lifeblood had not gone unnoticed by its deepest, most primal aspects. Certain areas, long dormant and slumbering, were stirred by the violent disruption. These were places where the Skywood's energy had pooled and concentrated over millennia, forming pockets of immense, untamed power, guarded by forces that predated even the oldest trees.

In the Whispering Caves, a network of subterranean caverns deep beneath the Skywood's roots, the dormant energies began to stir. These caves were not merely geological formations; they were conduits to a more ancient, chaotic layer of the Skywood's existence. The surge of vital essence, a raw and unrefined power, acted like a key, unlocking pathways that had been sealed for eons. From the deepest, darkest recesses, a low, guttural hum began to emanate, a sound that vibrated not through the earth, but through the very fabric of reality.

For centuries, the Whispering Caves had been home to the Lumina Worms, creatures of pure, phosphorescent light. They were not malicious, but their very existence was tied to a delicate balance. Their light, born from the slow, steady absorption of the Skywood's ambient energies, was a calming, stabilizing force. But the sudden, violent influx of raw essence was too much for them. It was like exposing a candle flame to a hurricane; their gentle glow was overwhelmed, their essence amplified to an unsustainable degree.

Their luminescence intensified, shifting from a soft, ethereal glow to a blinding, pulsating radiance. This amplified light, now infused with the uncontrolled energy of the surge, began to warp the very nature of the caves. The stone walls rippled and flowed as if they were liquid. The air crackled with a disorienting energy, causing illusions and phantasms to manifest from the heightened mental states of any creature that dared venture too close. The Lumina Worms, no longer passive guardians, became agents of a chaotic transformation, their amplified light a weapon of unintended destruction, twisting perception and distorting reality in their immediate vicinity.

Cael had always believed the Ashbound were the primary threat, their outward aggression a tangible danger. But his intervention had unearthed a far subtler, more insidious peril. He had inadvertently poked a sleeping dragon, not the lumbering, fire-breathing kind, but one whose breath was madness and whose scales were reality itself. This was the true 'unforeseen consequence' – not just a shift in water levels or a localized destruction, but the awakening of primal forces that operated on principles far beyond human comprehension.

The Lumina Worms' amplified light was also radiating outwards, subtly affecting the Skywood's more sensitive inhabitants. The Sylphs, ethereal beings of wind and mist who normally dwelled high in the canopy, found their senses overwhelmed. Their delicate communication, a symphony of rustling leaves and whispered breezes, was now a cacophony of discordant whispers and disorienting flashes of light. Their connection to the Skywood's natural rhythms was disrupted, and many were driven to disarray, their movements becoming erratic and unpredictable. Some even began to descend from their lofty perches, drawn by the hypnotic, pulsing light from the Whispering Caves, their delicate forms becoming vulnerable to the corrupted energies.

The consequences were cascading. The diverted water flooded the marshlands, displacing its inhabitants and creating a new source of ecological stress. The awakened primal energies in the Whispering Caves began to warp reality, transforming a hidden sanctuary into a zone of chaos. And the Sylphs, the Skywood's natural messengers and guardians of its atmosphere, were being driven mad, their disruption further destabilizing the already precarious balance. Cael's drastic measure, born of a desperate need to act, had not simply diverted a flow; it had unleashed a chain reaction, each consequence leading to another, each ripple expanding outwards, touching every aspect of the Skywood's intricate, interconnected existence. He had saved the Skywood from a slow death, perhaps, but at the risk of a sudden, catastrophic implosion. The choice had been made, and the price of that choice was only just beginning to be tallied. He had acted with the best intentions, but the Skywood, in its infinite complexity, was proving that good intentions were a poor shield against the brutal calculus of nature. The very essence of his intervention was becoming a poison, and he was the one who had administered it.

Mara's breath hitched, a phantom sting of ozone and damp earth pricking her senses even miles away. It was the faintest echo, a tremor that rippled not through the ground, but through the subtle hum of the world's own vitality, a sense she had honed since childhood. Cael. What had he *done*? The surge, the violent redirection of the Skywood's lifeblood, had been felt, a seismic shift in the elemental currents that made her stomach churn. It wasn't the gentle coaxing of nature she championed, the patient diplomacy of understanding delicate balances, but a brute-force assertion that felt inherently wrong, like tearing a wound open to staunch a bleeding finger.

She had spent weeks, months even, piecing together the fragmented accounts of the weather engines' disruption, carefully consulting ancient texts, deciphering the subtle language of wind patterns and moisture retention. Her approach was one of meticulous study, of seeking harmony before intervention, believing that any solution must be woven into the existing tapestry, not ripped from it. The idea of forceful change, of a unilateral act of power, grated against her deepest convictions. She had envisioned a council, a unified approach, where every faction, every perspective, had a voice in the delicate art of restoring balance. Cael's actions, as the tremor in the earth's pulse suggested, spoke of a very different path.

News, like water itself, found ways to seep through even the most fortified barriers. Whispers reached her from the western marshes, tales of sudden, inexplicable deluges, of amphibious villagers finding their homes submerged beneath energized water. The descriptions were fragmented, tinged with fear and confusion, but the underlying cause, Mara suspected, was Cael's desperate gamble. He had spoken of the Skywood's decay, of a life-giving flood, but what she was hearing spoke of a deluge, a destructive overflow. It mirrored the ecological textbooks she had studied, the cautionary tales of systems overloaded, of equilibrium shattered by a single, ill-considered act.

Her mind, usually a calm harbor for reasoned thought, was now a churning sea of doubt. Cael was brilliant, she couldn't deny that. His understanding of the Skywood's deep mechanics was profound, his dedication undeniable. But brilliance, she had learned, could be a dangerous companion to arrogance. Had he truly understood the implications of unleashing such raw, untamed energy? Or had he, in his haste to correct one imbalance, created a cascade of others, each more devastating than the last? The thought that he might be acting out of a desperate fear, a misguided belief that brute force was the only answer, sent a chill down her spine.

She pictured him, likely at the heart of the Skywood, amidst the groaning conduits, the thrashing flora. Was he observing the subtle shifts, the unintended consequences rippling outwards? Or was he blinded by the immediate, perceived success of his intervention, deaf to the cries of the displaced, the subtle fracturing of the natural order? Her diplomatic approach, the painstaking efforts to build consensus and foster understanding, felt suddenly fragile, almost naive, in the face of such overt, potent action.

The thought of the weather engines' manipulation, a subtle insidious force that had been so carefully uncovered, added another layer to her growing unease. Had Cael grasped the true nature of that interference? Was it a crude physical tampering, or something far more nuanced, a manipulation of subtle energies that required an equally subtle, informed response? If Cael's understanding of the *cause* was flawed, then his chosen *solution* was bound to be equally so. He might be fighting a phantom, or worse, misinterpreting the battleground entirely, his drastic measures only exacerbating the problem he sought to solve.

She recalled their last conversation, a heated exchange where she had urged caution, where she had stressed the interconnectedness of all things, the delicate symphony of the Skywood's existence. He had been dismissive, his eyes alight with the fervor of a man convinced of his singular purpose. "We don't have time for your philosophies, Mara," he had said, his voice sharp with urgency. "The Skywood is dying. I will save it." At the time, she had attributed his intensity to the dire circumstances. Now, she saw a different possibility: a desperate conviction that bordered on recklessness, a willingness to sacrifice nuance for expediency.

The implications of his actions gnawed at her. The Skywood was not just a forest; it was a living, breathing entity, its health intrinsically linked to the well-being of every creature, every ecosystem within its vast embrace. To forcefully alter its lifeblood was to risk not just physical damage, but a fundamental disruption of its very consciousness, its ancient rhythms. She had always believed that true healing came from understanding, from working *with* the natural world, not imposing one's will upon it. Cael's intervention, as described by the panicked whispers from the west, sounded less like healing and more like a violent surgery performed without a clear diagnosis.

The very fabric of her trust in him, a trust forged in shared purpose and mutual respect, began to fray. She had seen his dedication, his brilliance, his deep love for the Skywood. But now, she also saw the potential for hubris, the chilling possibility that his conviction had blinded him to the risks, to the delicate balance he was so intent on restoring. He was a man of action, decisive and bold, but was he a man who truly understood the subtle forces he was now wielding?

The marshlands, now teeming with disoriented amphibious folk and their waterlogged homes, were a stark testament to the potential dangers of his approach. This was not a minor inconvenience; it was an ecological disaster, a displacement of a community that had lived in harmony with its environment for generations. And it was a consequence that Mara, with her diplomatic sensibilities, could have foreseen, could have helped to mitigate, had she been consulted, had Cael not chosen to act alone.

Her heart ached for those affected, but also for the Skywood itself. This was not the restoration she had envisioned. This was a wound inflicted, however unintentionally, by a well-meaning hand. She feared that Cael, in his desperate attempt to mend what was broken, was inadvertently shattering it further, his drastic measures creating a new, perhaps more insidious, form of decay. The whispers of his actions were growing louder, each one a shard of glass in the smooth surface of her trust, leaving her to wonder if Cael, in his urgent quest to save the Skywood, was becoming its greatest threat. The very essence of his intervention, the raw power he had unleashed, was beginning to feel less like a cure and more like a poison, and Mara was starting to believe that she, and perhaps the Skywood itself, were the ones who would have to bear its bitter taste.

Her gaze drifted towards the distant, verdant expanse of the Skywood, a place she had always seen as a sanctuary, a testament to nature's resilience and enduring power. Now, a shadow of apprehension fell over it in her mind. The stories reaching her were unsettling, not just of floods, but of a subtle, unsettling change in the very air, a disorientation that even the Sylphs, those ethereal beings of wind and mist, seemed to be experiencing. These were creatures attuned to the faintest shifts, their existence a delicate dance with the Skywood's atmosphere. If they were disoriented, if their graceful ballet was faltering, it spoke of a deeper disruption, a dissonance that Cael's brute force might not be equipped to address.

She remembered the Lumina Worms, creatures of pure, gentle light that resided in the deepest caverns, their luminescence a product of the Skywood's slow, steady energies. The surge, as described in the scattered reports, had intensified their glow to an almost blinding degree, twisting their benevolent light into something chaotic. This was not a mere physical alteration; it suggested a fundamental change in the very essence of these creatures, a perversion of their natural state driven by the overwhelming influx of raw energy. It was like forcing a flower to bloom in a hurricane; the result was not beauty, but destruction.

This amplification of the Lumina Worms' light was a particularly disturbing detail. It implied that Cael's actions were not just altering the macro-level flows of water and essence, but were also impacting the most delicate, foundational elements of the Skywood's ecosystem. The light, once a calming beacon, was now a source of disorientation, a catalyst for illusion and perceptual distortion. It was a subtle yet profound weapon, capable of unmaking minds and realities, and it was a direct consequence of Cael's forceful intervention.

Her initial respect for Cael's decisive action began to curdle into a potent, unsettling fear. He had presented himself as a savior, a beacon of hope against the encroaching blight. But what if his understanding of the blight was incomplete? What if the weather engines' manipulation was a subtle disease, and Cael's cure was a violent purge that was killing the patient? The thought was a bitter pill to swallow, especially given her own belief in the power of diplomacy and reasoned intervention.

She found herself replaying their last significant discussion, the one where she had presented her findings on the weather engines. She had painstakingly laid out the evidence, the subtle anomalies in atmospheric pressure, the peculiar patterns of moisture distribution, the faint traces of foreign energies. Cael had listened, his brow furrowed, but his response had been focused on the immediate, tangible signs of decay. He had acknowledged her research, but had ultimately deferred to his own plans, his own immediate vision of how to address the crisis. At the time, she had interpreted his focus as a necessary pragmatism, a man prioritizing action. Now, she saw it as a potential blind spot, a refusal to grapple with the deeper, more complex realities of the situation.

He had spoken of an encroaching "rot," a physical decay that was visible and undeniable. But what if the rot was not merely physical? What if it was an insidious corruption of the Skywood's very spirit, a manipulation of its elemental heart that required a more nuanced, less aggressive approach? If Cael's understanding was limited to the visible symptoms, his drastic measures might be akin to amputating a limb to treat a fever.

The tales of the western marshlands, of the drowned villages and displaced peoples, were no longer just a sign of Cael's overreach; they were a chilling premonition of what could happen if his understanding of the problem was fundamentally flawed. He was wielding immense power, but was he directing it with wisdom, or with a desperate, misinformed urgency? The very idea that his well-intentioned actions could be causing more harm than good, that he might be exacerbating the very problem he sought to solve, was a terrifying prospect.

Her diplomatic instincts, honed through years of negotiation and mediation, screamed at her that this was not the way. True restoration required understanding, patience, and a deep respect for the intricate web of life. It required collaboration, not unilateral action. Cael's approach, while undeniably powerful, lacked these essential components. It was the path of the warrior, not the healer, and in the delicate ecosystem of the Skywood, the warrior's methods could prove to be the most destructive.

The more she learned, the more her initial admiration for Cael's boldness began to erode, replaced by a gnawing distrust. His actions were too extreme, his methods too forceful. He was playing with forces he might not fully comprehend, driven by a desperation that seemed to override caution and foresight. She had always believed in finding solutions that honored the Skywood's delicate balance, but Cael's actions suggested he was willing to sacrifice that balance for a quick, albeit potentially devastating, fix. The hope she had held for a united effort, for a measured response, was slowly giving way to the grim realization that Cael's 'drastic measures' might indeed be the most drastic mistake the Skywood had ever faced. The thought that his genuine desire to save it might lead to its ruin was a betrayal not just of their shared purpose, but of the very essence of the Skywood's intricate, interconnected being. She had to find a way to understand what he had truly done, and if possible, to mitigate the damage before his well-intentioned fury consumed them all.

The tremors that rippled through the earth were not merely seismic; they were echoes of a profound disruption, a violation of ancient pacts that resonated deep within the bedrock of the world. For the land dragons, beings intrinsically bound to the earth's pulse, Cael's actions were not just a political maneuver, but a visceral affront. Thryxal, his scales the color of ancient granite and his eyes like molten gold, felt the imbalance as a physical pain, a sharp ache in his very bones. He had been a silent observer for centuries, a guardian of the Skywood's deep roots, and the sudden, violent surge of its lifeblood was a cacophony against the slow, steady rhythm he had always known.

He had felt Cael's presence, a spark of fierce, unyielding will, at the heart of the Skywood. The human's ambition, his desperation, was palpable, a scent on the wind that spoke of both courage and a dangerous recklessness. Thryxal had always held a grudging respect for humanity's tenacity, their ability to adapt and innovate, but this was different. This was not adaptation; it was a forceful imposition, a brutal reshaping of forces that had remained in delicate equilibrium for millennia. He had warned his kin of the growing imbalance, of the creeping blight that threatened to consume the Skywood, but none had anticipated a solution so... immoderate.

"He tears at the Skywood's heart," rumbled Ignis, his voice like the grinding of tectonic plates, his breath a perpetual ember. Ignis, whose territory lay in the volcanic vents bordering the western fringes of the forest, had always been more volatile, his temper as fiery as his name suggested. "He seeks to heal a festering wound with a cauterizing flame, but the fire consumes the flesh it means to save."

Thryxal shifted, the movement sending ripples through the rocky terrain of his lair. "His intent, Ignis, is not malice. It is a desperate gambit to preserve what he perceives as lost."

"Perception is a fickle thing when wielded by mortals," Ignis retorted, a plume of smoke escaping his nostrils. "And their desperation breeds recklessness. The waters in the western marshes... they are not merely swollen; they are *energized*. My kin, the earth elementals who dwell there, are in disarray. The usual currents are corrupted, and their forms flicker like dying flames. They speak of unnatural storms, of skies weeping with a fury they have never known."

Another of their kind, the ancient and stoic Terra, whose massive form was a living landscape of moss and stone, added her voice. "The deep earth groans, Thryxal. The ley lines that carry the Skywood's essence are fractured. Cael has not redirected the flow; he has dammed it, and now he has broken the dam. The resulting flood is uncontrolled, unpredictable. The very earth beneath our claws shifts and buckles. Those who live in the Skywood's shadow, the burrowing folk, the root weavers... their homes are being torn asunder. They speak of a water that burns, a deluge that drowns not just the body, but the spirit."

Thryxal closed his eyes, the images conjured by their words playing out in his mind. He had felt the initial surge, a faint tremor that had belied the true extent of the devastation. He had sensed the Skywood's agony, a silent scream that had reverberated through the earth's core. Cael, in his hubris, had tapped into a power far greater than he understood, a force that demanded respect, not manipulation.

"He believes he is fighting the blight," Thryxal said, his voice a low, resonant hum. "But he may be unleashing a new one, born of his own making. The blight is a sickness of decay, of slow unraveling. What he has done is a shockwave, a violent disruption. The Skywood's resilience is immense, but even the strongest oak can be shattered by a sudden, catastrophic storm."

"And what of those who are caught in this storm, Thryxal?" Ignis pressed, his golden eyes narrowing. "The Sylphs, those ethereal beings who dance upon the Skywood's breath, are disoriented. Their patterns are broken, their whispers lost in the unnatural winds. They are the forest's lungs, and you say their breath is faltering. What of the Lumina Worms, whose gentle light has guided lost travelers for ages? Reports speak of their light growing wild, chaotic, a blinding glare that sows confusion and fear. This is not healing; it is madness."

"Humanity's ambition often outstrips their wisdom," Terra mused, her voice like the slow creak of ancient trees. "Cael is a man of great vision, and perhaps, great desperation. He sees the decay, and he acts. But he acts as if the Skywood were a machine to be repaired, not a living entity to be nurtured. He has bypassed the whispers of the wind and the murmur of the roots, and instead, he has roared."

The dragons exchanged glances, a silent understanding passing between them. Cael had sought to rally their support, to enlist their power in his desperate endeavor. He had spoken of a unified front against the encroaching darkness, of a necessary sacrifice for the greater good. But his unilateral action, his bold assertion of power without consultation, had alienated those whose respect he so desperately needed.

"He believes he has saved the Skywood," Ignis scoffed, a puff of acrid smoke clouding the air. "He has merely proven that humanity's capacity for destruction rivals that of any blight. He has taken the Skywood's lifeblood, its very essence, and hurled it about like a child with a broken toy. The rivers run with an unnatural force, the air crackles with displaced energy. The creatures of the deep earth, those who are most sensitive to the land's balance, are in turmoil. They speak of a pervasive unease, a discordant hum that vibrates through their very being. This is not the work of a savior; it is the work of a fool."

Thryxal raised a claw, a gesture that silenced Ignis's sputtering rage. "We have our own duties, Ignis. The Skywood's plight is dire, but our role is not to mirror humanity's rashness. We are the earth's anchors, its ancient heart. We must observe, and when the time is right, we must act to restore balance, not to amplify chaos."

"But Cael believes he *is* the restoration," Terra stated, her tone heavy with concern. "He has tapped into the Skywood's deepest wells, seeking to flood its veins with vitality. He has succeeded, in a way. The forest is teeming with energy, but it is a wild, untamed energy. The plants grow with unnatural speed, their leaves unfurling with a visible, almost violent, expansion. This is not healthy growth; it is a fevered blooming, a desperate surge before the inevitable collapse."

"He has always been so driven," Thryxal mused, his gaze fixed on the distant, shimmering canopy of the Skywood. "Even as a hatchling, he possessed a fierce will. I remember him, barely a sapling in human years, arguing with the elders of his village about the encroaching blight, his voice thin but filled with a conviction that belied his age. He saw the rot, and he could not bear to stand idly by."

"Conviction can be a dangerous companion when it blinds one to the path," Ignis growled. "He has not only disregarded the ancient pacts between our kind and his, but he has also sown discord among the lesser creatures of the earth. The water sprites are fleeing their homes, their sacred pools now churning with volatile currents. The burrowing moles, whose sense of direction is tied to the earth's subtle magnetic fields, are lost, their tunnels collapsing. This is not merely an ecological imbalance; it is a societal collapse for many who call the Skywood home."

"His actions have created a dilemma for us," Terra stated plainly. "To intervene now, to try and counter his brute force with our own, would be to engage in the very kind of destructive action he has taken. It would be to risk shattering the Skywood further, to become instruments of its undoing."

Thryxal nodded slowly, the weight of their shared responsibility settling upon him. "He has sought to impose order, but he has created chaos. He has sought to save, but he has endangered. We must be patient. We must understand the full scope of his actions, the ripples he has sent through the Skywood and beyond. The land dragons have always been the silent witnesses, the keepers of the earth's deep memory. We will watch. We will feel the earth's pain, and we will endure. For when Cael's drastic measures inevitably falter, it will be for us to mend what he has broken, to find the true path to restoration, the one that honors the Skywood's intricate song, not silences it with a roar."

The news of Cael's intervention had spread like wildfire, igniting a tempest of reactions amongst the dragon kin. For Ignis, whose fiery spirit burned with an almost insatiable intensity, Cael's unilateral actions were a profound betrayal. He saw it not as a desperate attempt to save the Skywood, but as a blatant act of human arrogance, a reckless disregard for the ancient order that governed their world. The very essence of the Skywood, the delicate tapestry of life and energy that Thryxal and Ignis had sworn to protect, had been ripped asunder by a single, ill-conceived act of brute force. Ignis had witnessed the initial surge, a violent jolt that had sent tremors through his volcanic domain, a far cry from the subtle, almost imperceptible shifts he was accustomed to. It was like a blacksmith's hammer striking a silken web, a crude imposition of power that had no place in the natural world.

"He has shown his true colors," Ignis had bellowed, his voice echoing through the molten chambers of his home. "This is not the act of a protector, but of a conqueror. He has taken the Skywood's very lifeblood, its elemental essence, and has redirected it with the clumsy hands of a child playing with fire. The consequences are already evident. The western marshlands, once a sanctuary of calm and natural ebb and flow, are now a churning cauldron of uncontrolled energy. The water sprites, the guardians of those sacred pools, have fled their homes, their voices a symphony of distress carried on the unnatural winds. They speak of a water that no longer nourishes, but burns, a deluge that drowns not just flesh, but spirit."

Thryxal, ever the pragmatist, the ancient guardian who understood the intricate balance of power, had attempted to temper Ignis's fury. "His intent, Ignis, is not to harm. He believes he is acting out of necessity, to combat a blight that threatened to consume us all."

"Necessity?" Ignis had scoffed, a plume of sulfurous smoke escaping his nostrils. "Is it necessary to shatter the very foundations of our world? Is it necessary to inflict such pain upon the creatures that dwell within its embrace? The earth elementals, those who are closest to the heart of the land, are in disarray. Their forms flicker and distort, their connection to the Skywood's currents severed by this... this unnatural flood. They speak of disorienting storms, of skies weeping with a fury they have never known. This is not a cure, Thryxal; it is a plague of his own making."

Terra, whose ancient form was a living landscape of moss-covered stones and gnarled roots, had offered her quiet, somber perspective. Her voice, like the slow grind of glaciers, carried a profound weight of sorrow. "The deep earth groans," she had stated, her gaze fixed on the distant, shimmering expanse of the Skywood. "The ley lines, the arteries of the Skywood's essence, have been fractured. Cael has not merely redirected the flow; he has attempted to dam it, and in his haste, he has broken the dam. The resulting deluge is uncontrolled, unpredictable. The very ground beneath our claws shifts and buckles. The burrowing folk, the root weavers, those who have lived in harmony with the earth for eons, have had their homes torn asunder. They speak of a water that is not merely wet, but corrosive, a flood that drowns not just the body, but the very spirit of the land."

Thryxal had listened intently, his golden eyes reflecting the grim reality of their kin's reports. He had felt the initial disturbance, a faint tremor that had belied the true extent of the devastation. He had sensed the Skywood's agony, a silent scream that had reverberated through the earth's core. Cael, in his hubris, had tapped into a power far greater than he understood, a force that demanded respect, not manipulation. He had always admired Cael's fierce will, his unwavering conviction, but this... this was beyond anything he could have anticipated. This was not a calculated risk; it was a reckless gamble with the fate of their shared world.

"He believes he is fighting the blight," Thryxal had said, his voice a low, resonant hum that seemed to vibrate through the very rock of his lair. "But he may be unleashing a new one, one born of his own making. The blight is a sickness of decay, of slow unraveling. What he has done is a shockwave, a violent disruption. The Skywood's resilience is immense, but even the strongest oak can be shattered by a sudden, catastrophic storm."

Ignis, however, remained unconvinced, his fiery spirit unwilling to accept any mitigating circumstances. "And what of those who are caught in this storm, Thryxal?" he had demanded, his voice laced with a dangerous edge. "The Sylphs, those ethereal beings who dance upon the Skywood's breath, are disoriented. Their patterns are broken, their whispers lost in the unnatural winds. They are the forest's lungs, and you say their breath is faltering. What of the Lumina Worms, whose gentle light has guided lost travelers for ages? Reports speak of their light growing wild, chaotic, a blinding glare that sows confusion and fear. This is not healing; it is madness. He has not merely disrupted the flow of water; he has corrupted the very essence of light and air within the Skywood."

"Humanity's ambition often outstrips their wisdom," Terra had mused, her voice like the slow creak of ancient trees. "Cael is a man of great vision, and perhaps, great desperation. He sees the decay, and he acts. But he acts as if the Skywood were a machine to be repaired, not a living entity to be nurtured. He has bypassed the whispers of the wind and the murmur of the roots, and instead, he has roared. He has not sought our counsel, not asked for our aid in the way that respects our nature. He has declared war on the blight, and in doing so, he has declared war on the Skywood itself."

The dragons exchanged glances, a silent understanding passing between them. Cael had sought to rally their support, to enlist their power in his desperate endeavor. He had spoken of a unified front against the encroaching darkness, of a necessary sacrifice for the greater good. But his unilateral action, his bold assertion of power without consultation, had alienated those whose respect he so desperately needed. He had approached them not as allies, but as tools to be wielded, and this had ignited a fury within Ignis that burned hotter than any volcanic forge.

"He believes he has saved the Skywood," Ignis had scoffed, a puff of acrid smoke clouding the air. "He has merely proven that humanity's capacity for destruction rivals that of any blight. He has taken the Skywood's lifeblood, its very essence, and has hurled it about like a child with a broken toy. The rivers run with an unnatural force, the air crackles with displaced energy. The creatures of the deep earth, those who are most sensitive to the land's balance, are in turmoil. They speak of a pervasive unease, a discordant hum that vibrates through their very being. This is not the work of a savior; it is the work of a fool who thinks he understands the heart of a dragon when he only grasps its claws."

Thryxal raised a claw, a gesture that silenced Ignis's sputtering rage. He understood Ignis's anger, his deep-seated respect for the natural order. But he also understood the precariousness of their situation. To retaliate with brute force, to meet Cael's drastic measures with their own, would be to engage in the very chaos they sought to quell.

"We have our own duties, Ignis," Thryxal had said, his voice a low rumble that conveyed a profound sense of responsibility. "The Skywood's plight is dire, but our role is not to mirror humanity's rashness. We are the earth's anchors, its ancient heart. We must observe, and when the time is right, we must act to restore balance, not to amplify chaos. Cael's actions have created a schism, a rift not only in the Skywood's natural order but also between our kind and his. He has shown a blatant disregard for the ancient pacts that have bound us for millennia, a pact that demands consultation and mutual respect, not unilateral decree."

"But Cael believes he *is* the restoration," Terra had stated, her tone heavy with concern. "He has tapped into the Skywood's deepest wells, seeking to flood its veins with vitality. He has succeeded, in a way. The forest is teeming with energy, but it is a wild, untamed energy. The plants grow with unnatural speed, their leaves unfurling with a visible, almost violent, expansion. This is not healthy growth; it is a fevered blooming, a desperate surge before the inevitable collapse. He has become a tempest, and he mistakes his own destructive force for the cleansing power of a storm."

"He has always been so driven," Thryxal had mused, his gaze fixed on the distant, shimmering canopy of the Skywood. "Even as a hatchling, he possessed a fierce will. I remember him, barely a sapling in human years, arguing with the elders of his village about the encroaching blight, his voice thin but filled with a conviction that belied his age. He saw the rot, and he could not bear to stand idly by. He has carried that same urgency, that same desperate need to act, into adulthood. But his actions today have demonstrated a profound misunderstanding of the forces he wields. He has mistaken the vibrant pulse of the Skywood for a mechanism to be controlled, not a living entity to be understood."

"Conviction can be a dangerous companion when it blinds one to the path," Ignis had growled, his frustration evident. "He has not only disregarded the ancient pacts between our kind and his, but he has also sown discord among the lesser creatures of the earth. The water sprites are fleeing their homes, their sacred pools now churning with volatile currents. The burrowing moles, whose sense of direction is tied to the earth's subtle magnetic fields, are lost, their tunnels collapsing. This is not merely an ecological imbalance; it is a societal collapse for many who call the Skywood home. He has become a force of disruption, and it is his very act of 'saving' that threatens to destroy."

Thryxal's sigh was like the slow shifting of mountains. He understood Ignis's outrage. Cael's actions had not only violated the sanctity of the Skywood but had also broken a centuries-old trust between humans and dragons. The unilateral nature of Cael's 'drastic measures' was the most egregious offense. It was a clear indication that Cael, despite his acknowledged brilliance, saw the dragons not as equals, but as pawns to be moved or ignored at his convenience.

"His actions have created a dilemma for us," Terra had stated plainly, her ancient eyes filled with a weary wisdom. "To intervene now, to try and counter his brute force with our own, would be to engage in the very kind of destructive action he has taken. It would be to risk shattering the Skywood further, to become instruments of its undoing. We are guardians, not wreckers. Our strength lies in our steadfastness, our ability to endure and to mend, not to break."

"He has sought to impose order, but he has created chaos," Thryxal had agreed, his gaze fixed on the distant, verdant expanse of the Skywood. "He has sought to save, but he has endangered. We must be patient. We must understand the full scope of his actions, the ripples he has sent through the Skywood and beyond. The land dragons have always been the silent witnesses, the keepers of the earth's deep memory.

We will watch. We will feel the earth's pain, and we will endure. For when Cael's drastic measures inevitably falter, when his grand design crumbles under the weight of its own imbalance, it will be for us to mend what he has broken, to find the true path to restoration, the one that honors the Skywood's intricate song, not silences it with a roar. He has played his hand with a reckless abandon, and now, we must simply wait for the consequences to reveal themselves, and for our moment to act."

CHAPTER NINE

SHARPENING TENSIONS

The air in the council chambers, once thick with the tension of shared purpose, now crackled with a different kind of energy—one of suspicion and accusation. Mara stood before Cael, her usual composure frayed, her eyes, normally pools of calm clarity, now flashing with a fierce, wounded light. The tremors that had shaken the Skywood, the unnatural surge of its lifeblood, the panicked whispers of the forest's denizens—these were not abstract concepts to her. She had felt them, too, a dissonant hum that vibrated in her bones, a palpable imbalance that spoke of a world thrown violently off-kilter.

"You call this healing, Cael?" Mara's voice was a low, dangerous murmur, each word carefully enunciated, laced with the bitter taste of betrayal. The ornate carvings on the chamber walls, depicting ancient pacts between humans and the forest spirits, seemed to mock her. "You have not healed the Skywood; you have wounded it anew, with a far more brutal hand than any blight could manage." She gestured with a hand that trembled slightly, the emerald sheen of her skin seeming to dim under the chamber's flickering torchlight. "The Sylphs are scattered, their ethereal songs now a cacophony of fear. The Lumina Worms, once beacons of gentle guidance, now blind with erratic, searing light. The very currents of the marshlands boil with an energy that sears the spirit. What madness drove you to such an act?"

Cael met her gaze, his own eyes hard and unyielding, a stark contrast to the desperate urgency that had fueled his actions. He stood his ground, a solitary figure against the tide of her accusation, his hands clasped behind his back, a posture of unwavering resolve that bordered on defiance. "Madness?" he echoed, his voice rough, carrying the weight of sleepless nights and agonizing decisions. "No, Mara. It was necessity. Look around you! The blight was not merely creeping; it was consuming. The Skywood was dying, its breath fading. I did what had to be done. I tapped into its deepest reserves, its latent power, and I forced it to surge. It was a gamble, yes, but a necessary one. To stand idly by and watch everything we hold dear turn to ash? That would have been the true madness."

"But at what cost?" Mara countered, stepping closer, her voice rising with her anguish. "You speak of necessity, but you acted alone. You consulted no one. You did not seek the wisdom of the dragons, the ancient guardians who understand the earth's pulse in ways we can only dream of. You did not even confide in me, your council. You played God with the heart of the Skywood, and now we are all left to suffer the consequences of your hubris." The word 'hubris' hung in the air, heavy and sharp, a testament to the chasm that had opened between them. She saw the desperation in his eyes, the raw fear that had likely driven him, but it did not excuse the recklessness, the sheer audacity of his unilateral decision. "The rivers are not merely swollen; they thrum with an alien power. The roots of the ancient trees weep sap that burns like fire. The earth itself groans under the strain. This is not life, Cael; it is a fevered delirium, a desperate, uncontrolled burst of energy that will surely lead to collapse."

Cael's jaw tightened. He understood her anger, her pain, but he could not concede the righteousness of his actions. He saw himself not as a reckless gambler, but as a surgeon wielding a desperate, albeit crude, scalpel against a terminal illness. "You speak of consultation, Mara, of patience," he said, his voice tight with frustration. "While you deliberated, the blight would have won. While you sought counsel, the Skywood would have withered. There was no time for measured debate. The time for action was *now*. And

I acted. I made the choice that had to be made, the choice that no one else was willing to make. Is it so wrong to fight for survival?"

"Survival at the expense of balance is not survival; it is a slow, agonizing suicide," Mara retorted, her eyes narrowing as she studied his face, searching for any flicker of doubt, any sign that he understood the depth of the damage he had wrought. "You have not restored the Skywood; you have merely replaced one threat with another. You have proven that humanity's ambition, when unchecked, is a force more devastating than any natural decay. You have demonstrated a terrifying capacity for destruction, masked by the guise of salvation. The creatures of the deep earth, those most attuned to the land's subtle rhythms, are in turmoil. They speak of a pervasive unease, a discordant hum that vibrates through their very being. This is not healing, Cael. This is annihilation dressed as progress."

A pained expression flickered across Cael's face, a brief crack in his steely facade. He knew Mara's dedication to the Skywood was as profound as his own, her understanding of its delicate ecosystems far deeper. Her words, though sharp, held a truth he could not entirely dismiss. But the specter of the blight, the memory of the encroaching rot, the desperate pleas of his people, still loomed large in his mind. "I understand your concerns, Mara, truly I do," he said, his voice softening slightly, though the underlying conviction remained. "But you did not see what I saw. You did not feel the despair that gripped our people as the blight advanced. You were not there, witnessing the slow, inexorable death of the very heart of our world. The choices were stark, and I chose to fight. I chose to believe that the Skywood, in its immense power, could withstand this surge, that it could adapt, that it could heal from this intervention, just as it has healed from countless other wounds throughout its long history."

"Adapt to what, Cael?" Mara pressed, her voice gaining an edge of desperation. "To a power it cannot control? To a force that tears at its very essence? You have not given the Skywood strength; you have given it a fever. You have accelerated its growth, yes, but into a wild, untamed frenzy. The plants bloom with unnatural speed, their leaves unfurling with a visible, almost violent, expansion. This is not healthy growth; it is a desperate, final surge before the inevitable collapse. You have become the storm, Cael, and you mistake your own destructive force for the cleansing power of nature."

Cael flinched at the accusation. He had always seen himself as a protector, a healer, and the idea that he had become a force of destruction was a bitter pill to swallow. "I did what I believed was right," he insisted, his voice regaining its earlier firmness, though a weariness now underscored it. "I took the risk, the burden. I did not ask for your approval, Mara, because I knew there would be debate, and debate would lead to delay. And delay would mean death. For the Skywood, and for my people. I have always believed that action, even drastic action, is preferable to inaction. You value balance, Mara, and I admire that. But sometimes, to restore balance, one must first create a significant disturbance. Think of a fractured bone; it must be broken cleanly before it can be set and healed."

"A fractured bone is a localized injury, Cael," Mara countered, her voice laced with a profound sadness. "You have fractured the entire body of the Skywood. You have disrupted the delicate interplay of energies that sustain it. You have disregarded the ancient pacts, the trust that has bound humans and the forest spirits for millennia. You acted as if you were the sole owner of this world, the only one capable of making decisions. You did not seek to understand the Skywood; you sought to command it. You did not listen to its whispers; you drowned them out with your roar." She paused, her gaze sweeping over his defiant stance, the weariness etched into his features. "I remember you, Cael. As a child, you were always so driven, so eager to protect, to act. You saw the blight, and you could not bear to stand idly by. But that urgency, that conviction, has blinded you to the wisdom of patience, to the necessity of collaboration. You have always been quick to act, but now, your actions have consequences far beyond your immediate sight."

The weight of her words settled upon Cael, a palpable burden. He understood her viewpoint, the emphasis she placed on harmony and interconnectedness. But he felt, with every fiber of his being, that his actions, however drastic, were justified by the dire circumstances. "And what of your inaction, Mara?" he challenged, his voice hardening again.

"What of your reliance on ancient rituals and whispered promises, while the blight gnawed at our very foundations? While the Skywood sickened and died? Did your pursuit of balance offer any solace to the villages that were slowly being choked by the decay? Did your respect for the Sylphs' ethereal songs offer any comfort to the people who were watching their world crumble around them? I made a choice. I chose to fight. I chose to risk everything, to embrace the chaos, in the hope of forging a new order, a stronger Skywood. You speak of the damage I have done, but I ask you, what damage would inaction have wrought?"

"Inaction is not what I advocate, Cael," Mara replied, her voice firm, though laced with a deep sorrow. "I advocate for understanding, for a measured approach, for working *with* the Skywood, not against it. You have not forged a new order; you have unleashed a tempest, and you have mistaken your own destructive force for the cleansing power of a storm. The Sylphs are disoriented, their patterns broken. The Lumina Worms' light is wild and chaotic. The creatures of the deep earth are in disarray. This is not the work of a savior; it is the work of someone who has fundamentally misunderstood the nature of the power he wields. You have not healed the Skywood; you have merely amplified its suffering, masked its decay with a desperate, frenzied vitality."

Cael looked away, his gaze fixed on the intricate patterns of the chamber floor. He saw not the carvings of pacts and alliances, but the chaotic swirl of energies he had unleashed. He had envisioned a controlled surge, a directed flood of power that would revitalize the Skywood, pushing back the blight and restoring its lost vitality. Instead, he had created a maelstrom, a wild, untamed force that threatened to consume everything in its path. The whispers of the forest creatures, the pleas of the displaced, the anguished cries of the earth elementals—these were no longer abstract reports. They were the echoes of his own failure, the bitter fruit of his ambition.

"You believe I have failed," he stated, his voice barely above a whisper, the fight draining out of him, replaced by a profound weariness. "You believe I have made things worse. Perhaps you are right." He looked back at Mara, his eyes filled with a depth of regret she had not seen before. "I acted with the best intentions, Mara. I believed I was saving us. But the path to hell, as they say..." He trailed off, the unspoken implication hanging heavy in the air. He had sought to control the forces of nature, to bend them to his will, and in doing so, he had broken them. He had become the very thing he had sought to fight—a force of uncontrolled destruction.

Mara watched him, her heart aching not for his defiance, but for the genuine despair that now clouded his features. The rift between them was deep, forged in the fires of their conflicting methods and the devastating consequences of his unilateral actions. She saw not a madman, but a man consumed by his own desperate ambition, a man who had made a terrible choice, believing it was the only choice available. "Your intentions, Cael," she said, her voice soft now, the anger replaced by a profound sadness, "do not absolve you of the responsibility for your actions.

The Skywood is a living entity, not a machine to be repaired with brute force. It requires understanding, respect, and patience. These are the qualities you have discarded in your haste." She took a deep breath, the scent of ozone and damp earth still clinging to the air, a constant reminder of the forces he had unleashed. "The dragons... they are not merely powerful beings, Cael. They are the keepers of balance, the anchors of the earth. Their wisdom lies not in their strength, but in their understanding of the natural order. You have alienated them. You have broken faith with them, and with us. And now, we are all caught in the tempest you have created."

Cael remained silent, the weight of his actions pressing down on him. He had expected resistance, perhaps even anger, but the depth of Mara's disappointment, the sorrow in her voice, struck him more profoundly than any accusation. He had believed he was acting for the greater good, but his actions had created a schism, not only within the Skywood but also between himself and those he had sworn to protect. He had sought to be a savior, but in his haste, he had become a source of discord, a harbinger of chaos. The clear, decisive path he had envisioned had dissolved into a tangled mess of unintended consequences, leaving him adrift in a sea of doubt and regret. The Skywood was vibrant, yes, but it was a fevered, uncontrolled vibrancy, a stark testament to his monumental miscalculation. The accusations, unspoken but heavy in the air, were more damning than any shouted word. He had played God, and now, he was forced to confront the terrifying reality of his very human fallibility.

Mara's chambers, usually a sanctuary of quiet study, had become a crucible of her escalating anxieties. The tremors that had wracked the Skywood, the erratic pulse of its lifeblood, and the unnerving silence that had fallen over the once-vibrant forest floor—these were not mere symptoms of a dying ecosystem. They were, she now suspected, deliberate acts. Cael's desperate gambit, his forceful infusion of raw power into the Skywood's core, had been a desperate, misguided attempt to mend what he perceived as a wound. But Mara's instincts, honed by years of communion with the land, screamed a different truth. His actions were a symptom, not a cure, and the true ailment lay hidden, festering beneath the surface.

Her gaze swept over the maps and arcane diagrams spread across her worktable, charts detailing atmospheric currents, energy flow diagrams of the ancient weather engines, and detailed illustrations of the Skywood's interconnected root systems. Each line, each symbol, represented a piece of a puzzle that was rapidly coalescing into a terrifying image. Cael had spoken of necessity, of the blight's relentless advance, and while she had acknowledged the severity of the threat, his solution had felt... brutal. It had bypassed the intricate, almost sentient, symphony of the Skywood, opting instead for a forceful, percussive strike. That approach, she now believed, had not only failed to address the root cause but had actively masked it, creating a chaotic surge of energy that could be easily mistaken for a desperate recovery.

She picked up a smooth, obsidian shard, its surface cool and unyielding against her fingertips. It was a fragment from one of the outer weather engines, one of the colossal, crystalline structures humming with an unseen power, designed to regulate the region's climate. The official explanation, the one Cael and the council had accepted, was that these engines were merely reactive, responding to natural fluctuations. But Mara had always harbored a deep-seated unease about their true nature, their immense capacity. And now, with the Skywood's unnatural fever, her suspicions had solidified. What if the engines were not just reactive, but *proactive*? What if they were being manipulated?

The idea was audacious, bordering on heretical. The weather engines were ancient, their origins lost to time, their workings understood only by a select few, and even then, with a healthy dose of reverence rather than absolute comprehension. They were the very breath of their world, regulating seasons, guiding rains, and warding off extreme climatic shifts. To suggest they were being deliberately influenced, twisted to serve an agenda, was to suggest an enemy far more insidious than any blight.

Yet, the evidence, however circumstantial, began to stack. The localized intensity of the recent storms, the unnatural patterns of wind shifts that defied all known meteorological models, the creeping desiccation of certain flora in areas far from the blight's reach, all pointed to an external influence. And the weather engines, positioned at strategic nexus points across the land, were the most likely conduits.

Driven by this nascent theory, Mara had begun a solitary, clandestine investigation. While Cael was busy tending to the immediate, volatile fallout of his actions, she was delving into the engine's deeper mechanisms, poring over ancient texts detailing their energy signatures, their symbiotic relationship with the Skywood's Ley lines. She had even begun discreetly observing the engines themselves, undertaking short, perilous journeys to their remote locations. These were not mere reconnaissance missions; they were pilgrimages to the heart of her suspicion.

Her first visit had been to the Azure Falls engine, a towering crystalline edifice nestled behind a cascading waterfall, its energies usually a gentle hum that soothed the surrounding valleys. Now, she had felt a distinct disharmony. The usual soothing resonance was overlaid with a subtle, discordant thrum, like a beautiful melody played with a single, jarring note. She had spent hours there, disguised as a wandering herbalist, noting the strange eddies in the mist, the way the water seemed to recoil from the engine's base, as if in pain.

Her subsequent visits to other engines had yielded similar observations. The Verdant Plateau engine, designed to draw moisture from the atmosphere, was emitting an unnaturally dry heat. The Whispering Dunes engine, meant to temper the desert's harsh winds, was generating gusts that felt... weaponized, carrying a fine, abrasive dust that stung the eyes. Each engine, in its own way, was exhibiting a subtle but undeniable deviation from its intended function.

Mara knew that confronting Cael directly with these suspicions would be met with dismissal, perhaps even anger. He was too entrenched in his belief that he had acted correctly, too focused on the immediate crisis he believed he had averted. He saw the Skywood's frenzied growth as a sign of recovery, not a symptom of deeper manipulation. To him, her focus on the weather engines would seem like a distraction, a desperate attempt to shift blame or avoid acknowledging the harsh realities they faced. He needed irrefutable proof, and that was what she was determined to find.

She spent her days in the council's archives, not searching for ancient prophecies or forgotten spells, but for schematics, for records of energy calibrations, for any anomaly in the engines' maintenance logs that might have been overlooked or deliberately obscured. She cross-referenced these with the accounts of the Skywood's forest tenders, seeking patterns in the plant life's distress, in the unusual behavior of the fauna. She sought out the hermitic scholars who studied geomancy and atmospheric magic, not for their pronouncements on balance, but for their understanding of energy conduits and potential interference.

One evening, poring over a brittle, leather-bound tome detailing the intricate workings of the weather engines, a passage caught her eye. It spoke of 'harmonic resonance amplification,' a concept that seemed to describe how external energetic frequencies could be amplified and channeled through the engines. The text warned of the dangers of such manipulation, of the potential for catastrophic ecological imbalance if such power was wielded without understanding or ethical consideration. It was an ancient warning, written in an era when such manipulation was a theoretical threat, not a present reality.

"Harmonic resonance amplification..." Mara murmured, tracing the elegant, archaic script with her finger. This was it. This was the key. Cael's surge of power, while crude, had been a massive influx of raw energy. If something else had been subtly influencing the engines, layering its own energetic signature onto them, then Cael's actions would have acted as a catalyst, amplifying that existing influence to an unprecedented degree. He hadn't *caused* the problem, but he had certainly exacerbated it, making the Skywood's symptoms appear as a direct result of his own actions.

The implication was staggering. It meant that the blight, the tremors, the disarray of the forest spirits – these were not the Skywood's death throes, but the amplified screams of a system under siege. The blight itself might be a byproduct of this interference, a symptom of the land's corrupted energy.

Mara decided she needed to see one of the engines up close, under the cover of darkness. She chose the Sunstone Ridge engine, a massive structure built into a mountain face, known for its ability to harness solar energy and distribute it as warmth and light to the surrounding regions. It was a considerable journey, and she made it alone, traveling by night, relying on her knowledge of the hidden trails and the subtle shifts in the air that warned of approaching creatures.

As she approached Sunstone Ridge, the air grew heavy, charged with an almost palpable tension. The usual gentle warmth emanating from the engine was replaced by an oppressive heat, and the light it cast was a harsh, pulsating orange, far from its natural golden hue. She found a vantage point on a rocky outcrop overlooking the engine, its crystalline facets glowing with an unnatural intensity. She noticed subtle, almost imperceptible pulses emanating from its core, not the steady thrum of a healthy engine, but a staccato beat, like a wounded heart struggling to pump blood.

She activated a small, handheld scrying device, a tool she had painstakingly crafted from enchanted quartz and silver wire. It was designed to capture and analyze ambient energy signatures. As she focused it on the Sunstone Ridge engine, the device began to emit a low, distressed whine. The reading on its surface flickered wildly, displaying a complex waveform that was unlike anything she had ever seen. It was a chaotic blend of natural solar energy and something... alien. Something that felt sharp, intrusive, and aggressively directed.

She spent hours observing, meticulously recording the energy fluctuations, the spectral patterns of the light, the very hum of the structure. She noticed faint, shimmering lines of energy, almost invisible to the naked eye, weaving around the engine's core. They weren't the natural currents of the Skywood; they were like tendrils, siphoning and redirecting the engine's power. And they seemed to originate from a specific point on the mountain's opposite slope, a seemingly unremarkable cluster of ancient, gnarled trees.

Her heart pounded. This was it. Direct evidence. Not just an educated guess, but observable, measurable interference. She needed to reach that point. The terrain was treacherous, a sheer cliff face in places, but Mara's determination was a force unto itself. She scaled the rocks, her movements economical and precise, her focus unwavering.

When she finally reached the cluster of trees, she found a small, hidden clearing. In the center of the clearing, nestled amongst the roots of the oldest tree, was a device unlike any she had ever seen. It was a compact, obsidian obelisk, no taller than her knee, etched with symbols that were unsettlingly familiar, yet subtly warped, as if they had been corrupted. It pulsed with a faint, malevolent energy, and from its apex, the shimmering tendrils of influence snaked out, disappearing into the earth and, she now realized, connecting to the Sunstone Ridge engine.

She touched the obelisk cautiously, her skin prickling with a sensation akin to static electricity. The energy emanating from it was cold, devoid of life, yet potent. It felt like a parasite, feeding on the natural energies of the Skywood, subtly twisting them to its own unknown purpose. She realized with a chilling certainty that Cael's intervention had not only amplified the effects of this device but had inadvertently provided it with a massive surge of energy to manipulate, thus causing the Skywood's violent, feverish reaction.

She carefully examined the obelisk, looking for a way to deactivate it, but it seemed impervious to direct interference. It was designed to be subtle, to operate in the background, its influence insidious rather than overt. Any attempt to smash it would likely only scatter its components and amplify the problem, or worse, trigger a more immediate, catastrophic reaction. She needed a more nuanced approach.

Returning to her chambers, Mara worked with renewed urgency. She studied the symbols on the obelisk, comparing them to ancient texts on forbidden magic and parasitic energies. She discovered that the symbols were a twisted form of warding magic, designed not to protect, but to corrupt and control. The device was an 'energetic siphon,' a tool for siphoning and redirecting the ambient magical energies of a region.

She realized that Cael's forceful infusion of energy had essentially acted as a beacon, drawing the siphon's full attention and amplifying its output. The Skywood's current state was a consequence of this amplified corruption. The blight, the weather anomalies, the disarray of the forest spirits – they were all symptoms of the land's lifeblood being systematically poisoned and redirected.

Mara knew she couldn't simply destroy the siphon. The energies it manipulated were too volatile. Instead, she needed to understand its mechanism of control, to find a way to disrupt its influence without causing further harm. She began to sketch out potential countermeasures, focusing on redirecting the siphon's own corrupted energy back upon itself, creating a feedback loop that would neutralize its effect. It was a dangerous proposition, requiring a precise understanding of the siphon's energetic output and a carefully calibrated counter-frequency.

She began gathering rare components: moon-kissed dew collected from the highest peaks, the heartwood of a lightning-struck elder tree, and the finely powdered dust of a fallen meteor. Each ingredient held a unique energetic property, essential for constructing a device capable of disrupting the siphon's parasitic drain. She worked in secret, the weight of her knowledge a heavy burden. She knew that once she revealed what she had found, the accusations against Cael would be overshadowed by the terrifying reality of a hidden enemy, and the fight for survival would take on a new, more perilous dimension. Her independent pursuit was not just about proving Cael wrong; it was about unmasking the true threat and finding a way to protect the Skywood from a danger it hadn't even recognized. The path ahead was fraught with uncertainty, but for the first time, Mara felt she was on the verge of uncovering the truth, a truth that promised a difficult but potentially brighter future for their beleaguered world.

The weight of his decisions pressed down on Cael like the unyielding stone of the mountain peaks. Each breath felt heavier, each dawn a stark reminder of the fractured trust and the growing chasm between himself and those he once considered allies. The Skywood, once a vibrant tapestry of shared purpose, now seemed to whisper accusations in the rustling leaves, its altered pulse a constant thrum of discord against his own conscience. He moved through the Canopy Accord Council chambers like a phantom, his presence eliciting hushed conversations that ceased the moment he drew near. The sharp, knowing glances, the averted eyes – they were more potent than any shouted condemnation. They spoke of a leadership compromised, a judgment clouded, a man who had, in his haste to save, inflicted his own wound upon the very heart of their world.

His attempts to explain, to reassert the necessity of his actions, fell on deaf ears, or worse, were met with a weary resignation that stung more than outright anger. He had presented his findings, the undeniable evidence of the blight's insidious spread, the desperate need for immediate intervention. He had spoken of the encroaching decay, the palpable fear that had gripped the forest tenders, the whispers of dying ley lines. But his words, once imbued with the authority of conviction, now sounded hollow, like the echoes of a past triumph that had curdled into present failure. The council members, their faces etched with a mixture of concern and resentment, saw only the chaos that had ensued, the unnatural surge of energy that had ripped through the Skywood, the disquiet among the forest spirits. They saw not a savior, but a reckless hand that had tampered with forces it didn't fully comprehend.

"The Skywood is not merely recovering, Cael," Elder Elara had said, her voice a low, steady tremor that belied the steel in her gaze. "It is convulsing. You have introduced a fever, not a cure. And now, the land dragons... they are not pleased."

The land dragons. The very mention sent a chill down his spine. Thryxal, their ancient, wise elder, had always been a steady anchor, a voice of reason and profound connection to the earth's deep rhythms. But even Thryxal's ancient eyes, usually filled with a patient understanding, now held a distant disappointment. Cael had sought him out in the sacred grottos, the air thick with the scent of damp earth and ancient magic, hoping to find solace, or at least comprehension. Instead, he had found a formidable, silent disapproval.

"You have disturbed the ancient balance, Cael," Thryxal's voice had rumbled, each syllable resonating with the slow, deliberate power of the earth itself. "You acted as a surgeon with a bludgeon, seeking to excise a tumor by shattering the bone. The Skywood's sickness is a delicate imbalance, not a swift infestation. Your intervention, while perhaps born of a noble intent, has amplified the discord, not healed it."

Thryxal had explained, his words painting a vivid, unsettling picture, of how the land dragons felt the Skywood's distress not as a singular wound, but as a cascade of discordant vibrations, an unnatural resonance that had been amplified by Cael's forceful energy infusion. The tremors, the erratic pulse, the unnerving silence – these were not the symptoms of a blight that Cael had tried to fight, but the amplified reactions of a system thrown into chaos by his own actions. Thryxal had spoken of the subtle currents of energy that flowed beneath the surface, the intricate network that connected every living thing, and how Cael's blunt approach had disrupted this delicate symphony.

"The dragons feel your disharmony, Cael," Thryxal had continued, his massive form shifting, scales the color of obsidian catching the faint, phosphorescent glow of the cavern. "They are creatures of deep connection, and they sense the disruption. They feel the Skywood's pain, and they feel the source of that amplified pain emanating from you."

The implications were a cold knot in Cael's stomach. He had sought to protect the forest, to preserve its lifeblood, and in doing so, he had become a source of its suffering. The land dragons, the ancient guardians of the earth's equilibrium, now saw him as a disruptor, a force of imbalance. Their trust, hard-won and deeply respected, had been eroded, replaced by a cautious distance, a palpable wariness. He could feel it in the way the earth seemed to hum with a low, protective energy whenever he walked, a subtle warning to tread carefully, to not inflict further damage.

His isolation wasn't just political; it was existential. He felt adrift, a solitary figure on a turbulent sea, the familiar shores of support and understanding receding with every passing tide. The weight of leadership, once a burden he bore with a sense of shared responsibility, now felt like a solitary yoke. He was the one who had made the decision, the one who had wielded the power, and now he was the one who had to carry the consequences.

He found himself spending more time away from the council halls, seeking the solitude of the ancient, unblemished parts of the Skywood, places that had not yet felt the tremors of his intervention. He would sit for hours beneath the colossal, moss-draped boughs of the elder trees, listening to the wind sigh through the leaves, trying to decipher its message. Was it forgiveness? Was it condemnation? Or was it simply the indifferent song of nature, a melody that continued regardless of the discord caused by its inhabitants?

He would trace the patterns of the bark, the intricate veins of the leaves, seeking a connection that felt increasingly elusive. The Skywood was a living entity, and he had always felt its pulse as his own. But now, that connection felt strained, like a frayed thread that threatened to snap. The vibrant life force that had once surged through him, a shared energy with the forest, now felt muted, a pale imitation of its former strength. He wondered if his own internal turmoil, the gnawing doubt and the weight of responsibility, was actively interfering with his ability to commune with the land.

His most trusted advisors, the younger members of the Accord who had once looked to him with eager admiration, now kept their distance. They had witnessed the fallout, the palpable unease that had settled over the forest, and they were hesitant to align themselves too closely with a leader whose decisions had created such division. Their loyalty, once a steadfast shield, had become a fragile barrier, easily breached by the winds of doubt. He understood their reticence; they had families, futures to consider, and a leader who had inadvertently fractured their world was a precarious gamble.

One evening, while walking through the twilight-dappled groves, he encountered Lyra, a young, gifted forester whose keen observations he had always valued. She had been tending to a grove of luminous moss, her face etched with a familiar concern. As he approached, her posture stiffened, her movements becoming more guarded.

"Cael," she acknowledged, her voice polite but distant.

"Lyra," he replied, his own voice raspy with a weariness he couldn't disguise. "How fares the grove?"

"It... it is as it is," she said, her gaze flicking towards the deeper woods, a subtle indication of her reluctance to engage. "The light is fainter than it should be, and the moss seems... hesitant to bloom."

Cael felt a familiar pang of guilt. This was the effect of his actions, the ripple of unease spreading through every corner of the Skywood. "I am trying to understand," he began, his voice laced with a desperate sincerity. "I know my actions have caused... disruption."

Lyra looked at him then, her eyes searching his face, and for a fleeting moment, he saw a flicker of the old camaraderie, the shared belief in his vision. But it was quickly replaced by a pragmatism that chilled him. "We all are trying to understand, Cael," she said softly. "But understanding does not always bring comfort. Some wounds... they are deep."

She returned her attention to the moss, her message clear: the conversation was over. Cael turned away, the silence of the grove suddenly deafening. He was a leader who had lost his footing, a beacon that had sputtered and dimmed. The certainty that had fueled his decisive action was now a haunting memory, replaced by a gnawing question: had he been wrong? Had his desperate attempt to save the Skywood from one peril inadvertently delivered it into the clutches of another, a more insidious, unseen threat?

He found himself poring over ancient texts in the solitude of his chambers, not seeking power or solutions, but understanding. He reread accounts of past ecological crises, of periods of imbalance and the arduous paths to recovery. He sought wisdom not in potent spells or forceful interventions, but in the quiet resilience of nature, in the slow, deliberate processes of healing. He read of civilizations that had risen and fallen, of leaders who had made grave errors and the long, often painful, journeys they had undertaken to mend the damage they had wrought.

He began to notice patterns, recurring themes that resonated with his current predicament. Many of these ancient narratives spoke of the dangers of haste, of the hubris that often accompanied power, and the critical importance of listening to the subtle whispers of the natural world, rather than imposing one's will upon it. He had been so focused on the visible threat, the blight, that he had overlooked the subtler signs, the deeper disquiet that Mara had hinted at, the unnerving harmony he now suspected was being manipulated.

The thought of Mara sent a fresh wave of regret through him. He had dismissed her concerns, her intuition, too readily. He had seen her as overly cautious, perhaps even fearful, while he had been driven by the urgency of the moment. Now, he wondered if her quiet observations, her deep communion with the Skywood, had held a truth that he, in his haste and self-imposed authority, had been blind to.

He remembered their last significant conversation, before he had enacted his plan. She had spoken of balance, of interconnectedness, of a gentle mending rather than a forceful purge. He had nodded, but his mind had already been made up, his course set. He had believed he was acting with the best of intentions, guided by logic and a desperate need for decisive action. Now, the consequences of that decisiveness weighed heavily upon him.

The isolation was a self-inflicted wound, a consequence of his own actions, but it was also a necessary period of introspection. He couldn't lead the Skywood back to health if he couldn't first understand the true nature of its illness, and his own role in its exacerbation. He had to shed the illusion of infallible leadership, the certainty that had driven him, and embrace the humility of doubt. He had to learn to listen again, not just to the council, but to the earth itself, to the subtle currents of energy that flowed beneath the surface, to the quiet wisdom of those he had sidelined.

He began to spend hours observing the weather engines, not with the intent to control them, but to understand their rhythms, their subtle shifts. He noticed inconsistencies, minute deviations from their usual operational patterns, anomalies that he had previously dismissed as minor fluctuations. He watched the way the Skywood responded to the subtle changes in atmospheric pressure, the way the forest spirits moved through the canopy, their energy fluctuating with an almost anxious rhythm.

He realized, with a dawning sense of dread, that his intervention hadn't just amplified the Skywood's existing ailments; it had potentially masked a deeper, more sinister manipulation. The energy surge he had unleashed, in his misguided attempt to combat the blight, might have served as a catalyst for something far more dangerous, something that had been lurking in the shadows, subtly influencing the very forces that sustained their world.

Cael stood alone, the vastness of the Skywood stretching out before him, a magnificent, wounded entity. He carried the burden of his choices, the isolation a stark testament to their gravity. But within that solitude, a seed of a new understanding began to sprout. He had to find the truth, not just about the blight, but about the forces that might be manipulating their world. And for that, he knew, he would need to rely on more than just his own strength; he would need to reclaim the lost connections, to find a way to mend the broken trust, and to listen to the quiet, profound wisdom of the land dragons once more. His isolation, though painful, was not an end, but a difficult, necessary beginning.

The whispers that had begun as a murmur within the Canopy Accord Council, fueled by Cael's controversial intervention, had now swelled into a torrent, and the Ashbound were not merely listening; they were orchestrating the gale. The deep fissure of mistrust that had opened between Cael and Mara, the profound disappointment radiating from the land dragons – these were not seen by the Ashbound as unfortunate side effects of a well-intentioned but flawed act, but as fertile ground upon which to sow their own seeds of discord and power. Their faction, a collection of pragmatic, often ruthless individuals who believed in radical, immediate solutions over the Skywood's traditional, slower paths to balance, saw in the current turmoil an unprecedented opportunity.

Elder Malakor, his face a roadmap of weathered cynicism, had been the first to articulate the Ashbound's nascent strategy. He had convened a clandestine meeting in a shadowed grove, far from the prying eyes of the Accord and the watchful gaze of the forest spirits. The air there was thick with the scent of damp earth and the metallic tang of apprehension. Around him sat a dozen of his most trusted lieutenants, their faces illuminated by the flickering glow of enchanted moss that cast long, dancing shadows.

"The Skywood is sick," Malakor began, his voice a low rumble that seemed to vibrate with the very impatience of the earth. "And the one tasked with its healing has, in his haste, only deepened the wound. Cael, blinded by a misguided sense of urgency, has alienated the very powers that sustain us.

The forest dragons, creatures of ancient inertia, have been disturbed. Mara, for all her connection to the land's whispers, has found herself isolated, her voice drowned out by the cacophony of Cael's blundering."

He paused, allowing the weight of his words to settle. "This is not a time for deliberation. This is a time for decisive action. The Skywood needs a firm hand, a guiding will that is not afraid to make the difficult choices, the necessary sacrifices. And who better to provide that hand than those who understand the true cost of inaction? The Ashbound."

A ripple of agreement passed through the assembled faction members. They had long advocated for more aggressive methods of managing the Skywood's resources, for bolder interventions to combat threats, and they had often found themselves at odds with the Council's more conservative approach, personified by Cael's earlier leadership. Now, they saw their philosophy validated, not by wisdom, but by chaos.

"Our message must be clear," Malakor continued, his eyes gleaming with a cold fire. "Cael's actions have proven the inherent weakness of the Accord's approach. His brute force has disrupted the delicate balance, and in doing so, has revealed the fragility of our defenses. The dragons' wavering loyalty is a testament to this weakness. They feel the disarray, and they see that the Council, under Cael's misguided leadership, is incapable of restoring order."

He leaned forward, his voice dropping to a conspiratorial whisper. "We will speak of the blight, of course. We will remind everyone of its insidious nature, of how it has been allowed to fester, of how Cael's actions, while intended to be a swift cure, have only served to destabilize the entire system, making it *more* susceptible to further decay. We will highlight Mara's isolation, not as a sign of her being unheard, but as proof that the established leadership is deaf to true wisdom, too proud to admit its mistakes."

"And what of the dragons, Elder?" a young woman named Lyra, her face sharp with ambition, inquired. Lyra was one of the newer recruits, drawn to the Ashbound's promise of swift, decisive change. She had been a talented forest tender, but her patience had worn thin with what she perceived as the Accord's dithering.

Malakor's lips curved into a sardonic smile. "The dragons are powerful, yes, but they are also creatures of habit, of deep-seated traditions. They fear change, but they fear chaos even more. We will portray Cael's intervention as a violent disruption of that sacred order. We will emphasize that his actions have angered the earth itself, creating a disharmony that the dragons, in their ancient wisdom, are struggling to comprehend or correct. We will suggest that their wavering support is not a judgment on Cael's intent, but a sign of their deep-seated fear that he has unleashed a force beyond their control, a force that threatens to unravel the very fabric of the Skywood."

He gestured to a map spread on a mossy log, a roughly drawn representation of the Skywood's various regions. "We will identify areas where the blight's resurgence is most apparent, or where the energy currents are weakest. We will then propose our own solutions – solutions that are direct, effective, and require the unified, unwavering commitment that only the Ashbound can provide. We will call for the establishment of specialized 'recovery zones,' overseen by the Ashbound, where we can implement our proven methods of accelerated growth and restoration, free from the bureaucratic infighting and indecisiveness of the Accord."

"Accelerated growth?" Lyra questioned, a glint in her eye. "What does that entail, Elder?"

"It entails a more… vigorous approach," Malakor stated, his tone leaving little room for further inquiry. "We will utilize methods that bypass the slow, organic processes of the forest. We will employ specially cultivated strains of growth catalysts, carefully managed energy conduits to accelerate ley line recovery, and, where necessary, focused clearing of 'unproductive' biomass to allow for faster regeneration. We will present these as necessary measures, born of the dire circumstances that Cael's folly has created.

We will argue that the Skywood can no longer afford the luxury of its traditional pace. It needs to be *forced* back into health."

The Ashbound's propaganda machine, subtle yet pervasive, began to grind into motion. They didn't directly accuse Cael of malice, but their carefully crafted narratives painted him as incompetent, a well-meaning fool who had inadvertently jeopardized everyone's safety. They spoke of his "reckless energy infusion," not as a healing act, but as a "violent disruption" that had "unsettled the ancient foundations of the Skywood." They highlighted the disquiet among the forest spirits, the erratic pulse of the ley lines, and the increasingly anxious tremors felt by the land dragons, framing these as direct consequences of Cael's hubris.

They began to circulate stories, whispered in the hushed marketplaces of the canopy villages and carried on the wind to the remotest outposts. Tales of forest tenders who had witnessed Cael's energy surge firsthand, their descriptions amplified and distorted to sound like the unleashed fury of a tempest rather than a controlled infusion. They spoke of weakened sections of the forest floor, areas where the blight's tendrils, though seemingly held at bay, were now reported to be subtly deeper, their roots reaching into the disrupted soil.

Crucially, they focused on Mara and Cael's fractured relationship. They presented Mara's concerns, her intuitive unease, not as a differing perspective, but as a profound disagreement born of Cael's stubborn refusal to acknowledge his mistakes. They subtly implied that Mara, a respected figure deeply attuned to the Skywood's well-being, had been sidelined and ignored by Cael, who was too consumed by his own pride to heed her warnings. This narrative was particularly effective, as many in the Accord had witnessed the visible tension between them, and the dragons' reticence towards Cael seemed to validate the idea that something was fundamentally wrong with his approach.

"The dragons are not communicating," was a common refrain, disseminated by Ashbound sympathizers within the Accord's lower ranks. "They used to speak to Cael with ease. Now, they are silent, or their rumblings are of discontent. This is not the sign of a healthy balance; it is the cry of a wounded earth, a warning that Cael has overstepped his bounds."

The Ashbound also began to leverage the perceived weakness of the land dragons. While acknowledging their ancient power, they framed their current state of agitation and distant disappointment not as a reaction to Cael's actions, but as a sign of their own declining influence, of their inability to maintain the Skywood's equilibrium in the face of Cael's disruptive presence.

"The dragons are ancient, yes," Malakor would say during his carefully staged public addresses, his voice resonating with a feigned concern. "But even the oldest trees can be weakened by a relentless storm. Their power lies in stability, in the predictable flow of nature. Cael's intervention has created a maelstrom. He has introduced an element of unpredictability that even the dragons struggle to master. They feel the discord, the disquiet, and they are withdrawing, perhaps out of fear, perhaps out of a weary resignation that their ancient wisdom is no longer enough to guide us through this chaos."

This narrative was designed to sow doubt about the very foundations of the Skywood's spiritual leadership. If the land dragons, the ultimate arbiters of natural balance, were faltering, then what hope was there? This created a void, a vacuum of certainty, that the Ashbound were eager to fill.

Their proposed solutions were presented as a stark contrast to Cael's perceived failures. They spoke of "controlled regeneration protocols," of "stabilization matrices for the ley lines," and of "proactive blight eradication." These were complex, technical-sounding terms that hinted at a scientific, unfaltering approach. They didn't shy away from the idea of "necessary sacrifices," of clearing diseased or weakened sections of the forest to allow for rapid regrowth.

"We cannot afford to coddle weakened branches," Malakor declared at a hastily called assembly in the Lower Canopy. "We must prune aggressively.

We must redirect vital energies, even if it means temporary hardship for certain areas. The Ashbound have the knowledge, the will, and the dedication to see this through. We will not be swayed by sentimentality or by the hesitant pronouncements of those who cling to outdated methods. We will act. We will restore. We will ensure the Skywood survives, even if it must be reshaped in the process."

He pointed to the scarred bark of a blight-ridden tree that had been brought to the assembly, a stark visual aid. "This is the consequence of hesitation," he boomed. "This is the result of indecision. Cael's actions have only proven that a gentle touch is no longer sufficient. The Skywood needs strength. It needs a clear vision. It needs the Ashbound."

The Ashbound's strategy was multi-pronged. They cultivated their image as the faction of action, the only ones willing to make the tough decisions. They actively spread misinformation, twisting Cael's intentions and exaggerating the negative consequences of his actions. They exploited the existing divisions within the Accord, particularly the growing unease surrounding Cael and the evident disapproval of the land dragons. They presented themselves as the logical, pragmatic solution to the escalating crisis, offering a clear path forward that, while potentially harsh, promised swift and decisive results.

One particular tactic involved sending out scouting parties, ostensibly to assess the blight's spread, but in reality, to identify and subtly exacerbate weaknesses in the forest's natural defenses. These Ashbound scouts, skilled in navigating the dense undergrowth, would deliberately disturb sensitive fungal networks, introduce minor soil imbalances in areas already stressed, or even subtly disrupt the territorial boundaries of guardian spirits, creating localized pockets of disquiet that they could later point to as evidence of the Skywood's deteriorating state, and further proof that Cael's intervention had weakened the entire ecosystem.

They also began a campaign of subtle recruitment, targeting those who felt disenfranchised by Cael's leadership or who were impatient with the Council's slow pace. They offered them a sense of purpose, a place within a movement that promised to take control and restore order. They appealed to their frustrations, validating their anger and their fears, and channeling it into a collective desire for decisive, even radical, change.

"Cael is a dreamer," one Ashbound recruiter was heard telling a group of disillusioned forest tenders. "He means well, but he is lost in the clouds. We are the ones with our feet on the ground, the ones who understand that the Skywood needs more than just gentle persuasion. It needs to be commanded. It needs to be saved, by force if necessary."

The narrative that the Ashbound pushed was one of pragmatism versus idealism, of necessary harshness versus naive sentimentality. They framed Cael as the embodiment of the latter, his actions a testament to his inability to grasp the brutal realities of ecological preservation. They, on the other hand, presented themselves as the embodiment of the former, their proposed methods rigorous, scientific, and ultimately, more effective.

They carefully avoided direct confrontation with Cael himself, understanding that a direct challenge might galvanize his supporters. Instead, they worked from the periphery, undermining his authority through insinuation, rumor, and the strategic exploitation of every setback the Skywood experienced. They became the voice of doubt, the chorus of caution that amplified every tremor of unease, every rustle of concern into a roaring testament to Cael's failure.

The division within the Canopy Accord grew. Those who still held faith in Cael's intentions found themselves increasingly isolated, their pleas for patience and understanding drowned out by the Ashbound's strident pronouncements of impending doom and the urgent need for a strong hand. The dragons' continued silence, their somber presence now a symbol of deep unease rather than wise counsel, served as a constant, visual reminder of the fractured balance, a narrative the Ashbound skillfully woven into their own agenda. They were not just waiting for an opportunity; they were actively manufacturing one, turning the Skywood's own distress into the very weapon they would use to seize control.

The air in Mara's solitary workspace, a small, overgrown nook carved into the root system of a colossal ancient sequoia, hummed with a different kind of tension. It was not the charged, volatile energy of political machitions or the rumbling discontent of the land dragons, but the quiet, focused intensity of a mind grappling with an impossible puzzle. Dust motes danced in the slivers of light that pierced the dense canopy overhead, illuminating stacks of ancient scrolls, worn leather-bound tomes, and peculiar, crystalline devices that pulsed with faint, residual energy. Outside, the Skywood teemed with a growing disquiet, a palpable unease that had seeped into the very sap of the trees, yet within this secluded sanctuary, Mara sought a different kind of truth.

Her fingers, stained with the earth and the faint iridescence of concentrated energy, traced the intricate patterns etched onto a small, obsidian shard. It was one of dozens she had meticulously collected from the periphery of the weather engines, each bearing the subtle, almost imperceptible signature of interference. The Accords' traditional methods of diagnostics, designed to detect gross malfunctions or natural decay, had proven utterly inadequate against the sophisticated sabotage she suspected. This was not a matter of wear and tear; it was a deliberate, intricate unmaking.

For weeks, she had poured over every scrap of data, every anomaly, every whisper from the forest spirits that hinted at unnatural disruptions. The Council, blinded by the Ashbound's escalating rhetoric and Cael's perceived failures, had largely dismissed her solitary investigations as the desperate attempts of an ostracized scholar. They saw her isolation as confirmation of her diminished standing, not as a necessary condition for unbiased inquiry. But Mara knew that true understanding often bloomed in the quiet spaces, far from the clamor of accusation and defense.

The breakthrough came not as a sudden revelation, but as a slow, dawning realization, like the first hint of dawn after a long, starless night. She had been studying the temporal signatures of the weather engines' energy flow, attempting to map the precise moments of their deviation from natural patterns. Most of these deviations were erratic, appearing as jagged spikes and dips, suggesting a chaotic, uncontrolled force at play. Yet, when she layered her data from the obsidian shards, a faint, recurring pattern began to emerge.

It wasn't the energy surge itself that was the primary point of sabotage, she realized, but the *timing* and *frequency* of subtle harmonic disruptions. These weren't brute-force attacks designed to overload the engines, but elegant, insidious manipulations that subtly altered the resonant frequencies of the weather-regulating crystals within. It was like a skilled musician playing a dissonant note that, while seemingly minor, could throw an entire symphony into disarray.

The obsidian shards, she now understood, were not merely byproducts of the energy interference; they were tools. Each shard contained a microscopic echo of the precise harmonic frequency used to destabilize the engines. By understanding the specific sequence of these frequencies, and the subtle amplifications that accompanied them, she could not only identify the saboteur's methods but potentially, and this was the breathtaking part, *reverse* the process.

Her heart hammered against her ribs, a frantic bird trapped in a cage of bone. This was it. This was the key. The Ashbound spoke of forced restoration, of radical interventions, and Cael, in his desperation, had attempted a forceful recalibration. But true healing, true balance, required understanding the precise nature of the wound. And the wound, it appeared, was a meticulously crafted disharmony.

She spent the next few days in a feverish daze, painstakingly cross-referencing the harmonic signatures on the shards with ancient texts on elemental resonance and ley line harmonics. She discovered references to "sympathetic resonance manipulation," a theoretical practice described as the most subtle and devastating form of elemental control, capable of influencing not just the physical manifestations of weather, but the very atmospheric equilibrium that sustained life. The texts warned that such manipulation required an intimate understanding of the Skywood's energetic matrix, an insight that few possessed.

The implications were staggering. If her theory held true, then Cael's attempt to force a balance had been akin to a physician attempting to mend a fractured bone by pounding it further into place. He had addressed the symptom—the erratic weather—but not the root cause—the deliberate sonic sabotage. His actions, born of a desire to *fix*, had only served to deepen the discord, making the underlying problem harder to perceive.

This realization brought a fresh wave of despair, yet it was tinged with a strange kind of clarity. The chasm between her and Cael, carved by his impulsive actions and her subsequent isolation, felt immense. He saw her as someone who had abandoned him in his time of need, and she saw him as someone who had acted without considering the profound, interconnected nature of their world. But this discovery, this understanding of the *how* behind the *what*, offered a potential bridge.

If she could meticulously demonstrate the precise mechanism of the sabotage, the exact frequencies and their amplification, it would be irrefutable evidence. It would not only expose the true culprits but also vindicate her own approach, proving that the Skywood's healing lay not in brute force, but in a nuanced understanding of its delicate energetic symphony. It would offer a path forward that was not about imposing will, but about restoring natural harmony.

She looked at the map spread out on her workbench, a complex topographical representation of the Skywood dotted with energy nodes and ley line convergences. The patterns she had deciphered on the obsidian shards now seemed to align with specific junctions, suggesting that the saboteur had targeted key points of atmospheric convergence, nodes where the Skywood's natural weather patterns were most easily influenced.

The Ashbound, she now suspected, were not merely exploiting the chaos Cael had created; they were the architects of it, using their understanding of elemental resonance to sow discord. Their talk of "accelerated growth" and "necessary sacrifices" took on a chilling new meaning. Were they not only manipulating the weather but also preparing to exploit the weakened state of the Skywood for their own radical agenda?

A tremor ran through the ground, a low rumble that felt less like geological instability and more like a deep sigh of distress from the earth itself. The dragons. Their presence, usually a source of grounding stability, now felt like a constant reminder of the imbalance, their silence a testament to the profound disquiet that permeated the Skywood. Mara understood now that their apprehension wasn't just a reaction to Cael's energy infusion; it was a primal sensing of the deeper, more insidious sabotage that had been occurring all along.

She carefully gathered the obsidian shards, arranging them in a specific sequence that mirrored the harmonic progression she had identified. Each shard, in its own silent way, was a piece of the puzzle, a testament to the sophisticated nature of the attack. This was not the work of a rogue element or a natural blight. This was a calculated, deliberate act of sabotage.

The hope she felt was fragile, a tiny spark in the encroaching darkness. It was the hope of knowledge, of understanding, of a truth that could cut through the Ashbound's manufactured narrative and Cael's misguided efforts. It was the hope that by deciphering the saboteur's song, she could begin to compose a new melody for the Skywood, a song of restoration and balance.

But the path to presenting this truth was fraught with peril. The Ashbound had already woven a potent web of misinformation, and the Accord Council was deeply entrenched in their mistrust of Cael, and by extension, anyone associated with his controversial actions. She was an outsider, isolated and seemingly without allies. The dragons, though they might sense the truth of her findings, were too distant, too profoundly disturbed by the Skywood's ailment to actively intervene on her behalf.

She would have to find a way to present her findings to Cael himself. It was a daunting prospect. The rift between them felt as wide and as deep as the canyons that scarred the lower reaches of the Skywood. His pride, his desperation, his sense of betrayal – these were formidable barriers. Yet, he was the one who had inadvertently exposed the vulnerability of the engines, the one whose actions, however misguided, had drawn attention to the very systems that were now being exploited. He had the authority, however compromised, to initiate a true restoration.

She imagined his face, etched with weariness and a fierce, often blind, determination. Would he be able to see past his own anger and accept that her approach, so different from his own, might hold the key to healing the very wound he had inadvertently widened? Would he recognize the sophisticated nature of the sabotage and understand that his forceful intervention had only served to obscure it?

The weight of this uncertainty pressed down on her, heavier than the ancient sequoia overhead. But beneath the doubt, a kernel of resolve hardened. She had discovered a truth that could potentially save their world. She could not let it be buried under layers of political maneuvering and personal animosity. The Skywood deserved more. It deserved a chance at genuine healing, a chance to rediscover its lost harmony.

She began to meticulously document her findings, sketching the harmonic waveforms, cross-referencing the resonant frequencies with ancient geomantic charts, and compiling a detailed report that laid bare the intricate mechanism of the sabotage. Each stroke of her stylus was a declaration of intent, a small act of defiance against the growing tide of chaos. This was not a plea for forgiveness, nor an accusation. It was a beacon of knowledge, a singular, fragile glimmer of hope offered to a world teetering on the brink. She knew it was a long shot, a desperate gamble, but sometimes, in the heart of the deepest darkness, the smallest light could illuminate the path forward. The Skywood's fate, she realized, might depend on whether two fractured souls could find common ground in the pursuit of its salvation.

CHAPTER TEN

RESTORING RESONANCE

The obsidian shards, no longer inert fragments of sabotage, now pulsed with a newfound potential in Mara's hands. Each was a key, a sonic imprint of the Skywood's dissonance. She had meticulously cataloged their resonant frequencies, charting their subtle, insidious deviations from the natural hum of the planet. The ancient texts, once arcane riddles, now spoke with the clarity of a whispered truth, detailing the precise methods by which sympathetic resonance manipulation could be employed to unravel the delicate atmospheric tapestry. This was not a crude assault, but a surgical strike, a precise unmaking of equilibrium by playing the wrong notes in the Skywood's grand symphony.

Her workspace, usually a sanctuary of quiet contemplation, now buzzed with a focused, almost frantic energy. The air itself seemed to vibrate with the echoes of her efforts. She had gathered a collection of crystals, not the complex, engineered components of the weather engines, but smaller, naturally formed specimens, each possessing a unique harmonic signature. These were the conduits, the physical anchors she intended to use to transmit her counter-frequencies. She envisioned them as tuning forks, capable of reasserting the Skywood's fundamental harmonic.

The process was a delicate dance between the empirical and the intuitive. She would take a data-etched shard, its surface cool and smooth against her calloused fingertips, and hold it near a particular crystal. Then, with a finely tuned stylus, she would gently trace the amplified harmonic pattern onto the crystal's surface, coaxing it to resonate with the recorded dissonance. It was a painstaking effort, akin to painstakingly recreating a corrupted musical score, note by agonizing note. The goal wasn't to simply negate the disruptive frequencies, but to *reharmonize* them, to weave the discordant notes back into the Skywood's natural melody.

She recalled Cael's frantic attempts to *force* equilibrium, his energetic recalibrations that had been akin to a blacksmith hammering a warped bell back into shape. Such blunt force had only deepened the fissures, making the original wound harder to discern. Mara understood that true healing required a subtler touch, a deep empathy for the Skywood's inherent nature. She was not trying to impose her will, but to remind the land of its own ancient song.

One particular shard, a sliver of obsidian with an almost imperceptible shimmer of violet, proved exceptionally challenging. Its frequency was deeply embedded, a persistent hum that seemed to resist any attempt at reharmonization. It spoke of a deeper corruption, a deliberate attempt to sow discord at a fundamental level. She spent an entire cycle of the twin moons working on this single shard, her brow furrowed in concentration, her breath shallow. The ambient light in her nook grew dim, then brightened again with the Skywood's diurnal rhythm, but Mara remained absorbed, her world reduced to the tiny shard and the faint pulse of energy within it.

She began to experiment with cascading frequencies. Instead of trying to directly counter the disruptive note, she would introduce a series of harmonically related tones, each one subtly shifting the overall resonance. It was like weaving a new tapestry, where the disruptive thread, once isolated and stark, was gradually integrated into a richer, more complex pattern. She discovered that by introducing a specific sequence of ascending tones, she could not only neutralize the disruptive frequency but also amplify the Skywood's inherent restorative vibrations.

This method, she theorized, would work by creating a sympathetic feedback loop. The initial counter-frequency would nudge the local resonance, and as it propagated through the Skywood's energetic matrix, it would amplify the land's own natural healing mechanisms. It was a form of energetic acupressure, stimulating the natural flow of vitality rather than attempting to force it.

The challenge was immense. The Skywood was a vast, interconnected ecosystem, and the weather engines were not isolated units but integral nodes in its complex circulatory system. A localized correction, however well-intentioned, could have unforeseen ripple effects. She meticulously studied the geomantic charts, tracing the ley lines that crisscrossed the land, noting the points where the weather engines' energetic conduits intersected with these vital arteries. The saboteur, she realized, had targeted these nexus points, maximizing the impact of their discordant frequencies.

Her breakthrough came not from a single shard, but from the synthesis of several. She noticed that the disruptive frequencies from different locations, when layered, created complex interference patterns. It was as if the saboteur was not just playing individual dissonant notes, but composing an entire symphony of chaos. This meant that her counter-measures would need to be equally sophisticated, not just a single note of harmony, but a complex chord that could address multiple dissonances simultaneously.

She began to work with larger, more potent crystals, drawing on the latent energies of the ancient sequoias that surrounded her workspace. These massive trees, with their deep roots and skyward reach, acted as natural amplifiers, their very being attuned to the Skywood's subtle energies. She carefully placed the obsidian shards onto the surfaces of these crystals, their dark facets stark against the pale, veined rock. Then, using a series of finely calibrated sonic emitters – devices she had painstakingly crafted from salvaged components of the weather engines themselves – she began to broadcast the counter-frequencies.

The initial results were subtle, almost imperceptible. A slight tremor in the air, a faint shift in the ambient light. But then, as the cascading frequencies began to propagate, something shifted. The air in her workspace seemed to clear, the oppressive tension easing. A faint, warm glow emanated from the crystals, a gentle hum that resonated deep within her bones. It was the sound of the Skywood breathing, of its ancient song reasserting itself.

She spent days refining the process, adjusting the amplitude and frequency of her emissions, monitoring the Skywood's energetic feedback through a series of sensitive crystalline sensors she had placed at strategic points around her nook. She discovered that certain combinations of frequencies had a more profound restorative effect, like finding the perfect harmony that resolved a lingering dissonance. It was like learning a lost language, each resonance a word, each sequence a phrase, and the entirety of it a powerful, restorative ballad.

One particular moment stands out, a testament to the profound interconnectedness of the Skywood. She was working with a crystal that had been exposed to a particularly virulent strain of the disruptive frequency, a lingering echo of the sabotage. As she introduced her counter-sequence, a faint tremor ran through the ground, not the usual rumble of the dragons' unease, but a subtle vibration that seemed to hum in time with her crystals. She looked up, and through a gap in the sequoia's canopy, she saw a flash of iridescent scales – one of the forest dragons, its head raised, seemingly listening. It was a silent acknowledgment, a sign that the Skywood itself was responding to her efforts.

Her understanding of the sabotage deepened with each successful reharmonization. She realized that the Ashbound's agenda was not just about controlling the weather, but about fundamentally altering the Skywood's energetic signature. They were not merely breaking the song, but trying to rewrite it, to replace its ancient melody with a harsh, alien cadence. Her work, therefore, was not just a repair; it was a reclamation.

The implications of her findings were staggering. If she could indeed prove that the weather engines were being manipulated through precise harmonic frequencies, it would shatter the Ashbound's narrative of natural disaster and Cael's supposed incompetence. It would reveal their deliberate act of ecological warfare. But more importantly, it offered a tangible path to healing, a method that respected the Skywood's inherent vitality.

She began to meticulously document her findings, creating visual representations of the harmonic waveforms, mapping the propagation of her counter-frequencies, and meticulously noting the precise sequence of restorative tones. Her workspace, once cluttered with the detritus of her investigation, now bore the organized precision of a laboratory. The scrolls and tomes were still present, but they were now consulted with a specific purpose, their ancient wisdom applied to the urgent task at hand.

She realized that her efforts, while scientifically rigorous, were also deeply rooted in a mystical understanding of the Skywood. The crystals, the ancient trees, the very earth beneath her feet – they all responded to more than just physical forces. They were alive, imbued with a consciousness that Mara, through her dedication and her unique sensitivity, was learning to commune with.

As she worked, the Skywood responded. The air grew cleaner, the dappled sunlight seemed to shine with a warmer hue, and the incessant whisper of disquiet that had permeated the forest began to recede, replaced by a more gentle, natural rustling. The dragons, she sensed, were stirring, their ancient slumber disturbed not by her presence, but by the faint, returning hum of equilibrium.

Her progress was not without its setbacks. There were moments when a particular frequency would refuse to harmonize, or when the feedback loop would become unstable, threatening to unravel her painstaking work. These were the moments when the weight of her isolation would press down, when the sheer scale of the Skywood's ailment would threaten to crush her fragile hope. But each time, she would return to her data, to the ancient texts, and to the quiet wisdom of the land itself, finding a new approach, a different sequence, a subtle adjustment that would bring her back from the brink.

She began to believe that the Skywood was not merely a passive recipient of her efforts, but an active participant. It was as if the land itself was guiding her, whispering the correct frequencies, showing her the most efficient pathways for her counter-measures. This symbiotic relationship, this dance between her scientific understanding and the Skywood's intuitive wisdom, was the true source of her breakthrough. She was not imposing a solution, but facilitating a rediscovery of its own inherent balance. The intricate tapestry of resonance was being mended, thread by painstaking thread, not by force, but by a profound understanding of its original, harmonious design.

The ambient light in Mara's nook, filtered through the ancient sequoias, cast long, dancing shadows that played across her meticulously arranged collection of crystals. Each facet, meticulously polished by her own hands, gleamed with an inner luminescence, awaiting its role in the grand symphony of restoration. The obsidian shards, the very instruments of discord, lay dormant now, their corrupted frequencies captured and translated into a language of light and vibration. Her stylus, tipped with a filament of refined sky-iron, hovered over a particularly large geode, its amethystine heart pulsing faintly. This was no mere rock; it was a repository of the Skywood's deep earth resonance, a conduit capable of channeling the land's own restorative energies.

Mara's breathing was shallow, her focus absolute. The process was less about imposition and more about persuasion, a gentle coaxing of the Skywood's inherent harmonic to reassert itself. She recalled her initial attempts, driven by a desperate urgency, to simply blast away the dissonant frequencies. It had been akin to shouting into a hurricane, a futile exertion of force against an overwhelming imbalance. Now, she understood that true restoration was a dialogue, a patient whisper that encouraged the land to remember its own song.

She began by tracing the amplified patterns from the obsidian shards onto the geode's surface. This was not a physical etching in the traditional sense, but a transfer of energetic signatures, a delicate dance between the captured dissonance and the crystal's innate vibratory matrix. Each line drawn was a carefully calibrated wave, designed to resonate sympathetically with the corrupting frequencies, not to cancel them out, but to subtly alter their pitch, to introduce a harmonic overtone that would begin to untangle the knots of discord. It was a painstaking endeavor, demanding a level of precision that made the most intricate of alchemical formulae seem crude by comparison. The stylus moved with a painterly grace, each stroke a testament to Mara's growing understanding of the Skywood's energetic language.

The geode responded. A low hum, deeper and more resonant than the ambient thrum of the forest, began to emanate from within. It was the sound of deep earth awakening, of ancient currents stirring. Mara monitored the subtle shifts in vibration with a series of smaller, finely tuned resonance stones scattered around her workspace. Their internal crystalline structures would quiver, their light flickering in a complex, rhythmic pattern that translated the geode's energetic output. She was essentially listening to the earth's heartbeat, guiding it back to a steady, healthy rhythm.

The challenge lay in the interconnectedness of it all. The weather engines, each a node in the Skywood's vast energetic network, had been twisted and perverted. Their dissonant frequencies weren't isolated incidents; they were ripples spreading through the land's energetic circulatory system. To mend one area, she had to consider the impact on countless others. Her geomantic charts, spread out on a low table, were a testament to this complexity. Ley lines, like glowing arteries, crisscrossed the parchment, marked with the points where the weather engines' conduits intersected with the earth's natural flows. The saboteur had targeted these nexus points with a chilling understanding of their vital importance.

Mara adjusted her approach. Instead of focusing on individual shards and their corresponding frequencies, she began to weave them together. She realized that the discordant notes, when layered, created intricate interference patterns, a cacophony of chaos. Her counter-measures, therefore, needed to be equally complex, a symphony of harmony designed to address multiple dissonances simultaneously. She began to select multiple obsidian shards, their captured frequencies representing different facets of the sabotage, and simultaneously trace their corresponding harmonic patterns onto the geode.

The effect was profound. The geode's hum deepened, becoming richer, more complex. The resonance stones around her flickered with a newfound intensity, their light coalescing into a unified glow. It was as if Mara was not just repairing a single broken string, but re-tuning an entire orchestra. She was not merely correcting errors; she was re-composing the Skywood's song, weaving the discordant notes back into a tapestry of breathtaking beauty.

She experimented with cascading frequencies, a technique she had gleaned from an obscure treatise on ancient elemental manipulation. Instead of directly countering a disruptive frequency, she introduced a sequence of harmonically related tones, each one subtly shifting the overall resonance. It was like guiding a lost traveler back to their path by illuminating a series of stepping stones, rather than trying to shove them in the right direction. This method created a sympathetic feedback loop, where the initial counter-frequency nudged the local resonance, and as it propagated through the Skywood's energetic matrix, it amplified the land's own natural healing mechanisms.

The sequoias surrounding her nook seemed to respond to this shift. Their leaves, which had been rustling with an anxious whisper, now swayed with a more serene cadence. A gentle breeze, carrying the scent of damp earth and pine, wove through the clearing, a stark contrast to the oppressive stillness that had often permeated the area. Mara felt a subtle shift in the air, a lightening of the atmospheric pressure that had weighed on her spirit for so long.

One particularly stubborn shard, imbued with a frequency that spoke of deep-seated corruption, resisted her initial attempts at reharmonization. It was a discordant note that seemed to echo with a malevolent intent, a deliberate perversion of the Skywood's life-giving energies. Mara spent an entire cycle of the twin moons locked in a silent battle with this single shard. She meticulously charted its complex waveform, its erratic pulses, its subtle yet persistent tendency to destabilize the surrounding resonance.

It was during this protracted struggle that she discovered the power of symbiotic resonance. She began to incorporate smaller, naturally occurring crystals – moss agates with their intricate internal patterns, smoky quartz imbued with the earth's deep memory – into her work. These weren't conduits for her carefully constructed counter-frequencies, but amplifiers of the Skywood's own inherent restorative vibrations. She would place these 'helper' crystals alongside the geode, allowing their subtle energies to interact, to create a harmonious background hum that would gradually envelop and neutralize the stubborn dissonance.

The breakthrough came not from a single, forceful counter-frequency, but from a series of gentle, undulating waves. She found that by broadcasting a specific sequence of ascending tones, each one slightly higher than the last, she could create a resonant cascade that effectively 'lifted' the disruptive frequency, drawing it out of its harmful pitch and into a more harmonious range. It was like coaxing a shy creature out of its hiding place by offering it a sweet melody.

As she worked, Mara felt a growing connection to the Skywood, a sense of partnership that transcended the purely scientific. It was as if the land itself was whispering guidance, nudging her towards the correct frequencies, revealing the most efficient pathways for her counter-measures. This symbiotic relationship, this dance between her empirical knowledge and the Skywood's intuitive wisdom, was the true engine of her progress. She wasn't imposing a solution; she was facilitating a rediscovery of its own inherent balance.

She began to document her findings with a new urgency. Her scrolls were no longer filled with abstract theories or historical accounts, but with precise diagrams of waveform propagation, meticulously charted sequences of resonant tones, and visual representations of the energetic feedback loops she was creating. Her workspace transformed from a den of investigation into a humming laboratory of restoration, where the ancient texts and modern scientific instruments worked in concert.

The air in her nook grew noticeably cleaner, the oppressive tension that had clung to it like a shroud began to dissipate. The dappled sunlight, filtering through the sequoia canopy, seemed to shine with a warmer, more vibrant hue. The incessant whisper of disquiet that had permeated the forest for so long was gradually receding, replaced by the gentle, natural rustling of leaves and the distant, contented murmur of the earth.

She observed a subtle yet significant change in the behavior of the forest's fauna. Birds, whose songs had been muted and anxious, now chirped with a clearer, more melodic cadence. Small forest creatures, which had been skittish and withdrawn, began to emerge from their burrows, their movements more fluid and less fearful. These were not dramatic shifts, but subtle indicators, like the first hesitant signs of life returning to a wounded organism.

There were moments of profound challenge, of course. Days when a particular frequency would refuse to harmonize, or when a carefully constructed feedback loop would threaten to unravel, sending ripples of dissonance through her delicate system. These were the moments when the weight of her isolation would press down, when the sheer scale of the Skywood's ailment would threaten to overwhelm her fragile hope. During these times, she would retreat to her data, to the ancient texts, and to the quiet wisdom of the land itself, seeking a new approach, a different sequence, a subtle adjustment that would pull her back from the brink.

She found solace in the patterns, in the inherent order that lay beneath the apparent chaos. The Skywood, she realized, was not a passive recipient of her efforts, but an active participant in its own healing. It was as if the land itself was guiding her, breathing its ancient song into her work, reminding her of the original, harmonious design that had been so brutally disrupted.

One such challenging moment occurred when she was attempting to reharmonize a particularly potent area of discord, a nexus point where several corrupted ley lines converged. The obsidian shard associated with this location pulsed with a dark, unsettling energy, its frequency resisting all her attempts at subtle manipulation. The resonance stones around her flickered erratically, their light dim and unstable. For a full day, she worked tirelessly, her brow furrowed, her hands trembling with fatigue, but the dissonance remained.

As dusk settled, casting long shadows that deepened the gloom in her nook, Mara felt a pang of despair. She looked up, her gaze falling upon the colossal trunk of a nearby sequoia. Its ancient bark, gnarled and weathered, bore the marks of centuries. She reached out, her fingers tracing the deep furrows, feeling the immense, silent strength of the tree. And in that moment, an idea sparked.

She remembered a passage in an ancient text, speaking of the 'Root Song' of the world trees, their deep, grounding resonance that acted as an anchor for all other natural frequencies. The sequoias, she realized, were not just passive amplifiers; they were fundamental pillars of the Skywood's energetic architecture. She carefully retrieved a handful of fine, powdery soil from the base of the sequoia, and mixed it with a drop of dew collected from its highest branches. This mixture, she theorized, contained the concentrated essence of the tree's own deep resonance.

She applied this earthy balm to the surface of the recalcitrant obsidian shard. The effect was immediate and remarkable. The shard's dark energy seemed to soften, its aggressive pulsing subsiding into a more gentle throb. The resonance stones around her steadied, their light coalescing into a warm, golden glow. The stubborn dissonance, previously an immovable barrier, now seemed to yield, like a stubborn knot unraveling under a gentle, persistent tug.

Mara's heart swelled with a mixture of relief and profound gratitude. This was not just a scientific solution; it was a collaboration, a testament to the interconnectedness of all things within the Skywood. The tree, the earth, the dew – they had all played a role in her breakthrough. She was not a solitary savior, but a conduit, a facilitator of the land's own inherent power to heal.

The process of re-establishing the flow of natural energy was a symphony in progress. Each successful reharmonization was a new melody added to the grand composition, a thread woven back into the intricate tapestry of the Skywood. She meticulously adjusted the amplitude and frequency of her sonic emitters, monitoring the Skywood's energetic feedback through her network of crystalline sensors. She discovered that certain combinations of frequencies had a more profound restorative effect, like finding the perfect harmony that resolved a lingering dissonance. It was like learning a lost language, each resonance a word, each sequence a phrase, and the entirety of it a powerful, restorative ballad.

She began to visualize the flow of energy as currents of pure light, weaving through the Skywood's energetic matrix. Her counter-frequencies acted as gentle guides, nudging these currents away from the corrupted pathways and back into their natural, life-sustaining channels. The process was akin to clearing a clogged riverbed, not by dredging and tearing, but by subtly altering the course of the water, allowing it to find its own path once more.

The ancient texts, once arcane and mysterious, now served as a living guide, their wisdom unlocking the secrets of the Skywood's energetic circulatory system. She pored over diagrams of geomantic flows, comparing them with her real-time readings of energetic propagation. The saboteur had not merely disrupted the system; they had rerouted it, creating artificial dams and diverting the lifeblood of the land into stagnant pools of discord. Mara's task was to break these artificial barriers, to restore the natural, unimpeded flow.

She realized that her understanding of the sabotage ran deeper than mere ecological warfare. The Ashbound, by manipulating the Skywood's harmonic frequencies, were not just aiming to control the weather; they were attempting to fundamentally alter the land's energetic signature. They sought to replace its ancient, life-affirming melody with a harsh, alien cadence, a reflection of their own sterile and utilitarian worldview. Her work, therefore, was not just a repair; it was a reclamation of the Skywood's very soul.

The implications of her findings were staggering. If she could prove that the weather engines were being manipulated through precise harmonic frequencies, it would shatter the Ashbound's narrative of natural disaster and Cael's supposed incompetence. It would reveal their deliberate act of ecological warfare, a crime against the very essence of the Skywood. But more importantly, it offered a tangible path to healing, a method that respected the land's inherent vitality and offered a future of genuine restoration.

As she worked, the Skywood responded. The air grew cleaner, the dappled sunlight seemed to shine with a warmer hue, and the incessant whisper of disquiet that had permeated the forest began to recede, replaced by a more gentle, natural rustling. The dragons, she sensed, were stirring, their ancient slumber disturbed not by her presence, but by the faint, returning hum of equilibrium. She felt a subtle shift in the wind, a gentle caress that seemed to carry the faintest echo of a roar, a sound that was no longer of anger or distress, but of a deep, resonant awakening. The Skywood was not just healing; it was remembering.

The air in Mara's clearing, once thick with a palpable oppression, began to thin, carrying with it the faint, sweet scent of damp earth and resilient pine. The suffocating dryness that had clung to the Skywood like a shroud started to recede, not with the dramatic deluge of a storm, but with a subtle, almost imperceptible exhale. It was the breath of a land slowly awakening from a deep, unnatural slumber. Tiny, ephemeral tendrils of mist, born from the newly-awakened moisture in the soil, began to weave between the colossal trunks of the sequoias, catching the filtered sunlight and shimmering like captured starlight. These were not the harsh, biting winds that had previously scoured the landscape, but gentle zephyrs that whispered secrets of returning life.

The shift was not a sudden eradication of the damage, but a delicate recalibration. The frequencies Mara had so painstakingly coaxed back into harmony were not erasing the wounds, but encouraging the natural healing processes to begin their slow, arduous work. The Skywood was not instantly restored to its former glory, but it was no longer actively decaying. A fragile, yet vital, equilibrium was emerging, a testament to the land's inherent resilience. The deep, resonant hum that emanated from the earth, once a mournful throb, now pulsed with a steadier, more hopeful rhythm. It was the sound of a heart finding its beat again, however faint.

Mara observed these changes with a quiet intensity, her gaze sweeping across the clearing and beyond, into the emerald depths of the forest. The obsidian shards, once buzzing with discordant energy, now lay dormant, their corrupted frequencies subdued, their power contained. They were like captured storms, their thunder silenced, their lightning leashed. The geode on her workbench, no longer emitting the strained, protesting hum, now vibrated with a deep, sonorous resonance, a constant, steady anchor in the re-emerging symphony of the Skywood. The smaller resonance stones, once flickering with erratic light, now glowed with a soft, consistent luminescence, their gentle illumination a visual representation of the returning harmony.

She noticed the subtle transformations in the flora. The undergrowth, which had been brittle and parched, showing the tell-tale signs of cellular desiccation, now exhibited a faint, verdant sheen. Delicate ferns, which had been curled and yellowed, began to unfurl their fronds, tentatively reaching towards the dappled sunlight. The bark of the ancient sequoias, which had seemed to crack and thirst, now appeared to hold a richer, deeper hue, as if the very sap within them was beginning to flow with renewed vigor. Even the mosses, clinging to the shaded sides of rocks and fallen logs, seemed to be regaining their plush, vibrant texture. These were not grand, sweeping changes, but the quiet, persistent resurgence of life at its most fundamental level.

The fauna, too, responded to this nascent stability. The anxious rustling in the undergrowth, a constant indicator of heightened fear, began to subside. Mara heard the hesitant chirping of birds, their calls clearer and less frantic than they had been for so long. A small, furry creature, its fur matted and dull from stress, emerged from the shadow of a broad-leafed fern, its movements no longer jerky and fearful, but cautious, yet fluid. It paused, sniffing the air, then tentatively began to nibble at a patch of newly revived moss. It was a small act, an insignificant moment in the grand scheme of the Skywood, but for Mara, it was a profound confirmation. It was tangible evidence that her efforts, however arduous, were making a difference.

This re-establishment of a semblance of balance was more than just a cosmetic change; it was a fundamental shift in the energetic landscape. The Ashbound's sabotage had created a volatile, unpredictable environment, a constant state of flux that preyed on the Skywood's natural systems. By reintroducing a core of stability, Mara had given the land a foundation upon which to rebuild. The weather engines, though still bearing the scars of their perversion, were no longer broadcasting disruptive frequencies. Instead, they were emitting a softer, more neutral hum, allowing the natural atmospheric processes to reassert themselves gradually. The violent storms, the unnatural droughts, the unpredictable temperature fluctuations – these were beginning to recede, replaced by the more gentle, rhythmic patterns of a healthy ecosystem.

The impact of this stability extended beyond the immediate ecological crisis. The Skywood was a living entity, its health intrinsically linked to the well-being of its inhabitants. The Ashbound's disruption had sown seeds of fear and uncertainty, not just in the soil, but in the hearts of all who lived within its embrace. The re-emergence of a stable resonance offered a flicker of hope, a tangible sign that the destructive forces could be countered. It was a message, broadcast through the very frequencies of the land, that the Skywood was not defeated, that its song was not silenced.

Mara allowed herself a moment of quiet contemplation, the soft glow of the resonance stones illuminating her face. The weight of her responsibility, which had felt like an insurmountable burden, now seemed to shift, to become more manageable. This was not the end of her work, not by a long stretch. The deeper corruption, the more insidious manipulations, would require far more intricate and prolonged efforts. But this... this was a turning point. This was the dawn after a long, dark night. The forest was breathing again, however shallowly, and in that breath, there was the promise of a future.

She began to meticulously document the changes, her stylus dancing across the parchment. She charted the subtle shifts in atmospheric pressure, the newly emerging patterns of moisture saturation in the soil, and the gradually decreasing amplitude of residual dissonant frequencies. Her geomantic charts, once filled with alarming red lines indicating corrupted ley lines, now showed faint, tentative green shoots of revitalized energy, weaving their way back into the established network. These were not yet robust flows, but delicate tendrils, reaching out like hopeful fingers, seeking connection and stability.

The obsidian shards, while contained, remained a potent reminder of the threat. They were inert for now, their malevolent energy dampened, but their potential for disruption was still present. Mara knew that vigilance was paramount. Her work was not a single act of restoration, but an ongoing process of maintenance and defense. She had merely cleared a path, and now she, and perhaps others, would need to protect it.

She observed how the re-established resonance seemed to be creating a subtle but significant magnetic pull, drawing dissipated energetic fragments back towards their source. It was like a vast, unseen net, gently gathering scattered threads of life-force and weaving them back into the greater tapestry of the Skywood. This process was gradual, almost imperceptible to the untrained eye, but Mara, attuned to the subtle vibrations of the land, could feel it deeply. It was a comforting sensation, a reassurance that the Skywood possessed an innate drive towards wholeness.

The changes, though subtle, were enough. The oppressive stillness that had characterized the sabotaged areas began to dissipate, replaced by a gentle, natural murmur. The air itself felt lighter, less charged with a sense of impending doom. Sunlight, when it managed to penetrate the dense canopy, no longer felt harsh and sterile, but warm and life-giving, dappled patterns dancing on the forest floor like benevolent spirits. Even the silence was different; it was no longer the silence of absence, but the quietude of peace, of a world holding its breath, waiting for full recovery.

Mara moved through her clearing, her movements less tense, her shoulders less hunched. She picked up a fallen sequoia cone, its scales dry and brittle from the previous unnatural conditions. She placed it on the geode, allowing the stone's steady resonance to wash over it. As she watched, a faint, almost imperceptible softening seemed to occur, a subtle rehydration. It was a minuscule change, easily overlooked, but it spoke volumes about the transformative power of restored harmony.

She imagined the Skywood as a vast, intricate instrument, its many components intricately tuned to produce a grand, harmonious symphony. The Ashbound had introduced jarring, discordant notes, shattering the melody and throwing the entire orchestra into chaos. Her work was to reintroduce the lost harmonies, to guide the instruments back into their proper place, and to coax the orchestra to find its lost song. The obsidian shards were like broken strings, their dissonance amplified; her task was to silence them, and to help the remaining strings resonate with their true pitch.

The concept of "balance" in the Skywood was not about a static, unchanging state, but a dynamic equilibrium, a constant interplay of forces that maintained life and vitality. The Ashbound had sought to break this equilibrium, to push the Skywood into a state of extreme imbalance that would ultimately lead to its collapse. By re-establishing a semblance of this dynamic balance, Mara had not only halted the immediate destruction but had also given the Skywood the capacity to heal itself, to adapt and to endure.

She understood that this was not a permanent victory. The Ashbound were cunning and resourceful, and they would undoubtedly seek new ways to disrupt the Skywood. But for now, there was a moment of respite. A chance for the land to breathe, for its inhabitants to feel a sense of safety, and for hope to take root once more. The resonance she had restored was a beacon, a signal that the Skywood would not be easily extinguished, that its spirit, its song, was too deeply embedded in the fabric of existence to be silenced forever. This quietude, this returning hum of life, was the most precious sound Mara had heard in a long, long time. It was the sound of a world remembering how to live.

Cael watched from the shadowed periphery, his usual vantage point now feeling less like a strategic position and more like a place of hesitant observation. The air, which had once thrummed with a brittle tension, now carried a subtle, almost reverent stillness. It was the kind of quiet that preceded a revelation, or perhaps, the aftermath of one. The Skywood, or at least this small, beleaguered clearing, was exhaling. He could feel it, not just in the softening of the light that dappled through the reawakening canopy, but in the very rhythm of his own breath, which no longer felt like a fight against a suffocating atmosphere.

He had come with his own agenda, his own ingrained certainties. The oath he had sworn, a tapestry of duty and ingrained suspicion, had painted Mara as a disruptor, a rogue element playing with forces she didn't fully comprehend. His training, his upbringing, the very essence of his order, had instilled in him a deep-seated skepticism of methods that didn't adhere to their rigid doctrines. Force, control, containment – these were the tools of his trade. He believed in the efficacy of brute strength, of overwhelming power to quell any deviation from the established order. He saw the Skywood's suffering as a symptom of something that needed to be excised, amputated, rather than healed.

But here, in this space that had been a testament to his order's failure, he witnessed something that defied his preconceptions. Mara's hands, stained with earth and sap, moved with a grace that was less about command and more about communion. The resonance stones, once dismissed by him as trinkets, pulsed with a steady, vital energy, a stark contrast to the volatile, chaotic surges he had expected. The geode on her workbench, a seemingly inert rock to his untrained eye, now hummed with a deep, resonant frequency that vibrated through the very soles of his boots. It was a sound that spoke of fundamental truths, of an ancient song being sung back into existence.

He saw the subtle, yet profound, changes in the flora. The almost imperceptible greening of the undergrowth, the tentative unfurling of fern fronds, the richer hue of the sequoia bark – these were not the result of a forceful imposition of order. They were the quiet affirmations of a land reclaiming its own natural processes. The Ashbound had sought to twist and break the Skywood, to shatter its inherent resonance until it crumbled into dust. Mara, on the other hand, was not fighting the decay; she was fostering the growth. She was not imposing her will, but listening to the land's own whispers, coaxing it back to its true voice.

His gaze drifted to the obsidian shards, those jagged symbols of corruption and destruction. He had envisioned them being shattered, ground to dust under the weight of his order's power. But Mara had contained them, not with brute force, but with a more sophisticated understanding of energy. They lay dormant, their malevolent hum silenced, their destructive potential leashed. It was a testament to a different kind of power, one that understood the intricate web of energies that bound the Skywood together, and knew how to mend rather than sever.

He remembered the fear that had gripped this place, a tangible miasma that had made even the bravest souls hesitate. He had felt it himself, a cold knot in his gut that had fueled his resolve to enforce order. But now, that fear was receding, replaced by a fragile, yet undeniable, sense of peace. The hesitant chirping of birds, the cautious emergence of a small forest creature – these were not signs of a land held captive, but of a land slowly, cautiously, returning to life. His order had offered security through subjugation. Mara was offering resilience through restoration.

The realization dawned on him, not with a thunderclap, but with the slow, steady erosion of his certainty. His oath, so absolute and unyielding, suddenly felt like a cage. It had been forged in a time of perceived crisis, a time when the Ashbound's influence was a visible, aggressive blight. But the Skywood's wounds, he now understood, were not always wounds of external invasion. They were also wounds of internal imbalance, of energies gone awry, of a delicate harmony disrupted from within. His order's approach, focused on external threats, had perhaps blinded them to the subtler, more pervasive forms of decay.

He had always viewed nature as something to be controlled, something to be bent to the will of civilization. The Skywood, in its wild, untamed essence, had always represented a challenge to that worldview. He had seen its power as a threat, its freedom as chaos. But Mara's work was a refutation of that assumption. She demonstrated that true strength lay not in domination, but in understanding. That the most potent force was not the one that imposed its will, but the one that harmonized with the inherent rhythms of existence.

His earlier mistrust, which had been a shield, now felt like a barrier. He had seen Mara's methods as a reckless gamble, a dangerous flirtation with the very forces his order was sworn to suppress. He had judged her by the standards of his own rigid framework, failing to recognize that her framework was entirely different. Her approach was not about erasing the damage, but about guiding the process of healing. It was about recognizing the inherent resilience of the Skywood and providing the conditions for that resilience to flourish.

He found himself stepping forward, his heavy boots crunching softly on the newly softened earth. The movement, small as it was, felt monumental. He was breaking protocol, stepping out of the shadows, not with aggression, but with a tentative curiosity. He saw Mara turn, her expression not one of surprise, but of quiet acknowledgement. There was no fear in her eyes, no defensiveness, only a weary strength and a profound connection to the land around her.

"The resonance," he began, his voice rough with disuse, a stark contrast to the gentle hum of the geode. "It's... different."

Mara offered a small, almost imperceptible nod. "It is finding its rhythm again. The Skywood is learning to sing its own song, Cael. Not the one the Ashbound tried to force upon it, but its own."

He looked around the clearing, his gaze sweeping over the subtle signs of recovery. The mist, ethereal and delicate, weaving between the ancient trees. The vibrant green creeping back into the undergrowth. The air, no longer heavy with oppression, but alive with a subtle, life-affirming energy. He had been so focused on the visible scars, on the evidence of the Ashbound's malice, that he had failed to see the deeper, more fundamental strength of the Skywood. He had been looking for a fight, for a tangible enemy to subdue. He had not been looking for a patient healer.

"Your method," he said, the words feeling strange on his tongue, "it's not... forceful. It's... coaxing."

"It is listening," Mara corrected gently. "The land has its own language, its own needs. The Ashbound sought to drown it out with their dissonance. I am simply trying to help it find its voice again. The Skywood is not a thing to be controlled, Cael. It is a living entity, and it deserves respect."

Respect. The word echoed in his mind, a concept that had been largely absent from his tactical lexicon. His order dealt with threats, with enemies. They did not typically engage in "respectful dialogue" with the very forces they were meant to contain. But watching Mara, seeing the undeniable efficacy of her approach, he began to understand that his order's rigid dogma might be their greatest weakness. They were so focused on the sword, they had forgotten the balm.

He thought of the rigid protocols, the unquestioning obedience that defined his life. He had always believed that these were the foundations of strength, the bulwarks against chaos. But perhaps, in their pursuit of absolute control, they had lost sight of the true nature of balance. True balance wasn't the absence of conflict, but the harmonious integration of all forces, even those that seemed opposing. It was about understanding the interplay, the give and take, the natural ebb and flow.

"My oath," Cael said, his voice barely a whisper, "it demands I... contain threats. That I neutralize them."

"And what if containment is not the only way?" Mara asked, her gaze steady. "What if understanding the threat, and then working *with* the inherent strengths of the system to overcome it, is a more lasting solution?" She gestured to the geode. "This stone does not destroy the corrupted frequencies. It harmonizes with them, then slowly, patiently, realigns them to a healthier resonance. It does not erase the wound, it helps it to heal."

Cael's gaze fell upon the obsidian shards again. He had seen them as instruments of pure evil, something that needed to be utterly annihilated. But Mara had contained them, not by destroying their essence, but by dampening their disruptive power, by preventing them from spreading their corruption. It was a subtle but crucial distinction. His order's approach would have been to shatter them, a violent act that might have released a final, catastrophic surge of energy. Mara's was an act of quiet suppression, of careful neutralization.

He remembered the discussions within his order, the debates about the Ashbound's methods. They had focused on the destructive intent, the clear malice. They had failed to see the intricate understanding of energy manipulation that underpinned the Ashbound's actions. Their own response had been reactive, a mirroring of the Ashbound's aggression, albeit in the name of order.

"We... we always assumed that the only way to deal with such corruption was to obliterate it," Cael admitted, the words tasting like ash. "To eradicate it completely. Your approach... it suggests a different path. A path of integration, of rebalancing."

"The Skywood is too vast, too interconnected, to simply be... excised," Mara replied, her voice filled with a quiet conviction. "Every thread is important. Even the broken ones, if they can be mended, can be rewoven into the tapestry. The Ashbound sought to unravel the whole. My work is to ensure that the threads remain, that they are strengthened, even if the pattern must change."

He looked at the resonance stones again, their soft glow now appearing less like exotic curiosities and more like beacons of a forgotten wisdom. His order had relied on calculated force, on predictable outcomes. Mara's work was an art, a delicate dance with forces that defied easy categorization. It was a demonstration that true strength did not always lie in overwhelming power, but in profound understanding and gentle persistence.

A slow, internal shift was occurring within Cael. The walls of his ingrained beliefs, so painstakingly constructed over years of training and indoctrination, were beginning to crumble. He had always seen himself as a guardian of order, a defender against chaos. But he was starting to question whether the order he served was truly the best way to preserve the Skywood. Perhaps his order's relentless pursuit of control had, in its own way, contributed to the imbalance.

He thought of the strictures of his oath, the rigid framework that defined his actions. He had always seen it as a source of strength, a guarantee of purpose. But now, it felt like a limitation, a blindfold that prevented him from seeing alternative solutions. Could his oath be reinterpreted? Could the concept of "containment" encompass more than just forceful suppression? Could it extend to understanding, to fostering growth, to restoring balance through less destructive means?

"I... I have always believed that the only way to protect something as vital as the Skywood was through absolute control," Cael confessed, his gaze fixed on the intricate patterns of moss slowly reclaiming a fallen log. "Through a constant, unwavering vigilance that leaves no room for error, or for... natural processes."

Mara met his gaze, her eyes holding a depth of understanding that Cael found both unsettling and strangely comforting. "Vigilance is important, Cael. But true protection comes from nurturing. From understanding the systems you are trying to protect. The Ashbound attacked the Skywood's resonance, its very song. My work is to restore that song, not to silence its inhabitants."

He looked at his own hands, hands that had been trained for combat, for swift, decisive action. They felt clumsy, ill-suited for the delicate work he was now witnessing. He was a warrior, not a healer. His order's purpose was to fight, to subdue. But what if the greatest fight was not against an external enemy, but against the internal forces that disrupted the natural order? What if the most effective form of "containment" was not through force, but through the restoration of balance?

"Your work," Cael said, the words forming slowly, deliberately, "it's... it's not about defeating the Ashbound. It's about healing the Skywood from their influence. It's about making it resilient again."

"Precisely," Mara confirmed, a faint smile touching her lips. "The Ashbound inflicted a wound. My task is to help the Skywood heal. And in doing so, to make it stronger than before. A truly resilient system does not fear disruption; it learns to adapt to it."

Cael looked out at the vast expanse of the Skywood, its ancient trees standing sentinel. He had always seen it as a territory to be secured, a resource to be managed. Now, for the first time, he saw it as a living, breathing entity, with its own intricate needs and its own inherent strength. His order's approach, so focused on the immediate threat, had perhaps overlooked the deeper, more fundamental aspects of the Skywood's well-being.

He was beginning to understand that his oath, while born of a noble intention, might have been too narrowly defined. The world was more complex than the black-and-white doctrines he had been taught. There were shades of grey, nuances that his order had failed to acknowledge. Perhaps there was a way to fulfill his duty, to protect the Skywood, without resorting to the same blunt instruments that had proven so ineffective.

"I... I have never considered this approach," Cael admitted, the confession a heavy weight lifted from his shoulders. "The idea of working with the land's own energies, rather than imposing our own will upon it. It's... revolutionary."

Mara inclined her head. "It is ancient, Cael. We have simply forgotten how to listen."

He watched her meticulously adjust a small resonance stone, its soft glow intensifying slightly. He saw the genuine connection she had with the very fabric of the Skywood. It was not a connection born of dominance, but of empathy. And in that empathy, he saw a power that his own order had never truly grasped. The power of life itself, the inherent drive towards healing and restoration.

The clearing, once a symbol of the Skywood's vulnerability, was now a testament to its resilience. And Cael, who had arrived as a skeptic, a guardian of a rigid order, was beginning to see the limitations of his own perspective. The path forward, he realized, might not be a path of forceful intervention, but a path of collaborative restoration. His oath, he mused, might require re-evaluation, a broadening of its scope to encompass the subtle, yet profound, power of harmonic resonance. The Skywood was not a battleground to be conquered, but a living symphony waiting to be restored.

Thryxal, ancient and weathered as the oldest peaks of the Dragon's Tooth range, watched from his secluded aerie. His scales, usually a formidable obsidian that blended seamlessly with the shadowed cliff faces, seemed to absorb the scant sunlight filtering through the canopy. His eyes, twin pools of molten gold that had witnessed millennia of shifting alliances and burgeoning civilizations, were fixed on the clearing below. He had expected to see defiance, perhaps even a foolish act of sacrifice. Instead, he observed a quiet miracle.

Mara. The human sorceress, as some of his kind still grumbled, was engaged in a dance with the very essence of the Skywood. Her movements were fluid, imbued with a grace that spoke of an intimate understanding of the forces she wielded. The air, which had for so long been thick with the cloying stench of Ashbound corruption, now carried a faint, sweet scent of ozone and burgeoning life. Thryxal could feel it, a subtle hum that vibrated not just in the earth beneath his claws, but deep within his own draconic core.

The Skywood was breathing again, its vital energies slowly reasserting themselves. He had seen this land scarred, its song fractured, its vibrant hues dulled by the insidious touch of the Ashbound. And he had witnessed the Ashbound's relentless assault, their philosophy of decay and dominion, with a cold, gnawing fury. He had also seen the futility of his own people's attempts to directly combat such pervasive corruption. Brute force, while effective against a tangible enemy, was a blunt instrument against a foe that twisted the very fabric of existence.

His gaze shifted, drawn to the figure at the periphery of the clearing. Cael. The young Ashbound Sentinel, whose presence had initially sent ripples of alarm through Thryxal's carefully constructed defenses. He had been a symbol of the very force that had nearly extinguished the Skywood's life. A living embodiment of the Ashbound's rigid, destructive doctrine. Thryxal had observed Cael's initial approach with a weary cynicism, expecting the predictable outcome: another attempt at forceful suppression, another clash of wills that would only further wound the already fragile land. He had braced himself for the inevitable confrontation, the inevitable disillusionment. He had seen enough of humanity's capacity for destruction to warrant such a bleak outlook.

But Cael was not acting as Thryxal had predicted. He stood not with the aggressive posture of a hunter, or the stern authority of a law enforcer, but with a stillness that bordered on reverence. His hardened stance, a testament to years of rigorous training and ingrained ideology, seemed to be softening. Thryxal, with his ancient senses, could detect the subtle shifts within the Sentinel. The rigid lines of his jaw had relaxed. The tension that had radiated from him like a heat haze was dissipating, replaced by a quiet contemplation. His eyes, which had once burned with the cold fire of conviction, now held a flicker of nascent wonder, a dawning comprehension. It was the look of a warrior witnessing a truth that defied his every battle-hardened instinct.

Thryxal unfurled a wing, a shadow passing over the clearing. He did not descend, not yet. His role was observation, a silent sentinel ensuring that the delicate balance being restored was not immediately shattered by outside interference. He had learned patience over his long existence, a virtue forged in the crucible of countless cycles of creation and destruction. He knew that genuine change, true healing, did not happen in a single, dramatic act, but in a slow, painstaking process. And he recognized the nascent signs of such a process unfolding before him.

He recalled the legends of the Skywood, of its inherent resonance, a song that had once echoed through the cosmos. He remembered the stories whispered among his own kind, tales of how the Ashbound had sought to silence that song, to twist it into a cacophony of despair. He had believed that such a profound wound could only be healed by immense power, by a force capable of eradicating the blight entirely. His own kin had offered their strength, their primordial might, but such power, untempered by understanding, could easily become another form of destruction.

Mara's approach was different. It was not a forceful negation of the corruption, but a delicate coaxing, a patient coaxing of the Skywood's own inherent resilience. The resonance stones, small and unassuming, pulsed with a steady light, a gentle counterpoint to the lingering whispers of dissonance. He could feel the geode on Mara's workbench, a conduit for the land's latent energies, humming with a low, steady frequency. It was the sound of nature recalibrating, of a wounded organism finding its way back to equilibrium.

And Cael. The Sentinel was not merely observing Mara's work; he was absorbing it. Thryxal saw it in the way Cael's gaze lingered on the subtle greening of the undergrowth, the tentative unfurling of leaves that had been brittle and scorched. He saw it in the almost imperceptible nod he gave when Mara spoke of listening to the land. This was not the grudging acknowledgement of an adversary; it was the dawning realization of a student.

Thryxal had always been wary of humanity. Their volatile nature, their tendency towards rapid advancement and equally rapid self-destruction, made them unpredictable. His people had witnessed their rise and fall countless times, their empires crumbling like dust in the winds of time. The Ashbound were merely a more virulent strain, a perversion of humanity's inherent drive for order. Thryxal had thus categorized all humans within that grim spectrum, a spectrum that offered little hope for genuine coexistence, let alone mutual trust.

But Cael was proving to be an anomaly. He was not a mindless enforcer of his order's destructive dogma. He possessed a capacity for introspection, for questioning the very foundations of his beliefs. This was a rare and precious quality, one that Thryxal had not seen in a human for many, many ages. The Ashbound Sentinel had come with a mandate of containment, of eradication. Yet, he was witnessing a different form of power, a power that did not seek to dominate, but to harmonize. He was seeing the efficacy of a method that did not seek to destroy the darkness, but to coax the light back into existence.

Thryxal remembered the animosity between dragons and the Ashbound, a conflict that had simmered for centuries. His people had fought them, bled for the lands they sought to corrupt. But the Ashbound were relentless, insidious. They seeped into the very soul of a place, twisting its natural order until it withered and died. Thryxal had long believed that only a direct, overwhelming force could counter such pervasive decay, a force that mirrored the Ashbound's own destructive power, but wielded with a righteous fury. He had advocated for such an approach, for a cleansing fire that would burn away the corruption, no matter the collateral damage.

Mara's methods, however, offered a different path. A path that acknowledged the interconnectedness of all things, that understood that true strength lay not in eradication, but in restoration. It was a philosophy that resonated with the ancient wisdom of his own kind, a wisdom that had often been overshadowed by the immediate need to defend against external threats.

He watched Cael step forward, his boots crunching softly on the revitalized earth. It was a small movement, almost insignificant in the grand scheme of the Skywood. But to Thryxal, it was a seismic shift. It was a Sentinel of the Ashbound stepping out of the shadows of his ingrained dogma, venturing into the light of a new understanding. He was not attacking, not interrogating, but observing, learning. His posture was not one of confrontation, but of hesitant curiosity.

Thryxal could feel the subtle shift in Cael's aura. The sharp edges of his military bearing were rounding, softening. The grim certainty that had been etched into his very being was being replaced by a hesitant inquiry. It was as if a deeply entrenched fortress of belief was beginning to show cracks, allowing in the sunlight of a wider perspective. This was the beginning of a profound transformation, a shedding of old skin that was far more significant than any physical molting.

He heard Mara's voice, calm and clear, a balm to the wounded air. He saw Cael respond, his voice rough, unused to words of observation rather than command. "The resonance," Cael said, his words carrying the weight of his newfound bewilderment, "it's... different."

Thryxal nodded, a silent affirmation that rippled through the ancient trees. Different, indeed. It was the difference between a dying ember and a roaring fire, between a choked whisper and a clear, strong song. It was the difference between despair and hope.

Mara's reply was gentle, devoid of accusation or judgment. "It is finding its rhythm again. The Skywood is learning to sing its own song, Cael. Not the one the Ashbound tried to force upon it, but its own."

Thryxal observed Cael's reaction. There was no immediate dismissal, no argument. Instead, a prolonged silence, a moment of deep contemplation. His gaze swept over the clearing, taking in the subtle signs of recovery that had previously escaped his notice, or perhaps, that he had been conditioned to ignore. The mist, no longer a suffocating shroud of despair, but a gentle veil of dew-kissed life. The vibrant green creeping back into the undergrowth, a testament to the land's indomitable will to survive. The air, no longer heavy with oppression, but alive with a subtle, life-affirming energy.

Cael's next words were hesitant, almost questioning. "Your method," he began, his voice tinged with an unfamiliar awe, "it's not... forceful. It's... coaxing."

"It is listening," Mara corrected, her voice soft but firm. "The land has its own language, its own needs. The Ashbound sought to drown it out with their dissonance. I am simply trying to help it find its voice again. The Skywood is not a thing to be controlled, Cael. It is a living entity, and it deserves respect."

Respect. The word hung in the air, a foreign concept in the lexicon of the Ashbound Sentinel. Thryxal had often wondered if humanity, in its relentless pursuit of dominion, had forgotten the meaning of the word. He had seen the Ashbound's disrespect for all life, their only allegiance to their own warped vision of order. Cael, by questioning Mara's methods, by acknowledging the concept of respect for the land, was stepping away from that ingrained ideology. He was showing a capacity for empathy, a willingness to see beyond the immediate threat and recognize the inherent value of what was being threatened.

Thryxal could almost feel the internal struggle within Cael. The clash between his upbringing, his oath, and the undeniable evidence before his eyes. His order had always believed in the absolute necessity of control, of rigid adherence to doctrine. They saw nature as a resource to be managed, a force to be subdued. Mara, however, was demonstrating that true strength lay not in domination, but in understanding and cooperation. She was showing that the most effective way to protect was not through force, but through fostering growth and resilience.

"My oath," Cael confessed, his voice barely above a whisper, "it demands I... contain threats. That I neutralize them."

"And what if containment is not the only way?" Mara's question was a gentle probe, designed not to challenge, but to invite deeper thought. "What if understanding the threat, and then working *with* the inherent strengths of the system to overcome it, is a more lasting solution?" She gestured to the geode. "This stone does not destroy the corrupted frequencies. It harmonizes with them, then slowly, patiently, realigns them to a healthier resonance. It does not erase the wound, it helps it to heal."

Thryxal's golden gaze drifted to the obsidian shards, those jagged remnants of the Ashbound's blight. He had seen them as symbols of pure, unadulterated evil, entities that deserved only annihilation. But Mara had contained them, not through brute force, but through a subtler understanding of energy manipulation. She had dampened their disruptive power, prevented them from spreading their corruption. This was a crucial distinction. His own order's approach would have been to shatter them, a violent act that might have unleashed a final, catastrophic surge of energy. Mara's was an act of quiet suppression, of careful neutralization.

He saw Cael's eyes follow his gaze, lingering on the obsidian. The Sentinel's internal conflict was palpable. He had been trained to believe that obliteration was the only solution to such corruption. Mara's work, however, suggested a path of integration, of rebalancing. It was a radical departure from everything he had ever known, everything he had been taught to believe.

"We... we always assumed that the only way to deal with such corruption was to obliterate it," Cael admitted, his voice laced with a newfound humility. "To eradicate it completely. Your approach... it suggests a different path. A path of integration, of rebalancing."

"The Skywood is too vast, too interconnected, to simply be... excised," Mara replied, her voice filled with a quiet conviction that resonated with

Thryxal's own deep-seated knowledge of the world's intricate systems. "Every thread is important. Even the broken ones, if they can be mended, can be rewoven into the tapestry. The Ashbound sought to unravel the whole. My work is to ensure that the threads remain, that they are strengthened, even if the pattern must change."

Thryxal watched as Cael looked at the resonance stones again, their soft glow now appearing less like exotic curiosities and more like beacons of a forgotten wisdom. His order had relied on calculated force, on predictable outcomes. Mara's work was an art, a delicate dance with forces that defied easy categorization. It was a demonstration that true strength did not always lie in overwhelming power, but in profound understanding and gentle persistence.

A slow, internal shift was occurring within Cael. The walls of his ingrained beliefs, so painstakingly constructed over years of training and indoctrination, were beginning to crumble. He had always seen himself as a guardian of order, a defender against chaos. But he was starting to question whether the order he served was truly the best way to preserve the Skywood. Perhaps his order's relentless pursuit of control had, in its own way, contributed to the imbalance.

He thought of the strictures of his oath, the rigid framework that defined his actions. He had always seen it as a source of strength, a guarantee of purpose. But now, it felt like a limitation, a blindfold that prevented him from seeing alternative solutions. Could his oath be reinterpreted? Could the concept of "containment" encompass more than just forceful suppression? Could it extend to understanding, to fostering growth, to restoring balance through less destructive means?

"I... I have never considered this approach," Cael admitted, the confession a heavy weight lifted from his shoulders. "The idea of working with the land's own energies, rather than imposing our own will upon it. It's... revolutionary."

Mara inclined her head. "It is ancient, Cael. We have simply forgotten how to listen."

Thryxal observed her meticulously adjust a small resonance stone, its soft glow intensifying slightly. He saw the genuine connection she had with the very fabric of the Skywood. It was not a connection born of dominance, but of empathy. And in that empathy, he saw a power that his own order had never truly grasped. The power of life itself, the inherent drive towards healing and restoration.

The clearing, once a symbol of the Skywood's vulnerability, was now a testament to its resilience. And Cael, who had arrived as a skeptic, a guardian of a rigid order, was beginning to see the limitations of his own perspective. The path forward, he realized, might not be a path of forceful intervention, but a path of collaborative restoration. His oath, he mused, might require re-evaluation, a broadening of its scope to encompass the subtle, yet profound, power of harmonic resonance. The Skywood was not a battleground to be conquered, but a living symphony waiting to be restored.

Thryxal let out a low, rumbling sound, a breath of ancient air that rustled the leaves on the trees below. It was not a sound of aggression, but of quiet acknowledgement, of cautious optimism. He had arrived with a grim certainty that humanity was a force of destruction, incapable of genuine healing. But Cael, in his willingness to learn, in his nascent empathy, had begun to chip away at that ancient prejudice.

It was a small crack, a fragile opening, but for Thryxal, it was a glimmer of hope, a promise that perhaps, just perhaps, a new era of understanding could dawn between his kind and humanity. He remained in his aerie, a silent guardian, his golden eyes fixed on the evolving scene, his ancient heart stirring with a cautious, unprecedented warmth. The possibility of trust, a concept long buried under the weight of conflict and suspicion, was beginning to stir within him.

CHAPTER ELEVEN

REFORGING THE OATH

The air in the clearing still hummed with the gentle thrum of restored energy, a stark contrast to the oppressive stillness that had clung to it only hours before. The scent of damp earth and nascent growth, a fragrance that had seemed a distant memory, now permeated the atmosphere, a subtle perfume of resilience. Cael stood at the edge of the clearing, a solitary figure against the vibrant resurgence of the Skywood.

His polished greaves, usually gleaming with the disciplined sheen of an Ashbound Sentinel, were scuffed with mud, a testament to his reluctant journey. His gaze was fixed on Mara, who was carefully tending to a cluster of newly unfurled mosses, her movements economical and precise, as if she were conducting a silent symphony with the very soil.

He had come expecting to find an enemy, a rogue element that needed to be brought to heel. He had arrived with the weight of his oath, the ingrained certainty of his order's doctrine pressing down on him like a physical burden. The Ashbound taught that corruption was anathema, an infection to be purged with absolute efficiency, leaving no trace behind. Their methods were swift, decisive, and often brutal, prioritizing the eradication of the disease over the preservation of the host. And Mara, with her unconventional methods, her seemingly gentle coaxing of the land's own energies, had been an affront to everything he understood.

Yet, the evidence was undeniable. The Skywood was healing. The Ashbound's blight, a creeping rot that had threatened to consume this ancient forest, was receding. And it wasn't through the forceful imposition of order, but through a process that felt more akin to nurture. He had witnessed it with his own eyes: the subtle greening of the undergrowth, the vibrant unfurling of leaves that had been brittle and scorched, the very air breathing with a renewed vitality. He had felt the resonance, the low, steady hum that emanated from the earth, a song that had been silenced for too long. It was a truth that gnawed at the foundations of his belief, a profound dissonance within his own carefully constructed worldview.

He took a hesitant step forward, his boots crunching on the damp, yielding earth. The sound, usually a sharp, percussive note in his patrols, seemed muted here, absorbed by the revitalized soil. Mara looked up, her expression one of quiet observation, devoid of surprise or alarm. There was no fear in her eyes, no defensiveness. It was the calm gaze of someone who understood the intricate dance of life and decay, of resilience and renewal.

"Sentinel," Mara acknowledged, her voice a soft, steady current against the rustling leaves. It held no accusation, no judgment, only a simple recognition of his presence.

Cael found himself struggling for words. The carefully honed phrases of command, interrogation, and pronouncement felt utterly inadequate, hollow against the reality unfolding before him. He had rehearsed this encounter in his mind countless times, each scenario culminating in a confrontation, a forceful assertion of his authority. But the reality was a humbling disarray of his expectations.

"Sorceress," he began, his voice rough, unused to this softer register. He cleared his throat, the sound betraying his internal turmoil. "I... I have observed. The land... it is healing."

Mara offered a small, knowing smile. "It is finding its balance again, Sentinel. It has a profound capacity for resilience, if only we allow it." She gestured to a patch of earth where tiny, pale blue flowers were tentatively pushing through the soil. "These are Skybells. They haven't bloomed here for decades. Their presence is a good omen."

Cael's gaze followed her gesture. He had always seen the Skywood as a battleground, a place of strategic importance that needed to be secured and controlled. The Ashbound's philosophy was one of absolute dominion, of bending nature to their will, of imposing a sterile order upon the wild. They saw inherent chaos in the untamed world, a threat to be managed. He had been trained to see the blight as an enemy to be eradicated, the land as a resource to be exploited, its natural rhythms a weakness to be overcome. But Mara's approach... it was one of profound respect, of partnership.

"Your methods," Cael said, the words tumbling out in a rush, born of a desperate need to understand. "They are... not what I was led to believe. We were taught that such corruption could only be cleansed by fire, by absolute destruction." He met her gaze, his own eyes mirroring the confusion and nascent wonder that had begun to bloom within him. "But you... you have not destroyed it. You have... coaxed it back."

Mara knelt, gently touching the damp earth. "Destruction is a blunt instrument, Sentinel. It leaves scars that may never truly heal. The Ashbound's approach, while seemingly decisive, often creates deeper wounds, fractures that can fester for generations. The Skywood is a complex ecosystem, intricately connected. To rip out one corrupted element without understanding its role, its connection to the whole, is to risk unraveling the entire tapestry."

She looked up at him, her eyes holding a depth of understanding that made him feel both exposed and strangely seen. "The Ashbound sought to silence the Skywood's song, to replace it with their own sterile silence. But the land has its own voice, its own rhythm. My work is to help it find that voice again, to harmonize the discordant notes, not to erase them."

Cael's mind raced, piecing together the fragmented truths he was witnessing. His oath, the very foundation of his existence as a Sentinel, was built upon the Ashbound's creed of ruthless eradication. He had been sworn to protect their vision of order, to eliminate anything that deviated from it. And Mara, with her gentle, yet potent, magic, was the antithesis of everything he had ever known.

"My oath," he began, the words tasting like ash in his mouth. "It binds me to... contain. To neutralize threats. To ensure the purity of the Ashbound's order." He paused, the weight of his past actions pressing down on him. He thought of the skirmishes, the forceful subjugation, the times he had acted with a certainty he now questioned. "I... I have failed to understand. I came here to... to stop you. To consider you a threat."

Mara's expression softened further. She rose to her feet, her gaze steady and compassionate. "I understand the burden of an oath, Sentinel. I understand the constraints of duty, the pressure of doctrine. The Ashbound, in their pursuit of order, have created a rigid framework, one that often blinds them to the nuances of the world they seek to control." She took a step closer, her presence not at all intimidating, but calming. "You were fulfilling your duty as you understood it. It is not your fault that the doctrine you were taught is incomplete."

This unexpected grace, this absence of condemnation, disarmed him more effectively than any physical force. He had braced himself for anger, for resistance, for the predictable clash of opposing wills. Instead, he found a bridge being offered, a hand extended across the chasm of his ingrained prejudice.

"Incomplete?" he echoed, the word a whisper of doubt against the edifice of his lifelong beliefs. "But our order... it has maintained stability for centuries. It has brought order to chaos."

"Order can be a shield, Sentinel," Mara conceded, her voice thoughtful. "But it can also be a cage. The Ashbound have imposed their order, their definition of perfection, upon a world that thrives on diversity and flux. True stability comes not from rigid control, but from a dynamic equilibrium, a constant process of adaptation and renewal. The Skywood has always adapted. It has weathered storms, endured droughts, and always, always found a way to bloom again. That is its strength."

She gestured to the obsidian shards, the remnants of the Ashbound's blight that she had contained within the geode. "These were shards of pure dissonance, fragments of the Ashbound's corrupting influence. My goal was not to obliterate them, though that would have been the Ashbound way. It was to understand the frequencies they emitted, to create a counter-resonance that would neutralize their harmful vibrations without shattering them. If they were destroyed, their residual energy might have caused further damage. Instead, they are now... inert. Their potential for harm contained."

Cael's gaze drifted to the geode, its crystalline surface pulsating with a soft, internal light. He had always viewed these fragments as symbols of pure evil, entities that deserved nothing less than utter annihilation. Mara's approach was a revelation. She had not engaged in a battle of wills, but a dance of frequencies, a subtle manipulation of energies that rendered the threat impotent. It was a demonstration of power that was both profound and elegant, a stark contrast to the crude, destructive force he was accustomed to wielding.

"So, you believe that... balance can be achieved through integration, rather than eradication?" he asked, the question a tentative exploration of a new frontier of thought.

"I believe that every element has its place, Sentinel," Mara replied, her voice firm. "Even the corrupted ones, if understood and reintegrated, can become part of a new, stronger whole. The Ashbound sought to prune away anything they deemed imperfect, fearing that it would weaken the structure. But in doing so, they weakened the very foundations they sought to protect. The Skywood's strength lies in its interconnectedness, its ability to absorb, adapt, and transform."

She met his gaze again, her eyes filled with a quiet conviction that resonated deep within him. "Your oath, Sentinel. It speaks of containment. Of neutralization. Does it not also speak of protection? Of safeguarding the land? Perhaps your definition of 'protection' has been too narrowly defined by the Ashbound's doctrine. Perhaps true protection lies not in sterile uniformity, but in fostering the vibrant, multifaceted life that the Skywood has always embodied."

The words struck him with the force of a physical blow, yet they were delivered with such gentle sincerity. He thought of his training, of the rigid interpretations of his sacred vows. He had always seen his oath as a rigid set of rules, an unyielding mandate. But Mara was suggesting a reinterpretation, a broadening of its scope. Could containment encompass understanding? Could neutralization be achieved through harmony, rather than brute force?

He looked around the clearing, really looking at it for the first time not as a tactical objective, but as a living, breathing entity. He saw the subtle interplay of light and shadow, the delicate dance of insects among the vibrant blooms, the ancient trees reaching towards the sky like weathered sentinels. This was not a sterile landscape devoid of imperfection; it was a tapestry woven with threads of life, decay, and renewal, each playing its part in the grand design.

"I... I have never considered it from this perspective," Cael admitted, his voice barely audible. The admission felt like a confession, a shedding of a heavy mantle he had carried for so long. "The Ashbound have always emphasized the absolute necessity of their order. Deviation was seen as weakness, as corruption in itself."

"And yet," Mara countered softly, "true strength often lies in adaptability. In embracing the unexpected. The Skywood's resilience is born from its willingness to change, to evolve. The Ashbound's rigid dogma, while offering a semblance of control, ultimately stifles growth. It is like trying to force a river to flow uphill – a futile endeavor that only leads to destruction."

She paused, her gaze sweeping over the newly vibrant clearing. "Your presence here, Sentinel, is a testament to that adaptability. You have come not with immediate hostility, but with a willingness to observe, to question. That, in itself, is a form of healing for this land. It is a sign that the Ashbound's influence is not absolute, that its hold on the hearts and minds of its Sentinels can be... loosened."

Cael felt a profound sense of humility wash over him. He had arrived as an enforcer, a symbol of an unyielding ideology, and he was leaving with the seeds of doubt, the nascent understanding of a different path. The clarity of Mara's vision, coupled with the undeniable evidence of the Skywood's recovery, had shattered his preconceived notions.

"I... I owe you an apology, Mara," he said, his voice laced with sincerity. "I misjudged you. I allowed my training, my ingrained beliefs, to blind me to the truth of your actions. You have shown me a different way, a path that does not require destruction, but fosters life."

Mara smiled, a genuine, warm expression that reached her eyes. "An apology is not necessary, Sentinel. Understanding is. We have both been bound by our respective oaths, our inherited doctrines. The important thing is that we can both see now that the Skywood is not a thing to be conquered, but a partner to be respected. Your order seeks order, and I seek balance. Perhaps, in time, we can find a way to achieve both, not by opposing each other, but by working together."

The idea of partnership, of collaboration between an Ashbound Sentinel and a sorceress of the wild, seemed almost heretical. Yet, as he stood there, breathing the revitalized air, feeling the gentle pulse of the earth beneath his feet, it no longer seemed impossible. It seemed like the only logical, and perhaps even the only truly honorable, path forward.

"A partnership," Cael mused, the word tasting new and strange on his tongue. "It is... an unconventional notion. But the results of your work are undeniable. If your methods can restore what the Ashbound have sought to corrupt, then perhaps there is merit in this unconventional approach."

"The Skywood has always been a place of ancient magic, Sentinel," Mara said. "A place where the boundaries between life and spirit, between action and consequence, are more fluid than your order might prefer. My magic is not about dominance, but about understanding the fundamental energies that bind all things. And those energies, when nurtured, have an incredible power to heal, to restore, to create."

She looked at him, a thoughtful expression on her face. "Your oath, Sentinel. It is a powerful thing. It binds you to a purpose. But purpose can be redefined. Protection can take many forms. If you can convince your order that true protection lies in fostering the Skywood's inherent vitality, in working *with* its natural rhythms, then perhaps your oath can be a force for healing, rather than for control."

Cael considered her words, his mind sifting through the implications. The Ashbound were not a monolithic entity. There were Sentinels who, like him, might be questioning the rigid adherence to destruction. There were those who, perhaps, harbored a quiet longing for a more nuanced understanding of their role. The thought of forging a new path, a path of restorative balance, began to take root within him, a fragile seedling pushing through the hardened earth of his indoctrination.

"It will not be easy," he admitted, his gaze fixed on the distant, verdant slopes of the Skywood. "The Ashbound value certainty. They fear the unknown. The idea of working with, rather than against, the very forces they have sworn to suppress will be met with... resistance."

"All change worthy of the name is met with resistance," Mara replied, her voice calm and unwavering. "But resistance can be overcome. You have seen the truth, Sentinel. You have witnessed the power of balance. Now, you must decide what you will do with that knowledge. Will you allow your oath to be a tool of suppression, or will you seek to redefine it as a force for restoration?"

Cael met her gaze, a newfound resolve hardening his expression. He had come seeking to contain a threat, and he had found something far more profound: a revelation. He had witnessed the limitations of his own order's doctrine and the potent efficacy of a gentler, more harmonious approach.

"I will seek to redefine it," he stated, the words firm and clear. "I will carry this understanding back to my order. I will speak of balance, of harmony, of a new way to protect the Skywood. And I will seek to forge a partnership, not of conflict, but of shared purpose. Your work here, Mara, has not just healed the land. It has begun to heal something within me, and perhaps, it can begin to heal the rift between our peoples."

A small, hopeful smile touched Mara's lips. "Then, Sentinel Cael, it seems we have a new oath to forge. Not one of opposition, but one of cooperation. A new understanding, born of mutual respect and a shared vision for the future of the Skywood."

As Cael turned to depart, the weight on his shoulders felt different. It was no longer the crushing burden of a rigid doctrine, but the hopeful anticipation of a new beginning, a profound shift in the ancient landscape of conflict and mistrust. He left the clearing with a renewed sense of purpose, the hum of the revitalized Skywood a comforting echo in his heart, a promise of a future where balance might, indeed, prevail.

Cael stood at the precipice of a profound redefinition, the words of his oath echoing in his mind not as a rigid decree, but as a melody waiting to be harmonized. The Ashbound's teachings, once the unshakeable bedrock of his identity, now felt like a brittle shell, cracked by the undeniable truth he had witnessed in the heart of the Skywood. His understanding of the Land Guardian's vow had been shaped by centuries of Ashbound doctrine: a mandate of absolute control, of forceful subjugation, of imposing a sterile order upon the wild. Protection, in their eyes, meant eradication of anything that threatened their vision of pristine, unblemished dominion. It was an oath forged in the fires of perceived chaos, designed to quell, to contain, and to conquer.

But Mara's gentle persistence, her almost reverent communion with the earth, had unraveled that tightly woven tapestry of belief. He had seen the Skywood not as a territory to be patrolled and secured against any perceived impurity, but as a living, breathing entity, a complex web of interconnected life that thrived on a delicate balance. His oath, he now realized with a dawning sense of revelation, did not demand the Ashbound's brand of ruthless enforcement. It spoke of guardianship, of stewardship, of safeguarding. And those terms, when viewed through the lens of what he had experienced, demanded a far more nuanced approach.

The concept of "domination" began to recede from his thoughts, replaced by a growing understanding of "protection" as a collaborative endeavor. He had always seen his role as that of a shield, a bulwark against corruption, a force that imposed its will upon nature to preserve it. This was a perspective of singular, top-down authority. Now, however, he began to perceive it as a partnership, a dialogue between the stewards and the land itself. His duty was not to bend the Skywood to his will, but to understand its will, to listen to its rhythms, and to work in concert with its inherent vitality. The very notion of "cleansing" shifted in his mind; it was no longer about the violent expulsion of what was deemed undesirable, but about restoring harmony, about fostering the land's own innate capacity for self-repair.

He traced the weathered inscription on his gauntlet, the familiar Ashbound sigil. It represented an order that prized certainty and efficiency above all else, an order that viewed nature as a force to be tamed, its wildness a flaw to be corrected. But Cael's journey through the revitalized heart of the Skywood had instilled in him a deep respect for that very wildness, a recognition that within its seemingly untamed essence lay a profound wisdom and a resilience that the Ashbound's rigid control could only ever suppress, never truly replicate. His oath, he began to believe, was not a tool of suppression, but a mandate for understanding and integration.

He recalled the Ashbound's fear of the "unraveling," the potential for a single corrupted element to destabilize the entire system. They preached that the only solution was swift and absolute eradication, a surgical removal of the diseased limb to save the body. But Mara had demonstrated a different path – one of delicate intervention, of understanding the interconnectedness, of coaxing the entire ecosystem back into health rather than simply excising the ailing parts. This was not about dominance; it was about a profound form of stewardship, one that acknowledged the inherent worth and purpose of every component, however seemingly flawed.

His oath, as a Land Guardian, was to protect the integrity of the natural world. But what was integrity? Was it the sterile uniformity the Ashbound enforced, or was it the vibrant, dynamic diversity he now saw flourishing? He began to see that the Ashbound's definition of protection was a cage, built by fear, that ultimately weakened the very things it sought to preserve. True protection, he mused, was not about imposing an external order, but about nurturing the internal strength, about facilitating the inherent processes of growth and renewal.

He thought of the Skybells Mara had pointed out, flowers that hadn't bloomed in decades, now tentatively pushing through the soil. This was not a sign of Ashbound victory, of a threat vanquished by their doctrine. This was a testament to the Skywood's own enduring spirit, a spirit that Mara had helped to reawaken. His oath, then, was not to be the shepherd who dictated the flock's every move, but rather a guide who understood the pasture, who knew when to let the flock graze freely and when to gently steer them away from a treacherous patch of ground.

The language of his oath began to reconfigure itself in his mind. "To guard the ancient ways" no longer meant to enforce the Ashbound's rigid interpretation of those ways, but to honor the Skywood's own ancient, cyclical rhythms. "To maintain the balance" was not about preventing any change, but about ensuring that change occurred within the natural ebb and flow of life, decay, and rebirth. His understanding of "stewardship" transformed from a position of ultimate authority to one of humble service, of tending to a sacred trust.

He had always viewed his role as one of a warrior, ready to draw his blade against any encroaching darkness. Now, he saw himself as a gardener, his hands skilled not just in wielding steel, but in understanding the soil, in recognizing the needs of the smallest sprout, in fostering growth. This shift was not merely semantic; it represented a fundamental alteration in his perception of power, of responsibility, and of his place within the grander scheme of the world. The Ashbound's philosophy was one of overcoming nature; his evolving oath was about cooperating with it.

He considered the subtle, yet potent, magic Mara employed. It was not a force that dominated or coerced, but one that persuaded, that harmonized, that worked with the existing energies. It was a magic that understood the language of the earth, and in doing so, coaxed forth its own latent power. This, he realized, was the essence of his own potential reinterpretation. His oath, if understood through this new paradigm, could empower him to act not as a blunt instrument of destruction, but as a subtle conduit of restoration.

The Ashbound believed that sentinels were the ultimate arbiters of natural order. But Cael now saw that true order arose organically, from the complex interplay of countless elements, each with its own purpose and place. His oath, therefore, was not to *impose* order, but to *facilitate* it, to ensure that the conditions were right for the Skywood's natural order to thrive. This meant recognizing the value of even those elements the Ashbound would deem corrupt or undesirable, understanding their role within the larger system, and finding ways to integrate them, or at least mitigate their disruptive influence, without resorting to brute force.

He imagined himself returning to his brethren, his words weighed down not by the arrogance of absolute certainty, but by the humility of newfound understanding. He would speak not of conquering the wild, but of befriending it. He would advocate not for the forceful imposition of Ashbound doctrine, but for a respectful dialogue with the living world. His oath, once a symbol of his unwavering adherence to a singular, unyielding ideology, was now becoming a testament to his capacity for growth, for adaptation, and for a deeper, more compassionate form of guardianship.

The word "protection" itself began to bloom in his mind, taking on new dimensions. It was not just about defending against external threats, but about nurturing the internal health of the ecosystem. It was about ensuring the continuity of life cycles, about respecting the inherent right of the Skywood to exist in its multifaceted glory, not in a state of Ashbound-imposed sterility. His oath was a promise, yes, but it was a promise that could be fulfilled in myriad ways, and the way he had been taught was, perhaps, the least effective and the most damaging.

He felt a profound sense of liberation from the heavy chains of his former dogma. The Skywood, in its resurgent glory, was not merely a landscape he was sworn to protect; it was a teacher, a mentor, a living testament to a wisdom far older and more profound than any Ashbound decree. His oath was not a rigid cage, but a vast horizon, an invitation to explore new possibilities for guardianship, a path towards a more meaningful and effective form of protection that embraced the very essence of what it meant for life to flourish. His reinterpretation of his oath was not a betrayal of his duty, but its ultimate fulfillment.

The air still hummed with the residual tremors of the Skywood's reawakening, a subtle thrum that resonated deep within Cael's bones. The scent of damp earth and newly unfurled leaves, once a mere backdrop to his duty, now spoke with a clarity that echoed the profound shift within him. His oath, no longer a rigid decree but a flowing current, guided his steps as he stood beside Mara, a silent testament to the burgeoning understanding between them. The urgent, almost frantic energy of their recent struggle had receded, replaced by a quiet determination to weave the threads of reconciliation, particularly with those ancient, powerful beings who had been wounded by the Ashbound's heavy hand: the land dragons.

Mara, her presence a soothing balm against the lingering unease, turned to him, her eyes holding a mixture of hope and trepidation. "They are wary, Cael. Their trust was not easily broken, and it will not be easily mended."

Cael nodded, the weight of generations of Ashbound actions settling upon his shoulders. He understood. The dragons, guardians of their own ancient territories, had witnessed firsthand the Ashbound's relentless pursuit of order, their invasive methods that carved through the land and its inhabitants without regard for the intricate web of life. They had felt the sting of their dominance, the arrogance of their pronouncements that nature was to be bent to their will, not respected as an equal.

"I understand their wariness," Cael replied, his voice low but firm. He looked towards the jagged peaks that pierced the azure sky, where the dragons had long retreated, their roars of defiance silenced by a weary resignation. "For too long, we have acted as conquerors, not protectors. We have viewed their power as a threat to be contained, their ancient wisdom as an obstacle to be bypassed.

The Ashbound saw them as raw, untamed force, and sought to bind it, to control it, to diminish it. They did not see the integral role they played, the symbiotic harmony they maintained with the very essence of the land." He paused, the words tasting new and yet profoundly true on his tongue. "My oath is to guard the land, but I have learned that true guardianship is not about imposing our will, but about understanding and cooperating with the will of the land itself. And the dragons are as much a part of that will as the deepest roots of the Skywood."

Mara's gaze softened. "Then you must speak to them, Cael. Not as a Sentinel who dictates terms, but as one who seeks to understand, to atone."

The task felt monumental, a climb more daunting than any physical ascent. The dragons were beings of immense power, their forms etched with the memory of ages, their hearts holding the fury of millennia. Yet, Cael felt a nascent courage, fueled by his transformed perspective. He was no longer the instrument of Ashbound dogma, but an evolving guardian, ready to acknowledge the errors of his predecessors and to forge a new path.

They made their way towards the dragon roosts, a journey that led them through landscapes still bearing the scars of past conflicts. Cael pointed them out, not with the usual Ashbound pronouncements of necessary eradication, but with a somber acknowledgement of what had been lost. He spoke of the Skywood's resilience, of its inherent drive to heal, a healing that had been hindered by the Ashbound's heavy-handed interventions.

"We believed we were cleansing," Cael admitted to Mara as they traversed a valley where once, a great oak, a dragon's sanctuary, had been razed to make way for an Ashbound fortification. "We thought we were removing imperfections. But we were, in fact, severing vital connections, disrupting ancient harmonies. The dragons, their very presence, were a part of that harmony. Their anger was not just a reaction to our intrusion; it was a cry of pain for the land itself."

As they approached the foothills where the great stone dragons often congregated, a palpable tension filled the air. The very rock seemed to emanate an ancient weariness, a deep-seated mistrust. Cael felt the familiar prickle of apprehension, but it was now tempered by a resolute calm. He stepped forward, his movements deliberate, respectful. He did not draw his weapon, nor did he adopt the imperious stance of a Sentinel. Instead, he offered his hands, palms open, a gesture of vulnerability.

And then, a shadow fell. It was Thryxal, the great earth dragon, his scales the color of weathered granite, his eyes like molten gold, blazing with an ancient fire. He landed with a tremor that shook the very ground, his immense form a testament to the raw power that pulsed through the land. His gaze, sharp and discerning, fell upon Cael, and Cael could feel the scrutiny, the silent weighing of his intentions.

"Sentinel," Thryxal's voice boomed, a rumble that seemed to originate from the very heart of the mountains. "You come again. What folly do you bring this time? More pronouncements of order? More attempts to chain what cannot be chained?"

Cael met Thryxal's gaze, refusing to flinch, but also refusing to meet it with defiance. "Great Thryxal," he began, his voice steady, imbued with the sincerity he now felt. "I have not come with pronouncements, but with understanding. And with a deep and heartfelt apology."

The golden eyes narrowed. "Apology? The Ashbound do not apologize. They conquer."

"The Ashbound of the past, perhaps," Cael conceded, his words carefully chosen. "But the land itself has taught me, and I have learned that our methods have been flawed, our understanding incomplete. We have sought to control what we should have sought to comprehend. We have sought to dominate what we should have sought to partner with. We have seen you, and all beings of this land, as forces to be subdued, when in truth, you are integral to its strength, its vitality, its very soul."

He gestured to the surrounding landscape, to the nascent signs of healing that Mara had so painstakingly nurtured. "Look around you, Great Thryxal. The Skywood is not a territory to be conquered, but a living entity, breathing, thriving, capable of its own resilience. And you, the dragons, are its ancient heart. Your power is not a threat to be contained, but a vital force that has long been suppressed by our ignorance."

Thryxal remained silent for a long moment, his gaze shifting from Cael to Mara, who stood a respectful distance behind him, her presence radiating a quiet support. The heat in his eyes seemed to lessen, replaced by a flicker of something akin to curiosity, perhaps even surprise.

"You speak differently, Sentinel," Thryxal rumbled, the suspicion still evident but no longer consuming. "Your words carry the echo of the land, not the harsh decree of your order."

"My oath is to protect," Cael explained, elaborating on the shift in his understanding. "But I have come to realize that true protection is not about wielding a sword to cleave away what we deem dangerous. It is about understanding the interconnectedness, about fostering balance, about respecting the inherent right of all beings to exist and to contribute to the whole. Your presence, your strength, your connection to the earth – these are not things to be feared or controlled. They are essential. And your absence, or your forced subservience, has weakened the land more than any perceived threat."

He took a step closer, his voice softening further. "For the harm inflicted by my order, for the disrespect shown to you and to the lands you guard, I offer my deepest regrets. I wish to forge a new path, one of true alliance, of mutual respect, and of shared guardianship. I do not ask you to forget the past, but to consider a future where our strengths can be combined, where we can work together to ensure the continued health and vitality of this world."

Mara stepped forward then, her voice gentle but firm. "Great Thryxal, the Skywood remembers. It remembers the songs of the earth that were silenced, the ancient rhythms that were disrupted. But it also remembers the power that lies dormant, waiting for its proper place. Cael speaks with a newfound truth. He seeks not to command, but to collaborate. He understands that the dragons are not tools to be wielded, but partners to be valued."

Thryxal's massive head lowered slightly, bringing his molten eyes closer to Cael's. The air crackled with his power, a restrained force that Cael now understood as a fundamental aspect of the land's health. He saw not just raw power, but ancient wisdom, a profound connection to the earth's deepest currents.

"You claim a new understanding, Sentinel," Thryxal said, his voice still a low growl, but the edge of pure anger had softened. "But words are easily spoken. Actions are what carve the stone. The Ashbound have carved deep wounds."

"I know," Cael replied, his gaze unwavering. "And I am prepared to demonstrate my commitment. My oath, when truly understood, is not a weapon of control, but a bond of stewardship. I wish to honor that bond with you, with all the dragons." He paused, then continued, "Tell me, Great Thryxal, what has been lost? What imbalances have been created by our interference that you, with your ancient knowledge, can help us to rectify? I am willing to learn, to listen, and to act not as a master, but as a humble servant of the land's true needs."

A long, profound silence stretched between them. The wind whispered through the rocks, carrying the scent of pine and the distant cry of a hawk. Thryxal's gaze swept over Cael, then Mara, and then the surrounding landscape, as if he were reading the very pulse of the earth. Cael held his breath, aware that in this moment, the fate of their fragile alliance, and perhaps the future of the Skywood itself, hung in the balance.

Finally, Thryxal let out a slow, resonant sigh, a sound like stones grinding together. It was not a roar of anger, but a sound of profound weariness, and perhaps, a flicker of hope.

"You speak of partnership, Sentinel," Thryxal finally said, his voice still deep, but with a newfound gravity. "You speak of listening. These are alien concepts from your order. Yet, I sense a truth in your words. The land has indeed suffered under the Ashbound's heavy hand. The streams that once flowed with vital energy have been diverted. The ancient groves where the earth's magic was strongest have been desecrated. The delicate balance between predator and prey, between growth and decay, has been disrupted by your sterile order."

He turned his golden gaze back to Cael. "The Ashbound believed in absolute purity, in the eradication of all that they deemed 'unnatural.' But life is not pure, Sentinel. It is a tapestry of countless threads, each vital, each contributing to the strength of the whole. Your order sought to unravel that tapestry, believing it was merely removing a few frayed ends."

Cael listened intently, absorbing every word, his mind already racing with possibilities. This was it – the opportunity he had hoped for. To move beyond the Ashbound's narrow vision and embrace a more holistic approach to guardianship.

"What imbalances do you speak of, Great Thryxal?" Cael asked, his voice earnest. "What needs must be addressed? I am ready to listen, to understand, and to dedicate my efforts, and the strength of any allies I can gather, to their restoration."

Thryxal's massive form seemed to relax, ever so slightly. He shifted his weight, the earth groaning beneath him. "There are the Whispering Falls," he began, his voice taking on a more measured tone, as if recalling a long-forgotten grievance. "Once, they were a nexus of life, their waters imbued with the earth's song. Your order, in their pursuit of resource extraction, rerouted the streams that fed them. Now, their song is a whisper, their vitality diminished. The creatures that depended on their unique waters are dwindling."

He continued, his narrative painting a vivid picture of past glories and present decay. "And the Sunstone Glade, a place where the earth's energy was amplified, a sacred space for the younger dragons to learn the ways of the land. Your fortifications, built with sterile stone and devoid of natural resonance, have disrupted the flow of energy. The glade lies dormant, its light dimmed."

Cael absorbed these details, his mind already mapping out potential solutions. Rerouting streams was a complex undertaking, but not impossible. Restoring the Sunstone Glade would require not just physical labor, but a reintroduction of natural energies, something he now felt more equipped to understand.

"These are grave matters," Cael said, his voice resonating with a newfound purpose. "And they are wrongs that must be righted. I pledge to you, Great Thryxal, that I will bring the matter of the Whispering Falls to the attention of those who can help redirect its waters. And I will dedicate myself to the restoration of the Sunstone Glade, not as a Sentinel imposing order, but as a guardian working with the land's own inherent strengths."

He looked directly into Thryxal's golden eyes. "This is not a promise made lightly, but a commitment born of a transformed understanding. My oath demands that I protect the integrity of the land, and I now see that you and your kind are not obstacles to that integrity, but essential pillars of it. I seek your guidance, not your subservience. I seek your alliance, not your subjugation. Will you consider this, Great Thryxal? Will you grant us a chance to prove that the Ashbound of today are not the Ashbound of yesterday?"

The air grew heavy with anticipation. Mara watched, her expression one of quiet hope, her faith in Cael's transformation evident. Thryxal's gaze lingered on Cael, a silent assessment that seemed to pierce to his very core. Then, slowly, the tension in his massive frame began to ease.

"The earth remembers, Sentinel," Thryxal rumbled, the sound still deep and resonant, but now carrying a different cadence. "It remembers the arrogance, but it also remembers the balance. Your words... they hold a different resonance. You speak with respect, not with the usual Ashbound decree. You acknowledge the harm, and you offer a path towards healing."

He took a deep breath, the sound like a subterranean wind. "The dragons have long been estranged from your order. We have watched your sterile interventions with sorrow and with anger. But the Skywood calls for balance. And perhaps, just perhaps, your new perspective can be the beginning of that balance."

He lowered his head further, a gesture that Cael recognized as a significant concession. "I will not immediately embrace this alliance, Sentinel. Trust, once shattered, takes time to rebuild. But I will observe. I will watch your actions. If you indeed work to restore the Whispering Falls, if you strive to rekindle the light of the Sunstone Glade, then perhaps, and only then, can we speak of a shared future. The earth is generous, Sentinel, but it is also unforgiving. Your actions will speak louder than your words."

A profound sense of relief washed over Cael. It was not a full embrace, not yet, but it was a crack in the millennia-old wall of mistrust, a tentative extension of a clawed, yet hopeful, hand. "I understand, Great Thryxal," Cael said, bowing his head in a gesture of profound respect. "And I will not fail you, or the land, in this endeavor."

He looked to Mara, a silent acknowledgement of their shared journey. Together, they had faced down a crisis born of imbalance, and now, they were beginning the arduous but essential work of restoring harmony, one alliance, one whisper of the wind, one flowing stream at a time. The path ahead was long, and fraught with the ghosts of past wrongs, but for the first time in a long time, Cael felt the steady pulse of true hope, not as a fleeting emotion, but as the deep, abiding rhythm of a land beginning to heal.

He knew the Ashbound elders would balk at his every word, at his every action, but he also knew, with a certainty that resonated deep within his soul, that this was the only path forward, the only way to truly fulfill the spirit of his oath. The dragons, once viewed as adversaries, were now potential allies, their ancient wisdom and power crucial to the Skywood's enduring health. It was a radical shift, born of necessity and illuminated by a deeper understanding of the interconnectedness of all things. He would work tirelessly, not to prove the Ashbound wrong, but to prove that protection, true protection, was about fostering life, not extinguishing perceived threats.

The rustling of leaves outside the council chamber, once a mundane sound, now seemed to carry a new resonance. It was the sound of the Skywood breathing, of its ancient systems recalibrating, a subtle symphony that had begun to play louder in the days since the Skywood's heart had pulsed anew. Inside, the Canopy Accord Council, a collection of individuals whose lineages were as deeply rooted in the Skywood as the oldest arboreal giants, were in session. The air, usually thick with the sharp debates and entrenched ideologies of its members, carried a different kind of charge – one of dawning realization, and tentative, yet undeniable, acceptance.

For generations, the Accord had been a fragile bulwark, designed to maintain a precarious balance between the encroaching needs of burgeoning settlements and the wild, untamed spirit of the Skywood. Their mandate was to protect, to preserve, and often, to enforce the rigid doctrines that had shaped the Ashbound's relationship with the natural world. But the Ashbound's philosophy, a rigid adherence to order and control, had been revealed as a brittle facade, easily shattered by the raw, untamed power of a land pushed too far.

Eldrin, his face a roadmap of a hundred seasons, the patriarch of the Willowbrook settlement, leaned forward, his gaze fixed on the intricate aerial map of the Skywood projected onto a shimmering disc of solidified moonlight. His usual skepticism, a well-honed tool of council deliberations, seemed to have dulled. "The Lumina Bloom," he began, his voice raspy with age and a touch of wonder, "it has returned. Not a single, struggling sprout, but a cascade of light, as the ancient texts foretold. Mara's efforts... they were not merely cosmetic. They were a balm to a festering wound."

Across from him, Lyra of the Sunstone Enclave, a woman whose connection to the crystalline energies of the mountain peaks was as profound as her sharp intellect, nodded slowly. Her initial resistance to Mara's unconventional methods, rooted in her own deep understanding of geological forces, had been steadily eroded by the irrefutable evidence. "The resonant hum," she stated, her voice clear and precise, "it has stabilized. The disruptive frequencies that plagued the northern passes have subsided. We have felt it in the very stone. It is as if the Skywood itself is breathing easier."

This was the crux of the shift. It wasn't just anecdotal reports or the emotional testimonies of those who had witnessed the reawakening of the Skywood's dormant life. It was the tangible, measurable impact of Mara's work, coupled with Cael's profound, and frankly, surprising, transformation. His interactions with Thryxal, the earth dragon, had been the most contentious point, a radical departure from the Ashbound's long-held animosity towards the ancient beings. Yet, the dragons' presence, once a source of fear and perceived threat, was now being viewed through a new lens – as guardians of a balance that the Ashbound had so carelessly disrupted.

"The tremors from the Skywood's heart," spoke Kaelen of the Ironwood Dominion, a man whose clan's strength was derived from their mastery of metal and timber, his tone gruff but devoid of its usual accusatory edge. "They were not the prelude to destruction, as many feared. They were... a recalibration. A reassertion of ancient energies. And Cael's approach, his willingness to listen to the land, to the dragons... it has been instrumental in preventing a catastrophic backlash." He paused, running a hand over the polished wood of the table. "My scouts report that the northern dragon roosts, once a place of extreme danger, are now showing signs of... coexistence. Not outright alliance, mind you, but a cessation of hostility. The patrols have not been attacked. The livestock remain undisturbed."

This was a monumental admission. The Ironwood Dominion had always been at the forefront of the Ashbound's efforts to contain, and if necessary, subdue, the land dragons. Their territory bordered some of the most volatile dragon nesting grounds. For Kaelen to speak of "coexistence" was to acknowledge that the Ashbound's policies had not only failed, but had actively been detrimental.

"It is not merely coexistence," Mara interjected softly, her voice carrying a quiet authority that had grown with her newfound connection to the Skywood. "It is the beginning of understanding. Thryxal has spoken of imbalances, of disrupted flows of vital energy. The rerouting of the Whispering Falls, the desecration of the Sunstone Glade – these were not acts of ecological necessity, but acts of arrogance. Cael has pledged to address these, not through brute force, but through intelligent, collaborative restoration. And the dragons, they are not merely passive observers of this change. They are the earth's ancient memory, and their knowledge is invaluable."

The council chamber was filled with a quiet murmur. The concept of "collaboration" with beings they had been taught to fear and subdue was a seismic shift in their collective understanding. It was one thing to acknowledge the Skywood's sentience, quite another to propose working *with* its oldest inhabitants.

Eldrin stroked his beard, his eyes reflecting the projected image of the Lumina Bloom. "The legends spoke of a time when the Sentinel and the dragons walked in harmony, guardians of the land together. We dismissed it as allegory, as a children's tale. Perhaps, we have been too quick to dismiss the wisdom of the ancients, especially when it conflicted with our own pursuit of dominion."

Lyra tapped a long, slender finger on the table. "The crystalline structures beneath the Sunstone Glade have been dormant for centuries. The disruption caused by the Ashbound's fortifications not only blocked the flow of ambient energy, but also severed a crucial link between the earth's core and the Skywood's upper canopy. If Cael can facilitate the removal of those structures, and if the dragons can guide the re-establishment of that energy flow, the potential for revitalization is immense. It could impact weather patterns, nutrient cycles, even the very growth rate of the Skywood's flora."

The debate, which had so often devolved into arguments over territorial boundaries, resource allocation, and the perceived threats of the wild, was now focused on a different kind of planning. The conversation wasn't about how to *control* the Skywood, but how to *nurture* it. The rigid lines that had defined the Ashbound's approach were softening, becoming more fluid, more responsive to the subtle cues of the environment.

"Cael's transformation is... unprecedented," Kaelen admitted, a note of reluctant respect in his voice. "The Ashbound have always valued discipline, adherence to doctrine. But true strength lies in adaptability, in recognizing when a path, however long-trodden, leads to ruin. He has shown a willingness to unlearn, to listen, and to act with a humility that is... commendable. I propose that we not only sanction his efforts to restore the Whispering Falls and the Sunstone Glade, but that we actively offer our support. The Ironwood Dominion has skilled engineers, those who understand the principles of water flow and structural integrity. We can offer our expertise, not to build fortifications, but to dismantle them, and to guide the natural restoration."

A ripple of agreement spread through the chamber. The thought of the Ironwood Dominion, the very embodiment of Ashbound control, lending their engineering prowess to a project spearheaded by a reformed Sentinel and supported by dragons, was a testament to the magnitude of the shift.

"And the Lumina Bloom," Eldrin added, his voice growing stronger. "Its resurgence signals more than just a return of a rare flora. It is a beacon. Its petals, when they are at their peak, are said to hold a potent, life-affirming energy. If Mara can harness even a fraction of that energy, it could be a vital component in the healing of weakened ecosystems, a catalyst for growth in areas that have been barren for too long."

Mara looked at Eldrin, her eyes shining. "The Lumina Bloom thrives on balance, Eldrin. It requires not just light and water, but a specific energetic signature that is only present when the Skywood is in harmony. Its return is a direct result of the efforts to mend the rifts, both physical and spiritual. And yes, its essence, when carefully collected and prepared, can indeed be a powerful restorative."

The council members, who had once viewed Mara as an outsider, a practitioner of esoteric arts that bordered on heresy, were now looking at her with newfound respect. Her work, once dismissed as the ramblings of a nature-worshipper, was proving to be the very key to the Skywood's survival.

"We must also consider the broader implications," Lyra stated, her gaze sweeping across the council. "If the dragons are willing to engage, to share their knowledge, it opens up possibilities that were unthinkable mere months ago. Their understanding of geological formations, of subterranean currents, of the very pulse of the earth... it far surpasses our own. This is not just about restoring a few ecological sites. This is about forging a new era of coexistence, one where the Sentinel, the Accord, and the ancient beings of this land can work in concert."

The words hung in the air, heavy with the weight of generations of conflict. Coexistence. Alliance. Partnership. These were not terms that had ever been spoken within these hallowed halls, not in earnest, at least.

"The Ashbound elders," Kaelen said, his voice tinged with a hint of apprehension, "they will not find this easy. Their adherence to tradition runs deep."

Cael, who had remained largely silent, listening intently to the unfolding discourse, finally spoke. His voice, though still carrying the weight of his recent experiences, was now imbued with a quiet resolve. "The Ashbound's traditions were built on a foundation of fear and misunderstanding. If we are to truly protect the Skywood, we must embrace the truths that have been revealed, however uncomfortable they may be. My oath is to guard the land, and I have learned that true guardianship requires not just strength, but wisdom, humility, and the willingness to form alliances with all who share that purpose. The dragons are not our enemies; they are integral to the land's health. Their knowledge, their power, is not a threat, but a vital component of the balance we seek."

He looked around the chamber, his gaze meeting each member's in turn. "I will present my proposals for the restoration of the Whispering Falls and the Sunstone Glade to the Ashbound Council. I will speak of the dragons not as adversaries, but as partners. I will not shy away from the changes that have occurred, but will embrace them as the path forward. And I ask for your support, not just in sanctioning these efforts, but in advocating for this new understanding. The Canopy Accord must be a testament to adaptability, to growth, and to the enduring power of a Skywood that thrives in balance, not in subjugation."

A profound silence descended upon the chamber, broken only by the soft, rhythmic rustling of leaves outside. It was the sound of a new chapter beginning, a chapter written not with the harsh lines of control, but with the vibrant, interwoven threads of understanding and respect. The Canopy Accord was no longer merely a council of keepers of the old ways, but the nascent architects of a new, more harmonious future, a future where the oath to protect was finally understood in its truest, most profound sense. The acceptance was not universal, not yet, but the seeds had been sown, watered by tangible proof and nurtured by the undeniable wisdom of a land finally allowed to breathe.

The path ahead would undoubtedly be challenging, filled with the friction of old beliefs clashing with new realities, but for the first time, the Canopy Accord Council felt a collective sense of purpose, a shared vision of a Skywood reborn, not through dominance, but through genuine partnership. They began to discuss logistics, not of enforcement, but of collaboration. Eldrin suggested a joint delegation to observe the restoration efforts at the Whispering Falls. Lyra offered to coordinate with Cael on the energy flow studies for the Sunstone Glade. Kaelen pledged his engineers, with a clear directive: to assist in dismantling, not building. The Accord was shifting, transforming, reforging its oath not in stone, but in the ever-growing, ever-adapting spirit of the Skywood itself.

The debates that followed were not about whether to act, but how best to act in concert, how to leverage the unique strengths of each faction, and crucially, how to communicate this seismic shift to the wider settlements and the reluctant Ashbound elders. The future was uncertain, but it was no longer a future of dwindling hope; it was a future of hard-won, deeply earned, possibility.

The council chamber, moments before filled with the hum of nascent agreement, now settled into a quieter, more reflective cadence. The immediate crisis had receded, leaving in its wake a profound silence, the kind that follows a tempest, where the air is cleansed but the landscape bears the undeniable scars of the storm. This was the breath of a fragile peace, a delicate truce brokered not by force of arms or the weight of decree, but by the undeniable resurgence of life that had bloomed where despair had threatened to take root.

Eldrin, his gaze no longer fixed on the shimmering map but resting on his clasped hands, spoke with the quiet authority of a man who had witnessed the ebb and flow of seasons, and now, of ecological and societal tides. "The immediate danger has passed," he stated, his voice a low rumble, acknowledging the immense relief that had swept through the council. "The Skywood breathes again, not with the ragged gasps of a dying world, but with the steady, vital pulse of a land awakening. The dragons, once perceived as harbingers of destruction, have become our unexpected allies, their roars now a resonant chorus to the land's healing. This is a victory, one we have earned through a willingness to shed old fears and embrace a new understanding."

Lyra, ever the pragmatist, nodded, her eyes distant, as if still attuned to the subtler energies of the earth. "A victory, yes, but not an end," she cautioned, her words a gentle counterpoint to the prevailing sense of triumph. "The Skywood's resonance pathways, those intricate veins of life force that connect every living thing within its embrace, have been deeply scarred. The disruption caused by generations of Ashbound influence, their relentless pursuit of order and control, has left fissures that will take time, and a sustained commitment to balance, to mend. We have merely stanched the bleeding; the true healing is a long and arduous journey."

Kaelen, the gruff facade of the Ironwood Dominion softening, chimed in, his voice surprisingly devoid of its usual defensive edge. "Indeed. The Ashbound Faction, though their influence has been demonstrably detrimental, is not a force that can be simply wished away. Their beliefs are deeply ingrained, their adherence to tradition a formidable obstacle. They see our current path as a betrayal of their ancestral doctrines, a dangerous deviation from the established order. While many within the council have embraced this new paradigm, we must not underestimate the resistance we will face. Their numbers are still significant, their networks far-reaching."

Mara, her connection to the revitalized Skywood now a palpable aura, added her perspective. "The land dragons, while our allies now, are sentient beings with their own ancient memories and grievances. Their cooperation is a testament to Cael's extraordinary efforts, but it is also a trust that must be continuously nurtured. They have felt the pain of the Skywood, the disruption of their ancestral territories, the imbalance in the elemental flows. Their continued alliance is contingent upon our genuine commitment to restoring what has been broken, not just for our benefit, but for theirs, and for the Skywood as a whole." She paused, her gaze sweeping across the assembled council members. "The Lumina Bloom's resurgence is a powerful symbol, a beacon of hope. But its radiance, while potent, is finite. It thrives on the restored harmony, and its continued flourishing depends on our vigilance. We have proven that the Skywood can heal, but we have also learned how easily that healing can be undone."

Eldrin sighed, a sound that carried the weight of centuries of Ashbound dogma. "The Ashbound Faction. They are the lingering shadow, the specter of the old ways that still haunt our pronouncements. Their fear of the untamed, their deep-seated belief that nature must be subjugated to human will, is a deeply entrenched ideology. To convince them that true strength lies not in dominion but in symbiosis, that the wild is not an enemy to be conquered but a partner to be respected, will be our greatest challenge. They have seen the evidence, the undeniable proof of the Skywood's revival, yet many will cling to their prejudices, their established narratives of control."

Lyra traced an invisible pattern on the polished surface of the table. "Their resistance stems from a fundamental misunderstanding of the Skywood's true nature. They view it as a resource to be exploited, a force to be harnessed, rather than a living, breathing entity with its own inherent rights and needs. The resonance pathways, which we have begun to mend, are not merely conduits of energy; they are the very lifeblood of this world, and their disruption has had profound, far-reaching consequences, not just for the flora and fauna, but for the subtle atmospheric conditions, the very quality of the air we breathe, the predictable patterns of the seasons. The Ashbound's actions, though perhaps born of a desire for security and prosperity, have inadvertently sown the seeds of instability."

Kaelen grunted, a sound of grudging agreement. "My own people, the Ironwood clan, have always prided themselves on their mastery of the wood and metal, their ability to shape the Skywood to their will. We built the fortified settlements, the logging camps that encroached upon dragon territories, the dams that diverted vital waterways. These were acts of progress, or so we believed. Now, we must acknowledge that our 'progress' came at a devastating cost. My clan's engineers, skilled in construction, must now learn the art of deconstruction, of aiding nature's reclamation, not its subjugation. This is a paradigm shift that will not be easily accepted by those who have always defined themselves by their ability to dominate."

Mara looked towards Cael, who had been listening intently, his presence a quiet anchor in the chamber. "Cael, your journey has been the catalyst for this change. You have seen firsthand the consequences of the Ashbound's approach, and you have forged a new path, one of understanding and cooperation. But the path you walk is still fraught with peril. The dragons have offered their aid, but their patience is not infinite. The land itself, though healing, is still vulnerable. And the Ashbound Faction, with their ingrained fear and their unwavering belief in their own righteousness, will seek to reassert their control."

Cael finally spoke, his voice steady, though a flicker of the immense burden he carried was visible in his eyes. "I understand the challenges that lie ahead. The Ashbound elders will demand answers, and some will be unwilling to hear them. They will see the dragons not as allies, but as a renewed threat, their collaboration with us a sign of our weakness, not our wisdom. They will view the restoration of the Whispering Falls and the Sunstone Glade not as acts of healing, but as a return to a chaotic, uncontrolled state. My oath as Sentinel was to protect the Skywood, and I have learned that true protection requires more than just strength; it requires foresight, empathy, and the courage to challenge deeply held, yet fundamentally flawed, beliefs."

He rose from his seat, his posture conveying a quiet determination that resonated through the chamber. "I will not shy away from confronting the Ashbound Faction. I will present the evidence of their actions' detrimental effects, the undeniable proof of the Skywood's suffering under their dominion. I will speak of the dragons not as beasts to be feared, but as ancient stewards of this land, whose knowledge and power are vital to its continued health. I will advocate for the dismantling of their fortifications, for the restoration of the natural pathways, and for a future where the Sentinel and the ancient beings of the Skywood work in concert, not in opposition."

Eldrin leaned forward, his gaze thoughtful. "Your resolve is commendable, Cael. But we must also consider the broader implications. The peace we have achieved is fragile, a thin veneer over deep-seated animosities. If we are to truly secure the Skywood's future, we must address the underlying causes of this discord. The Ashbound Faction, for all their misguided zeal, represents a segment of the population whose fears, however irrational, must be acknowledged. Simply dismissing their concerns will only drive them further into opposition."

Lyra nodded in agreement. "The economic implications are also significant. The Ashbound's methods, while ecologically destructive, did provide a certain level of predictable resource extraction and settlement expansion. Our new approach, one of collaborative restoration and respect for natural cycles, will require a fundamental reevaluation of our societal structures and economic priorities. This is not merely a matter of ecological balance; it is a societal transformation. The settlements that have grown accustomed to the Ashbound's control will need time to adapt to a world where nature is not a commodity to be endlessly harvested."

Kaelen rubbed his chin, a thoughtful expression on his face. "Perhaps, we can offer a compromise, a path that acknowledges the Ashbound's need for order while still respecting the Skywood's needs. We can involve them in the restoration efforts, not as overseers, but as participants. Their engineering skills, honed for construction, can be repurposed for constructive endeavors – aiding in the careful removal of barriers, in the re-establishment of natural waterways, in the sensitive regrowth of damaged ecosystems. By giving them a role in the healing process, we might begin to shift their perspective, to demonstrate that true order arises not from subjugation, but from the harmonious integration of all living things."

Mara smiled faintly. "That is a wise approach, Kaelen. The Skywood's healing is not a solitary endeavor, nor should it be. It requires the collective effort of all its inhabitants. If the Ashbound Faction can be guided to understand that their actions can contribute to the Skywood's revitalization, rather than its destruction, then we have a chance to truly mend the rifts, not just in the land, but in our society."

The air in the council chamber seemed to lighten, the weight of past conflicts slowly dissipating, replaced by the nascent hope of a shared future. The fragile peace was not merely an absence of war, but a budding understanding, a testament to the Skywood's enduring resilience and the capacity for change within its people. The dragons, the Lumina Bloom, the reawakened earth – these were all powerful signs, but they were also a call to action, a reminder that the journey towards true balance was ongoing, a continuous act of reforging the oath, not just in words, but in deeds. The path ahead would be challenging, undoubtedly, but for the first time in generations, it was a path that led not towards further destruction, but towards a genuine, and hard-won, harmony. The whispers of the wind through the leaves outside no longer sounded like a lament, but like a promise, a gentle encouragement to embrace the dawn of a new era.

CHAPTER TWELVE

WHISPERS FROM THE DEEP

The immediate crisis had receded, a tempest that had churned the Skywood's heart and then, miraculously, relented. A fragile peace now settled over the land, a quiet interlude that felt less like a victory and more like a held breath. Yet, beneath the surface of this newfound calm, a disquietude lingered, a subtle dissonance that resonated deeper than the newly mended pathways. The Skywood, though breathing with renewed vigor, was not yet whole. The very act of healing had revealed new scars, not of physical wounds, but of an insidious imbalance that had been merely contained, not eradicated.

The resonance pathways, once muted and choked by the Ashbound's suffocating control, now pulsed with a vibrant energy. It was a powerful, almost overwhelming surge, a testament to the land's innate resilience and Cael's tireless efforts. However, this revitalization was not a simple return to the status quo. The restored conduits hummed with an energy that felt... alien. It was as if the Skywood, in its desperate struggle for survival, had tapped into a source of power previously unknown, or perhaps, deliberately suppressed.

The hum was not the steady, melodic song of ancient earth; it was a more complex, sometimes discordant melody, laced with undertones that spoke of a power yet to be understood, and a potential for chaos that had not been entirely banished. Lyra, her senses attuned to the subtlest shifts in the earth's energetic tapestry, found herself constantly on edge. The familiar currents that once guided her now swirled with an unfamiliar intensity, the echoes of forgotten magic interwoven with the raw power of renewal. It was like listening to a symphony where a new, powerful instrument had been introduced, its notes both breathtakingly beautiful and unnervingly unpredictable.

Eldrin, too, felt it. The ancient wisdom that had guided him for centuries now offered only partial explanations for the Skywood's current state. He would sit for hours, his fingers tracing the patterns on the revitalized pathways visible beneath the forest floor, trying to decipher the new language they spoke. "It is as if the Skywood has awakened to a new consciousness," he mused one evening, his voice a low rumble that blended with the rustling of the rejuvenated leaves. "The Ashbound's methods were crude, brutal, but they imposed a predictable order. In their absence, the Skywood's own inherent magic has surged forth, untamed and unfamiliar. We have replaced subjugation with freedom, but this freedom carries its own weight, its own inherent dangers."

The barren patches remained. These were not the vast, desolate expanses left by the Ashbound's more egregious acts of ecological devastation, but smaller, more localized pockets of an unnatural emptiness. In these areas, the soil was sterile, the air unnervingly still, and even the most resilient of mosses refused to take root. They were like small, dark wounds on the Skywood's recovering body, areas where the new life force seemed to recoil, unable to penetrate the lingering blight. Cael had personally investigated several of these zones, his dragon allies by his side. The dragons, creatures intimately connected to the earth's vital energies, seemed particularly disturbed by these barren patches. Their rumbling growls, usually expressions of contentment or concern, would deepen into a guttural disquiet when they approached these sterile areas. Some of the younger dragons, less experienced in the ways of the Skywood, would even refuse to enter them, their scales bristling with an instinctual fear.

One such area, nestled within the shadowed heart of the Whispering Falls region, had become a particular focus of Cael's unease. Even after the falls had been coaxed back to their former glory, their cascading waters now singing a joyous song, this particular glade remained stubbornly lifeless. The water that trickled through it seemed to lose its vitality, becoming thin and colorless as it passed over the parched earth. The air hung heavy, devoid of the usual forest scents, and the only sound was an unnerving silence, as if the very life force of the Skywood had been leached away. Mara, her connection to the land so profound that she could feel its every tremor, described the sensation as akin to a persistent, low-grade fever. "It is not dead, not entirely," she explained to Cael, her brow furrowed in concentration. "But it is sick. The very essence of life is struggling to take hold, as if there is an invisible barrier, a lingering poison that the Lumina Bloom's light cannot penetrate."

Kaelen's engineers, their skills now redirected from construction to careful ecological restoration, had examined the soil in these barren areas. Their instruments, designed to detect the most minute mineral deficiencies, revealed nothing out of the ordinary. The composition of the earth was sound, the water table adequate. Yet, life refused to flourish. It was a mystery that gnawed at the edges of their scientific understanding, a stark reminder that the Skywood's intricacies extended beyond the realm of tangible measurement. "It's as if something has fundamentally altered the earth's ability to nurture life," one of Kaelen's most trusted engineers reported, his voice laced with frustration. "The Ashbound's methods were destructive, yes, but they left behind tangible evidence of their impact – soil depletion, blocked waterways, fractured rock. This... this is different. It's a void, a negation of life's very potential."

This subtle but pervasive unease was beginning to ripple through the council. The initial elation of averting disaster had given way to a more somber reflection. They had achieved a remarkable victory, but the victory felt incomplete, precarious. The whispers that echoed from the deep places of the Skywood were no longer just the gentle murmurings of a recovering forest, but carried an undertone of warning. The dragons' newfound cooperation was a powerful alliance, but their ancient wisdom also spoke of cycles, of balance, and of the consequences that inevitably followed any disruption. If the Skywood was not fully restored, if these barren pockets represented a deeper, unresolved malignancy, then the dragons' patience might not be as eternal as they hoped.

Lyra, ever the astute observer, noticed the subtle shifts in the demeanor of the council members. The confident pronouncements of a few weeks prior had been replaced by a quiet anxiety, a shared sense of navigating uncharted territory. The fear of the Ashbound's overt control had been replaced by a more profound, existential fear: the fear of the unknown, of a darkness that lurked just beyond the edges of their understanding, a darkness that their hard-won peace had merely held at bay, but not vanquished. She saw it in Eldrin's increasingly furrowed brow as he pored over ancient texts, searching for any mention of such lingering blight. She felt it in Mara's quiet meditations, her connection to the Skywood now tinged with a sorrow that spoke of a deeper, unhealed wound. Even Cael, whose resolve had been the bedrock of their recent successes, carried a new weight in his gaze, a silent acknowledgment of the battle that was far from over.

The resurgence of the Lumina Bloom, once a triumphant symbol, now also held a note of urgency. Its brilliant light, while pushing back the encroaching shadows, seemed to be struggling against an unseen force in these barren areas. It was as if the bloom itself, the very embodiment of the Skywood's restorative power, was being tested, its luminescence dimmed by an encroaching decay. This wasn't a sudden collapse, but a slow, insidious erosion, a creeping dread that whispered of a foe far more cunning than the Ashbound's overt aggression. The Ashbound had sought to control and dominate, their actions driven by a flawed ideology. But this new threat, this lingering shadow, felt more primal, more fundamental – a force that seemed to actively resist the very essence of life.

The dragons, in their wisdom, had spoken of the Skywood's deep memory, of the echoes of past wounds that could fester for generations. Cael recalled a hushed conversation with the elder dragon, Ignis, whose scales shimmered with the wisdom of millennia. Ignis had spoken of times when the Skywood had been sickened by forces that had left no visible trace, but whose effects had rippled through the land for centuries. "The earth remembers," Ignis had rumbled, his voice like shifting stones. "And sometimes, the deepest wounds are not those that bleed, but those that lie dormant, waiting for the right moment to awaken." Cael had dismissed it then as a cautionary tale, but now, as he looked upon the unnervingly barren glades, Ignis's words took on a chilling new significance.

The fragile peace, it seemed, was a deceptive calm. The Skywood had been coaxed back from the brink, but the journey to true recovery was proving to be far more complex than anyone had anticipated. The restored resonance pathways, the revitalized flora and fauna, the returned dragons – these were all steps forward, but they were steps taken on ground that still held unseen dangers. The lingering shadows were not merely the remnants of the Ashbound's dominion, but something deeper, something that had always been present, or perhaps, had been awakened by the very act of healing.

The true test of their commitment, Cael realized, would not be in the grand gestures of restoration, but in their ability to confront these subtle, persistent threats, to delve into the lingering shadows and unearth the truths that lay hidden beneath the surface of their hard-won peace. The whispers from the deep were no longer just the stirrings of a recovering world, but the echoes of a profound, unresolved mystery, a challenge that would demand every ounce of their courage, their wisdom, and their unwavering belief in the enduring power of life. The council chamber, though quieter, now hummed with a different kind of energy – not the buoyant triumph of victory, but the steady, determined resolve of those who understood that the real fight had only just begun, and that the deepest scars were often the most insidious.

The council chamber, usually a place of urgent debate and strategic planning, had fallen into a hushed reverence. Eldrin, his ancient eyes holding the distant flicker of forgotten stars, unfurled a scroll brittle with age. The parchment, unlike any the assembled leaders had ever seen, shimmered with an inner luminescence, its script a serpentine dance of symbols that spoke of a language predating spoken words. He had discovered it, not through conventional research, but through a series of increasingly vivid dreams, visions that had tugged at his subconscious like the roots of an ancient tree seeking water. These dreams had led him to a hidden chamber beneath the oldest roots of the Skywood, a place he had previously believed to be merely a geological anomaly. Instead, he had found this repository, a vault of knowledge guarded by an energy that felt both protective and profoundly sorrowful.

"These," Eldrin began, his voice a low thrum that resonated with the earth's own deep vibrations, "are not mere records. They are echoes. Whispers from the world's genesis." He gestured to the shimmering script. "This language, it predates even the oldest dragon tongues. It speaks of the Deep Places, of the primordial heart of Aethel. And it speaks of guardians, and of what they guarded."

Cael leaned forward, his gaze fixed on the scroll. The Lumina Bloom's light, so vital to their recent victory, seemed to dim in comparison to the ethereal glow emanating from the parchment. "Guardians? Guarding what, Eldrin?"

"Entities," Eldrin replied, his brow furrowed with a familiar blend of awe and apprehension. "Beings woven from the very fabric of Aethel's creation. They are not of flesh and blood, nor are they spirits in the way we understand them. They are... fundamental. Tied to the planet's inherent forces, to the currents that flowed before the first mountain rose or the first ocean formed." He paused, letting the weight of his words settle. "And these texts suggest they do not slumber eternally. They awaken. They stir when the world's balance is critically threatened, or when something within them is disturbed."

Lyra, her senses tingling with an awareness that transcended the physical, felt a ripple of disquiet run through her. The new, unpredictable energy pulsing through the resonance pathways now seemed to carry a deeper, more ancient rhythm, one that was both awe-inspiring and terrifying.

"The barren patches," she murmured, her voice barely audible. "The places where life recoils. Could this be connected?"

Eldrin nodded slowly. "The portents speak of 'Rifts of Stillness.' Places where the primal energies have been... inverted. Where creation falters not from lack of vitality, but from a presence that actively negates it. These are not merely ecological wounds, but echoes of a far older malaise, a disruption that has been dormant for eons, yet remains intrinsically linked to the planet's very life force."

He pointed to a particular section of the scroll, where a series of swirling glyphs pulsed with a slightly more intense light. "This speaks of the 'Children of the Unmaking.' They are not destroyers in the conventional sense, no more than a black hole is a destroyer. They are forces of entropy, of absolute stillness, of the void that preceded existence. They were not banished, Cael, Lyra, Kaelen. They were... contained. Held in a state of quiescence by the ancient guardians, within the deepest strata of Aethel."

Mara, who had been quietly observing, her connection to the Skywood usually a source of solace, now radiated a deep unease. She felt the subtle resonance of Eldrin's words as if they were tectonic shifts within her own soul. "The dreams I've had," she whispered, her voice strained. "Not of Ashbound shadow, but of an ancient, crushing weight. A silence so profound it felt like the end of all sound. I thought it was a lingering echo of the devastation. But perhaps..."

"Perhaps it is the stirring of that which was contained," Eldrin finished, his gaze meeting hers. "The Ashbound's actions, their perversion of the Skywood's life force, may have inadvertently weakened the ancient seals, or perhaps, the very act of healing the land has disturbed the slumber of these primordial entities. The resonance pathways, now thrumming with renewed energy, may be inadvertently broadcasting a signal that stirs them from their deep, silent rest."

Kaelen, the pragmatic engineer, shifted uncomfortably. His instruments had found no anomalies in the barren patches, no logical explanation for the sterile earth. But the concept of primordial entities, of forces that existed beyond scientific measurement, was a humbling, and frankly, terrifying, proposition. "If these are not creatures that can be fought with steel or elemental magic, how do we defend against them? How do we even comprehend them?"

"That is the gravitas of these portents," Eldrin said, his voice grave. "The ancient lore does not speak of direct conflict, but of balance. The guardians were not warriors, but conduits. They maintained a delicate equilibrium. Their power lay in understanding the fundamental harmonies of existence. To counter the Unmaking, one must not fight it with destruction, but with creation. With life. With a resonance so profound it reasserts the very principle of being."

He gestured to the Lumina Bloom, now a symbol of their recent triumph. "The bloom's light, the Skywood's renewed vitality, the dragons' ancient wisdom – these are all manifestations of creation's power. But if these entities are stirring, it suggests our current efforts, while vital, may be insufficient. The Skywood is healing, yes, but if its deepest heart is being disturbed, then the healing itself may be attracting a far more ancient and profound threat."

The weight of this revelation settled heavily upon the council. The Ashbound had been a tangible enemy, their motivations understood, their tactics predictable. But this was something else entirely. This was a threat woven into the very fabric of reality, a force that predated their understanding of good and evil, of life and death. It spoke of a cosmic dance, a cyclical ebb and flow that they had only just begun to glimpse.

"The dragons," Cael said, his voice resonating with a newfound urgency. "They have always spoken of balance, of the earth's deep memory. Have they ever spoken of such primal forces?"

Eldrin inclined his head. "Their oldest tales hint at 'The Great Sleepers,' entities that shaped the world in its nascent stages. They are spoken of with reverence, not fear, but with a profound understanding of their immense power. The dragons learned to live in harmony with these forces, to respect their presence, to understand that their slumber was as vital to the world's existence as the sun's warmth. But they also knew that a prolonged imbalance, or a deliberate disturbance, could awaken them. And when they awaken, the world reshapes itself around them."

Lyra looked towards the windows, towards the vibrant green of the recovering Skywood. The Lumina Bloom, planted with such hope, now seemed to shimmer with a desperate plea. "So, the fight isn't over," she stated, not as a question, but as a somber realization. "The Ashbound were a symptom. This... this is the disease."

"A disease that has been dormant for millennia," Eldrin corrected gently. "And one that may require a far deeper understanding of the Skywood's true nature than we have ever possessed. These portents are not a condemnation, but a warning. A call to look beyond the immediate, to understand the deep currents that flow beneath the surface of our world. The entities in the Deep Places are not inherently malevolent. They are fundamental. Their stirring signifies a profound disharmony, and our task is to restore that harmony, not to wage war upon the primordial forces of existence."

The implications were staggering. They had emerged from a conflict that had nearly shattered their world, only to find themselves facing a danger that dwarfed it in scale and antiquity. The fragile peace they had fought so hard to achieve was not an end, but a preamble. A moment of quiet contemplation before a storm that had been gathering since the dawn of time. The whispers from the deep were no longer just the murmurs of a recovering forest, but the thunderous pronouncements of a world reawakening to its most ancient truths. The portents, shimmering on the ancient parchment, offered not a map to victory, but a profound challenge to their understanding of existence itself. They had to learn to listen not just to the pulse of the living forest, but to the silent, powerful rhythm of the world's oldest heart.

Mara's Unease

The council chamber, accustomed to the urgency of immediate threats, now reverberated with the ancient anxieties unearthed by Eldrin's scroll. While the elders grappled with the implications of primordial forces and their potential awakening, Mara felt a subtler, yet equally profound, shift. It wasn't a sound, nor a visible phenomenon, but a sensation that rippled through her very being, a discordant hum beneath the renewed vibrancy of the Skywood. It was a feeling she'd come to recognize, a primal alarm bell that had first sounded with the creeping drought, but now, it was amplified, deeper, and far more unsettling. It resonated not from the wilting leaves or the parched earth, but from a place far below, a place she couldn't name, a darkness she couldn't fathom.

Her connection to the Skywood, normally a source of grounded comfort, felt... frayed. The lifeblood of the ancient forest, now flowing with renewed vigor thanks to the Lumina Bloom and the dragon's ancient magic, had always sung a clear, resonant song to her. But now, interwoven with that song was a dissonant undertone, a low frequency vibration that felt alien and menacing. It was like a shadow cast upon a sunlit glade, a silent predator lurking just beyond the periphery of vision. Her mind, ever seeking logical anchors, struggled to categorize this new sensation. It lacked the distinct signature of the Ashbound's corrupted energy, nor did it possess the raw, untamed power of the dragons she had come to know. This was something else entirely, something that felt... *old*. Older than the trees, older than the mountains, perhaps even older than the Skywood itself.

She tried to draw strength from the Skywood, to feel its roots anchoring her, but the connection felt tenuous, as if the very earth beneath her feet was humming with an unfamiliar, unsettling tremor. It was a profound sense of unease, a primal intuition that screamed of an impending danger originating from a realm beyond her current understanding, a realm that existed not in the tangible world of earth and sky, but in the deep, unseen currents of Aethel itself. The concept of "Rifts of Stillness" and "Children of the Unmaking" felt abstract, intellectual constructs, but this sensation, this deep, vibrating disquiet, was visceral. It spoke of a primal force stirring, a power that defied her attempts at scientific classification, a force that whispered of oblivion.

Mara closed her eyes, trying to filter out the hushed murmurs of the council, the rustling of Eldrin's ancient scroll, and focus on this internal disturbance. She pictured the Skywood's roots, plunging deep into the earth, reaching for the heart of the world. Usually, this visualization brought a sense of peace, a connection to the planet's enduring strength. But now, her mind's eye saw those roots encountering something dense, something unyielding, something that pulsed with a cold, silent rhythm. It was like reaching into impossibly deep water, where the pressure intensified with every descent, and the darkness became absolute. She felt a phantom pressure in her chest, a heaviness that mirrored the oppressive stillness Eldrin had described.

This wasn't the familiar ache of ecological imbalance, the desperate cry of a wounded ecosystem. This was something more fundamental, a disturbance at the very core of existence. It was the antithesis of the vibrant life she nurtured, the very essence of being. The Lumina Bloom, a beacon of hope and resilience, seemed to flicker in her mind's eye, its brilliant light unable to penetrate this profound, encroaching darkness. She felt a chill that had nothing to do with the ambient temperature, a creeping dread that settled deep within her bones. It was the unsettling awareness that the battle against the Ashbound, while crucial, had perhaps only cleared the stage for a far more ancient and terrifying drama to unfold. The whispers Eldrin spoke of were becoming a deafening roar within her, a primal warning that resonated with the deepest, most instinctual parts of her being. The earth, her constant companion, her source of power and understanding, was now a conduit for an ancient, unfathomable unease.

Cael's breath hitched, the rhythmic inhale and exhale that usually grounded him in the present moment suddenly felt clumsy, out of sync. He was in the Heartwood, the very core of the Skywood, a place usually alive with the thrumming pulse of ancient life, a symphony of rustling leaves, chattering creatures, and the deep, resonant sigh of the earth. Today, however, the symphony was marred by a jarring, almost imperceptible discord. It wasn't a sound that assaulted his ears, but a vibration that seeped into his bones, a chilling tremor that resonated not from the sprawling canopy above, nor the moss-laden earth beneath his boots, but from a place far, far deeper.

His oath, renewed and reshaped by the crucible of near-destruction, now bound him more tightly than ever to the well-being of this ancient forest, and by extension, the very bedrock of Aethel. As a Land Guardian, he was meant to be its shield, its sentinel, its conduit to the natural world. He felt the Skywood's every heartbeat, its every surge of energy, its every whisper of distress. But this... this was different. This was not the familiar ache of a wounded limb, a drought-stricken root, or a blighted branch. This was a primal shudder, a deep, unsettling tremor that felt like the awakening of something vast and slumbering, something that predated even the Skywood's ancient existence.

He knelt, his calloused hands pressing flat against the cool, damp soil. The earth, usually a source of unwavering strength and connection, felt... uneasy. It was a subtle disquiet, like the nervous twitch of a sleeper on the verge of a nightmare. He could still feel the vibrant thrum of the Skywood, the renewed vitality brought by the Lumina Bloom and the echo of the dragons' potent magic. The forest was healing, its emerald tapestry rewoven with threads of vibrant green and silver light. But beneath that reassuring hum, a darker, more potent vibration was stirring. It was a low frequency thrum, a persistent tremor that spoke of immense pressure, of immense age, of immense, unfathomable power.

His Land Guardian oath, once a sacred pact of protection, now felt like a fragile barrier against a tide he could barely comprehend. He had fought the Ashbound, had witnessed their destructive hunger, their insatiable need to unravel the threads of life. He had believed, with a fierce certainty born of experience, that their corruption was the greatest threat to Aethel. But now, a gnawing dread, cold and sharp, began to coil in his gut. The Ashbound, he realized with a sickening lurch, were merely the surface ripples of a much deeper, far more ancient disturbance. They were the gnats buzzing around the slumbering leviathan.

Cael closed his eyes, his focus sharpening, pushing past the surface sensations of the forest. He sought the deeper currents, the subterranean arteries of Aethel. He felt the roots of the Skywood, ancient and gnarled, plunging into the darkness. Usually, their descent was a passage into a realm of quiet strength, of geological patience, of the slow, steady growth that built mountains and carved valleys. But today, as his awareness followed their downward path, he felt them brush against something alien, something immense and inert, yet pulsing with a silent, latent power. It was like a colossal stone, buried for millennia, beginning to shift in its deep, earthen bed.

He pictured the layers of rock and soil, the veins of mineral and hidden water, the ancient, compressed memories of the earth. He imagined himself descending with them, through strata of time, through epochs of creation and decay. And with each deepening descent, the unsettling vibration intensified. It was a palpable pressure, a force that seemed to push back against his very essence, against the life force that courhomed within him. It was not the chaotic energy of destruction he had faced before, but a profound, absolute stillness that was terrifying in its potential. A stillness that was the antithesis of life itself.

This was the "Rift of Stillness" Eldrin had spoken of. Not a tear in the fabric of reality, as he had first imagined, but a profound, abyssal void, a place where the very concept of motion, of life, of existence, was held in abeyance. And from this void, a subtle but insistent pressure was building, like the slow accumulation of water behind an immense dam, threatening to breach its ancient, earthen walls.

He remembered the ancient texts, the fragmented lore he had studied in his youth, tales of primal forces that existed before the Skywood, before the dragons, before the very concept of Aethel was sung into being. He had dismissed them as myths, as cautionary tales designed to inspire awe. But now, the whispers of those forgotten tales seemed to echo in the deep, resonant thrum beneath his feet. They spoke of the "Children of the Unmaking," not as malevolent entities, but as an absence, a void that sought to reclaim all that was.

Cael felt a profound vulnerability, a stark realization that his oath, his strength, his very existence as a Land Guardian, was rooted in a world that was now facing a threat that transcended physical form. The Ashbound had sought to corrupt and consume, to twist and pervert. But this... this was a force that sought to *unmake*. It was the slow, inexorable erosion of existence, the silent erasure of all that was. And it was stirring, not in the ravaged lands of the Ashbound, but from the deepest, most sacred heart of Aethel.

He pulled his hands from the earth, the sensation lingering on his skin like a phantom chill. The vibrant energy of the Skywood, which usually flowed through him like a river, now felt like a thin, fragile membrane stretched taut over an unfathomable abyss. He looked at the ancient trees, their colossal forms reaching towards the heavens, their roots plunging into the depths. They were the embodiment of life, of resilience, of time. But even they, he now understood, were anchored to something that was beginning to tremble.

A sense of isolation washed over him. He was the Land Guardian, sworn to protect the living world. But how could he protect it from an absence? How could he fight a stillness that threatened to absorb all motion, all life? The Ashbound were an enemy he could see, an enemy he could confront with blade and magic. But this was an enemy that existed in the realm of being and non-being, an enemy that operated on a scale of time and space that dwarfed his own understanding.

He rose slowly, his gaze sweeping across the sun-dappled glade. The Lumina Bloom, so recently a symbol of hope and renewal, seemed to cast a fainter light now, its brilliance struggling to pierce the encroaching shadow that Cael felt radiating from the deep. He could almost see it, not with his eyes, but with his mind's eye: a vast, silent expanse, a negation of all form and energy, slowly, imperceptibly, pressing outwards.

This was not a battle that could be won with force, or even with cunning. It was a battle for the very concept of existence, a fight against the primal urge of the void to reclaim its dominion. And Cael, the Land Guardian, felt a chilling premonition. The peace they had fought so hard to achieve, the healing they had so painstakingly nurtured, might be nothing more than a fleeting moment of light before an eternal, silent darkness. The deep earth, his sanctuary, his source of power, was now whispering a terrifying secret – a secret of an end that had no beginning, a stillness that predated motion, an unmaking that was the ultimate, inevitable end.

His oath, once a beacon of hope, now felt like a desperate, fragile promise made against the backdrop of an unimaginable cosmic silence. He was a guardian of life, and the greatest threat was not a destroyer, but an absence. And that absence was beginning to stir. The earth beneath him continued its low, insistent hum, a constant reminder of the vast, ancient forces that lay dormant, and were now, irrevocably, awakening. He felt a cold dread seep into his very soul, the chilling certainty that the battles of the surface were but a prelude to a conflict of cosmic proportions, a conflict waged not in the light of the sun, but in the crushing, silent depths of Aethel's forgotten heart.

The forest breathed again. The vibrant pulse of the Heartwood, which Cael had felt falter and then surge with the triumphant bloom of the Lumina, now beat with a steady, reassuring rhythm. The scars left by the Ashbound's insidious corruption were already fading, the emerald tapestry of the Skywood reweaving itself with an almost miraculous speed. It was a testament to the forest's inherent resilience, a power Cael, as its Land Guardian, had sworn to uphold. Yet, even as relief washed over him, a disquiet settled in the aftermath. The Ashbound were gone. Not vanquished, not defeated in a pitched battle, but simply... absent. Their once-rampant presence, their shrieking propaganda, their very distinct and terrifying ideology of unmaking, had receded as if a storm had abruptly ceased, leaving behind an unnerving calm.

This vanishing act, however, was more unsettling than any direct confrontation. The Ashbound had been a tangible enemy, a force of destructive hunger that Cael understood. He knew their motivations, their twisted desire to return Aethel to a primal, unformed state, to unravel the intricate tapestry of life they so vehemently despised. He had met their fervor with his own grounded strength, his own unwavering commitment to preservation. But now, their absence left a void not of peace, but of unanswered questions. Where had they gone? Had they simply retreated, licking their wounds and regrouping in some shadowed corner of the realm, biding their time until the next opportune moment to spread their blight? Or was their disappearance a symptom of something far more profound, something that transcended the superficial battles they had waged?

The tremors Cael had felt from the deep, the unsettling resonance that spoke of an ancient, immense power stirring in the hidden heart of Aethel, returned to his thoughts. He had dismissed the Ashbound's ideology as a destructive fringe element, a chaotic eruption born of desperation and nihilism. He had believed their corruption was the greatest threat. But now, their abrupt departure felt less like a strategic retreat and more like a response, or perhaps even a consequence, of that deeper stirring. Were the Ashbound merely gnats buzzing around the slumbering leviathan he sensed below? Were they a manifestation, a symptom, of a much larger, more fundamental imbalance that was beginning to assert itself?

The whispers from the deep had spoken of a stillness, an unmaking, a negation of existence itself. It was a concept so alien, so antithetical to everything Cael stood for, that it had been difficult to fully grasp. He had confronted beings who sought to destroy, to corrupt, to consume. But this was different. This was an absence, a void that threatened to erase the very definition of being. And if this force was awakening, a force that predated the Skywood, predated the dragons, predated the very song of Aethel's creation, then the Ashbound's radical agenda suddenly seemed less like an independent threat and more like a chaotic echo of a far more potent, primordial force.

He walked through the Heartwood, his boots sinking slightly into the soft, damp earth. The air, once thick with the acrid scent of the Ashbound's corruption, was now sweet with the fragrance of damp soil and burgeoning life. Yet, beneath the surface of this revitalized beauty, Cael felt a persistent unease. The forest's healing was a testament to its strength, but it was a strength rooted in a world that was now demonstrably precarious. The Ashbound had been a fire, raging and destructive, but a fire that could be fought, a fire that consumed and left ashes. This new threat, the one stirring from the deep, felt like a slow, inexorable frost, a chill that permeated to the very bone, an unmaking that promised not ash, but an absolute, profound emptiness.

He recalled the fragmented prophecies, the hushed tales of the "Children of the Unmaking" that he had once dismissed as allegorical warnings. These were not beings with malice, but rather an existential negation, a primal urge for the universe to return to its pre-creational state of absolute stillness. The Ashbound's rhetoric, their desire to "cleanse" Aethel, to "return it to its true form," now seemed to take on a chilling new resonance. Had their radical actions been an unconscious, or perhaps even a deliberate, attempt to appease or facilitate this deeper, more fundamental force? Had they, in their nihilistic fervor, recognized the stirring of the void and sought to hasten its arrival?

The thought sent a shiver down Cael's spine, a coldness that had nothing to do with the lingering dampness of the forest floor. He had always believed that the greatest threats to Aethel would come from those who sought to dominate or destroy its living essence. He had faced warlords and sorcerers, creatures of shadow and blight. But the Ashbound, with their seemingly nonsensical ideology of unmaking, had always been an anomaly, a disturbing outlier in his understanding of conflict. Now, their disappearance felt like a confirmation that they were not the primary threat, but rather a secondary phenomenon, a symptom of a deeper malaise.

He stopped by the base of a colossal Skywood sentinel, its bark gnarled and ancient, its branches reaching like skeletal fingers towards the dappled sunlight. This tree, and countless others like it, were the embodiment of life's tenacity, its ability to endure, to grow, to adapt. They were living history, their rings a chronicle of centuries, millennia. Yet, Cael felt a sudden, chilling empathy for their immense roots, plunging deep into the earth, anchoring them to a world that was now revealing its most terrifying secret. What if their very foundation, the bedrock of their existence, was beginning to shift, to erode not from external attack, but from an internal dissolution?

The Ashbound's disappearance was a puzzle piece that didn't fit, a sudden silence in the cacophony of chaos they had represented. It was too neat, too absolute. Their fervor, their zealotry, had been a force that Cael could understand, a force that he could counter. But the quiet, the absence of their destructive presence, now felt more insidious. It allowed the deeper unease to fester, to grow. It allowed the whispers from the deep to be heard more clearly.

He closed his eyes, attempting to reconnect with the earth, to feel its pulse, its rhythm. The Skywood's heartbeat was strong, vibrant. The Lumina Bloom's energy, though now subdued after its initial burst of power, still resonated, a beacon of healing. But beneath it all, that low, persistent thrum persisted. It was a vibration that seemed to resonate with the very absence of the Ashbound. It was as if the forest, having shed the Ashbound's outward corruption, was now more acutely aware of the profound, silent pressure from below.

Perhaps the Ashbound hadn't simply retreated. Perhaps their radical ideology, their fervent belief in unmaking, had been a twisted form of attunement. Perhaps they had been drawn to, or even acted as conduits for, the nascent force stirring in the deep. Their goal of returning Aethel to a primal, unformed state was, in its own perverse way, a mirror of the void's own drive towards stillness and non-existence. Their disappearance, then, could be interpreted not as a surrender, but as a completion of their role, a merging with the greater, primordial force they had so fervently served. They had been the vanguard, the initial disruption, a prelude to the true unmaking.

This thought was a bitter pill to swallow. Cael had dedicated his life to protecting the living world, to preserving its intricate beauty and complex vitality. The idea that a group of extremists, driven by nihilistic despair, could have inadvertently paved the way for a force that sought to erase existence itself, was a devastating prospect. It suggested a hierarchy of threats, a cosmic order of destruction, where the Ashbound, whom he had considered the apex of danger, were merely pawns in a much larger, much older game.

He opened his eyes, gazing at the canopy above. The sunlight filtered through the leaves, painting shifting patterns on the forest floor. It was a scene of profound peace, of vibrant life. But Cael could no longer see it with the same unblemished clarity. He saw now the fragile boundary between existence and non-existence, the delicate balance that held the world together. The Ashbound's disappearance had removed a visible threat, a tangible enemy. But in its place, it had amplified the presence of an invisible one, a threat that operated on a scale of time and being that dwarfed all his previous understanding.

The forest was healing, yes, but it was healing on the precipice of something ancient and terrifying. The Ashbound's radical presence had been a blight, but it had also been a warning, a scream from the edges of sanity. Their silence now was a deeper, more chilling premonition. It suggested that the true battle was not one of survival, but of existence itself. And that battle, Cael feared, was not being fought on the surface, where he had always stood as guardian, but in the silent, crushing depths of Aethel's forgotten heart, a heart that was now pulsing with the rhythm of unmaking.

He was a guardian of life, and the greatest threat was not a destroyer, but an absence. And that absence, he now understood, was not merely stirring, but was beginning to exert its profound, silent influence, drawing the world, and perhaps even the Ashbound themselves, into its abyssal embrace. The very stability of the Skywood, the very breath of the Heartwood, felt like a temporary reprieve, a moment of defiant life against an encroaching, eternal stillness. The Ashbound's disappearance was not an end to their story, but a shift in the narrative, a fading from the foreground to become a part of the deeper, darker currents that now threatened to overwhelm Aethel.

CHAPTER THIRTEEN
A NEW HORIZON

The earth beneath Cael's feet no longer felt like the stable, yielding ground of a healthy forest. Instead, it had taken on a subtle, disquieting vibratory quality, a low hum that resonated not just through the soles of his boots but deep into the marrow of his bones. It was a resonance that had been growing in intensity since the abrupt disappearance of the Ashbound, a silence that spoke volumes more than their guttural pronouncements ever had. The Heartwood, once a bastion of vibrant life and the locus of Aethel's spiritual energy, now felt like a delicate shell, its profound healing a mere outward manifestation masking an underlying tremor of unrest. The Lumina Bloom's residual power, a soothing balm that had quelled the Ashbound's corruption, now seemed to be engaged in a desperate, holding action against a far more ancient and pervasive influence.

Cael had always conceived of threats as discrete entities – creatures of malice, ideologies of destruction, forces that could be named, understood, and confronted. The Ashbound, for all their terrifying nihilism, had fit this paradigm. They were a disease, a cancerous growth on the body of Aethel. But this... this was different. This was not an invasion, but an emergence. It was the planet itself groaning under an unimaginable pressure, a deep seismic ache that spoke of tectonic plates shifting not by geological time, but by the awakening of forces that predated even the oldest mountains. He had felt the tremors before, faint and distant, dismissed as the echoes of the Ashbound's machinations. Now, however, they were undeniable, a persistent thrumming beneath the surface, a rhythmic pulse that felt less like a heartbeat and more like a slow, inexorable grind.

He ventured beyond the familiar embrace of the Skywood, his intuition pulling him towards the jagged peaks of the Obsidian Range, a mountain chain that had always been a stark, alien presence against the verdant backdrop of the forest. The Ashbound had occasionally used the foothills of these mountains as staging grounds, their dark banners a jarring contrast against the stark, volcanic rock. But the deeper recesses, the treacherous, shadow-choked valleys and soaring spires, had remained largely unexplored, avoided by the forest dwellers due to an innate, primal sense of dread. Now, as Cael approached, the very air seemed to thicken, carrying with it a faint, metallic tang, the scent of something ancient and mineral, something that had been buried for eons.

The ground here was not merely vibrating; it was actively contorting. Cracks, impossibly straight and deep, spiderwebbed across the obsidian plains, some emitting a faint, phosphorescent glow. These were not the chaotic fissures of a natural earthquake; they seemed too precise, too deliberate, as if the earth itself were being systematically unstitched. From some of these fissures, a strange, viscous substance oozed – not lava, nor mud, but a shimmering, obsidian-like fluid that seemed to absorb light rather than reflect it. It pooled in iridescent puddles that reflected distorted images of the sky, images that seemed to ripple and warp with a disturbing fluidity.

A guttural roar, unlike any creature Cael had ever heard, echoed from the heart of the range. It was a sound of immense power, a sound that seemed to tear at the very fabric of reality. It was not a roar of aggression or territoriality, but of something primordial being disturbed, something ancient and slumbering being roused. Cael drew his warding blade, its familiar weight a comfort against the rising tide of unease. The blade, forged from the heartwood of a fallen elder tree, pulsed with a faint, emerald light, a beacon of life against the encroaching darkness.

As he pressed further into the Obsidian Range, the geological anomalies intensified. Entire sections of the mountainside seemed to have undergone a rapid, unnatural crystallization. Jagged, perfectly formed geometric shapes jutted from the rock face, some resembling colossal, interlocking teeth, others like impossibly intricate, crystalline lattices. They pulsed with a faint, internal light, a cold, crystalline luminescence that offered no warmth, only an alien beauty that was deeply unsettling. These were not the chaotic formations of nature; they were too ordered, too deliberate, suggesting an intelligence at work that operated on principles utterly foreign to Aethel's organic existence.

Then he saw them. Emerging from a fissure that glowed with an internal, amethyst light, were creatures of living obsidian. They were not biological in any sense Cael understood. They moved with a stiff, jerky gait, their forms composed of sharp angles and unyielding surfaces. Their bodies were a mosaic of polished black stone, etched with intricate, glowing veins of amethyst. They had no discernible faces, no limbs that mimicked those of Aethel's fauna, only blunt protrusions and sharp, crystalline edges. They were constructs, or perhaps elemental beings, born from the very heart of the disturbed earth.

These Obsidian Sentinels, as Cael began to call them in his mind, moved with a single purpose, their glowing veins pulsing in unison as they approached one of the crystalline formations. They seemed to be tending to it, their movements precise and methodical, as if they were part of some grand, geological operation. They did not seem to notice Cael, or perhaps they simply did not perceive him as a threat. Their focus was entirely on the strange, mineral growths that were rapidly transforming the landscape.

Cael watched, his heart a heavy stone in his chest, as one of the Sentinels placed a multi-faceted appendage against a colossal, crystalline spire. The spire pulsed brighter, and the ground around it vibrated with a deeper resonance. It was as if the earth was not just being shaken, but being fundamentally reordered, its very substance being transmuted. This was not a localized phenomenon. The tremors he felt were a symptom of a planet-wide awakening, a shift in the very foundations of Aethel.

The Ashbound's nihilistic desire to "unmake" had been a crude, destructive echo of a far more profound force. They had sought to return Aethel to a state of primal chaos, a void of nothingness. But this... this was not chaos. This was a different kind of unmaking, a systematic dissolution of organic life, a replacement of vibrant, living matter with inert, crystalline structures. It was a transformation, not into nothingness, but into something else entirely, something cold, sterile, and eternal. The Ashbound had been a symptom, a frantic, misguided herald of this deeper, more insidious threat.

He remembered the fragmented prophecies he had found in the oldest texts of the Skywood, tales of the "Children of the Deep," beings of stone and shadow that slumbered beneath the world's crust, waiting for the opportune moment to reclaim Aethel. He had always dismissed them as myth, as allegorical warnings about the earth's volatile nature. But the reality unfolding before him was far more terrifying than any myth. These were not mere subterranean beasts; they were manifestations of a fundamental planetary shift, a reordering of existence driven by an intelligence that operated on geological timescales and with an alien logic.

The further Cael ventured, the more pronounced the crystalline growths became. They no longer merely jutted from the ground; they formed sprawling, intricate structures that twisted and intertwined, creating a bizarre, alien architecture that seemed to swallow the natural contours of the mountains. The phosphorescent fissures widened, revealing glowing veins of pure energy pulsing beneath the surface, like the arteries of a dying world. And then, he saw it. In the center of a vast, natural amphitheater, a colossal structure was rising from the earth. It was a spire of pure, crystalline light, impossibly tall, its apex lost in the swirling, ethereal clouds that now perpetually hung over the Obsidian Range. It pulsed with a resonant hum, a sound that vibrated through Cael's very soul, a siren song of utter stillness.

Around this central spire, hundreds of Obsidian Sentinels were moving in a synchronized dance, their glowing veins flaring in response to the spire's pulse. They were not simply tending to the structures; they were actively constructing them, their mineral bodies shaping and refining the nascent crystalline forms. It was a hive mind, a collective consciousness operating in perfect harmony, driven by a singular, unfathomable purpose.

This was no longer just a regional crisis. The scale of this emerging threat was planetary. The Skywood's struggle, the Ashbound's corruption – these had been mere localized outbreaks, symptoms of a deeper rot that had been festering for millennia. The disappearance of the Ashbound was not a victory for the forest, but a sign that their purpose had been fulfilled, that they had served their role in the prelude to this grand, terrifying transformation. They had been the initial disruption, the chaotic element that had weakened the world's defenses, allowing this ancient, primordial force to stir and begin its slow, inexorable reordering of Aethel.

Cael felt a profound sense of isolation, a chilling realization that his role as Land Guardian, as a protector of living things, might be fundamentally insufficient against such an existential threat. He could fight a dragon, a blight, a corrupted sorcerer. But how did one fight the very earth itself, when it decided to shed its skin of life and embrace a new form of existence? The energy emanating from the crystalline spire was not malevolent in the way he understood it; it was simply... indifferent. It was the ultimate expression of entropy, a slow, inevitable march towards a state of perfect, crystalline order that would consume all organic life.

He looked back towards the distant, verdant silhouette of the Skywood. It represented everything he fought for – life, growth, the intricate, messy beauty of a thriving ecosystem. But that beauty, that vitality, now seemed incredibly fragile, a temporary anomaly in the grand, geological timescale of Aethel. The crisis was no longer confined to the forest, or even to the land. This threat whispered of realms beyond, of forces that operated on scales that dwarfed the Skywood, the dragons, even the very essence of Aethel as he knew it. The Obsidian Range was merely the first manifestation, the initial tremor of a coming seismic shift that would reshape not just the land, but the very definition of what it meant to exist.

The Ashbound's dramatic departure was now chillingly clear: they had not been defeated; they had been absorbed, their destructive fervor a minor ripple in the face of this ancient, elemental tide. Their unmaking had been a foreshadowing, not an end. The true unmaking had just begun, not as annihilation, but as a profound, alien transformation. The horizon, once filled with the promise of rebuilding and renewal, now stretched out towards an unknown, crystalline future, a future where the very soil of Aethel might sing a song of stillness, and the Skywood would be but a memory etched in fading emerald. He was no longer just the guardian of a forest, but a solitary witness to the earth's terrifying metamorphosis. The scope of the challenge had expanded exponentially, demanding a new understanding of his role, and perhaps, a journey into realms he had never conceived of, realms where the very ground beneath his feet was not made of soil and root, but of an ancient, immutable crystal.

The tremors that had seized Cael's senses were not merely geological; they were seismic shifts in the very fabric of his understanding. The Obsidian Range, once a stark but familiar boundary, now felt like a wound in the world, a gateway to depths far exceeding the familiar root systems of the Skywood. The crystalline formations, the sentient obsidian constructs – these were not aberrations of nature, but rather the first whispers of a force that had always been present, yet hidden, slumbering beneath the veneer of organic life. His perception of Aethel, once grounded in the tangible reality of soil, leaf, and flowing water, was being irrevocably altered, expanding to encompass a dimension of existence he had never before considered. The threat was not simply to the Skywood, or even to the known lands; it was to Aethel itself, in a way that transcended the immediate concerns of survival and spoke to the fundamental nature of its being.

This realization was as exhilarating as it was terrifying. If the problem was not confined to the surface, then the solution could not be either. The Ashbound's nihilistic desire to unmake had been a clumsy echo, a blunt instrument wielded by those who misunderstood the true nature of dissolution. What Cael was witnessing was not destruction, but a profound transmutation, an evolutionary leap driven by an intelligence as ancient as the planet's core. This implied that the answer might lie not in combating this new order, but in understanding it, and perhaps, in finding a way to integrate or coexist. The thought was audacious, bordering on blasphemy to his ingrained role as guardian of life, yet the evidence before him demanded such radical re-evaluation. He had to venture beyond the known, to seek out the origins of this crystalline awakening, and in doing so, potentially find a new horizon for Aethel's future.

The sheer scale of the transformation was humbling. The towering crystalline spire at the heart of the Obsidian Range was a monument to an alien artistry, a testament to an objective far grander than mere territorial conquest. It suggested a purpose that operated on geological timescales, a methodical unfolding that had been underway for eons, patiently awaiting the opportune moment. This moment, it seemed, had arrived with the weakening of the world's organic resilience, a vulnerability exploited by the deep-seated forces that now asserted themselves. The Ashbound, in their misguided fury, had inadvertently cleared the path, their destructive acts serving as a catalyst for a far more significant, and far less understood, emergence.

Cael's mind, accustomed to the immediate challenges of the forest – the blight that threatened the ancient oaks, the territorial disputes between elven clans, the lingering shadows of the Ashbound – struggled to encompass this new paradigm. The concept of "realms" that had been hinted at in ancient lore, once abstract notions of mystical dimensions or far-off lands, now felt starkly real. If the crystalline intelligence resided deep within the earth, it was logical to assume that it might have connections to other hidden places, to realms that lay beneath the surface, within the churning depths of the oceans, or perhaps even beyond the veil of the sky. The Obsidian Range, it seemed, was not an isolated phenomenon but a nexus, a point of connection to a vaster, more intricate network of existence.

The implications for the Skywood's future were immense. Its survival could no longer be guaranteed by its own internal strength or the vigilance of its guardians. The challenges to come would demand a far broader understanding of Aethel, a willingness to explore the unknown and to forge alliances with forces and beings that lay outside the familiar confines of the forest. He had to consider that the "enemy" was not a singular entity to be vanquished, but a fundamental shift in the planet's being, a transformation that might necessitate a redefinition of what it meant to be alive. The Lumina Bloom's residual power, while a potent force against corruption, might prove to be a mere flicker against the encroaching geological eternity.

His thoughts turned to the ancient prophecies, the fragments of lore that spoke of the world's deep history. He had always interpreted these as allegorical warnings, cautionary tales designed to instill respect for the natural world. Now, he saw them as literal accounts, imperfectly translated echoes of events and forces that had shaped Aethel long before the rise of the current civilizations. The "Children of the Deep" were not metaphors; they were the architects of this crystalline emergence, their awakening a cosmic inevitability.

The journey ahead would not be one of simply defending a territory, but of exploring the very foundations of Aethel's existence. He needed to understand the mechanics of this crystalline transformation, the principles that governed the obsidian constructs, and the ultimate goal of this deep-earth intelligence. This would likely involve journeys into the earth itself, into the labyrinthine caverns and subterranean seas that had always been the subject of fear and speculation. It might also involve venturing to the ocean's floor, where pressure and darkness might have fostered similar, as-yet-undiscovered forms of life or intelligence. Or perhaps, the influence was even more pervasive, reaching out into the celestial spheres, where cosmic energies might interact with Aethel's core in ways he could not yet fathom.

The very act of continuing his exploration of the Obsidian Range was a step into this new, expanded reality. Each crystalline shard, each pulsing vein of light, was a clue, a piece of a puzzle that spanned millennia and continents. He could no longer afford to see Aethel as a single, unified entity in the way he once had. It was a complex tapestry of interconnected realms, each with its own unique ecology, its own histories, and its own hidden powers. The Skywood was but one thread in this grand design, and its fate was inextricably linked to the health and balance of the whole.

The path forward was uncertain, fraught with dangers he could only begin to imagine. But within that uncertainty lay the seeds of hope. If this transformation was a natural, albeit alien, process, then perhaps it was not an inherently destructive one. Perhaps it was a necessary evolution, a shedding of one form for another, more enduring one. His role, then, might not be to halt this change, but to guide it, to ensure that some echo of life, some memory of Aethel's vibrant past, could endure within the crystalline future. This would require a profound shift in his perspective, a willingness to shed his preconceived notions and embrace the alien, the unknown, and the potentially incomprehensible.

The Lumina Bloom's power was a testament to Aethel's resilience, its ability to generate and sustain life against overwhelming odds. But what if Aethel's resilience lay not just in its organic forms, but in its very substance, in its capacity for change and adaptation? The crystalline structures, while seemingly inert, pulsed with a vibrant, internal energy, a different kind of life, perhaps. The task before him was to understand this duality, to bridge the gap between the organic and the crystalline, and to find a way for them to coexist, or at least, to transition in a manner that preserved the essence of what Aethel was.

He considered the possibility of other realms, other worlds that might have faced similar transformations or that held knowledge crucial to understanding his current predicament. Were there beings who had already navigated such a shift? Were there ancient civilizations that had either succumbed to or mastered the forces he was now encountering? The questions multiplied, each one opening a new avenue of inquiry, a new direction for his journey. This was no longer a localized crisis; it was an existential one, demanding a cosmic perspective. The horizon had indeed expanded, not just in distance, but in depth and scope, stretching into realms that defied his wildest imaginings. The true adventure, the one that would define the future of Aethel, was only just beginning, and it would take him far beyond the familiar forests and mountains, into the very heart of the world and perhaps, beyond.

The thought of subterranean exploration sent a shiver down his spine, not of fear, but of anticipation. He pictured vast, echoing caverns lit by bioluminescent flora, teeming with creatures adapted to eternal darkness. He imagined the possibility of ancient ruins, remnants of civilizations that had thrived in the deep, their knowledge lost to the surface world for millennia. What secrets might they hold about the earth's core, about the origins of the crystalline entities, about the very nature of Aethel's existence? This was a new frontier, a realm of mystery and potential discovery that dwarfed anything he had ever encountered.

And then there were the oceans. The crushing depths, the alien landscapes of hydrothermal vents, the colossal creatures that swam in the perpetual twilight – these were worlds unto themselves, teeming with life that had evolved in complete isolation from the terrestrial sphere. Could there be a connection between the crystalline emergence and the hidden life of the seas? Perhaps the same ancient forces that stirred in the earth's crust also influenced the oceanic abyss, shaping its inhabitants and its geological formations in ways that mirrored the changes he was witnessing in the Obsidian Range. The thought of descending into that alien environment, armed with only his courage and his warding blade, was daunting, but the potential rewards – the answers that might lie in those unfathomable depths – were too great to ignore.

The idea of celestial realms, while more abstract, was no less compelling. Ancient texts often spoke of the stars as watchers, as influences that governed the ebb and flow of life on Aethel. Could the current transformation be linked to cosmic events, to the alignment of celestial bodies, or to the influence of energies from beyond the sky? The very air above the Obsidian Range seemed to have shifted, becoming charged with an ethereal quality, a subtle luminescence that hinted at something otherworldly. This suggested that the crisis might not be confined to Aethel's physical body, but might also extend to its connection with the wider cosmos, a disruption in the celestial balance that manifested in the geological upheaval below.

This broadening of scope meant that his understanding of "balance" had to evolve. It was no longer solely about the harmonious interplay of flora and fauna within a defined ecosystem. It was about the intricate relationships between the earth, the sea, the sky, and perhaps even the distant stars. The crystalline emergence was not an invasion, but a rebalancing, a reassertion of forces that had been dormant for too long, and the true challenge lay in understanding the complex dynamics of this new equilibrium. His journey was no longer simply a quest to save the Skywood, but to comprehend Aethel in its entirety, to embrace its vastness and its myriad interconnected parts. This was the promise of the new horizon – a terrifying, awe-inspiring vista of a world far grander and more mysterious than he had ever dared to imagine.

Mara met Cael's gaze, the flicker of understanding passing between them like a whispered secret. The chasm that had once separated them, a divide forged in suspicion and misunderstanding, had finally bridged. It wasn't just the tremors of the earth that had shaken the foundations of their beliefs, but the seismic shift within their own hearts. Cael's eyes, once clouded with defensiveness, now held a quiet resolve, a clarity born from the terrifying revelations of the Obsidian Range. And Mara, who had learned to trust the whispers of ancient earth and the resonance of forgotten energies, saw in his steadfast presence not a threat, but a promise. Their shared journey through the heart of the crystalline awakening had stripped away the pretenses, leaving behind a raw, unyielding truth: they were two halves of a necessary whole, their destinies irrevocably intertwined with the fate of Aethel.

"The whispers were right, then," Mara murmured, her voice soft but steady, an echo of the ancient stones that had guided her. "Not an end, but a transformation. And it's not an enemy we face, Cael, but... a profound change." She gestured towards the pulsating heart of the spire, the alien light casting an ethereal glow on their faces. "This isn't destruction. It's emergence. Something ancient, vast, and deeply rooted in Aethel's very being has awakened." Her fingers traced the intricate patterns on her bracers, imbued with the Lumina Bloom's residual essence, a testament to her own journey of healing and discovery. The path she had walked, once fraught with the pain of betrayal and the burden of her people's legacy, had led her here, to this unexpected alliance.

Cael nodded, his hand instinctively resting on the hilt of his warding blade. The weight of it was a familiar comfort, but the nature of its purpose had fundamentally changed. He was no longer just a guardian of the Skywood, a defender against external threats. His oath, once sworn to protect the organic life of the forest, now felt broader, more encompassing. He understood that true protection meant understanding, and sometimes, it meant adapting to forces far beyond the scope of simple combat. "The Ashbound were a symptom, a chaotic expression of a deeper unrest," he acknowledged, his voice a low rumble that resonated with the earth's own tremor. "They sought to unravel, but what's happening here is... reweaving. A fundamental shift in the world's very composition." He looked at Mara, a newfound respect in his gaze. "Your insight, Mara, has been invaluable. You heard what I could not, saw what I was blind to."

Mara offered a small, wry smile. "We both heard different songs, Cael. Yours was the song of the forest, the lifeblood of the canopy. Mine was the deeper hum, the heartbeat of the stone. And it seems those songs have finally found harmony." She remembered the fear that had gripped her when she first encountered Cael, the ingrained mistrust of those who walked different paths. But his actions, his willingness to listen, to learn, had chipped away at her defenses, just as the crystalline growth was reshaping the familiar landscape. His reformed oath, she knew, was not a dilution of his commitment, but an expansion of it, a testament to his growth. He had chosen understanding over ignorance, adaptation over stagnation, and in doing so, had become a far more potent force for balance than his previous rigidity allowed.

"The Skywood," Cael continued, his brow furrowed as he considered the implications, "it thrives on the old ways. But the old ways may not be enough. This crystalline consciousness... it operates on timescales we can barely comprehend. Its objectives are not those of conquest, but of... deep, geological evolution." He paused, a moment of profound introspection settling over him. "If this is a natural progression of Aethel, then our role cannot be to fight it. It must be to understand it. To find a way for the old to coexist with the new, or at least, to transition with minimal loss." The thought was audacious, almost heretical to the deeply ingrained protective instincts of a guardian, yet the evidence before them was undeniable. The sheer scale of the crystalline spire, its alien artistry, spoke of a purpose far grander than any he had previously encountered.

Mara reached out, her hand hovering over a shard of obsidian that pulsed with a soft, internal light. "And that's where we come in, isn't it?" she said, her voice imbued with a quiet confidence. "You, with your connection to the living world, your understanding of its intricate systems. And me, with my resonance with the earth's deeper energies, my ability to interpret the silent language of stone and crystal."

She met his gaze directly. "Our mistrust has been our greatest obstacle, Cael. Now, it is gone. We are a united front, not just for the Skywood, but for Aethel itself. We will be the bridge between the world that is fading and the world that is emerging." Her fingers, lightly brushing the crystal, sent a faint warmth through her arm, a confirmation of the deep currents of energy that flowed through this place. She felt a kinship with this awakening, a sense of awe rather than terror. It was a language she was only beginning to understand, but one she felt compelled to decipher.

Cael's gaze swept across the transformed landscape, the familiar peaks of the Obsidian Range now adorned with impossible structures of light and crystal. It was a breathtaking, terrifying sight. He had spent his life guarding the vibrant, organic tapestry of the Skywood, understanding its delicate balance, its intricate web of life. But now, he saw that tapestry was part of something far larger, something woven from threads of stone and primal energy that lay beneath the surface, pulsing with an ancient, alien life. "The Ashbound sought to destroy," he mused, his voice low. "They saw only emptiness. But you, Mara, you saw the potential for something new. Your people, the earth-kin, have always understood the deep currents.

You carry that knowledge." He felt a pang of regret for his past blindness, for the superficial understanding he had held of the world. The Skywood was a vital part of Aethel, but it was not the entirety of it.

"We are the custodians of balance, Cael," Mara replied, her voice firm. "And balance is not static. It is a dynamic, ever-shifting interplay of forces. What we are witnessing is not an imbalance, but a recalibration. The earth is finding a new equilibrium, and it is our responsibility to ensure that this transition is one of evolution, not annihilation." She looked at him, her eyes reflecting the ethereal light. "We will need to understand the full extent of this emergence. What lies deeper within the earth? What other realms are connected to this crystalline network? Your understanding of the surface world, coupled with my sensitivity to the subterranean, can unlock these secrets." Her mind was already racing, piecing together fragments of forgotten lore, whispers of underground kingdoms and ancient pacts.

Cael took a deep breath, the crisp mountain air filling his lungs. It tasted different now, charged with an energy that hummed beneath his skin. He thought of the Lumina Bloom, its radiant power a symbol of Aethel's resilience, its ability to push back against the encroaching shadows. But this was different. This was not a corruption to be purged, but a fundamental shift in the planet's very nature. "My oath," he said, the words a solemn vow, "was to protect life. I believed that meant preserving what we know. But Aethel is far more than just the Skywood. It is the mountains, the oceans, the very core of the world. If life is to endure, it must adapt. And we... we must guide that adaptation." He extended his hand, palm open. "My strength, my knowledge of the wild places, they are yours, Mara. Together, we can navigate this new horizon."

Mara placed her hand in his, a spark of energy passing between them, a silent affirmation of their pact. The touch was grounding, a reminder of the tangible world amidst the awe-inspiring strangeness. "And my path will lead us deeper," she promised, her gaze unwavering. "I feel the resonance of ancient cities beneath the mountains, the echoes of civilizations that once walked hand-in-hand with the earth. There are answers there, Cael, answers about the origins of this awakening, about the architects of this crystalline emergence. We will not be fighting an enemy; we will be learning from a forgotten past, integrating its wisdom into Aethel's future." She felt a surge of exhilaration, a sense of purpose so profound it eclipsed any lingering fear. The Ashbound had been a destructive storm, but this was a deep, slow tide, and they would learn to ride its currents.

"The lore speaks of 'Children of the Deep'," Cael said, recalling fragments of forgotten tales. "I always dismissed them as myth. But now..." He looked at the spire, its crystalline facets reflecting the sky like a thousand eyes. "Now, I see they were not metaphors. They are the architects. And they are stirring." The thought of venturing into the earth's hidden depths, into realms of perpetual darkness and unknown inhabitants, sent a thrill through him. It was a stark contrast to the sun-dappled tranquility of the Skywood, but a necessary one.

"And they are not alone," Mara added, her eyes alight with discovery. "The earth's song is not the only one I hear. There is a symphony beneath the waves, a deep-sea chorus that has evolved in isolation. The forces that stir here, Cael, they resonate in the crushing depths as well. The balance of Aethel extends to its oceans, to its abyssal plains. We may find answers not just in the stone, but in the brine and the darkness." The prospect of plumbing the ocean's depths, of confronting the colossal and the unknown, was daunting, but the potential for understanding was immense.

Cael gripped Mara's hand a little tighter. "Then our journey will be one of exploration, not conquest. We will seek knowledge, forge understanding, and strive for a harmony that encompasses all of Aethel, from its highest peaks to its deepest trenches." He felt a lightness he hadn't known in years, a shedding of the burden of solitary defense. With Mara by his side, their mistrust dissolved, their strengths complementary, they were ready. The horizon had indeed expanded, revealing a vista of a world far more complex and wondrous than he had ever imagined. It was a future fraught with peril, yes, but also brimming with the promise of a profound, new beginning. The earth's heart was beating anew, and they would be there to witness, and to guide, its grand rebirth.

"The Lumina Bloom," Mara mused, a soft glow emanating from her bracers, "was Aethel's defense against decay. But this... this is Aethel's embrace of change. It's not about warding off the inevitable, but about guiding it. We must learn to dance with the geological eternity, to find the echo of life within the crystalline heart." She squeezed Cael's hand. "Our shared path has just begun, Guardian. And it will lead us to places we never dreamed existed, to truths that will redefine everything we thought we knew." The alliance was forged, not in fire, but in the quiet resonance of shared purpose, a beacon of hope against the vast, unknown future. They stood on the precipice of a new era, two unlikely allies bound by the fate of their world, ready to face whatever lay beyond the horizon.

The crystalline spire pulsed with a new intensity, not a surge of raw power, but a subtle, almost imperceptible shift in its resonant frequency. It was a change that Mara felt deep in her bones, a tremor that vibrated beyond the physical, into the very fabric of her being. Cael, standing beside her, his hand a steady anchor on her arm, mirrored her unease. The tremors that had once signified the awakening now felt like the prelude to something far more volatile, a prelude to a storm that threatened to engulf not just the Obsidian Range, but all of Aethel. The fragile alliance they had forged, born from the ashes of mistrust and nurtured by shared revelation, now faced its first true test: a confrontation that would eclipse the localized ecological disasters they had witnessed, and propel them into a conflict of an entirely different magnitude.

"It's... accelerating," Mara breathed, her voice barely a whisper against the thrumming energy of the spire. Her bracers, usually a source of comforting warmth, felt cool against her skin, as if the ambient energy of the awakening had shifted, recalibrating itself in a way that was both alien and unsettling. "The growth, the expansion... it's no longer contained. It's reaching out." She could feel tendrils of crystalline energy, subtle as spider silk but infinitely more potent, extending beyond the immediate vicinity of the spire, probing the surrounding landscape, seeping into the very bedrock of the mountains. It was a silent invasion, a cosmic expansion that spoke of intent far beyond mere geological evolution. This was not a passive emergence; it was an active, albeit subtle, assertion of dominance.

Cael's gaze was fixed on the horizon, his jaw tight. "The Ashbound were a localized blight, a symptom of imbalance. But this..." He trailed off, his eyes scanning the newly formed crystalline structures that adorned the peaks, structures that seemed to writhe with an inner luminescence. "This is a tide. And it's rising faster than we anticipated." He remembered the Ashbound's frenzy, their desperate, chaotic attempts to unravel the world. That had been a destructive force, yes, but a force that operated within the familiar paradigms of conflict. This was different. This was an alien intelligence, a geological consciousness that operated on scales that dwarfed mortal comprehension. Its very expansion was a form of warfare, a slow, inexorable conquest that rendered conventional defenses obsolete.

The air grew heavy, charged with an invisible pressure that pressed down on them, a tangible manifestation of the escalating threat. The familiar scent of pine and damp earth was being slowly, insidiously, replaced by a faint, metallic tang, the smell of nascent crystal. It was the scent of a world being rewritten, its fundamental composition altered by an unyielding, alien will. Mara felt a prickling sensation across her skin, as if a thousand tiny needles were probing her senses, seeking out vulnerabilities, assessing her resistance. The whispers of the earth, once a comforting chorus of ancient wisdom, now carried a discordant undertone, a frantic murmuring of a world struggling to adapt to an overwhelming presence.

"The crystalline resonance," Mara explained, her voice strained, "it's not just affecting the stone and the minerals. It's interacting with the life force of Aethel itself. I can feel it... the way it's subtly influencing the flow of elemental energies, redirecting them, reshaping them. It's like a vast, cosmic parasite, drawing sustenance and power from the very essence of our world." She closed her eyes for a moment, focusing, trying to pinpoint the epicenter of this encroaching influence. "It's not just the Obsidian Range anymore. The influence is spreading, Cael. It's seeping into the deep veins of the earth, reaching out towards the Skywood, and I fear...

I fear it's not stopping there." The implication hung in the air, heavy and suffocating: the entire planet was now the target.

Cael gripped his warding blade, its familiar weight a stark contrast to the intangible nature of the threat. His oath, once to protect the organic life of the Skywood, now felt woefully inadequate. How could he defend against a force that was not an invading army, but a fundamental alteration of reality? "We underestimated the scope of this awakening," he admitted, his voice grim. "We thought it was a localized event, a response to some imbalance within the mountains. But it's a world-shaping phenomenon. The stakes are no longer about preserving the Skywood; they're about the survival of Aethel as we know it." He looked at Mara, his gaze filled with a newfound urgency. The quiet understanding that had passed between them now had to be forged into action, into a desperate fight for a future that was rapidly slipping away.

The landscape around them began to shimmer, the solid rock and earth distorting as the crystalline growth advanced with startling speed. What had been a slow, deliberate transformation now felt like a rampant eruption. Crystalline tendrils snaked across the ground, encasing trees and boulders in shimmering prisons of light. The air thrummed with an audible hum, a low-frequency vibration that resonated deep within their chests, inducing a sense of unease, of profound disorientation. This was not a natural growth; it was an aggressive, geometric expansion, a manifestation of an alien will bent on remaking the world in its own image.

"This is beyond a simple ecological shift, Cael," Mara stated, her voice ringing with a desperate clarity. "This is an invasion, not of armies and legions, but of consciousness and form. The very laws of nature as we understand them are being rewritten by this... crystalline entity. It's imposing its own order, its own logic, on Aethel. And if it continues unchecked, there will be nothing left of the world we know." Her fingers traced the patterns on her bracers, the Lumina Bloom's essence a faint, flickering ember against the overwhelming surge of crystalline energy. It was a reminder of the life that was at stake, of the vibrant, chaotic, beautiful tapestry of Aethel that was now threatened with erasure.

Cael felt a cold dread creep into his heart, a premonition of the immense struggle that lay ahead. The Ashbound had been a tangible enemy, their motivations understandable even if their methods were abhorrent. But this was an enemy that defied easy definition, an enemy that was both the environment and the force altering it. "We need to understand its purpose, Mara," he said, his voice a low growl of determination. "Why is it doing this? What is it trying to achieve? Simply fighting it, if that's even possible, won't be enough. We need to find its weakness, its core objective, or we will be swept away by this... geological tide." He looked towards the distant peaks, now gleaming with an unnatural, multifaceted light. The horizon, once a symbol of hope and new beginnings, now represented an encroaching threat, a visible manifestation of a world-altering conflict.

The subtle shift in the spire's energy had not gone unnoticed by the wider world. Whispers, once confined to remote villages and nomadic tribes, began to coalesce into a chorus of concern, then fear. The tremors that had once been a curiosity were now a harbinger of disaster, causing sinkholes in the plains and unsettling the deep-sea currents. Coastal communities reported strange phosphorescent blooms in the ocean, an eerie reflection of the crystalline glow on the mountain peaks. The Ashbound had been a localized plague, a scar on the land. This, however, was a systemic fever, a contagion that threatened to consume the entire planet. The scale of the conflict was no longer a matter of conjecture; it was an undeniable reality.

"The ancient texts spoke of 'The Great Unraveling'," Mara murmured, her gaze distant, as if she were seeing visions in the pulsating light of the spire. "But I always interpreted it as a catastrophic event, an end. Now, I see it differently. It wasn't an end to be feared, but a transformation to be guided. Yet, this... this feels like a forced unraveling, an imposition of an alien order that seeks to erase the old altogether." She shivered, not from the cold, but from the chilling certainty that the challenges ahead would dwarf anything they had faced before. The confrontation was no longer just about survival; it was about the very essence of life and consciousness on Aethel.

Cael nodded, his resolve hardening. "If this is a new form of existence, a new way of being for Aethel, then we must understand it, not just oppose it. But the current path it's forging is one of erasure, not evolution. The intensity of its growth, the speed at which it's consuming the landscape... it leaves no room for the existing life forms to adapt. It's a conquest, pure and simple, disguised as natural progression."

He met Mara's gaze, their shared purpose a fragile but potent shield against the encroaching dread. "We're moving beyond regional threats, Mara. This is a global confrontation. The conflicts we face now will determine the very future of Aethel, whether it will be a world of vibrant, diverse life, or a sterile, crystalline monument to a forgotten past." The promise of a new horizon had not faded, but it was now shrouded in the shadow of an unprecedented war, a war for the soul of their world. The stakes had been raised beyond measure, and the coming battles would be epic in scale, their consequences rippling through the very foundations of existence.

The palpable shift in the Obsidian Range wasn't just a change in the earth's composition; it was a seismic alteration in the very rhythm of Aethel. The crystalline tendrils, once creeping with unnerving slowness, now pulsed with a vibrant, almost aggressive luminescence, extending their reach like the roots of an ancient, hungry god. Mara felt it as a tightening in her chest, a phantom pressure mirroring the geometric expansion she could sense permeating the land. The Lumina Bloom's quiet hum, once a comforting presence against her skin, now felt like a desperate whisper in a hurricane, its familiar energy struggling to assert itself against the overwhelming, alien resonance.

Cael, ever watchful, observed the horizon not with the steady gaze of a guardian, but with the sharp, assessing eyes of a strategist. The crystalline formations, once marvels of an uncontrolled awakening, now appeared as fortifications, silent sentinels of an encroaching dominion. He had seen the raw power of the Ashbound, the destructive chaos of a dying world lashing out. This, however, was different. This was an architect, a builder, a force with an intent so profound and alien it bypassed the conventional understanding of conflict. It was a geological intelligence, a consciousness woven from mineral and light, and its expansion was not an act of war, but an act of *becoming*.

"It's not just consuming the land," Mara said, her voice tight with the weight of her understanding. "It's *repurposing* it. Every atom, every molecule, is being drawn into its pattern. The water that flows through the mountains, the very air we breathe... it's all being assimilated. The Lumina Bloom is fighting it, trying to maintain the old frequencies, the old connections, but it's like trying to hold back the tide with a single grain of sand." She looked at her bracers, the intricate Lumina Bloom patterns glowing with a faint, defiant warmth. They were a testament to Aethel's vibrant, organic past, a stark contrast to the shimmering, sterile beauty that was beginning to dominate the landscape.

Cael ran a hand over the weathered leather of his bracers, a familiar anchor in this sea of unsettling change. His purpose had always been clear: protect the Skywood, its ancient trees, its vibrant life. But now, the very ground beneath his feet was becoming alien. The Skywood itself, though distant, felt the tremors, the subtle shifts in elemental flows that Mara had spoken of. The interconnectedness of Aethel was its greatest strength, but in the face of this encroaching crystal, it was also its greatest vulnerability. "If it assimilates everything," he mused, his gaze sweeping across the now glittering peaks, "then it's not just changing the landscape, it's changing the fundamental nature of Aethel. What happens to the life that cannot adapt? What happens to us?"

The question hung in the charged air, heavy with unspoken fear. Mara could feel the subtle hum of the spire, a sound that had once been a source of awe, now a low thrum of dread. It was a siren song, luring Aethel towards a transformation it was not equipped to handle, a metamorphosis driven by an alien imperative. "The ancient prophecies spoke of a time when the earth would shed its old skin," she murmured, recalling fragmented verses from texts long dismissed as myth. "I thought it was about renewal, about a cyclical rebirth. But this... this is not shedding. This is erasure. This is a hostile takeover of reality itself."

Their immediate crisis, the contained chaos of the Ashbound and the localized ecological unraveling, felt like a distant memory, a prelude to a storm of unimaginable scale. The crystalline growth was no longer confined to the Obsidian Range. Mara could sense its insidious creep, its tendrils reaching out like spectral fingers towards the fertile plains, towards the whispering heart of the Skywood, and beyond, towards the distant, uncharted territories that lay beyond the known world. This was no longer a battle for a single mountain range; it was a war for the soul of an entire planet.

"We need to find the source," Cael declared, his voice firm, a beacon of resolve in the encroaching uncertainty. "Not just the spire, but the *origin* of this... consciousness. If it's a geological awakening, there must be a heart, a core. And if it has a core, it has a weakness." He looked towards the north, a direction that had always represented the untamed, the unknown. For generations, the nomadic tribes of the Frostfell had spoken of ancient earth-songs, of primal forces that lay dormant beneath the frozen plains. Perhaps, in those forgotten lands, lay the answers they desperately needed.

Mara nodded, her eyes, once filled with the quiet wisdom of the earth, now held a spark of fierce determination. "The spire is a conduit, not the source," she confirmed. "It amplifies, it shapes, but the true impetus lies deeper. I can feel the echoes of its intent, a vast, silent ambition that predates even the oldest mountains. It desires... integration. But not in a way that allows for coexistence. It seeks a singular, crystalline perfection." She paused, her gaze sweeping across the jagged, now gleaming peaks, the crystalline structures reflecting the ethereal light of Aethel's dual moons. "We have to go beyond the Obsidian Range. We have to venture into the heart of this new horizon, to find what lies at its very foundation."

The path ahead was daunting, shrouded in the shimmering haze of crystalline transformation. The familiar landscapes they had fought to protect were being irrevocably altered, their very essence rewritten. Yet, within the chilling beauty of this change, a new understanding was beginning to dawn. The world was not merely under attack; it was undergoing a profound, albeit violent, metamorphosis. And in this metamorphosis, lay the potential for a future, however uncertain.

Cael's attention drifted to a faint, almost imperceptible shimmer on the distant horizon, beyond the Obsidian Range. It was a subtle distortion in the atmosphere, a whisper of something new, something untamed. He knew, with a certainty that settled deep in his bones, that their journey would lead them there. This crystalline menace, this cosmic architect, was not just reshaping the immediate world; it was opening up entirely new frontiers, vast, unexplored territories that would test their resolve and their understanding of Aethel to their very limits.

"The nomadic tribes," Cael said, his voice gaining a new edge of excitement, "the ones from the Sunken Valleys. They spoke of 'Earth-Weavers,' beings who could shape stone and mountain with song. I always dismissed it as folklore. But what if... what if they were the first to sense this? What if they knew how to communicate with these... geological intelligences?" The idea, once fantastical, now held the weight of desperate possibility. If such beings existed, and if they understood this new force, they could be the key to bridging the chasm between the old Aethel and the new.

Mara felt a jolt of recognition. "The Sunken Valleys," she echoed. "The legends there speak of a profound connection to the earth, a reverence that goes beyond mere cultivation. They believe that every stone has a voice, every mineral a song. If this crystalline entity is a new song, a new voice of Aethel, then perhaps they are the only ones who can truly listen, and perhaps, even respond." The implications were staggering. A new alliance, forged not in shared fear of a common enemy, but in a shared understanding of a fundamental shift in the planet's being.

"And what of the other factions?" Cael mused, his mind already racing through the complex political tapestry of Aethel. "The High Council in Aeridor, the merchant guilds of Port Azure, the reclusive scholars of the Whispering Archives. They have always operated within their own spheres of influence, their own ideologies. This threat, however, transcends all of that. It demands a unity of purpose that has never been seen before."

He envisioned the High Council, their gilded halls and ancient traditions, grappling with a force that defied their laws and their decrees. He saw the bustling markets of Port Azure, their commerce reliant on the stable flow of resources, now threatened by a geological upheaval that rendered their trade routes obsolete. And the Whispering Archives, their vast repositories of knowledge, might hold the fragmented truths they needed, but their keepers were notoriously insular.

"We will need to convince them," Mara stated, her voice carrying a newfound authority. "The Lumina Bloom showed me the interconnectedness of all things, Cael. It showed me that balance is not just about preserving what exists, but about facilitating adaptation, about finding harmony within change. This crystalline emergence, while aggressive, is still a part of Aethel's unfolding story. We cannot simply fight it; we must understand its place in the grand design, and help Aethel find a new equilibrium." Her vision, once focused on the immediate preservation of life, had expanded to encompass the very future of the planet, a future that would inevitably be shaped by this new, crystalline force.

The immediate threat of the crystalline spire's accelerated growth was undeniable, a visible manifestation of an encroaching power. But as they stood on the precipice of this new horizon, Mara and Cael recognized that the true challenge lay not in combating a singular enemy, but in navigating an era of profound transformation. The world was changing, not just around them, but *within* them. The Lumina Bloom's essence pulsed within Mara, a fragile beacon of organic life in a world increasingly dominated by geometric perfection. Cael's warding blade, a symbol of protection, now felt like a relic of a bygone era, its purpose needing to adapt to an enemy that was not flesh and blood, but stone and light.

"This is more than just a new threat, Cael," Mara said, her gaze fixed on the shimmering horizon, a horizon that now promised not just danger, but also discovery. "It's a new era. The old ways of understanding our world, of interacting with its forces, may no longer be sufficient. We are on the cusp of something unprecedented, something that will redefine what it means to be alive on Aethel." The Lumina Bloom's whispers had always been about cycles, about renewal. Now, they spoke of evolution, of a profound, planet-wide metamorphosis.

Cael nodded, his hand resting on the hilt of his blade. The weight was familiar, grounding. "And we will face it," he vowed, his voice resonating with a quiet strength. "We will seek out the Earth-Weavers, we will speak to the scholars of the Archives, we will rally those who can still hear the heartbeat of Aethel. For the Skywood, for the plains, for all the life that has flourished and will continue to struggle for existence." He turned to Mara, a shared understanding passing between them, a silent acknowledgment of the immense journey that lay ahead.

"We will forge this new horizon, Mara. Not as conquerors, but as custodians. We will ensure that Aethel's future is not a sterile monument, but a vibrant, living testament to resilience, to adaptation, and to the enduring power of life, in all its forms." The Obsidian Range, once a symbol of a localized crisis, had become the launching point for a global endeavor. The seeds of the future had been sown, not just in the crystalline growth that now defined the mountains, but in the hearts and minds of those who refused to let their world be erased. The horizon stretched before them, vast and unknown, a testament to the enduring spirit of Aethel, a promise of trials to come, and the enduring possibility of hope.

GLOSSARY

Aethel: The planet on which the story takes place.

Ashbound: A destructive, chaotic elemental force previously a primary threat.

Crystalline Growth: The new, geometrically perfect mineral formations rapidly expanding across Aethel.

Earth-Weavers: Legendary inhabitants of the Sunken Valleys, believed to communicate with geological forces.

Lumina Bloom: An organic energy source and life-force conduit, vital to Aethel's native ecosystems.

Obsidian Range: A mountainous region now experiencing rapid crystalline transformation.

Skywood: A vast, ancient forest crucial to the planet's biodiversity.

Spire: A structure within the Obsidian Range that amplifies and directs the crystalline growth.

Sunken Valleys: A region inhabited by the semi-mythical Earth-Weavers.

REFERENCE

The Lumina Bloom Cycles: Fragmentary texts detailing Aethel's natural energy flows and historical ecological shifts.

Whispers of the Deep Earth: Oral traditions and ancient carvings from the Sunken Valleys, hinting at geological sentience.

The High Council Archives: Records of historical planetary events and diplomatic efforts.

Aeridorian Meteorological Logs: Data on atmospheric and geological anomalies.

www.ingramcontent.com/pod-product-compliance
Lightning Source LLC
Chambersburg PA
CBHW030114310726
48970CB00004B/1282